P9-CQP-443

"Force has no place in the feelings between us," he said huskily.

Tory couldn't bear the implications of that. For the first time in her life, she'd found a man she was drawn to, in will, mind, strength, and, oh, so much in body—and that man stood for everything she despised.

Clasping her arms, Sinan pulled her back against him. "Don't be so troubled, little one. Remember, being a prisoner is a state of mind as much as a condition of the body. Give yourself to me freely, and I'll no longer have need to hold you."

Tory almost lifted her hand to his. She longed to give in to him . . . but she knew if she did, she'd start a journey to her own ruin from whence she'd never return. She, a pirate's plaything? The Grenville blood bestowed by her noble ancestors fired in her veins. Never could she humiliate her name and herself in such a way.

She flung up her head, clasping her hands behind her back. "No, there can never be peace between us as long as you hold me against my will . . ."

THE HAWK'S LADY
COLLEEN SHANNON

Nominated as Best New Historical Romance Novelist by *Romantic Times*

*Books by Colleen Shannon
from Charter*

WILD HEART TAMED
THE TENDER DEVIL
THE HAWK'S LADY

The Hawk's Lady

Colleen Shannon

CHARTER BOOKS, NEW YORK

THE HAWK'S LADY
A Charter Book/published by arrangement with
the author

PRINTING HISTORY
Charter edition/February 1989

All rights reserved.
Copyright © 1989 by Colleen Shannon.
This book may not be reproduced in whole
or in part, by mimeograph or any other means,
without permission. For information address:
The Berkley Publishing Group, 200 Madison Avenue,
New York, New York 10016.

ISBN: 1-55773-158-6

Charter Books are published by The Berkley Publishing Group,
200 Madison Avenue, New York, New York 10016.
The name "Charter" and the "C" logo
are trademarks belonging to Charter Communications, Inc.

PRINTED IN THE UNITED STATES OF AMERICA

10 9 8 7 6 5 4 3 2 1

To a wonderful woman:
my own Greaty, Lorraine Fuglaar.
For the love,
and the belief in myself
that made this possible.

ACKNOWLEDGMENT

With warmest thanks to Mr. Michael Alford,
curator of North Carolina's Maritime Museum.

PART I

"The Moving Finger writes; and, having writ,
moves on: nor all your Piety nor Wit shall lure
it back to cancel half a Line, nor all your Tears
wash out a Word of it."

—*THE RUBAIYAT,*
Omar Khayyam

Chapter 1

That lovely June day began perfectly. A smiling Nature beamed down on Tory, blessing her with a warm but not hot sun and a cool but not cold breeze. The serene Mediterranean horizon hinted of no danger beyond. Turquoise seas and cornflower skies mixed into a sublime blue palette; the air sparkled with purity after London's fumes; and the boundless waves were a buoyant escort to freedom.

Porpoises frolicked alongside the *Defiant Lady,* their dark hides skimming the waves. Occasionally one leaped into the air, flaunting a pale belly before diving again. When one rascal arced and turned his perpetual grin on her, Tory smiled back, wanting to shout her joy to him and all creation. How good it felt to be mistress of her own destiny at last!

Tory spun exuberantly, arms flung wide, and laughed. In her clinging yellow muslin gown, red-gold hair ablaze, she seemed as brilliantly untouchable as the sun. Sailors admired her tall, lush figure, grinning at her joy until a stern look from their captain sent them hastily back to work.

The tiny woman at her side, however, was immune to Tory's contagious mirth. She watched her charge sourly, fearing this moment would be scant recompense for the inevitable sorrow to come.

Tory took Becky's hands in hers and said cajolingly, "Don't spoil the *Defiant Lady*'s maiden voyage with those sour looks, please? We're almost to Majorca, so your dire warnings have come to naught. I can't wait to see Eleni! It's been so long since our academy days, letters or no. How surprised she'll be to see me!"

Plump and pugnacious as a bulldog, Becky pulled away to prop her fists on ample hips. "That smile won't wheedle you out of this mess, Victoria Alicia Grenville. You've gone too far this time. Your grandmother will cut you off for sure for embarrassing her by leaving poor Baron Howard at the altar."

Tory's smile faded. She narrowed eyes as turquoise as the

Mediterranean at her friend and companion. "She has no one to blame but herself. I told her I wouldn't marry Cedric and I meant it. Besides, since I've attained my majority, she can cut me out of her will if she pleases. I'll live on my mother's bequest."

Her bravado won but a rude snort from Becky. "There speaks a lady who's never known a moment's want. Well, Her Grace will indulge you no longer. Had she known to what use you'd put this pretty new yacht, she'd never have bought it for you, peace offering or no. As for living on that piddling income from your mother . . . pshaw! You've no idea how to economize. And you'll be ostracized to boot, at least for a time. There's a limit to what the ton will stand for, even from Tory the Terror."

Tory the Terror grimaced at the detested appellation and opened her mouth to speak, but Becky cut her off.

"Yes, yes, I know you don't care a farthing for their opinion, but that will change when you meet the right man. *If* we survive this ill-conceived voyage and make it back to England."

When Becky paused in her pacing to cast a scared look over her shoulder, Tory's scowl faded. Her famous grin flashed again, as wild and bright as her red-gold mane. "Smile, you old crosspatch, we've won!"

This time she earned a glower. Tory put a bracing arm about Becky's shoulders. "We're too close for Greaty to drag me back now. Napoleon is too occupied in Egypt to notice one small British yacht. And I daresay those tales about the Barbary pirates are exaggerated."

As if cued, the lookout cried, "Sail ho, to starboard!"

Stony gray eyes clashed with dancing turquoise ones before both women rushed to the starboard side of the vessel to await Captain McAllister's verdict.

The captain snapped his eyeglass closed and roared, "All hands on deck! Hoist every rag she'll carry, men!"

McAllister wheeled and strode up to the women. He'd argued volubly against this voyage, as had Becky, with as little effect. Grimly he watched his mistress whiten when he growled, "She's showin' nae colors, but she's a xebec, a ship favored by the corsairs, and she's bearin' doon fast. Wi' her tonnage, in this brisk wind she'll run us doon in a trice. I trust ye understand noo how foolhardy ye were to insist we leave wi'out obtainin' a pass. We hae nae choice but t' try t' repel them hand to hand, but we've little hope o' that, since they outnumber us probably five t' one.''

Removing a pistol from his belt, he offered it, butt first, to Tory. "If we fail, I suggest ye use this. On yourself." He offered some extra shot, which Tory ignored. Some instinct, however, bade her accept the pistol.

Becky moaned and clutched her bosom, but Tory tilted her chin high, stared into McAllister's condemning brown eyes, and snapped, ''Don't be idiotish! As British subjects, we're duly protected by our treaties with each of the Barbary States. Doubtless once they see our colors they'll leave us be.''

"It wouldna be the first or last time these pirates hae abrogated a treaty. We showed our colors upon sightin' them, but they still pursue. And wi'out a pass . . .'' His voice trailed off into ominous silence, and he stalked off to organize his crew.

Tory ignored Becky's pleas to go below and stayed to watch, unable to believe she was to be captured now, when they were so close to their destination.

The seamen harbored no such illusions and scrambled to hoist all sail. To a man, they were scared. The Barbary States were notoriously ruthless to captives.

But the xebec was built for speed. Inexorably it closed the gap, long black bow and stern crowded with boarders, triangular sails puffed by the wind. Turbaned figures swarmed about the deck, scimitars winking at their sides. Final confirmation of their identity came: The crescent and star of the Algerian flag fluttered brazenly up the xebec's mainmast.

"Oh, God, no,'' Tory whispered. She didn't protest when McAllister marched her to the companionway leading to the hold, Becky clasped to his other side.

Despite his anger, he offered what little reassurance he could. "When we refuse t' open fire, they'll realize this ship is unarmed, an' perhaps they'll be merciful. Hide as best ye can, but if ye're discovered, tell them your identity immediately. Perhaps greed for the handsome ransom ye'll bring will—'' He bit the words back and hurried off to help his men prepare for boarding.

Tory's pallor increased as she finally realized the danger she'd brought upon them all, herself and Becky especially, in her headlong flight from a distasteful marriage. As the xebec drew alongside, Tory chanced one last look—and almost fell into the hold as glittering green eyes locked with hers. Shocked, Tory stared. The brigand stood out from his swarthy mates not only by his assurance but by his stunning golden beauty as well.

His features were the most regular she'd ever seen, Roman nose balanced perfectly by a wide, full-lipped mouth and high cheekbones. It was a strong face, an arrogant face, a face that asked and gave no quarter. His forehead was broad, his jaw as unyielding as the muscular, bronzed torso revealed by his scanty vest.

His honey-brown, sun-streaked hair glittered in the sun, curling in riotous disregard of the red band he wore about his forehead. Their mutual appraisal only took a second, but in that moment, Tory trembled. He wore a threatening arsenal: a dagger at his side, two pistols in his belt, and a cutlass in one hand. But she was frightened more by his expression as he hovered in the rigging of the xebec like a golden hawk preparing to swoop. He touched his brow insolently, his eyes dropping to her body. *I look forward to a closer acquaintance,* he said as plain as words.

Pure terror broke his spell. Tory scrambled behind Becky into the hold, convinced of her folly at last. She'd seen lust before in men's eyes, but it had been veiled; the blond pirate had made his intentions plain in one blistering look. Her station would not save her this time . . . She hunkered down beside Becky behind the crates and rigging in the hold, her head bowed in uncharacteristic humility, praying as she never had before.

Only then did she remember the pistol . . .

Unreasonably comforted, she straightened her shoulders and pushed Becky behind her. Grenville heirs had remained true to their motto, ''Honor above all,'' through centuries of war, pestilence, and natural disaster. She was the last direct descendant of that proud line, and no gang of cutthroats would shake her loyalty to her heritage. She clutched the pistol to her bosom like a talisman and waited.

She held her panic at bay when the *Defiant Lady* shuddered as the other ship scraped alongside; when the terrifying yells of the boarding pirates resounded; and even when she heard the clang of cutlass and pike and the screams of wounded men. The battle was mercifully short. Savage whoops proclaimed the pirates' victory, and the English travelers' doom. Tory met Becky's tearful eyes, ignoring her friend's outstretched hand.

''Whatever they do to us can't be worse than death,'' she reprimanded.

Becky shook her head sadly at this innocence, but they had

no time to argue. Tory shoved Becky prone behind her and braced the pistol on a low crate. She'd been taught to shoot by her grandmother's head groom, but she'd never aimed at a moving—especially a human—target before.

Booted feet tromped down the companionway, followed by a tall lithe body. Only her nervousness saved the pirate captain's life. When that ash-brown head cleared the hatch, Tory held her breath and tried to squeeze the trigger, as she'd been taught, but her sweaty finger slipped and jerked it instead. She flinched at the report, but the bullet merely sheared off one gleaming curl as the pirate froze on the steps. Tory watched it flutter to the deck and form an exclamation point. She dropped the spent pistol and raised her eyes.

They traveled up and up, over strong calves encased in knee-high brown boots, up muscular breeches-clad thighs, past a flat, taut midsection, over a wide, blood-streaked chest, and came to rest finally on the face she expected to see grimacing with rage. Her mouth dropped open as she again met sparkling green eyes and a wide mouth quirked in . . . amusement? Amusement!

Tory shot up to a sitting position. She watched disbelieving as he lithely jumped the last few steps, bent, picked up the lock of hair, and sauntered over to her as casually as a strolling dandy. Two swarthy pirates had followed him into the hold. If their leader was unconcerned, they were not. They leveled angry black eyes and steady pistols on her.

Ignoring Becky's warning look, Tory rose. She was tall for a woman, yet even standing ramrod straight, she felt dwarfed. However, she was too furious at the pirate's rude appraisal to be intimidated. Thorough green eyes ran down and down, from her curly mane to her graceful neck, paused on her large, heaving breasts, descended past her small waist to the rich curve of her hips, slid down to her long feet, and glided back up to her full mouth. Finally, his eyes met hers.

He astonished her yet again when he cocked his head and murmured in flawless English, "A veritable Amazon. I'm surprised you missed. Still, you should praise Allah that you did. My crew would not have been . . . pleased had you killed me." He twirled the lock of hair between forefinger and thumb absentmindedly as he spoke, but his stare was challenge direct.

Something dangerous flickered in his eyes, and she shivered as she got the strangest feeling he had a grudge against her that he was eager to settle. Ridiculous. When he smiled and bowed, she dismissed the notion as incredible. She opened her mouth to tell him her identity, but he beat her to it.

"Sinan Reis, commander of the xebec *Scorpion,* subject of that most noble of deys, Bobba Mustapha of Algiers, informs you, madam, you are my prisoner." When she sniffed disdainfully, he added, "To do with as I will."

Before she realized his intention, he stepped closer, tweaked her bodice open, and dropped the lock of hair inside. He patted the spot, his smile widening when she jerked away. "A memento of the man to whom you belong—until I honor you with my attention again." He turned to walk away.

Tory was unused to such insolence from any man, and in her fury she forgot her precarious position. "I belong to no one!" she spat. "You filthy freebooter, predator upon women, you would not be so cocky were I still armed."

Becky groaned, but Tory shook off her restraining hand. The dark pirates understood the universal tone of contemptuous defiance. They grumbled and started forward, but Sinan Reis stayed them with an outflung hand.

He swiveled. Tory refused to look away from the gimlet stare lancing her in two, even when he closed the gap between them. She backed up a step before she could stop herself, and her fury raged hotter when he smirked.

"Like all women, you're show without substance. You bray like a jackal until faced with a stronger opponent," he goaded, backing her up another step, and another, until the bulkhead prevented further retreat.

Putting his palms on either side of her head, he leaned into her, every muscle pressing into her shrinking body. Tory clenched her teeth and tried to shove him back, but he smiled and leaned closer. She shied away from the touch of his smooth, warm skin. No power on earth would have made her admit she was curious to see if the bulging muscles in his arms were as hard as they looked.

Tory drew a deep breath, flung up her head, and fixed him with the glare that had cowed many a London dandy. "Release me, pirate, and we shall see how brave I am."

He raised his eyebrows and settled more comfortably against her. "Indeed? What will you do? Scratch my eyes out? Kick me where it hurts most?" He threw back his brown head and laughed scornfully.

Tory's eyes narrowed to incandescent turquoise slits. Words

were useless against this man. He twisted them and wrapped them about her. Since this barbarian recognized no rules but his own, she would beat him at his own game. It was time he learned a lesson men through the centuries had ignored at their peril: Not all women were weak and cowardly.

Suiting her action to his words, she went for his face, simultaneously lifting her knee. He caught her hands before they connected and tried to dodge the knee she rammed into his groin, but he was standing too close. Her knee connected solidly. He groaned and doubled over, releasing her.

Two cries of rage preceded the turbaned whirlwind that engulfed her. One brigand caught her hair and jerked her head back; the other whipped a dagger up to slit her throat.

Becky screamed. Tory closed her eyes, waiting for the cold slice. Sinan Reis straightened painfully before the knife could connect and ordered his men sharply away. They protested, but at his repeated command they let Tory go and stepped back to his side, their stares inimical.

Putting an arm about Tory, Becky urged, "Tell him who you are, and for God's sake don't anger him further. Your wealth and title are meaningless to these savages. You're just another woman to them—"

Sinan Reis interrupted, "On the contrary, madam. Lady Victoria Alicia Grenville is not just another woman to them. They think her a demon and want to exorcise her before she casts her spells upon me."

Becky and Tory stared at him in astonishment. "How do you know my name?" Tory demanded.

He shrugged, but that dangerous glimmer in his eyes was now twice as bright. Tory stared into that threat and promise as long as courage allowed, but finally dropped her eyes to his torso. No comfort there, for the size and strength of him posed a threat of another kind. Masculine aggression vibrated from the powerful physique, though he didn't move. Why did she suddenly feel like a battle to be won or a wall to be scaled?

"It matters not how I know your name. What does matter is the handsome ransom you'll bring—when I'm finished with you and ready to let you go. *If* you survive long enough for me to collect it. Normally, we treat Christian women gently— especially *rich* Christian women—but I may make an exception of you."

The provocation was so blatant, his white teeth bared in a

nasty smile, that Tory reacted exactly . . . as he wanted her to? She sensed that he was goading her, but she was too furious to care.

"If you lay a hand on me, you'll not live to crow about it." She reached inside her bodice and flung the lock of hair at his feet like a gauntlet. "Are my threats still empty, mighty reis?"

She sent a derisive look at the bulge in his buff-colored breeches. Becky gasped; the pirate stiffened. Tory smiled. Magenta stained his throat and face in an angry tide, but her triumph was short-lived.

"Make good on your threats, mighty Amazon," he mocked her tone of voice. He drew his dagger from his belt and sent it whizzing into the plank between her feet, which were spread in a challenging stance. Point first, the blade stuck and quivered. Tory was too innocent to catch the sexual innuendo, and she looked at the pirates in bewilderment when they guffawed. Becky clasped her hands to her red cheeks and worried her lower lip with her teeth.

Tory looked from the knife to Sinan Reis, who had his thumbs hooked in his belt. His hips made one blatant little grind; his eyes dropped to her bosom. Comprehension hit her like a slap in the face. She paled, then reddened as fury swept the vestiges of caution away. Snarling, she bent down and heaved the knife free.

"No!" Becky yelled, trying to catch her arm, but the turbaned pirates dragged her aside. She could only watch this inevitable battle.

Sinan Reis braced his feet and spread his arms for balance, smiling languidly. "You'd kill an unarmed man? Tsk, tsk!"

"Arm yourself, pirate!" Tory cried. "If I must die, I'll go honorably by sending your black soul where it belongs!"

Sinan shook his head. "Wishful thinking, my lovely Amazon. You'll not die, nor will you kill me. Come, vent your spleen and turn your passions in a more pleasurable direction." He didn't reach for the dagger one of the other pirates offered, but he did remove his leather vest and wrap it around his right arm.

Tory gripped the knife firmly. They circled each other. Tory's loosened hair flowed around her shoulders like a fur cape, and her eyes snapped with the primitive need to avenge herself and her crew. That wide chest was too smooth. It needed some scratches in it to make it less appealing. Not too deep, just enough to scar him a little.

Calculating green eyes never left hers, and when she made her first strike, he turned neatly aside. The knife slashed thin air. She inched forward, hoping to corner him against the bulkhead, but he danced around her before she could maneuver herself into striking position. Teeth gritting, she turned and stalked him. He rarely allowed her close enough to strike, and when he did, his shielded arm blocked the point of the dagger or he dodged at the last moment.

He taunted, admiring her heaving bosom, "What creamy white skin. I shall enjoy licking your sweat away, fair captive." His arm blocked her furious jab.

A red haze clouded Tory's vision as she realized he was toying with her. She was indeed a weak woman compared to him; he'd challenged her merely to humiliate her. The knowledge gave her strength. Before he'd regained his balance from her last jab, she slashed his left wrist, which was all she could reach. Blood welled up along the gash, delighting her. His mouth tightened as he, too, watched.

When his eyes met hers, they no longer teased. He had become deadly earnest in his intent to disarm her. Now it was she who retreated and he who stalked. She jabbed wildly, but always he foiled her. She lunged in a desperate attempt to break past his guard, but found herself caught at the waist, her knife hand manacled in a ruthless grip. Tighter and tighter he squeezed until she moaned and dropped the dagger.

Defeated, she bowed her head and bit her lip, but he gave her no time for self-pity. He flung off the vest and forced her head up. Triumph glittering in his eyes, he crooned, "So, do you still want to kill me?"

Tory hated her weakness, despised his strength, and she had spirit aplenty left to cry, "Yes, yes, I hate you!"

A tug on her hair bowed her body, fitting her curves to his disturbing angles. "You'll get your chance, lady hellion. You will make me die a little death every time I take you." He consumed her defiant cry with hungry lips.

Tory struggled to hit him, but he clasped her wrists behind her back. She tried to turn her face aside, but he bent her over his arm until she couldn't move, couldn't breathe, couldn't think. She told herself she was revolted, that his lips tasted as bland as the other lips she'd known, but slowly, curiosity grew. How could his mouth be so hard, yet so persuasive? Who ever heard of a gentle pirate? Her resistance weakened.

The mingled smell of their sweat, the feel of his soft chest hair tickling her breastbone, and the wooing heat of his mouth combined to disarm her of her righteous, flaming sword and sear her with the need to respond to him. No, Tory, no, he's a murderer, a renegade, she tried to tell herself, but her senses didn't care. They enjoyed the nibbles he took from her mouth; they urged her to open her lips to his bold exploration.

She resisted, forcing her eyes open. Her willpower rebounded at his calculating look. He didn't care about giving her pleasure. He wanted to humiliate her, and she'd almost helped him do exactly that! Tory went limp. He lifted his head. Her considerable weight seemed to pain his wrist, but his grimace smoothed into a smile as, blushing, she met the kindling green eyes.

"Ah, you surprise me, Amazon. Stripped of sword and buckler, are you a woman after all? A tender, round armful made for man's delight?"

Tory ignored the first genuine smile he'd bestowed on her and hurled back, "Neither of which you know anything about!"

When he raised an inquiring eyebrow she sneered, "Tenderness *or* being a man!"

Instead of bursting into a rage as she expected, he let his smile deepen. This time it was the smile of a man who knew he was a man and could therefore ignore her puny insults. "Before we are quits, milady, you'll see I have intimate knowledge of both." He leaned down to whisper in her ear, "How much of the first I show you will depend on how well you please the second."

Tory struggled so furiously he let her go. God, she hated him! Even her worst insults he dismissed. What manner of man was he? Torn between rage and fascination, she backed away. "I'll see you hang for that!"

He shrugged into his vest with total unconcern. "Indeed? That will be a neat trick, since the combined forces of Europe have been unable to defeat the Barbary States in over three centuries."

His men grabbed Tory and bound her hands behind her back, smiling at her cries of rage. Sinan turned to Becky. "I'll leave you unbound, madam, if you give me your word that you will not try to release this hellcat." His gentle tone won Becky's reluctant nod.

When he turned back to Tory, his face hardened. "You'll remain in your cabin until we reach Algiers. If you try any tricks, I'll personally see to your punishment." He cupped her chin and forced her head up so he could meet her glare. "Our methods of disciplining slaves are not pleasant. It would be a shame to mar that lovely skin." Another raking glance and he added, "Especially when I have such plans for it."

Bending, he pressed his lips to the V-shaped neckline of her bodice, teasing her bountiful flesh with his mouth, her ears with his words. "Farewell milady. I leave you my favor."

Tory gasped in shock when she felt a gentle but unmistakable nibble on the upper curve of one breast. "You bragging ass, you dare to liken yourself to a knight?" Her arms were bound, but not her feet . . .

He choked into the skin he still nuzzled when she kicked him. He lifted his head. The blinding beauty of the smile he bestowed on her made her blink. She had not kicked him that hard, but to laugh?

He took two steps back, crossed his arms, and braced his feet, indeed laughing softly—as would a man who looked forward to untold delights. He leaned close to rim her lips with one tanned finger, pulling his hand away when she tried to bite it. His smile still in place, he said, "Knights extended gallantry to the weak, the helpless, and the womanly. The first two you are not. As to the last . . . we shall see. But one similarity between our sport and the tourneys of old does exist, milady."

Though she tried, she couldn't resist. "Well?" she snapped when he waited.

"If I'm the knight, milady, don't you realize what that makes you? No?" He stepped up to her and wrapped one strong thigh about her legs to keep her still. He paused again, and only when she looked at him did he finish softly, "My conquest. And make no mistake, milady. A conquest it will be." He planted one last burning kiss on her bosom before he walked away, turned, and blew her a cocky kiss from the companionway.

Then he was gone, but the imprint of his lips, the promise in those eyes, burned long after in Tory's flesh and mind. She squirmed to free her hands so she could wipe his touch away, but the pirates hauled her up the companionway to the deck. Tory swallowed and braced herself. The carnage she dreaded did not appear. At first she was relieved to see no bodies, but her cheeks bloomed with color when she spied her crew, stripped to drawers and socks, huddled in a miserable group. Some were wounded, but all, thank God, were alive.

Tory glared at their captors. She was surprised at their diversity: aquiline-faced, dark-skinned Moors; full-blood Negroes; Turks, like the escorts of the captain, who apparently served as officers; even pale and tawny-skinned Italians and Spaniards babbling in their own languages. Tory's mouth firmed with contempt for these most of all, for they had turned on their own kind. Like their captain. Tory squelched her curiosity about her adversary and watched, her anger growing apace with her frustration.

The pirates danced around in their stolen clothes, pointing derisively at their prisoners. Tory gritted her teeth at the indignities and stood tall despite her bonds. She'd show these pirates what an Englishwoman was made of!

When the brigands caught sight of her, their merriment subsided. Aah's and grunts of astonishment sounded at her fiery beauty; she was a little rumpled now, but striking to the men nonetheless. Pirates crowded about her, tweaking her flowing locks, testing the resiliency of her arms, stroking the softness of her cheek.

One corsair, taller and cockier than the others, closed his hand over her breast. Tory gasped and tried to shrink away, but she was surrounded by a wall of rank male flesh. The tall pirate grinned, his strong white teeth as rapacious as a wolf's, and elbowed the other pirates aside to cup both her breasts. Tory was frightened, but angrier still, and she kicked him in the shin.

He grunted in broken Spanish, "Woman not be so proud when sold at *besistan*. Perhaps I buy you and teach you respect." He tugged her head back and shoved his face into hers.

Tory had never thought she'd be thankful to hear that smooth voice, but she closed her eyes in relief when Sinan came on deck and spoke to the pirate in Arabic. The man answered in Spanish, a language Tory spoke fluently. "She not yours, either. Great dey keep her himself or send her to Constantinople."

Sinan pulled Tory away from the pirates, his hold as possessive as his encompassing look. "Not this time. I intend to ask for her as my share of the capture. I think you know our generous master will not deny me."

The other pirates who spoke Spanish gasped at such foolishness. As captain, Sinan was due a larger share of the booty than anyone other than the ship's owners and the dey, and to fritter it away on a mere woman, even such a beautiful one, was beyond their ken.

Ahmet was not appeased. "Perhaps I ask for her myself. I,

too, am respected.'' He hawked and spat at Sinan's feet. The spittle oozed down the toe of Sinan's boot.

The crew looked warily from Ahmet to Sinan. Ahmet was a favorite of the Janissaries, the Turkish military elite respected even by the sultan of Turkey. Ahmet was jealous of Sinan's influence with the dey and the *ta'ifa*, the corsair council established by Barbarossa. If Ahmet defeated Sinan in a fair fight or made him lose face in the eyes of his crew, he'd be a step closer to winning his own command.

Though Tory understood none of this, she felt the anger emanating from the powerful body behind her, and her heart raced. If he was killed, what would become of them? Arrogant as he was, Sinan at least was clean, and he had a measured control that she sensed the sly Ahmet could not match. Thus, Tory, Becky, and the crewmen, both Christians and Moslems, watched and awaited Sinan's response.

Setting Tory aside, Sinan strode up to Ahmet and ordered softly, ''Clean my boot of your spittle, dog, or I will cleanse it in your blood.''

Ahmet paled, but he snarled, ''It is you, infidel, who will bleed until your skin is as pale as your wit.'' Ahmet unsheathed his cutlass and brandished it, his hatred at last bare for all to see.

Sinan removed his own weapon and gestured with his arm for everyone to clear a circle for them. ''I've been patient too long. Your kind understand only one thing!'' Sinan bared his teeth in a snarl as feral as Ahmet's. Each man circled the other.

Cutlasses rang in the silence as Sinan blocked Ahmet's vicious stab. Sinan slammed Ahmet's cutlass aside and made a swift strike at his exposed middle, but the pirate leaped back a step. Sinan followed, slashing, jabbing, forcing Ahmet to retreat. Ahmet turned away from a thrust, striking at Sinan's torso simultaneously, slipping under his opponent's guard. The wicked point of the two-edged blade lashed the left side of Sinan's chest. Sinan knocked the cutlass aside, not pausing, though blood oozed from the shallow gash and trickled down his body. Ahmet recovered quickly, arcing his sword at Sinan's belly.

Sinan sucked in his middle, clasped his weapon in both hands, and whammed Ahmet's extended blade down so hard that its point was embedded in the deck. The Arab had no time to pull it free; he backed away and removed a small dagger from his belt. He flipped it toward Sinan's heart, but the captain pirate ducked and the dagger stuck in the mainmast.

Ahmet retreated, searching frantically for another weapon. He swooped down to claim a discarded pike, but Sinan stepped on the hilt and set the tip of his own cutlass against Ahmet's throat.

Ahmet straightened gingerly, red with hatred, and spat, "Finish me, then!"

Sinan leaned on his sword until a bright speck of blood appeared. He lifted his foot and wiped his boot on Ahmet's dirty pantaloons; then he lowered the sword and shook his head. "No, I'll let you live to face the *ta'ifa*. Bind him! Take him back aboard the *Scorpion* and let him reflect on his greed and foolishness." Ahmet was dragged away.

"Does anyone else challenge my right to the woman?" Sinan propped his sword, point down, against the deck and leaned casually on it. When none of the other pirates stepped forward, he sheathed it. "Lock these men in the hold and set sail for Algiers. Tonight we celebrate!"

Cheering, the pirates scrambled to obey. Tory's relief dissolved into apprehension when Sinan stepped up to her and lifted her chin.

"You are mine by right of capture and by right of battle now, woman. It's time you learned what that means." Sinan hoisted Tory over his shoulder, ignoring McAllister's threats, Becky's pleas, Tory's curses, and his crew's laughter. He took his booty below to her own spacious cabin.

And what a cabin it was! He flipped her down on her capacious poster bed and looked appreciatively about. Sea-green silk hung over the portholes and around the bed, and emerald-green brocade chairs sat opposite a gold sofa. The bulkheads were paneled in black walnut, the ceiling banded at the top with gilded molding. The ebony dressing table and bed were inlaid with ivory and mother-of-pearl.

Sinan walked to the vanity and riffled its contents, searching until he discovered a false drawer bottom. He pulled out her jewel case, ignoring Tory's outrage, and dumped her jewels on the dresser. He whistled as rainbow hues of green, blue, purple, gold, pink, and other colors sparkled even in the muted light.

He put the jewels away, went to her washstand and poured water into the fine Chinese porcelain bowl. After cleansing himself, he dried off on her clean white towel, shrugging at the rusty stain. Still ignoring Tory, he investigated her armoire. Her clothes were a mess, for other pirates had already flipped through them and filched a gift for wife or sweetheart. Finally he found something that pleased him and threw it over his shoulder.

The whisper of azure silk looked ludicrous against his decidedly masculine frame, but Tory was in no humorous mood. She rose and matched him look for look when he strode up and tossed the negligee on the bed. He slit her bonds with his knife and pointed with the tip of the weapon at the garments.

"Put them on." He sheathed the knife, folded his arms, and waited.

Stalling for time, Tory rubbed her tingling wrists as she considered her best course of action. She wondered if her own little pistol remained in the bottom of her wardrobe, and she couldn't hide the betraying flicker of her eyes.

He clicked his tongue. "Is this what you seek?" He pulled her pistol out of his breeches pocket and dangled it in the air just above her head.

Tory's gaze went from the gun to his superior expression and then to the floor in apparent defeat. She said huskily, "Yes, but, as usual, you've outwitted me."

His eyes widened at this response. He smiled slowly. "Ah, you show some sense at last. Do you yield to me, madam?"

Sighing sadly, Tory inched closer to him, her eyes still lowered. He was taken off-guard when she whipped her hand to his belt and seized his own weapon. "Never while I live, pirate," she sneered, nudging him in the chest with his pistol. All her frustrated pride and all her hatred were visible in her eyes.

Calmly, he dropped his remaining weapons behind him and leaned into the barrel pressed against his chest. "The advantage is yours. Take your revenge," he whispered.

Tory nibbled her lip. She didn't want to kill him, for she knew the other brigands would show her no mercy if she did. She looked at his chest, rising and falling steadily with his unhurried breathing, and knew she couldn't put a gaping hole in it and drain all breath, all life, from that magnificent form. Groaning in frustration, she would have lowered the pistol, but he held her hand level.

"Come, you'd best pull the trigger, for it's the only way you'll be free of me before I've taken what I want," he whispered, his eyes compelling.

Tory struggled to free her hand. To her astonishment, she felt his finger forcing hers to contract. She screamed and closed her eyes, cringing away. But no report sounded. An empty click was followed by deep chuckles. Her eyes opened. Blood lust glowed from her pupils.

Hissing, she flung the weapon away and flew at him, teeth bared, nails curled, but he was waiting for her. He tripped her neatly, caught her hands behind her back and pressed her into the soft mattress with his own body. Tory spat vitriol, but he might have been stone deaf for all the heed he took. He smiled and held her until her struggles slowed, then ceased.

His gaze lowered from her glorious, tempestuous face to the white flesh above her breasts, bared by her position with her hands behind her back. Inhaling shakily, he ripped the muslin with a capable hand. Her dainty chemise parted like leaves before a whirlwind. Her full, pearly breasts, dusky pink circles crowned by enraged nipples, were bare to his eyes, a feast to all his senses.

Sight alone didn't satisfy him long. He traced one pink rim, touch leading naturally to the most basic urge: taste. His mouth sampled a roseate crest.

Tory struggled, terrified at the feel of the warm mouth sucking the flesh no man had seen or dared touch. Humiliated tears bedewed her eyes. He consumed her like a famished man presented with a banquet.

When he ceased tugging at one puckered crest only to torment the other, Tory could bear no more. "Please, please, let me go. I'll do whatever you say, but stop!"

He laved the hard tip of her breast one last time, then, panting, he sat up, released her arms, and pressed her shoulders into the mattress. "You will obey me?"

Tory nodded wildly. "Yes, yes, anything you ask if you'll let me go."

His eyes went compulsively to her voluptuous display, but he stood and whirled away, commanding over his shoulder, "Dress yourself in the garments I selected." He poured fresh water into the basin to wash his face.

Eyeing him, Tory rose on trembly legs. She looked longingly at the door, but only more—and perhaps worse—danger awaited outside. Nerving herself, she flung off her ruined clothes and pulled the gown over her head. As it slithered to her feet he turned to look at her. The fine azure silk nightgown had a high bodice yoked with pleated chiffon. An upstanding ruffle framed her face, and azure ribbons were tied under her breasts, their streamers falling to the flowing hem. It was a garment meant to tease a man. From the look on his face, it succeeded despairingly well.

"So much the lady," he murmured, "yet so much woman, too. If only . . ." So softly he spoke, as if to himself. But all too soon his face set indomitably again.

Tory brushed her tangled hair away from her face and braved a look into his eyes, but the hunger there struck her like a blow. She looked away. Pulling the robe over the gown, she tied it shakily. She froze like a cornered animal when he flung his forehead band off and advanced. She clenched the robe as if sheer willpower could keep it on, but he brushed her hands away and pulled the ribbons open.

A different emotion made him tremble, too, as he stared at the tall figure that was as richly curved as the sirens who lured seamen to their doom. Her heart thundered with hatred, but, for the moment, she was defeated by his aggressive masculinity.

"Please, you promised . . ." she croaked. He seemed not to hear as he raised his hands and cupped her breasts, kneading the firm flesh and testing its weight in his palms. He thrust his arousal against her.

Nuzzling the hollow of her throat, he whispered, "And I'll keep my promise . . . for now. Your initiation will be no rushed affair, my lovely captive. Only patience will teach you the delights of submission. The day will come when you'll no longer wish to escape me. You will see."

He pressed a passionate kiss to her cleavage. Stepping back, he swept one last look over her, then turned, collected his weapons, and exited.

Tory crumpled where she stood. He had spared her . . . but for how long?

Chapter 2

Tory paced her cabin, eager and afraid. They were approaching Algiers, the Turkish officer had informed her in idiomatic Spanish. He had been her sole visitor these past days. He'd brought her disgusting meals of black olives pounded into paste and mixed with olive oil, unleavened bread, dates, and figs. The fruit and bread had been her only sustenance for two days, and her frustration was exacerbated by hunger.

She peered out the porthole yet again. Surging waves glittered like a sun-sequined mantle of the deep, but Tory was blind now to nature's beauty. The cotton-puffed skies and the skirling wind were false enchanters that had lured her into complacency once. They would not do so again. Tory focused all her considerable concentration on the coming battle. Her real enemy loomed ever larger in her thoughts, both fascinating and repelling her.

Who was Sinan Reis? Why had he threatened her, then left her alone? Something about him didn't fit. Was he the ruthless renegade Christian he appeared to be, or a fair-skinned Circassian Arab fluent in English? Was he as venal and greedy as the corsair heirs of Barbarossa, or was he ambitious but true to his own code of honor? Tory pressed her nose to the glass, grimly aware his motivations didn't much matter. The facts were stark: Pirate he was, for whatever reason; she was his captive.

Until, that is, she could escape.

Simultaneous with the thought, Tory sighted a gracefully swooping gull. She stiffened. Land! Tory raced to the armoire and withdrew a voluminous green cloak. Feverishly, she stuffed her jewels into the deep pockets, so intent on her task that she didn't hear the cabin door open. She was holding an exquisite ruby necklace that had been in her family for generations when a silky voice bound her in place.

"Your efforts are quite useless, my lovely Amazon. Once we reach Algiers, you'll be stripped, and garbed as befits a slave. You'll have only one place to hide your jewels. Even that, in time, will know my touch."

Tory stared at her captor uncomprehendingly. He was dressed as an Arab, in baggy white pantaloons, red sash, gold-banded white *kaffiyeh* headdress and richly embroidered blue silk coat. The easy way he wore the garments frightened her more than his threats. With his hair covered, and with his deeply tanned skin, he was the ruthless East personified.

The cloak dropped from her numb fingers as his meaning penetrated: She was to be stripped and enslaved. Panic swamped even her anger as she stared into those implacable green eyes. Tory was unaware of the plea in her own that brought a quiver of regret to his hard face. She knew only that she couldn't bear such humiliation and would do anything to avoid it.

"But," she quavered, "I thought I was to be ransomed."

Sinan's face became expressionless, but the large hand that brushed back a curl from her temple was gentle. When Tory flinched, the hand dropped back to his side. "You misunderstand me. I'm not going to sell you. It is my clothes you will wear, my slave you will be." His voice lowered to rasp across her nerves like grit. "And it is my command you will obey."

It was too much. The tension of the last two days and the shock of his words culminated into a challenge as bold as a tossed gage. Her practical half warned her that only forbearance could serve her now, but Tory had lived life in defiance of such restrictions. Her instincts came to the fore.

She braced her feet, crossed her arms over her bosom, and plumbed eyes as impenetrable and dangerous as the sea. She mimicked his tone, "*You* misunderstand *me*. I'm not going to obey you. You can take my clothes and keep me naked, but I will never be your slave."

"Really?" Sinan raised a brow, his warning all the more chilling for its casualness. "Perhaps I shall sell you at the market, then. I've no need of discord in my harem. If you persist in this defiance, you may find your next master less patient."

He picked up the cloak, removed the jewels from the pockets, and put them back in the case. He flung the cape over the simple muslin day dress she'd chosen from her depleted wardrobe, and held a black silk square before her face.

Tory shied away. "I'm not a heathen ashamed to show my face!"

Jerking her chin around, he warned harshly, "You'll wear it unless you want to be thought a whore."

Shocked, Tory subsided. He tied a loose knot behind her head. She wondered at the quick breath he took when their torsos brushed. He jerked away, flushing.

"That's a good, docile slave," he taunted. "Perhaps you'll make a fine addition to my harem after all." When Tory stiffened, he grated a laugh and pushed her to the door.

He led her to her jailer and delivered a curt order. The Turk, Kahlil, stood guard over her at the rail. Tory craned her neck, sighing with relief when she saw Becky sitting in the stern, unharmed but likewise guarded and veiled.

Sinan returned to the cabin. Opening the jewel case, he examined each piece with an experienced, appreciative eye. Selecting the ruby necklace and several of the oldest, most valuable pieces, he undid his red sash and secreted the jewelry in the hidden slits. He wound the sash back around his waist, the bulge in the back concealed by his wide-sleeved coat. If he felt any remorse at stealing from his pirate brethren, he gave no sign. Patting the sash, he picked up the jewel case, climbed to the deck, and went to Tory's side.

So did Tory arrive at one of the most seductive, exotic cities of the Mediterranean. The *Scorpion* followed them into the bay, a green standard embroidered with sayings from the Koran proclaiming her capture, flying jubilantly above the British flag. The corsairs on both ships whooped and slapped one another on the back. The sailors in Tory's crew were herded to the deck like cattle to market, their faces as pale with dread as their captors were flushed with triumph.

Situated on a deep bay, the port of Algiers jutted out into the Mediterranean like an authoritative finger. The city meandered up hills overlooking the bay. Morning sun sparkled on the mosques and whitewashed houses lining the hills like a tiered amphitheater. The high city walls seemed but a frame for the artistry of azure-splashed skies, ivory minarets, and jade greenery—until they drew nearer and Tory saw the battlements atop the walls. A large castle dominated the city from a southern hill.

Sinan pointed to it. "The Casbah." The name meant nothing to Tory, but she edged away from him.

A fortified, walled pier—the mole—extended down to the water. It was shadowed by the city walls above and dominated by a tall tower on the roof of an octagonal fortress. Batteries of cannon were mounted on the fortress; others pointed seaward from the roofs of old warehouses. The walled road extending between fortress and city was built high atop the mole. A fortified buttress shielded the mole gate.

Workers on the water's edge paused in tarring the hulls of small beached ships to wave and shout. Hawk-faced Moors and Arabs wearing caps and turbans, shirts and pantaloons, swarmed over the road. Both ships anchored in the mole's shelter, where rowboats bore the triumphant pirate crew to their celebration and the English captives to their fate. Tory barely had time to glimpse her men, disheveled but unharmed, before she, too, was lowered into a boat. Sinan dropped lightly down beside her.

To Tory's relief, Becky, squawking at the indignity, was lowered into the boat as well. The women embraced.

"Are you unharmed, Tory?" Becky asked urgently.

Afraid to trust her voice, Tory nodded.

Becky held her hand, whispering, "We'll be ransomed soon enough, you'll see."

As she looked at Sinan's profile, clearly delineated against the sky, somehow Tory knew she would not escape him so easily. Unwilling to distress Becky by voicing her suspicions, she turned to watch the approaching town, choking back fear of the present and terror of the future.

When they reached the pier, the mob hooted, pointing at the pale Westerners. Tory and Becky drew the most attention. The universal language of curiosity—and, in some dark eyes, lust— told both women they were the objects of speculation. For once, Tory was grateful for Sinan's protective arm and the bared scimitars of the Turks imperiously forcing a passage through the crowd. They went up a flight of stone steps into the octagonal fortress. A heavy brass-studded door slammed behind them, quieting the spectators.

They had arrived at an open courtyard where a canvas awning shaded a stone bench along the wall. Almost dizzy with thirst and hunger, Tory was ready to slump down on the bench when the fresh sound of rushing water from an adjacent pillared chamber pricked her ears. Tory wandered in that direction, gasping in delight when she saw a lion's-head fountain spouting water into a marble basin. Tory's men were allowed to rush to the fountain and partake of the sweet refreshment, but when Tory moved to join them, a firm hand halted her.

Did he have eyes in the back of his head? she wondered irritably. Sinan was being questioned by a richly garbed man, and she had thought his attention elsewhere. Fuming, Tory glared down at the hand on her arm. She wriggled. The steel band tightened into a vise. Tory licked her dry lips, watching bitterly as another man wrote Sinan's answers in a huge ledger. Obviously he was bragging about his capture, giving an account of the vessel, crew, and cargo. As if to emphasize the richness of the prize, he gestured at the jewel box, which he carried under his other arm.

Infuriated, Tory snapped, "Am I listed as an asset or debit?"

Both Turks gasped at her rude interruption. Sinan appraised what he could see of her defiant face, then made a leisurely survey of her cloaked figure as if charting familiar territory. He said something out of the corner of his mouth to the men, who guffawed and returned to business.

When he finished and the two men left the courtyard, Tory demanded, "What joke did you make at my expense?"

Sinan's eyes ran over her again, lingering on her breasts. "I told them I had decided to be lenient with you since your passions matched your hair—in all things."

Tory flushed. "That's something you'll never know, pirate!"

Raising a brow at the boast they both knew was idle, Sinan snapped his fingers at a hovering servant. He picked up a cup from a brass tray brought to them, and offered it.

Tory eyed the cup speculatively. She reached for it, but Sinan held on to the handle and, with their hands in warm contact, whispered, "It will taste much better in your throat than on my face. If you toss it at me, I'll force you to lick every drop away." He released the cup and leaned close, his eyes issuing a dare.

Could he read her mind? Tory gritted her teeth and rotated the cup, peering down into the pale liquid, mightily tempted to throw it at him despite his threat. But she was too thirsty, she told herself. She lifted her veil and took a deep swallow of the refreshing, tangy juice, reluctantly aware she was learning the value of prudence. She'd never had to consider every word and action before. It irked her to learn such a lesson at *his* hands.

Sinan nodded approvingly. "So, even lofty aristocrats can learn submissiveness. There may be hope for you yet."

Tory's head shot up. "Submissiveness! I'll never submit to you!"

A gentle finger followed the high cheekbone, which was barely visible through her veil. "Perhaps it's not submissiveness I want. The man who tames a wild mare to his hand has a faithful companion indeed." His hand dropped away. "But what does such a woman as you know of faithfulness?"

"More than you know of honor, to be sure!"

The strong mouth quirked sardonically. "Honor is a subjective thing. Perhaps my honor would seem like betrayal to you."

Again, that hint of sadness mystified her, but he gave her no opportunity to question him. He turned away to hand Becky a cup of juice. Tory gripped the cup so tightly her nails marked her palms. Giving the cup to a servant, she stuffed her hands into her cloak pockets. Somehow, some way, she would escape this fiend and show *him* the Grenville code of honor in action.

Minutes later, Tory and Becky were ushered into the bright sunlight, and down the road into the city, Kahlil again forging a passage for them through the crowd of curious bystanders. The East had always fascinated Tory, so she followed meekly at first, engulfed by the world she'd always longed to see.

The city streets were as narrow as alleys. No carriage was used in the whole of Algiers, the favored means of transport being that most ancient one, the foot. A few goods-laden donkeys lumbered about. The houses all looked alike: whitewashed and windowless, or with a fanlight set over a massive oak door. The upper floors of many of the buildings were interconnected, spanning the streets to deepen the gloom. The odor of refuse arising from the drains fouled the air with its stench, but as they passed a series of open doorways, Tory scented strong coffee and exotic spices. She glimpsed robed figures lounging about, drinking from small cups, smoking water pipes. Strange musical instruments whined inside these buildings, which Tory deduced were the Algerine equivalents of English public houses.

Dark-skinned artisans—carpet makers, metalworkers, weavers—hastened out of cavernous workshops to watch them pass. Silk-dressed Turks, Berbers in coarse white burnooses, and bearded, black-garbed Jews all turned to stare at the odd sight of Western women walking the streets. By the time they passed a corner vendor, enticing sweetmeats spread on the table before him, Tory had seen enough. Her stomach growled, reminding her of the indignity of being paraded through the city, hungry, tired, and scared, a sideshow for these . . . these savages.

"I demand to know what you've done with my crew! Where are we going?" Tory tugged at the hand on her wrist.

Sinan didn't respond by so much as a flicker of an eyelash, though the crowd of men gasped and shook their heads at such defiance from a mere woman. Tory tried again to pull away, fruitlessly. She assessed the steep street, then collapsed to the ground, a dead weight. Sinan stopped and looked over his shoulder at her.

Audacious blue-green eyes gleamed over the veil. "There are many ways of resisting tyranny," Tory murmured.

Sinan reached out to force her up, but paused when the gleam in her eyes brightened to a sparkle. She braced herself, expecting him to pick her up. She had just begun to learn he seldom did the obvious, so she was stunned when he shrugged, seized the back of her cloak, and dragged her willy-nilly up the cobbled street. Tory suffered the bouncing abuse to her posterior for three whole steps before, cursing, she leaped to her feet.

He faced her, his mouth twisted in that mocking smile she was fast learning to hate. "There are many ways of enforcing obedience," he said softly. He caught her outstretched hand before she could swing her fist at him, warning, "I cannot suffer such insolence in public. If you strike me, I'll repay you in kind."

He'd outwitted her yet again. Tory knew it, she hated it, and she hated him the more for it. She jerked away and stalked ahead of him. He let her go several feet before he put two fingers to his mouth and whistled rudely. When she turned, he bowed.

"Your disdain would be more effective if you walked the right way, Highness." He swept an arm in the opposite direction. Sniffing, Tory pivoted, head held high, and stalked that way.

Becky trotted along, her worried eyes on the small area of Tory's face that she could see. She looked from Tory's eyes to Sinan's broad back to the ground. Becky swallowed the counsel she longed to give, for she knew Tory very well: The tighter one tried to bridle her, the harder Tory fought the bit. Tory had never met anyone in the whole of her twenty-one years with a will as strong as her own. Worse, she'd seldom been denied what she wanted. As a result, Tory was a little selfish, quite arrogant, and very disdainful of men in general.

Becky suspected Tory had, at last, met her match. If that man had not been her captor and a pirate, Becky would have rejoiced. Only such a man would win Tory's respect. He would humble her a little and make her a better person for it. But under the circumstances, Becky could only await with growing trepidation the outcome of this contest. These two were so dissimilar, the bold pirate and the refined lady, yet so much the same—strong personalities who recognized no limits but the ones they themselves imposed. When two such people clashed, chaos would result for them and for those around them. The captain had shown amazing restraint so far for a pirate, but the battle had just begun . . .

Even bleaker thoughts plagued Tory. Never had she felt so helpless. For the first time ever, she was in a situation where her wealth, her standing, and her beauty were useless. In fact, her appearance seemed to be a liability. Tory wished she were as ugly as Medusa so that she could turn Sinan to stone with just a look. Her absent smile faded as they reached their destination.

The building they were approaching could only be the palace. The walls were white, like those of the other houses, but the similarity ended there. The palace was two-storied, both floors graced with Moorish arches supported by elegant columns with ornate capitals. The upper story was surrounded by a latticed wooden balcony, and the roof cornice was crenellated. Two small towers atop the main entrance were tiled in a zigzag pattern that matched the tilework band extending around the roof. Trees and flowers added the final touch to the landscape of this Eastern potentate's abode.

Turkish soldiers lounged on benches near the entrance. Their splendid uniforms befit their roles as the dey's military police. Their arrogant heads were topped with pyramid-shaped turbans, and the wide cuffs of their shirts were turned back to show strong brown forearms.

Sinan smiled at Tory's worried look and taunted, "Do you find the dey's new palace imposing, fair captive? It was built with the sweat of slaves."

Tory looked at him defiantly, but her heart knocked against her ribs as they climbed the steps to the entrance. Kahlil spoke briefly to an officer who was set apart by his swagger and the red strip hanging from the peak of his turban. He peered curiously at Tory and Becky, but waved them through. Inside, more soldiers guarded a courtyard crowded with men.

The drone of conversation ended as two-score dark eyes turned to look at them. Word had already circulated about the prize won by Sinan, dubbed "the Hawk" by friends and foes alike for his uncanny ability to hunt and catch whatever prey he chased. In the few months since his promotion to reis, he'd already filled the dey's coffers with a share of booty exceeding that won in a whole season by less able captains. Among the men in the courtyard there was considerable resentment and suspicion of this Christian who had risen so quickly through the ranks. He seemed to have few weaknesses, Nazrani though he was.

It was thus a comfort to them that, if the rumors were true, Sinan was a man like any other. He had that most insidious weakness of all—desire for this beautiful woman. The men studied Tory clinically, gauging her charms to see if she was worth an entire share of the rich prize. Most concluded that no woman could be worth so much.

However, one pair of dark gray eyes, set in a swarthy face, kindled with interest as they examined her. Their owner was a tall Arab in a silk burnoose with a gold and silver *agal* about his striped silk *kaffiyeh*. When his eyes went to Sinan, they narrowed to steel slivers.

Tory was too preoccupied with curiosity and concern to note the interest she aroused. The courtyard was as beautiful as she'd expected. The floor was inlaid with six-sided stones, and the galleries were embellished with geometric designs. The fountain in the middle of the courtyard was covered and terraced, its wide, carved columns and zigzag design at the base and roof complementing the palace. Flowers overflowed corner urns. The arches supporting the galleries were harmonious works of art.

They ascended another stairway, then walked along the gallery into a small room leading onto an imposing audience chamber. Tory swallowed. There the ruler of Algiers sat on a low platform that was covered with Oriental rugs and silk cushions. His raiment was heavily jeweled, as was that of his hovering secretaries.

An arm embraced Tory, but she barely noticed Becky's effort to soothe her. Her nerves clamored with fear and with the need to do something to stop all this. She watched Sinan walk forward, bow, one hand to his forehead, and kiss the plump, bejeweled hand of the dey. Her fate was being decided before her very eyes by two savages who considered her a pawn in their game of wealth and power. She must outwit them. She *must*.

"*Salaam aleikum*, Excellency," Sinan murmured.

"Greetings to you as well, Sinan." Bobba Mustapha, dey of Algiers, smiled at his favorite corsair. "Sit beside me." As Sinan obeyed, Mustapha's smile faded. "Did you not take a risk by capturing a British prize when we have a treaty with that government?"

Sinan nodded an agreement, then averred, "I thought the prize worth the risk, Excellency." Sinan opened Tory's jewel case. "Everything aboard the vessel is as fine as these jewels. The treasure should fetch a handsome price." While the dey admired the contents, Sinan continued boldly, "Luckily, we've broken no treaty. They didn't carry a pass, nor was the vessel a merchantman. Our treaty doesn't cover private vessels foolish enough to travel the Mediterranean at this time, surely. And England is too busy with France to send a fleet to attack us, even if the ship had carried a pass."

Chortling, Bobba Mustapha slapped his knee. "You're right, as I will take pleasure in telling the British consul, when that dog arrives. The English have been too arrogant of late. They should know our patience is not unlimited and that we can break our treaty with them as easily as we do with those of less favored nations."

The dey fondled the jewels again. "You have done well, Sinan. I will have my secretary personally log every item in this case and add it to the other inventory. I have heard it rumored you wish something . . . unusual for your share this time." Mustapha's dark, hooded eyes wandered to Tory.

"Yes, if it pleases you, Excellency. I wish to keep the woman for my own. Considering the high ransom she'd bring, it is a rich share after all."

"I am glad you've found one woman, at least, who appeals to you," Mustapha said dryly.

Sinan flushed at the subtle reproach. "Lahtil is beautiful, effendi, and I am grateful for the gift, but she is such a child. Whereas this one . . ." Sinan, too, turned to look at Tory.

Mustapha saw his face set into grim lines that were, incongruously, uncertain. He sensed turmoil in this man who'd always seemed so immune to human weakness. His curiosity about the woman who inspired it increased. Mustapha gestured to Tory to approach.

Tory's shaking knees were not apparent in her confident walk. She stood before this fleshy, bearded Turk, meeting his dark eyes fearlessly. He looked surprised at such boldness from a woman, and a sudden thought struck her. These men seemed disconcerted by a spirited woman. If she proved intractable, perhaps he would let her go, fearing she'd inspire other women to rebellion?

Running her eyes over the dey contemptuously, Tory spoke in loud, taunting Spanish. "I thought the master must be as amoral as the servant. I see I was right." Her eyes scorned the hand fondling one of her favorite bracelets.

Sinan stiffened at her insolence, and Mustapha's cold eyes stabbed into hers. "Woman, I forgive you, since you are new to our land, but speak to me so again, and you'll be considered the man you think yourself, and you will be treated accordingly."

Tory wavered but an instant at the threat. "Why should I bear such humiliation? My ship captured, my crew enslaved, my jewels stolen. You have no right!"

The dey rose to his unimposing height, his stocky figure stiff with menace. "Perhaps a taste of the bastinado will make you see things differently." Such harsh treatment of a Christian woman was rare, but the dey looked furious enough to order it. Sinan—the Hawk—swooped down on Tory like his namesake, fastened talonlike hands in her shoulders, and forced her to her knees. She hissed at him, but he jerked her head back and snarled in her ear, "Apologize if you value your skin. He has absolute authority here."

Tory clamped her mouth shut.

Sinan released her. "Very well, the choice was yours. I cannot save you. After your feet have been beaten to a bloody pulp, you may still fetch a few sequins when you're stripped and sold in the marketplace." He moved away and watched impassively, but one hand played with his sword hilt and his eyes scanned the room as if searching for the nearest exit.

Tory looked from Becky's tearful face to the dey's furious one. The combination of worry for her friend and fear for her own skin defeated her wobbling resistance. She bowed her head. "I apologize, Excellency."

A soft sigh of relief escaped Sinan, but Tory was too miserable to hear it. She let him help her to her feet, numbly aware that nothing could save her now. Sinan spoke in gibberish again, but even if he had used Spanish, she'd have paid no heed. She didn't see Mustapha's cold dark eyes warm as Sinan spoke.

"She is like all women, effendi—her mouth outpaces her brain. But her beauty makes up for her foolishness." Sinan asked the other men to move away. Then he lowered Tory's veil to reveal her face, for the dey's eyes alone.

Mustapha's brows shot up. His eyes warmed further as he looked at the flawless skin, the stubborn red mouth, and the stunning turquoise eyes. "Indeed, a man can forgive much for such a face." After Sinan had raised the veil, Mustapha shook his head. "Still, I do not envy you your task. See she doesn't poison you with your own tea some night when you are weak from delight. You are sure you want this? We cannot send her back to her family dishonored. Such a woman will not mellow with the years, either."

Lambent green eyes belied Sinan's calm reply. "I've never been a man to like smooth wines. I prefer a young vintage with a sharp bite."

"Very well, Sinan, I will so instruct. You must keep the

woman hidden for now. If the British learn we have her, they could become difficult."

Sinan asked idly, "Is this a ruse that's worked before? I've heard it rumored another Christian woman lives in the house of your brother."

Mustapha's half-smile faded. "You know how unreliable city gossip is. I allow you liberties enough, Sinan. Do not press me further."

"Forgive my rudeness, effendi." Sinan bowed.

Appeased, Mustapha said briskly, "I will tell the consul when he arrives that we were unaware of the woman's identity and have already shipped her to Constantinople for the Sultan's harem. They'll know I'm lying but will have no way of proving it." Mustapha barked a laugh as sly as that of the fox he was. He indicated the pale-faced Becky. "What of the other?"

Sinan looked from Tory to Becky. "This woman will be easier to manage with her friend there. I will purchase her from the owners, if you've no objection."

Mustapha sat back down and waved a negligent hand. "Fine. She's too old to bring much. May Allah go with you."

Sinan bowed deeply. "And with you, effendi. Many thanks for your graciousness." Sinan ushered both women out of the room.

When they reached the courtyard, Kahlil joined them again. They hurried to the door, but were blocked by the tall, richly dressed Arab.

"*Andak*, corsair, I want a word with you."

"Yes, Sheikh Hassan?" Sinan halted.

"It is said you intend to keep this woman for your own. Is that true?"

Sinan sighed regretfully. "Would that it were so. The dey denied my request. The sultan has been growing restless, feeling he has not been given enough respect of late. She is to be sent to him this very night. She'll make a handsome gift, will she not?" Sinan turned to look at Tory warmly.

So did Hassan. His nostrils flared. Even cloaked and veiled, Tory's beauty was vibrant. Eyes as turquoise as the Arab's ring inspired a fervent "Most handsome!"

Sinan's fingers tightened at the look on Hassan's face. "We must leave to ready the woman for her journey." Sinan bowed slightly from the waist, the courtesy so casual it was insulting, and urged Tory out the door.

Angry gray eyes shadowed them. Hassan issued a curt, quiet order to a man in a dirty burnoose, who nodded and exited. Hassan dipped his fingers in the fountain's spray, smiling sensually.

Western women fascinated the sheikh, perhaps because his mother was half French. He had a Spanish girl in his harem now, but he had tired of her. She had no spirit. This woman, if the rumors were true, was both beautiful and courageous, a rare combination in a female. Particularly rare in a Westerner, he thought contemptuously. He longed to see more than that lovely pair of eyes. If the Hawk was lying, as he suspected, perhaps he would get the chance. It would be gratifying to steal her from the man who'd humiliated so many good Moslems in his ruthless climb to a captaincy. Hassan had strained his finances to fund a rival captain, and he did not appreciate being made a laughingstock by the owners of the *Scorpion*. Indeed, it was time someone lessened the Hawk's arrogance. Soon the pampered infidel would know his inferiority. Hassan fingered the end of his *kaffiyeh*, wondering if the woman's skin would be as silky.

Some distance away, Sinan opened the door of yet another white-walled, flat-roofed house. He stepped aside and swept a hand before him. "Your new home, madam."

Tory looked from the gaping door to the large, finely shaped hand, and could think only of Dante's famous line, "All hope abandon, ye who enter here." Her eyes beseeched as sincerely as the words of her plea. "Please don't do this. My grandmother will pay you handsomely for my return."

Sinan's face hardened. "And what of your crew? I know this voyage was your idea and very much against your captain's wishes. Don't you feel an obligation toward them?"

Well aware that she was at fault, Tory winced. But she had never intended to desert them. Why did he have such a poor opinion of her? Rashly she revealed her half-formed plans. "After I'm released, I'll ransom them one by one, if I have to beggar myself."

Sinan said grimly, "That will take time. What if they are dead by then?"

Tory cried, "How can I help them as your slave?"

Sinan reached under the veil and ran a finger over her lips. The light caress somehow seemed unbearably intimate, concealed as it was. Sinan's eyes riveted Tory to the spot as he leaned close to whisper, "You can help them, and yourself, in

only one way—by pleasing me. Under the laws of Islam, a slave
who bears her master a son becomes free.''

Taking advantage of Tory's shock, he urged her inside his
home. Kahlil and Becky followed. None of them noticed the
bearded man who hunkered down in the street nearby to watch
and wait.

Tory's ears roared as they emerged into the courtyard. Vaguely
she noticed a magnificent fountain, a dolphin spouting water
down to a sea horse, square in the middle of the blue-tiled floor.
The heat of the day was at its height, but the fountain gave an
illusion of coolness abetted by the thick walls. Spiral columns
of stone supported the second-floor balcony. Cedar balustrades,
elaborately whorled, decorated the overhead gallery. Flowers
gave color to the peaceful ambience.

But Tory knew nothing of peace. She felt smothered, hemmed
in, desperate. She tore off the veil, gasping for air. Impressions
crowded into her tired brain until her head felt too heavy for her
shoulders. She was weighted down by myriad images, all of
them terrifying. She saw her gaunt crew laboring in the stone
quarries outside the city. She saw Becky, ill from one of the
many plagues for which Algiers was notorious, dying despite
Tory's care. And she saw herself, bulging with a pirate's seed,
pale, haggard and hopeless.

The images pressed closer, smothering her. Her vision blurred,
but she struggled gamely until one last burden, the heaviest of
all, crushed the very air from her lungs. She saw herself aboard
the *Defiant Lady*, laughing as she led them all to ruin by her
willfulness. Guilt, compounded by hunger, fear, and tiredness,
overcame her normally strong constitution. For the first time in
her life, Tory fainted. And in a brief moment of comprehension,
she welcomed the darkness and hoped never to awaken.

She didn't hear Becky's cry of alarm or see the concern in
Sinan's face as he caught her. Cursing, he took the stairs two at
a time, then ran along the gallery to a heavy pair of brass-
studded doors, Becky hurrying behind him. He kicked the doors
open and strode through, passing several more doors on his way
to a chamber at the end of a short hall. When Becky opened the
door he indicated, Sinan entered and laid Tory gently on a low
divan piled with silk cushions. He opened Tory's cape, unbuttoned her dress, petticoats, and chemise, picked up a stunning
peacock-feather fan, and wielded it briskly.

Becky bit back a protest, then, looking around, scorned her

own foolishness. Much deeper intimacy awaited her charge. This room had obviously been designed for one purpose only: the pursuit of carnal delights.

The carpets covering the floor were vividly patterned in blue, red, and green, as were the seating cushions scattered about. Low tables were cluttered with knickknacks: sweetmeat boxes of crystal and silver, fans, ostrich eggs carved in beastlike allegorical figures, silver lamps and candelabra. The few windows in the room were high, narrow, and arched. They were covered with an elaborate wood tracery that blocked the light, giving the chamber a seductive dimness even now. Against the wall, lay a wide, very low bed covered with a gold-embroidered blue silk spread that matched the hangings winging out from each side. They soared in shiny folds to the ceiling where they were tucked under a brass plaque set high on the stucco wall.

Chilled, Becky turned back to Tory and was almost sorry when she awoke.

Tory's first sight was Sinan's face leaning over her. She blinked at the intensity with which he watched her, thinking vaguely that no corsair should be so handsome. Full awareness returned. She, too, shivered when she sat and took in the room's sensual opulence. A coolness at her bosom alerted her. She looked down, gasped, and covered her breasts.

Sinan's mouth quirked. "Relax, I only wanted to make you comfortable. I feel guilty enough for having starved you. I should have realized you'd eaten little the past couple of days." He stood and said blandly, "I'll have a tray sent up immediately. Then you may both bathe. I'll have the clothes I want you to wear left in the bathhouse. I'll see you again this evening." He strode from the room and shut the door. There was the distinct click of the outer double doors being locked, then retreating footsteps.

Burying her face in her hands, Tory muttered, "Oh, God, Becky, I'd give all I have to turn the clock back a week. I can't bear the knowledge that I've brought ruin upon us."

"Don't blame yourself too much, Tory." Becky touched her shoulder. "If we were fated to be captured, we would have been, whether here or at home in bed. In years past, these pirates have raided as far away as Ireland. Besides, things are not totally hopeless. Sinan may still let us go."

Tory lifted her head and dashed her tears away. "After he's used me like a whore. Of what good will my freedom be then?"

Unable to reply to that, Becky stood and wandered about the room. She said half humorously, "Things could be worse. I never dreamed captivity could be so luxurious."

She won but a glare for her efforts to lighten Tory's spirits. "I'd rather be beaten and starved, for then I'd keep my integrity. This fiend wants me to gladly participate in my own despoiling. Well, I won't! I'll defeat him yet." Tory surged to her feet, swayed, put a hand to her forehead, and took an unsteady step, then another, growing more confident. She was eyeing the high windows speculatively when a gentle knock sounded.

At Becky's call, a lovely Arab girl entered carrying a tray. She said in soft, fluent Spanish, "Welcome to the home of my master." She set the tray down on a low table.

Tory gaped at her. It hadn't occurred to her that she'd be one woman among many. Her lip curled at her own stupidity. Of course that pirate wouldn't be content with one body to plunder. Well, she was glad. Perhaps if this sloe-eyed, graceful creature kept him busy, he'd have no time for her. So why, when she visualized Sinan's bright head bent over this lustrous dark one, was she irritated?

Puzzled, Tory sat down on the divan and picked up a large slice of melon. She nibbled it, appraising the girl who stood near the door, kohl-darkened eyelids discreetly lowered as she waited for them to eat. Tory wondered why she was not veiled. She wore wide, loose trousers and soft, embroidered slippers. A long rust-colored tunic came almost to her knees; its full sleeves flowed with lace from the peach-colored blouse beneath. A beige sash encircled her narrow waist and matched the small embroidered cap on her head. She wore a tinkling array of jewelry: bracelets on both arms, anklets on one slim leg, and long, dangling earrings. All in all, it was a demure, elegant costume, surely strange attire for a harem girl. It didn't match Tory's vague notions from the Arabian Nights tales she'd read.

Tory looked through the items on the tray for utensils. Finding none, she shrugged and picked up a roasted chicken leg, too ravenous to be worried about such niceties as knives and forks. Becky sat beside her and ate hungrily. When they'd had their fill, they rinsed their hands in the copper finger bowl.

Strengthened, Tory wiped her mouth. The girl peeped at her in fascination. It was time for them to satisfy their mutual curiosity. Tory rose and approached her.

The slanted eyes widened in the dusky rose face when Tory demanded boldly. "Where are the other women?"

She shook her head. "There are no others. Only myself. My name is Lahtil." Her musical voice was as shy as the black gaze that lit on Tory's face before fluttering away.

Disconcerted, glad and uneasy all at once, Tory turned away to hide her confused emotions. She picked up an ostrich-feather fan and twirled it idly. "Tell me, do you ever leave the house?"

Lahtil frowned. "Rarely, and then I am accompanied by the master or Kahlil." Her voice softened on the name.

Tory swung around to look at her. "Who keeps the key to the outer door?"

Lahtil flushed and hurried on, "The master keeps the key. But there will be time enough for questions later. Now you must bathe and prepare yourself." She smiled sweetly at Becky. "There is room enough for you, too, *señora.*"

A chill began at Tory's neck and shivered down to her toes, freezing her questions in her throat. "Prepare myself? For what?" she asked hoarsely.

"For the master's return, of course. He dines with you after the celebration at the coffeehouse." Lahtil opened the chamber door and waited for Tory to pass.

Tory didn't budge. Her eyes narrowed as rage superseded fear. He crowed about his material conquest and expected to return to a sexual triumph. This pirate had much to learn about her. Tory sauntered over to the divan, sat down, and selected the plumpest fig off the tray. "I'll not be prepared like a lamb for slaughter. I can wait to bathe."

Shocked, Lahtil shut the door. "You would defy the master?"

Tory popped the fig in her mouth and chewed slowly. She swallowed, licked her fingers, and slanted a smile at the scandalized girl. "With relish."

Lahtil glanced at Becky as if for verification of such madness. "Is this the way of all Western women?"

"Only of the foolish ones," Becky answered wryly.

"Surely you don't expect me to just give myself to him and make his victory complete?" Tory glared at Becky.

Becky sat down beside her and took her hand. "No, but I hope you'll let common sense rule you for once, instead of pride or temper. What do you think you'll accomplish by refusing to bathe?"

"He'll not assume I'm compliant, at least. Perhaps my appearance will deter him." Tory glanced at her wrinkled, sweat-stained dress.

Becky looked at Lahtil. "Correct me if I'm wrong, but is the captain not likely to strip her and bathe her himself?"

Lahtil shifted uncomfortably. "The master is a fair man to those who obey him. To those who don't . . ." The sentence hung in the air.

"Listen to her, Tory," Becky urged. "You've never had to learn that a woman can turn her weaknesses into her greatest strengths. Anger bestirs anger. Compliancy begets gentleness. He warned you himself you'll only win your release by pleasing him. I'm thinking of you, Tory. I don't want this night to be any more difficult for you than it has to be."

Tory shook her head desperately. "Becky, you know me better than that. I'll not cooperate in my own humiliation, whatever the reason. Whether I am bruised or unmarked in the morning matters not to me as much as how I feel about myself." Tory couldn't bear to look into Becky's worried eyes. She turned away, muttering, "Besides, you assume too much. If I fight hard enough, perhaps he'll leave me alone."

They spent the rest of the afternoon arguing, with Lahtil as an interested observer. By the time heavy footsteps approached the door, they were both close to tears. Sinan entered, his brows shooting up at their distressed expressions. His eyes landed gently on Tory.

"Did you not find the baths to your liking?"

"I cannot say, as I have not seen them," Tory answered calmly.

"Indeed? That's an oversight I can correct." He held the door for her.

Tory clenched her teeth to still their tendency to chatter. "I am comfortable as I am, thank you. Perhaps later."

"But I am not comfortable with your appearance." Sinan strode forward and pulled her to her feet. He wrinkled his nose. "Or your smell."

Tory stiffened. Who had wrapped her in a heavy cape and hurried her through dirty streets? When Sinan tried to pull her to the door, Tory planted her feet. "I have no desire for a bath at the moment."

Veiled green eyes locked with hers. He ran a questing finger down her chin to her high-necked gown. "I had hoped with reflection would come wisdom. Will you not make things easy on both of us and obey me?''

His tone was mild, but his fingers played with the first button on her dress. Tory's eyes went beyond him to Becky. Her friend displayed no satisfaction at being proven right; instead, she pleaded with Tory to acquiesce, for both their sakes. Tory looked at Sinan again, wavering. A small, anticipatory smile played about his lips as he watched her, assessing her. She would not give him another chance to humiliate her as he obviously hoped to do.

Moving one step back, Tory put her palms together and su laamed. ''As you wish, master,'' she gibed.

He inclined his head. ''You learn quickly, sweet slave. Let us hope you will be as facile in other areas.''

Reluctantly, Tory let him take her arm and escort her out of the chamber. To her surprise, they continued out the double doors, down the stairs to an alcove on the ground floor. Tory peeked at the entrance as they passed and saw two red-capped Turks, scimitars at their sides, on guard, eyes averted from her unveiled face.

They passed beyond a heavy door into an antechamber containing several divans. Each was piled with cushions. Clothes hooks lined the walls. The entire room was inlaid with white marble, the walls decorated with geometric tiles of blue and green. The domed roof was inset with glass stars and crescents tinted in rainbow shades. Diffused, multihued patterns danced on every surface. An enormous gilded mirror reflected yet more soft light. Tory gasped in admiration and spun slowly around, feeling as though she'd stumbled inside a jewel-encrusted seashell. The sweet smell of incense added to the seductive atmosphere.

Sinan smiled at Tory's pleasure. He picked up a huge piece of linen and handed it to her. ''The next room is the bathing chamber. Leave your clothes here, take this with you, and don it after you've bathed. I can summon Lahtil to assist you, if you like. Your new attire awaits.''

At least he would allow her privacy to bathe. Tory sighed with relief. She glanced at the pile of clothes on one divan and turned toward the bath, suddenly eager to be clean again. ''No, no, I can manage.''

Sinan caught her arm. ''Disrobe here,'' he repeated.

Tory stiffened. She turned her head until their eyes clashed.

"I will not undress in front of you. If you want to make sport of me, you'll have to do it by force." The challenge rang in the stone room, bold as the turquoise gaze that refused to be cowed by commanding green eyes.

Sinan's grip tightened. He pulled her so close their torsos brushed together. " 'Force' is such an ugly word. Shall we say 'persuasion?' " He reached for the buttons at her neck, but found himself clutching air when Tory pulled away and backed up two steps.

"Force itself is ugly," she pointed out. "I won't let you dress up what you're trying to do to me in pretty words. You may think you've won my body as your plaything, but you will never, ever win my submission."

His nostrils flared. He took a step forward. Tory braced herself, her hands curling into claws. They stood like that for a dozen wayward heartbeats. Then something strange happened. Sinan barked a bitter laugh and turned away.

"I will wait outside. You have fifteen minutes," he grated, leaving the room and banging the door shut.

Tory removed her clothes and entered the next chamber. It was identical, but it contained only a slab of marble in the middle and deep basins on the walls, each with two copper spigots. She turned two of them on, and to her delight, hot water gushed out of one, cold out of the other. Water soon brimmed over the basin and drained out the holes in the marble floor. Tory scooped water over herself with a wooden dipper, lathering well with rose-scented soap. The pleasure she might have found in the activity was spoiled not only by the need to hurry but also by the memory of Sinan's face as he turned away.

Tremors ran through her despite the rising steam. For a moment, she'd glimpsed in his face the same host of emotions that troubled her whenever she was with him: anger, frustration, confusion, attraction. Other feelings had lain bare for her to see in that split second, but she wasn't sure she understood them. Self-disgust, perhaps? But would he be disgusted with himself unless his bold act of ruthless piracy was exactly that—an act?

Surely she'd felt a powerful urge in him to reach out to her, not to punish, but to reassure. She sensed he was as disconcerted by this last emotion as she was troubled by her reaction to his touch. It was almost as if they both struggled to deny feelings that surely had no place between captor and prisoner. Tory wet and soaped her hair, scrubbing so hard she hurt her scalp, then rinsed it, trying to drown her thoughts.

She returned to the antechamber and dressed hurriedly in the unfamiliar garments. A sheer V-neck overblouse secured by a single pearl button. A short, heavily embroidered waistcoat of turquoise brocade designed to fit snugly beneath her breasts. The tiny row of pearl buttons held it so tightly that she felt corseted. Tory looked around for drawers. To her horror, she found only a very full pair of sheer trousers that extended barely below her knee. She looked around for her own clothes, but they were gone. Flushing, she pulled the overblouse down over her bottom and slipped the trousers on, binding her waist with the long, tasseled red sash. She slipped her feet into pointed red slippers. Fearfully, she went to the mirror.

Her gasp mingled with a masculine one as Sinan reentered. Tory's horrified eyes were fixed on her thrusting breasts, framed so temptingly by the tight vest. The silk was so sheer Tory could see the imprint of her nipples; through the translucent trousers her thighs gleamed even in the dim chamber. From the knees down, her shapely legs were bare.

When she noticed Sinan, her flush continued down to her toes. Lahtil had worn no such seductive garments. Again, he humiliated her. But she'd naught to fight with except feigned indifference; it settled over her like the mantle she longed for. When Sinan put his hands on her shoulders, Tory met his forest-dark eyes in the mirror, stifling her urge to cover herself from his appreciative stare.

"You look as lovely as I knew you would," he said huskily. He put a cloak over her shoulders, smiling when she wrapped it around herself with a sigh of relief. He affixed a sheer veil to her face by a band behind her head and escorted her back to her chamber.

They found Becky and Lahtil chatting. Sinan indicated the door with a flick of his head. Lahtil exited. Becky, however, rose and faced Sinan, her little figure stiff with determination.

"I want your word by whatever code of honor you live by that you will not harm her," she pleaded.

"The word of a pirate?" Sinan sneered.

Becky's eyes remained steady. "The word of a man who does not harm those who are weaker than he."

Tory flung up her head at that, drawing Sinan's attention.

"I will be as gentle or firm with her as she warrants," he said ominously.

And Becky had to be content with that, for he ushered her out the door. He locked it behind her and pocketed the key. Then, slowly, he turned to face Tory.

So this was it. The time had come for her, a time so different from her girlish dreams. There was no ring on her hand to sanctify this moment; there would be no exchanged words of tenderness to quiet her maidenly fears. Only desire, hot and lusty, in the green eyes that came closer, closer . . .

Chapter 3

The cloak fell from Tory's numb shoulders. She shakily lowered her veil, unaware of how tempting she was burnished by the sun's fiery retreat. It seemed the Earth Herself had favored this loveliest of daughters with precious elements: hair of fire, skin of alabaster, eyes like oasis pools. Tory's cheeks were tinged rosebud pink with her inner conflict. Her trembling bosom promised earthy delights to the all too human man who longed to rest his head there.

A bare foot away from her, Sinan stopped. She stared at him in fear, frozen even when his lips brushed her temple. "Don't look at me so. I'm but a mortal man, but I'd never dream of defiling such loveliness," he whispered.

His gentleness broke her spell. Perhaps he would spare her if she could distract him? She flew to their supper tray and picked up a silver cup to sip the thick liquid. Looking surprised, she took a deeper sip.

Smiling indulgently, Sinan allowed her the diversion—for now. He sipped from another cup. "It's called sherbet. Do you like it?"

Tory nodded, hurriedly fixing him a plate of roasted lamb, rice pilaf, black bread, and dates. While he sat down, she lit every candle and lantern. Somewhat reassured, she sat next to him on the divan and nibbled a piece of lamb. She licked her fingers when she'd finished, unaware of the kindling in his watchful eyes.

"Don't you people believe in utensils?" She wiped her hands and mouth.

"The so-called conveniences of the West are not needed and are seldom wanted here. Have you ever considered that English ways seem strange to us? We are not the heathens here, milady. You are."

Tory was much struck by his words. Truly, she had not looked at things in that light before. She said hopefully, "Why, then, don't you let me go?"

Sinan choked on a sip of sherbet. Eyes brimming with laughter, he put the cup down. "You never give up, do you?" He ran one finger down her exquisitely molded cheekbone. "I've every hope of civilizing you eventually."

Disgruntled, Tory picked up a piece of molded candy and bit into it gingerly. Eagerly, she took a bigger bite. "What is it?"

"It's called *rahat lokum* in Turkish. It's a concoction of fruit pulp, semolina, honey, rose water, and apricot kernels. Do you like it?"

She reached for another piece in answer. He waited until she'd finished it, then took her hand to suck the stickiness from her fingers. "Would you like to know the English translation of the name?" he asked between licks.

"Yes," she croaked, shivering at the feelings inspired by his mouth. She tried to pull her hand away.

Gently he restrained her, pulling her wrist behind his back, pressing his other hand beneath her chin to tip her face up. "It's called Turkish delight. And there are many other delights in store for you." He uttered the last word into her mouth.

Tory strained to pull away, but he did not allow it. Very well, she would suffer his touch in silence, she decided. He would soon grow tired of embracing a statue. But his warm, tugging mouth proved she was very much a woman, with a woman's weaknesses. Tory's mouth trembled under the gentle assault. His skillful lips tasted of the candy, but the male manna they offered to her new hunger was sweeter still. Even as she castigated herself—*He's using you, Tory*—her lips opened to sample more.

Groaning, he pulled her closer, both hands roaming over her back, waist, and lower spine. Tory was filled by the taste of him, petted by the feel of him, and eager to know more. Why did her curves delight so to the pressure of hard angles and planes? Was that smooth brown skin as pleasing to touch as to look at?

She was lifting her hands to the opening in his shirt when he made a strategic error. He removed the lulling warmth of his mouth and seared a path of kisses down her throat to the luscious globes his hands lifted to cup. Tory stiffened, her hands in mid-air. Her eyes flew open to see his wheat-colored head bent to her breasts. His seeking lips seemed to rip the silk away, stripping her of the hatred that had girded her, forcing her to face the sensual stranger he made her with a touch.

Moaning in self-disgust, she shoved him back on the divan and ran to the locked door. She clawed at it, desperate to escape. Strong hands eased her away, but Tory shrank from them and retreated across the room.

Trembling like a cornered gazelle, she pleaded, "Don't! Please, take me and get it over with, but don't make me hate myself any more than I already do. A ravishing, gentle or rough, is still a violation of all I am and all I believe in. You can seduce my body, but my mind will know what you're doing and hate us both." Misty turquoise eyes beseeched him.

His features wavered before her gaze, so she didn't see him bend his head in brief indecision. He clenched shaking hands against his thighs, but then his face hardened.

When he looked at her again, he was implacable. "Or you may learn that what you believe in is no more immutable than the foolish aspirations of many a woman before you. Pride, courage, self-determination, loyalty—yes, these things are important for a woman as well as a man. But what of compassion, tenderness, maturity? Do you not need to learn these as well?"

Tory wiped her eyes on her sleeve. "Of course. But who gave you the right to be my teacher? Why do you even care what I am?"

"My motivations are no concern of yours. You were foolish enough to think yourself invincible, and now you must face the consequences. I have won you. You are mine to do with as I please." Arrogant, determined, he stalked her.

Tory flung an ivory statuette at him. He dodged and was upon her before she could do more than cry out. He slung her over his shoulder, grunting at her pounding fists, and carried her to the bed. He pulled back the covers and laid her face down on the mattress, ignoring her furious abuse.

"You poor imitation of a man! Filthy freebooter, I hate you! I'll see you pay for this, no matter what it takes!"

He anchored her with a knee in her back and flung off his coat and shirt. More carefully, he removed his sash and laid it on the low chest next to the bed. Then, and only then, did he allow Tory to turn over.

She flopped over like a landed barracuda, teeth bared to bite. He pinioned her wrists and halted her thrashing legs with his own. Keeping his head out of range of her teeth, he watched her clinically, as if gauging how long her strength would last.

Tory used words she wasn't aware she knew. Aside from an occasional wince, Sinan didn't react. Later, Tory would realize how patiently he subdued her. He held her just tightly enough to restrain her; how much easier it would have been for him to cuff her and enforce obedience.

Only when her overworked lungs gasped for air did she give up. Even then, her eyes sparked with defiance as she huffed, "Enjoy your victory while you may. But I warn you, you'd best look to your back and hire a food taster after this night." Her eyes widened when, instead of snarling as she expected, Sinan threw back his bright head and laughed.

Tory watched his brown throat, appraised the yards and yards, it seemed, of muscular, hair-dusted chest, and turned her head away with a disgusted grunt. Damn him, why did he weaken her so? Her vocal abuse he ignored; her physical defiance he quelled with insulting ease; her logical arguments he countered. And always, even as she hated him, he attracted her more than any man she'd ever known. Dimly she knew this last fact disturbed her most of all.

When he spoke, laughter still trembled in his voice. "The dey would be pleased to know his judgment is as acute as ever." When Tory's eyes jerked to his face, he drawled, "He warned me to take care lest you poison me. Does it please you to be thought a murderess?"

"Does it please you to be thought a rapist?" she hurled back.

His mirth died. "I've never raped a woman in my life. But I'm beginning to see the advantages." His face changed with frightening suddenness. Salacious eyes stripped her as he let her see what real lust looked like.

"Shall I show you what rape is? You seem to prefer it." He held her wrists above her head with one hand and swooped down on the revealed cleft between her breasts. His open mouth was both insult and brand as he conquered her supple flesh with none of the tenderness he'd shown before. He nudged the blouse aside, playing with her other breast with his free hand as if she were a toy bought for his pleasure. Tory struggled again, impotently.

When he lifted his head and looked at her, a measure of her pain was reflected in his face before he shuttered all emotion. "Is that what you want?" he challenged.

Tory went still. Her eyes pierced his like new-forged blades. "Yes, let us be honest. I'll wear my bruises like badges of honor, proof of my refusal to be dominated. And every time you take me will be a repeat of the first until you tire of bedding a scratching, biting wildcat. When you let me go, I'll be ruined, but at least I'll be able to look at myself in the mirror."

Sinan blinked. He shook his head, but reluctant admiration chased across his face. Ruefully, he smiled. "Such courage for a woman! I salute you, my Amazon, but you'll not enrage me into allowing your sour victory. You're but a woman, as you'll admit before our time together is over. But only your pride will be bruised. That I promise you."

To her amazement, he stood. His eyes flickered to her blouse as she sat up. She fastened it hastily.

Propping a casual hand on his bare waist, he taunted, "You've many lessons still to learn, but tonight has been beginning enough, I warrant. Have you never heard of the delights of anticipation? Delightful for me, at least. I fear you may find the wait somewhat . . . anxious. Every day you'll wonder—will this be it? And every day you retain your *purity*"—Tory wondered at his mocking stress on the word, as if he doubted it—"you'll worry more with each setting sun. When our time together comes, as it will, you'll be glad to have the waiting over."

Tory rose, tangled hair a-bristle with rage. "You flatter yourself, corsair. I'll count my blessings and say my prayers with every hour you don't touch me."

His chuckle sounded fiendish to her ears. "We shall see, sweet thorn. It will be an interesting contest of wills. But I warn you, I've never lost such a battle yet."

"Nor have I! And I won't lose it to a dirty pirate who hasn't sense enough to respect his betters!" Tory smiled nastily when her wild shot finally found a mark in his angry flush. He paced forward, then, cursing, stalked out, slamming and locking the door behind him.

More eager to escape than ever, Tory shoved a chest below a

window and pushed at the wooden gate. It wouldn't budge. Besides, it was far too small for her to slip through. She jumped down to wander the room, more bothered by his words than she would admit. It would be difficult indeed to live each day in fear of the next, but it was better than losing everything now, certainly. She'd have time to plan an escape . . .

Idly, Tory fondled the items on the chest beside the bed, lingering on Sinan's sash. Why did it bulge? She turned the sash over and shook it. Something heavy thunked against the chest. Tory's eyes widened. Her great-great-grandmother's ruby necklace! Feverishly she searched the other slits in the sash and found several more choice pieces of jewelry.

She quelled a sick disappointment. What else could she expect from a corsair? She should rejoice, for she had her first weapon against him. She'd no idea what code governed pirates, but surely the penalty for stealing must be harsh. Tory visualized Sinan upended, naked, the bastinado slashing at his feet and buttocks. She shuddered. No, even to win her freedom, she couldn't do that to him.

There was another way to turn this discovery to her advantage. They were her jewels, after all. Tory moved to search the room, still puzzling over why he had taken such a risk. If he'd been greedy, surely he could have slaked his lust and then sold her, satisfying both appetites? No, she would have sworn Sinan was neither foolhardy nor greedy. So why had he done it?

Beaufort Avery Cochran, alias Sinan Reis, asked himself a similar question as he slipped out of the house. His groin ached with unsatisfied desire. Why the hell hadn't he left her to the fate she deserved? He'd been a fool to accede to their demands and risk two years' work. Still, as long as he was committed, Lady Victoria Alicia Grenville would not leave him as she'd arrived. Too many men before him had been devastated by that bright wit and sensual beauty, but he would not be among their number.

Instead, the fine English lady would learn humility at the hands of a man whose nationality she despised and whose calling she reviled. He was armed against her undoubted charms because he knew her for what she was—cold, vain, and selfish. Again, he asked himself cynically if she really was the outraged virgin she portrayed so well. Even four years ago, on that disastrous London visit, he'd wondered. And from other London visitors he'd heard unsavory rumors about her. How could any woman scatter her attentions so freely among so many and remain pure? Surely no innocent could boldly defy both him and the dey.

Sinan tried to deny his anger at the thought, but he was not a man who lied to himself. Despite his wariness, he was attracted to her for the beauty and spirit that remained vibrant under shocks that would have stunned a weaker woman. He might as well admit it: The thought of any man but himself caressing that lush form enraged him.

Moreover, he'd risked everything to keep her safe. When she'd angered the dey, his hand had gone reflexively to his sword. He probably would have used it, too, if the dey had called for the bastinado as he'd threatened. And then, again, he'd committed folly to keep her heirlooms safe for her. He paused in midstride, too lost in thought to notice the footsteps that halted behind him, as he realized he'd left the sash in her room. Cursing, he debated going back, but he was already late. He could only hope she wouldn't find it. He walked on. Quiet footsteps shadowed him, impinging on the edges of his consciousness as his inner debate raged on.

Idiot, he scolded, quit lying to yourself. She attracts you more than any woman ever, despite her flaws. When you touch her, it's not her character you think of. Wistfully, he indulged a fleeting wish that her nature matched her stunning exterior. He sighed at his own foolishness. It was just as well she was a she-cat. Should she by some miracle be the one woman he couldn't live without, he'd really have cause to repine.

She'd never forgive his deception, or his rudeness four years ago.

Sinan glanced idly around, marveling yet again at the reluctance of most Algerines to be out after dark. Only rogues and drunkards frequented the winding streets when night fell, but the other inhabitants stayed inside more out of preference than fear. They were early risers and retirers, which suited his purposes.

So, why, then, were quiet footsteps trailing him? Sinan's spine tingled as his faint uneasiness crystallized into wariness. He rounded a building and flattened himself against the wall. When his pursuer peeked around the corner, Sinan caught his head in a neat wrestler's hold.

"Why are you following me?" he demanded in Arabic. When there was no response, he squeezed until the man's breath gurgled in his throat. He eased the pressure, gripping just enough to warn of the consequences should he be denied an answer again.

"The woman!" the man croaked. "She does not go to Turkey, as you claimed!"

Sinan's eyes narrowed. So Hassan hadn't believed him and had sent one of his watchdogs to get proof. How careless of him not to have considered that possibility.

Sinan released the man and stepped back. Without sympathy, he watched the bedouin rub his neck. "Tell Sheikh Hassan the woman's fate is no concern of his. Whether mine or the sultan's, she is beyond his reach. The dey has so decided. If Hassan persists in his interest, he'll have us both to deal with. Follow me farther at your peril." Sinan caressed his sword hilt suggestively, then whirled and strode off, his steps ringing on the cobblestones.

Dammit, he didn't need this! Sheikh Hassan despised Christians, especially the "renegade" who'd humiliated his own captain. As the leader of several bedouin tribes, and the owner of a farm and three vineyards, Hassan was both powerful and wealthy. Such an enemy was the last thing Sinan needed now. If Hassan should ever kidnap Tory . . .

Sinan huddled into his cloak, chilled at the thought. Hassan was rumored to be insatiable and cruel to the women in his harem. He would never understand a woman like Tory. His lovely wildcat would end up broken, or dead. His. Odd, with every passing moment, she seemed more truly his.

He'd begun this farce with the intention of frightening the aristocratic Victoria Grenville to within an inch of her pampered life. He had his own reasons for doing so, both practical and personal. Never again would she encourage, then coldly reject, a suitor; never again would she put so many innocent lives at risk out of foolish pride. But with every kiss they exchanged, every inch of silken flesh he touched, his resolves, justified as they were, became less compelling than this gnawing hunger. So what had begun as a lesson in humility for her was becoming the same for him. Indeed, he wondered now who was being enmeshed in his silken web. He'd best be careful lest he end as the black widow's feast after the courtship!

When Sinan reached the locked marketplace gates, he paused. Hearing nothing but the wind and a bird's hoarse caw, he eased down a side alley to rap on a small door. The door opened a suspicious crack, then wider.

A tall man in a tattered shirt and baggy pantaloons pulled him inside the metalworker's hut. Heavy tables were laden with tools: hammers, tongs, files, crucibles, small and large anvils. Gleaming copper pots hung from hooks on the walls. The metalworker's full nut-brown beard almost covered his face. His skin was dark like that of a Moor, but his snapping eyes were a curiously pale brown, strikingly light in their inky setting.

"Well, man, what news have you?" the dark-skinned man drawled in English, his cultured voice clashing with his appearance.

"I have the woman, but I want her removed as soon as possible. She's endangering everything." Sinan related her defiance of the dey. "Further, she's incited the interest of none other than Sheikh Hassan. The sooner we rid ourselves of her, the safer we'll both be."

"We can't leave now. Don't you return to sea soon?"

Sinan sighed, concurring, "Yes, I finish overseeing the refitting tomorrow. We sail the next day."

"And I have to go to Tripoli. Didn't they make plans for getting her out?"

"They left that up to my discretion." Sinan snorted in disgust. "Discretion, hell! Why didn't they just ransom her and be done with it?"

"It is odd. Perhaps your father wants you to bring her out so he can see you. It has been over two years, after all. Have you gleaned more information about Helen?"

"No, only rumors that a Christian woman is living with Saud, the dey's brother." When Sinan's face tightened with worry, the other man clapped him on the shoulder.

"She's being treated well, I'm certain. Unless she's changed greatly from when we were kids, even a jaded Turk won't be able to resist her. You'll find her, Beau. Win more of the dey's trust and you may even obtain an invitation to Saud's house."

"But hardly to his harem, Terence," Sinan pointed out.

A rakish smile displayed white teeth through Terence's beard. "I wouldn't put it past you to win entrée even there, old friend, considering the way you made the ladies' hearts flutter four years ago when you went to London. By the by, is the Lady Victoria as lovely as rumored?" Terence watched with interest as Sinan flushed and turned away.

"Yes, she's lovely, but she has the tongue of an asp and the will of a mule." He fingered a copper sheet.

"She sounds perfect for you," Terence teased. When Sinan whirled on him, he held up a placating hand. "I couldn't resist it, Beau. Where's your sense of humor?"

"Disappearing rapidly. Too much has happened of late that worries me. How are things in Tripoli? Is the Bashaw still making the same demands?"

"Yes. The treaties Congress made with these rascals weren't worth using up good parchment, much less the millions in tribute. Congress was crazy to be so generous to the dey. Now every Barbary State is clamoring for the same terms. A thirty-six-gun frigate in addition to the tribute! This madness has led exactly where we predicted: The Bashaw is threatening to take American vessels again unless Cathcart persuades Congress to supply him a brig."

"That's what happens when you let diplomats negotiate terms that should be settled at sword point. Though I must confess to a grudging respect for the tiger dey. He's a wily devil. I've got to get back. Be careful in your trading. I want you in one piece when we meet again next month. I hope we both have better news then."

Terence nodded an agreement, following Beau to the door. They went outside, peered around, then leaned back against the shop wall. The moon was a glowing crucible, plating the labyrinthine streets in mellow gold and gilding a minaret in the distance. An old fountain nearby frothed serenely, as it had for decades, night birds performing their ablutions in the life-giving spray as they had for millennia. Overhead the stars seemed to glitter more brightly than they did in northern climes, as if Allah had taken the jewels from his crown and recently polished them, returning them to their settings for the delectation of the faithful.

Sinan reflected, "There's much that's seductive about this land, despite its cruelties. People dress, eat, and intermingle much as they have for centuries. There's something appealing about that."

"I know what you mean. It will be a shame for change to come here, as it must. Something about this air makes a man want to throw a woman over his saddlebow and whisk her to his desert tent."

Sinan's body flushed despite the cool sea breeze, and he knew Terence had put into words part of what troubled him. Abruptly, he said good-bye and departed.

He brooded as he walked back to his house. The last two years had changed him, and not for the better. As expected he'd suffered deprivation and cruelty after he, and the Danish ship he'd sailed with, were captured. In some ways that had been easier to bear than the power he now wielded. It was heady, this ability to mete out life and death, leniency and punishment. The slaves in his household were utterly in his power, of course, and even the men of his crew were more subject to his whims than an American crew would have been.

He'd abused no one, nor would he, but still he'd been hardened by his experiences. Tory was a temptation more difficult to resist than she would have been three years ago. Had he been so seduced by the East's male code that he would repress the gallantry instilled in him at his father's knee and choose instead the transitory delights of the flesh? When he kissed her earlier, he had not been intent on teaching her a lesson; he'd been as hedonistic as he believed her to be. The feel of that warm body incited many emotions in him, but none, unfortunately, resembled righteous indignation.

Yes, Terence had defined what Sinan wanted to do with Tory—sweep her away to a primitive place where there was no right and wrong, only man and woman wanting to please each other as nature intended. No matter who she was or what she'd done in the past, she was here now with him. By the laws of this exotic land, he had every right over her. Despite all his fine lectures to himself, he could not argue away one simple fact: His body burned for this one woman above all others. Now what the hell was he to do about it?

Sinan entered the house, bade his sleepy Turkish guards a good night, picked up a lamp, and climbed to the seraglio. He quietly unlocked the double doors, then opened Tory's door even more cautiously. He set the lantern down beside her bed and was relieved to find his sash apparently undisturbed. Pocketing it, he reached for the lantern, promising himself he would leave without peeking. But again, his primal urges humiliated his honorable ones.

He looked at her sleeping face. How could she seem so sweet when he knew her for a scheming witch? His hand reached out with a will of its own to touch her soft cheek. She slept on her side, one arm under her pillow, her breasts pressed together. One peeped out of the blouse she had loosened to wear as a nightgown.

Sinan's body, already heated, responded to her unknowing display. Even as he told himself not to do so, he reached out to trace the pink velvet trim where it lay against the creamy silk globe. His male flesh ignored his will, standing to full attention in homage to her beauty. A strangled groan caught in his throat as he forced himself to pull away. Raising the lantern, he escaped, locking the doors as he went.

When he reached his own large room, he pulled a rug aside, lifted a small trapdoor, and dumped the jewelry into the cavity below, not bothering to examine it. His hands shaking, he undressed and threw himself on his bed. The sooner the *Scorpion* was ready for sea again, the better, he decided grimly. On that happy note, he slept. But his was not the serene sleep of the just; it was the tossing and turning of the guilty—of a man who knows his days are numbered.

When Tory woke the next morning, the first thing she noticed was the missing sash. She sat up, spine tingling as she realized Sinan must have entered her chamber while she slept. She threw the covers back and hurried to the ostrich egg on the table beside the divan. She turned it over and sighed with relief as three large, perfect rubies fell into her palm. Tory replaced them and set the egg back in its holder.

She dressed in her brief garments, and was buttoning the last button of the vest when the door opened. Lahtil entered bearing a tray. A silver coffee service, embossed with copper whorls, sat next to a plate of fruit and bread.

Setting the tray on a table, Lahtil said shyly, "The master says we may sit in the courtyard this morning, if you wish. You must wear your veil and cloak."

In eager reply, Tory attacked the light breakfast. God, it would be good to get out of this room. Luxurious it might be, but it was still a cage. Besides, a visit to the courtyard would give her an opportunity to further her plans. Surely this fortress had more than one exit? And perhaps even the loyal Kahlil would not be averse to a light flirtation?

Tory soon discovered otherwise. Kahlil ignored her overtures, staring coldly through her. Only when his dark eyes landed on Lahtil did they warm. Tory saw anguish in his face before he looked stoically ahead again, ignoring them. Tory glanced at Lahtil in time to see hopelessness dull her bright eyes. Tory felt a surge of sympathy for the pair. How cruel were the laws of

this land! Tory had always thought England indifferent to the
fate of women, but that misty isle seemed advanced in comparison to this country.

Troubled, Tory wandered around the courtyard. She saw several doors, but whenever she approached one of them, a soldier
courteously but firmly escorted her away.

When Becky joined them, Tory pulled her aside. "Help me
watch the servants' movements. We need to figure out where
these doors lead."

Becky nodded, but caught Tory's shoulder and asked gently,
"And how are you this morning, my dear?"

Tory understood her meaning. She smiled into Becky's worried eyes. "Fine, Becky. It seems our 'master' has little stomach
for feminine aggression. He left me be last night." She wandered away before Becky could probe deeper into what was still
raw in her mind.

For the rest of the morning, she and Becky lounged by the
fountain in apparent indolence, but they watched the traffic
closely. When a girl carried out a tray of refreshment from one
door, Tory assumed it must lead to the kitchens. When another
entered with fresh linens over her arm and walked up to the
living quarters, Tory deduced it led to the storerooms. Only one
door remained shut. That, Tory decided, would lead to the outside. It must be locked, or surely it would have soldiers guarding
it as well?

Tory patted her mouth to hide a yawn. "Lahtil, where does
that door go?"

Lahtil followed her pointing finger. "To the stables."

"But I've seen no horses here. Why are they kept?"

"The master seldom rides in Algiers, but he sometimes takes
his leisure in the countryside outside the city walls."

Tory held out her hand to Becky. "Shall we walk?"

Becky took Tory's hand, but the minute they were out of Lahtil's earshot, she warned, "What you're scheming won't work,
Tory. There are mountains and desert to the interior and more
pirates along the coast. Where would you go?"

"Surely anywhere is better than here. I've something now to
bargain with. If I can make it to the next city, I can bribe a
fisherman to take me to Majorca."

Becky frowned. "Something to bargain with? What?"

Tory opened her mouth to respond, but a movement behind
the tall potted plant they'd passed alerted her. She put a finger

to her lips and walked on, whirling a second later. Instead of
the listening soldier she expected, a small, dirty face peeped out
at her.

Huge brown eyes widened with fright when she took a step
forward. The little boy, who looked about ten, dashed around
her and out the kitchen door, brown legs flying under tattered
pants.

Frowning in concern, Tory walked back to the fountain. The
child probably wouldn't have understood if he had heard them.
But what had she done to frighten him so?

"Who was that child?" Tory sat next to Lahtil.

Lahtil tore her gaze away from Kahlil. "What child?"

"A little boy, about ten, brown hair and eyes."

The Arab girl's normally kind face hardened. "That's Jarrod,
the orphan boy the master brought home last month. He was
begging in the marketplace."

Tory wondered at the disapproval in her voice. "Is there
something wrong with him?"

She shrugged. "No more than there is with the rest of his
race. He's a Jew." She made no attempt to hide her disdain.

Tory's eyes softened with pity. Poor little mite. To be hated
for your very existence was a fate no one should suffer, especially a helpless child. On the heels of that thought came one as
disturbing. How did Sinan's compassion for the boy reconcile
with her image of him?

A ruthless pirate who cared only for himself would have tied
her down last night and taken his pleasure. A heartless savage
who recognized no laws but his own wouldn't have given an
orphaned child, much less a Jew in an Arab land, a second
thought. Who and what was this man who controlled her fate?

As if her thoughts had conjured him up, Sinan entered the
courtyard and strode to her side. His hair was lustrous in the
sunshine. His long legs were clad in tight breeches today, and
his thin white cotton shirt clung to the awesome power of his
torso. Kid boots hugged his legs.

Why couldn't he be old and ugly, sporting an eye patch and a
scar from cheek to jaw as a pirate should? Tory thought despairingly. He had no right to appeal to her senses so. Her hands
tingled to touch him; her eyes drank in the sight of him; her nose
quivered at the smell of coffee and sea spray that clung to him;
her ears pounded with her quickened heartbeat; her lips longed
to feel that hard, masterful mouth again.

Tory tore her eyes away from his steady gaze, damning him and herself equally. She must escape him. Soon!

"I hope you've had a pleasant day." The rumble of his voice made her wonder if he, too, fought some strong emotion.

A blessed surge of anger rescued Tory from herself. She rose to her feet. "Oh, yes, delightful! My every step dogged by your bloodhounds, unable to breathe in this heavy cloak and veil, stifled in the heat, bored, and always, always imprisoned!"

Sinan smiled tauntingly. "I can relieve all of your discomforts but one. Would you like to accompany me to the bath?"

Tory eyed that inviting hand distrustfully. "No, thank you. I shall suffer my discomforts alone."

"Pity. I do so enjoy company when I bathe. Perhaps you'll find your room more to your liking. I'll soon join you there." Sinan looked at Kahlil and pointed to the stairs.

Tory was led back up to her cage accompanied by the refrains of Sinan's cheerful whistling. She was not even allowed the comfort of Becky's presence. She paced the afternoon away, fuming more with every passing moment. She flung off the veil and cloak, wadded them into a ball, and threw them against the door.

When Sinan finally entered, she was in a rare state of distress. "God, if you don't let me out of here I'll go mad! I'm not used to inactivity. I demand you at least let me ride!"

Sinan propped one booted foot behind him and leaned against the door. "Demand?" he reiterated mildly.

"Yes, demand!" she hissed back. "Unless you want a lunatic captive rather than a reasonable one."

Sinan levered himself away from the door and approached her. Locking his thumbs in his belt, he taunted, "One man's—or woman's—reason is another's folly. Since your idea of reason has resulted in folly so far, maybe you should try lunacy."

He caught Tory's hand when she tried to slap him and pulled it behind his back, bending her over his other arm. "Better still," he whispered, "try not to think at all." When Tory turned her head away from his mouth, he nuzzled the curve of her jaw, nibbling down to her collarbone.

Gritting her teeth, Tory forced herself to be still. Struggles and pleas had been pointless, but there were other defenses. When he teased the rim of her ear with the tip of his tongue, not a quiver betrayed her pleasure. Even when he held her head still to find her mouth, she didn't protest. She let him bend her farther over his arm and kiss her ardently. She told herself repeatedly who he was and what he was trying to do, and the catechism was fervent enough to drown out her clamoring need to respond.

When, with a disgruntled look, he released her, she smirked at him. "Is my reasoning still so faulty?"

"No, only specious. When you discover what you're denying us both, you'll realize how much more attractive submission is."

"To an Eastern woman, perhaps, but never to me," Tory scoffed. "Submission is the result of coercion, and I despise force. Besides," she added softly, "it has been my experience that force is generally the last resort of the weak. The strong seldom need to use it."

Sinan lifted a skeptical eyebrow. "Indeed? What a utopian society England must be, then, despite its . . . checkered history. Isn't it odd that the very man who envisioned utopia lost his head as Henry the Eighth proved beyond doubt his own power over the weak?"

Tory groaned inwardly. She'd walked square into that trap. Energized by an argument of the sort she had all too rarely with the males of her acquaintance, she riposted, "And that same history has since proven Sir Thomas More right. It is he we venerate over the king who beheaded him."

"I'm certain Sir Thomas was comforted by the assurance of a future place in history as he was marched to the block," Sinan said dryly.

Tory flounced over to the divan and plopped down. "How ridiculous to argue with a pirate over the merits of force!"

A smile played about Sinan's lips as he sat down beside her and watched her mutinous face. No other female, except his mother, could participate in such an argument with him. What a rare woman this arrogant English girl was!

He couldn't resist needling her one more time. "Indeed, it is rather ironic. Were it not for the efficacy of force, you would not be sitting here beside me." He picked up a plump date and held it to Tory's lips, leaning near to whisper, "But you don't seem to realize that you have a power of your own that puts mine to shame."

When Tory opened her mouth to reply, he popped the date in. Something in her longed to satisfy the hunger with which he watched her chew. Hastily, she swallowed and tried to move away, but he lowered her to the divan, then eased deliciously down atop her.

"The power of a woman over a man is well documented throughout history. Cleopatra, Theodora, Madame de Pompadour, to name but a few. Aren't you curious to see if I'm susceptible?" He pulled her hands under his shirt, flattening her palms against the smooth-rough textures there.

They stayed like that, tingling from the pleasurable contact of hard against soft, neither sure any longer who was tempter, who was tempted. And when Tory's hands began to move, they realized it didn't matter.

Sinan growled and rubbed against her like a great, contented cat. "Ah, sweet, you make a man forget everything and care not that he does . . ." He buried his lips in the pounding curve between her neck and shoulder, catching her hands between their bodies. His tongue flicked her delicate bones and soft skin, outlining one collarbone, then the other.

When he pulled away, he was panting a little. He moved to lie beside her on the wide divan, freeing her of all restraint, yet captivating her by the feel of him warming her from head to toe. He played with a lock of her unbound hair, giving her no warning of the coming shock.

"Tomorrow I return to sea. I'll be gone several weeks at least. Will you not give me one taste of your lips to warm me on the long voyage? One kiss, freely given. That's all I ask. You have my word I'll carry it no further."

Steady green eyes held hers. Tory's heart leaped in her breast. She was glad he was going, she tried to tell herself, for surely she could put her plans into motion before he returned. So why did her throat close with something akin to regret as she realized this would be the last time she saw him? Her eyes dropped to that wide mouth that held such indomitable will, yet such kindness, too. Was a kiss so much to ask? Somehow, it never occurred to her to doubt his word. One kiss it would be, one embrace to give her a taste of how it could have been had he been other than a pirate.

Shyly, Tory cupped his cheeks in her hands and pulled his head to hers. When their lips touched, they quivered as lightning crackled between them. Groaning, Sinan pulled her full length on top of him, holding her head to deepen the kiss. Hesitantly, his tongue crept inside her open mouth.

Tory gasped against his seeking lips, stunned at the sensations inspired by that intimacy. Eyes closed, she rubbed herself against him, burying her hands in his hair, slanting her mouth over his to begin her own shy investigation. Their tongues danced as they exchanged their first kiss that was not a contest, a punishment, or a seduction. Instead, this was a seeking kiss, a hungry kiss, a gift between two people eager to please each other.

For minutes on end they lay entwined, Tory's hair a silken rain upon Sinan's face, his hands in firm possession of her waist, as if afraid to wander further. And in that exchange of bodies and lips came a revelation to them both: The power that drew them together mocked their brave words and foolish pride. It was a need that knew no limitations. It mattered not that he was a pirate and she a lady, or that he was her captor and she his prisoner; the only consequence was this need of two hungry bodies and two lonely spirits for each other.

Tory drew her head away first, but her willful body stayed put atop him. Her eyes misty, she watched Sinan's lids flutter open beneath her. Dazed, they stared at each other, uncertain, unaggressive, as each sought in the other the truth of what had happened between them. Sinan lifted a shaky hand to trace Tory's cheek. The gesture was so tender, almost loving, that she longed to cry.

"Perhaps you are right, after all," he said huskily. "Force has no place in the feelings between us."

Tory couldn't bear the implications of that. She scrambled to her feet and turned away, head bent. Dear God, why had she met him now? She found herself almost wishing she could remain with him. What folly! She recalled his words—reason had availed her little, so perhaps she should try lunacy. Her trembling lips tried to form a smile. "Lunacy" described perfectly this situation. For the first time in her life, she'd found a man she was drawn to, in will, mind, strength, and, oh, so much in body—and that man stood for everything she despised.

Sinan, too, rose from the bed. Clasping her arms, he pulled her back against him. He lowered his chin atop her head. "Don't be so troubled, little one. It's natural for you to feel such things. Think on them hard while I'm gone. Remember, being a prisoner is a state of mind as much as a condition of the body. Give yourself to me freely, and I'll no longer have need to hold you."

He turned her to face him, green eyes as tender as the first sprouts of spring. "And I promise, I'll think of you, as well.

I'll try very hard to understand your need for respect. Truce?''
He let her go, backed up a step, and held out his hand.

Tory almost lifted her hand to his. She longed to give in to
him, even plead with him not to go, but she knew if she did,
she'd start a journey to her own ruin from whence she'd never
return. She, a pirate's plaything? The Grenville blood bestowed
by her noble ancestors fired in her veins. Never could she humiliate her name and herself in such a way.

She flung up her head, clasping her hands behind her back.
''No, there can never be peace between us as long as you hold
me against my will. You go with my blessing.''

And she turned away, biting her lip over the lie, so she didn't
see Sinan's stricken look. His hand drooped back to his side.
Angry green flames burned the tender shoots to ash.

''As you wish, milady.'' He put sneering emphasis on the title
as he strode around to meet her eyes. ''Since you have no use
for tenderness between us, remember this: When I return, you
will be mine, force or no. Understood?''

When a hostile stare was his only response, he tapped her
cheek in warning. ''If you're foolish enough to attempt escape,
I'll not be gentle when I catch you. Rebellious slaves are not
much valued here. The choice is yours.''

And he strode from the room, shutting the door with a bang
that sounded to Tory like the gates of hell closing. She grieved
at the loss of the intimacy that had been so brief, so forbidden,
so sweet. But then she gritted her teeth. Good, let him rant,
rave, and threaten. Her victory would be all the greater when he
returned to find her gone. Ignoring her own misgivings, she sat
down, propped her elbow on her knee, her chin on her hand,
and planned. And if her eyes burned a little, she told herself she
was tired.

Chapter 4

By dawn, Tory was ready to admit defeat and get up. But when
decisive footsteps neared, she hastily closed her eyes, every nerve
tingling with awareness as her door was opened and steps ap-

proached. For ages, it seemed, Sinan stood over her. She caught a glimmer of light through one slitted eye and knew he held a candle. He stared down with an intensity brighter than the flame.

Her breathing quickened, and she was ready to leap away from him when he put the candle down and bent low. Warm lips caressed her forehead with a tenderness that troubled her. Huskily he said, "Good-bye, my Amazon. Dream of me in your chaste bed."

Picking up the candle, he retreated quietly, locking the door behind him. Silence descended, a lonely silence. Tory bit her lip to keep from calling him back. She wondered if he'd hoped to torment her after their bitter parting, but she really didn't think he had known she was awake.

He had indeed left her much to think about. Pirate he might be, but there were complexities to his nature she could only wonder about. She chewed her knuckles, telling herself to stop thinking about him, but she might as well have whistled to stop the wind.

His lust, his anger, his arrogance, she could deflect, but she had no shield against that damnable tenderness. It stirred up too many longings, too many dreams of how it might have been between them if she'd met him in other circumstances. Were he commoner, cit, or nobleman, Tory would have defied the world for the chance to know him better—in London.

But she wasn't in London. She was trapped in Barbary, in peril of her very life, and her only hope of escape lay in deceiving her captor. If he was also the very man who made her shiver with emotions she'd never known before, well, she had all the more reason to guard against him.

Tory dressed, but her fingers faltered as she stared in the mirror. What would Greaty say if she saw her so attired? Tory giggled at the thought of her grandmother's horror. Somehow, after that, the day was lighter. Tory smiled when Lahtil entered and set a breakfast tray on the low table before the divan.

"Good morning, Lahtil. And what joys are planned for today?" Tory attacked the rolls and coffee.

Lahtil met Tory's teasing look with a puzzled frown. "We will indeed be busy while the master is away. He's ordered that I instruct you in dance and in the ways of pleasing a man."

Sputtering coffee back into her cup, Tory glared over it at Lahtil. "I already know how to dance, and I've no interest whatever in pleasing our beloved master."

Lahtil paled. "But you must learn. I am to instruct you. I will be blamed if you refuse."

Tory set her cup down to clasp Lahtil's trembling hand. "The captain will know whom to blame. Besides, I suspect you know little more about pleasing a man than I do."

A red tide replaced Lahtil's pallor. She averted her head with a humiliated moan and pulled her hand away. "So even you perceive my shame. Does all the world know?"

Tory gently turned Lahtil's face back to hers. "And who is 'all the world'? Kahlil?"

"How did you know?" Lahtil croaked.

"I'm a woman. I see how you look at him, and I see how he looks back. But don't worry. I doubt Sinan suspects. I'll certainly not tell him."

"I am worse than nothing." Lahtil bowed her shining dark head. "I not only fail to please my master, I betray him by casting my eyes upon another man, his own trusted officer. If my master knew, he'd have me beaten, or drowned."

"Nonsense! You've done nothing wrong. You can't help it that Kahlil attracts you more than our beloved master." Again, Tory put sarcastic emphasis on the title. "The question is, what are we to do about it?"

Lahtil watched dully as Tory strode up and down. "Do? There is nothing we can do. *In'shallah.*"

Tory paused to stare. "What does that mean?"

"It is God's will."

Tory was so exasperated she spoke in English. "Balderdash!" Tory waved aside Lahtil's question. "A peculiarly English expression that, roughly translated, means 'donkey dung.' "

Lahtil looked shocked, but the mischievous sparkle in Tory's eyes clashed so with her haughtiness, nose stuck in the air, that Lahtil had to laugh. "You English are a peculiar race, indeed."

When Lahtil winked impishly, Tory was so delighted she grabbed the other girl's hands and pulled her to her feet. "That's the spirit! There is more to life than pleasing men, and, by heaven, before we part, you'll know it."

"Before we part?"

Tory flushed. "Another figure of speech. Now, when is an acceptable time for you to meet with Kahlil?"

Looking at Tory's bland face suspiciously, Lahtil answered, "The only time we are ever together is when I go to the *souq.* He always guards me as I make my purchases."

"Indeed?" Tory turned away to finger a feather fan. "And did our beloved master give his permission for us to go there?"

"He didn't say. Kahlil will know."

"And when can I see Kahlil?"

"We are to go down to the courtyard today."

Tory watched the sparkle return to Lahtil's eyes. "How exciting. I can hardly wait." Again, sarcasm was lost on her gentle companion, so simple were her joys and dreams. What would it be like, Tory wondered, to live with no thought but to please a man?

Shuddering at the mere thought, Tory turned away to comb and braid her hair. But when she looked in the mirror above the chest, it wasn't just her own reflection she saw. A tall figure with streaked hair stood behind her, his hands caressing her shoulders, breasts, waist, and . . .

Dammit, enough! Tory slammed the brush down and turned away. Broodingly, she garbed herself in cloak and veil. If the East's law of male supremacy was so lopsided, why had women not rebelled? It was against human nature to be satisfied with giving, but receiving nothing in return. Even Lahtil, who yearned for a man who was beyond her reach, was more contented with her lot than Tory had ever been in her English manor house. The conclusion was unavoidable: Women who were naught but the chattels of men had their own rewards.

The thought was so distasteful that at first she wouldn't accept it. When she and Lahtil arrived in the courtyard, she strode up to Kahlil with more aggression than tact. "We wish to go to the *souq*. Will you take us?"

Kahlil straightened haughtily. "It is not wise for you to leave the house." He turned back to his men.

Tory gritted her teeth but forced into her voice the husky timbre that had served her so well in the past. "But what could happen to us? With you as our guard, no one would dare to approach us."

When Kahlil turned back to her, his stiffness had relaxed a bit. Tory looked down. Really, men were so easy to manipulate. Feed their conceit and they would follow you around like lambs. With a few rare exceptions, of course . . . Tory forced her thoughts away from one such exception to listen expectantly.

"Perhaps, if you prove yourself diligent in learning to please the captain, you may go to the market as a reward." Kahlil smirked into Tory's shocked eyes. "It seems you know less of men than you think, hmm? You could learn much from Lahtil."

Lahtil drew Tory away before she could do more than sputter. Her giggles infuriated Tory further, but a grudging respect was born in Tory for this handsome Turkish officer with the dashing mustache and trim beard.

Still laughing, Lahtil teased, "He's not so easy to influence, no? Kahlil suspects you refused to learn to dance, and he will do whatever is necessary to get you to obey." Lahtil turned to look at the subject of her conversation.

And Kahlil looked back, his black eyes wild and ravenous before he hastily turned away. The merry gleam in Lahtil's eyes died like a snuffed candle. She slumped down on a marble bench by the fountain and stared at her feet.

Tory knew then that she couldn't leave until Sinan returned. Two people who loved each other so much should not be kept apart, especially when Sinan seemed to have no desire for Lahtil himself. If Tory disappeared now, Sinan would be furious with Kahlil and perhaps even with Lahtil. But when he returned, perhaps she could get him in a mellow mood . . . Once he had given his word, she could leave. Tory didn't question why she trusted Sinan. She only knew his word would be his bond.

But how would she elicit that mellow mood? Tory knew of only one thing Sinan wanted of her. She trailed a hand in the fountain to cool her sudden flush. That she could not give him. But perhaps she could make him believe she'd relented? If she agreed to dance for him . . . Then, while they ate, she'd discuss Lahtil. Tory knew little of how men reacted to passion, but surely he'd be eager to please her? After she persuaded him to give Lahtil to Kahlil, she would escape.

It sounded so easy, Tory thought wryly. But she knew her plan was rife with dangers. She'd thus far thwarted Sinan's advances because he chose to let her. If she enticed him, and escaped before . . . Heaven help her if he caught her! Tory shuddered as she remembered the strength in those big hands. So far they'd handled her gently, but after such a trick, he'd be furious.

Tory thrust her doubts away along with a sudden cowardly impulse to leave now, while she had the chance. She looked at Lahtil's bent head. She'd come to care for this sweet Arab girl. Those sad dark eyes would haunt her if she didn't at least try to help her.

And if honor bound her to stay until Sinan's return, she'd no reason to blame herself for weakness . . .

She sat down next to Lahtil. "I know when I'm beaten. You and Kahlil win, Lahtil. I'll learn to dance."

"Oh, thank you, Tory." Lahtil threw her arms about Tory. "You will not regret it. Dancing is fun, truly!"

"My only condition is that you use your influence to persuade Kahlil to take us to the market."

Lahtil's arms dropped away. "My influence? I have none. I am but a woman."

Tory's eyebrows rose at the new bitterness in Lahtil's voice. Could it be she was learning to resent her position of subservience? Tory's lips twitched at the thought of Kahlil plucking his sweet Arab rose only to find himself pricked by her thorns. "Kahlil is very aware of that. What more can you ask for?"

Before Lahtil could reply, they were interrupted by a yawning Becky. "Goodness, I haven't slept so late in years. It must be this sea air. How are you, my dears?" The subject changed, but it was not forgotten by either woman.

In the days that followed, Tory nurtured the seed of doubt she'd planted. "Isn't it odd that women are so little respected? We, after all, wield the ultimate power over the continuity of humanity." And, later: "I've always thought we're partly to blame for our own helplessness. Only when we insist upon respect will we receive it." Or: "Women can be so much more effective than men. You may have heard of our English queen, Elizabeth? She was a mere girl when she took the throne, yet by the time she died, she'd rallied our people to defeat the world's most powerful nation, Spain, and she led our country to its place as a world power. She was our best monarch, so much more effective than these bungling Georges."

Tory didn't mention, of course, that her ideas were considered radical even in England. And while Lahtil soaked up her lectures like a parched desert flower, she taught Tory a lesson that was equally salutary: Feminine wiles were a potent weapon in the ancient battle of the sexes.

While showing Tory how to undulate her arms and shoulders to display their delicate strength, she'd say, "We are taught that Allah sent us here to nurture and pleasure our men. A happy man has no need to beat his wives; he showers his favorites with gifts." As she demonstrated how to bend back from the waist and flick the hips, she said, "Women of my race are not powerless. Have you not heard of our sultanas, the favored wives and mothers of the heirs of the Ottoman Empire? Some of our sultanas have been the real rulers behind the throne. They attained their power by learning to please their men.''

But her most persuasive argument was the one that bothered Tory most: One day, as she demonstrated the proper alignment of hands and feet, Lahtil said idly, ''Though I have not yet experienced the delights of the flesh, I know from others that a skillful lover can make what you call our 'bondage' enjoyable—why, even women of your own race have gladly entered the sultan's harem and felt honored to be chosen.''

The movements of her dance became even more seductive after this speech. Eyes closed, hair trailing past her hips, Lahtil swayed to a sensual inner music. Tory watched her lick her lips and knew, suddenly, that Lahtil was thinking of Kahlil. Tory's cheeks burned when Lahtil made suggestive thrusts with her hips, yet she couldn't look away. Lahtil no longer seemed a servant to male lust; rather she joyously challenged her lover to match and fulfill the mystical power of woman.

Succumbing to a sudden urge, Tory leaped to her feet. Tory didn't hear Lahtil's murmured encouragement as she, too, became lost in the intricate rhythms thrumming in her blood. Eyes closed, she danced, enjoying the sensual slide of the hair down her back, the softness of the sumptuous carpets beneath her feet, the scent of the sweet incense Lahtil had lit. Tory felt as wild, as exotic as this land that called to her. She almost wished . . . Tory's eyes flew open. She froze, then slumped to a cushion. Hands pressed to flushed cheeks, she tried to quiet the tempest in her blood.

Thank God Sinan wasn't there. For a shocking, traitorous instant, she'd have gladly ended her dance in his arms and sunk to the carpets with him. Tory wasn't precisely sure what happened next, but she knew she was shameless to dream about it. Did she dare dance for Sinan? She could fight his seduction, but how could she defend herself against her own traitorous body?

Tory was restless the next day as she tried to come to terms with the changes taking place within her. When she glimpsed a brown little face peeking at her from behind a pillar, she welcomed the diversion. She turned away, then whirled and snatched the boy's shirt before he could run.

He struggled, as if afraid she'd beat him. Tory said in Spanish, ''Hush, *niño*, I won't harm you. Calm yourself.''

Her gentle tone finally quieted his struggle, but his trembling did not cease. Tory's throat ached with compassion as she drew him to a shadowed bench. "Come, sit."

He sat on edge, ready to bolt at the slightest threat. Tory stroked his thin wrist with her thumb. "I only wish to talk. You are Jarrod?"

A wary nod was his only answer.

"Why do you hide and watch us instead of walking up to satisfy your curiosity?"

That drew a response. He finally looked at her, his huge brown eyes wide. "The soldiers would beat me if I imposed myself on you. You are the master's favorite, and I am beneath your notice."

Tory snorted. "Ridiculous. They would not beat you for such a reason. Why are you beneath my notice?"

"I'm a Jew." He said it so simply, as if the three words explained everything. Then a tinge of bitterness crept into his voice. "Worse, I'm a homeless Jew."

A guttural command interrupted Tory's rebuttal. Jarrod tensed, but Tory held him firmly and turned to the Turkish guard. She'd never liked or trusted this stocky, swaggering lout. His shirt was dirty, his body odor overpowering, but it was the look in his eyes when he watched her that repulsed her most.

Tory said coolly, "He's doing no harm. I wish to talk to him. Leave us." Whether he spoke Spanish or not, he could hardly mistake her tone.

The Turk's obsidian eyes glittered. He took a menacing step, but a familiar voice interrupted.

"Ali! Return to your post. I will handle this."

Tory stared Ali down, refusing to let him see her fear, but she breathed a sigh of relief when Kahlil approached. With a last glower at Tory, Ali retreated. Kahlil crossed his arms and stared down at the pair. Jarrod tried to shrink into the stone bench, but Tory sat straighter.

"Don't glare at me. I'm but trying to pass the time in the only way allowed me."

"Do not think to use this little one in some scheme for escape," Kahlil warned softly.

For once, Tory was glad for the veil. She affected innocence. "I? Try to escape your eagle eye?"

Kahlil stiffened. "Woman, do not mock me. I do not like

serving as eunuch to a she-cat. I should be at Sinan's side to help protect him.''

Subdued, Tory muttered, ''Protect him? From what?''

''His enemies. Many resent his quick promotion to captain. If he's hurt, you'll be partly to blame. Remember that as you 'pass the time.' '' Kahlil whirled away, firm steps ringing on the tiles.

''The master will be fine, *sitt*. No one can harm him.'' Jarrod peered into Tory's troubled eyes.

Disturbed both by the news that Sinan was in danger and by her reaction to the news, Tory asked slowly, ''How do you know?''

The boy's dark eyes fired with youthful adoration. ''Because he is as strong as a lion, as wily as a fox, and as wary as a jackal.''

Tory had to smile at Jarrod's utter confidence in Sinan. ''Doubtless he can walk on water as well.''

Jarrod flushed at her gentle mockery. ''No, but he has a measure of the kindness of the one who did.''

''Yes, it's kind to go pillaging others' belongings,'' Tory scoffed.

Jarrod shrugged with the same fatalism Tory had seen in Lahtil. ''These seas belong to us. You Europeans exploit us for your own profit. Why should we not do the same?''

Tory knew Jarrod was referring to the centuries-old European philosophy that if one's own nation's shipping was protected, the pirates would then ravage one's competitors, leaving more of the rich Mediterranean market to the protected nation. Paying tribute to the Barbary states for safe passage was thus as much a matter of politics as it was expedient. Even that new nation that prided itself upon its independence—America—had meekly paid what amounted to a bribe. It was a cowardly, despicable policy. Tory wondered why so few had challenged it. If nations had united instead of trying to best each other, doubtless the whole nest of pirates would have been wiped out centuries ago. But, as usual, commerce played the decisive role in European politics.

When Tory didn't reply, Jarrod rose. Tory raised a hand to stop him. ''Please, may we meet again? Will you tell me more of this land and its people?''

Jarrod nodded shyly, then melted away into the early evening shadows.

They had many such conversations in the weeks that followed. Daily Tory grew more intrigued by and more fond of Jarrod. He had a wisdom far beyond his ten years. Once only did she question him about his background, for the pain in his face pierced her to the quick.

"What happened to my family?" he repeated dully. In a singsong voice that was all the more distressing for its lack of inflection, he droned, "My mother died in the plague of '96. My father followed her shortly after. He was a carpet merchant. An important Turk agreed to purchase carpets for his entire house, but when my father delivered them, he refused to pay the agreed upon price. When my father wrapped his wares to return them to our shop, the Turk began haggling. My father refused to lower his price. He turned to leave, but the Turk demanded my father kiss his feet in penance for trying to rob him. My father refused and the guards beheaded him."

Tory choked back nausea at the tale. "But that's monstrous! Was the Turk brought to justice?"

Jarrod laughed harshly. "Justice for a Turk and justice for a Jew are two different things. The Turk claimed that my father attacked him, a heinous crime for a Jew. There was no one but my father's slave to say him nay."

"But why were you left homeless? Didn't you inherit your father's business?"

"His creditors took everything. I had no relatives to help me, so I had to beg in the marketplace or starve. I would probably be dead now if the master had not taken me in. So you see, *sitt*, I owe much to him."

After that, Tory didn't test Jarrod's loyalty, for she sensed his growing fondness for her. How could she make him choose between her and the man he idolized? They discussed neutral subjects. He related stories of his travels with his father, and he described the beauty of the coastline and the grandeur of the Kabylia.

"You know Spanish from accompanying your father?"

Jarrod nodded, admitting proudly, "I speak Turkish, Arabic, Spanish, Italian, and some English."

"I'm impressed. We English are unfortunately an insular people. Aside from a smattering of French, we rarely trouble to learn other languages. I speak Spanish only because I insisted I learn so I could read Spanish literature and because I have a close Spanish friend."

''What are your people like?''

And so Tory told her youthful but rapt audience of the proud but bloody history of her people, the modern conveniences she was used to, and her love for horses.

''The world's most beautiful horses come from here.''

''Yes, I know. Yet I can't even see one.''

He said nothing at her obvious frustration.

Thus passed the days. Tory was amazed to find captivity so pleasant. She split her time between Lahtil and Jarrod, growing closer to each. Jarrod was a stimulating conversationalist who satisfied the hunger of Tory's mind; Lahtil was a comforting companion who helped Tory come to terms with the needs of her body.

Somehow, during Lahtil's gentle lectures and her demonstrations of how to massage the body, Tory accepted her own femininity. Finally, she admitted she was a woman of deep passion. Someday, perhaps, she'd meet the right man to tap that hidden wellspring. Someday, when these sultry days were as much a dream as the long, scented nights. Someday, when the golden image burning brightly in her mind was dimmed by the mists of time . . .

And so, as Tory awaited Sinan's return, slowly but vitally she changed. Dimly, she knew she and Lahtil, different as they were, English and Arab, fire and soft night, were bonded like sisters. As their kinship deepened, each endowed the other with a completeness, an acceptance they'd lacked before: Lahtil learned to respect her womanhood; Tory learned to enjoy hers. With that assurance came a new confidence to them both. When they sat in the courtyard, Lahtil no longer peeked at Kahlil; she boldly sought his gaze.

Tory watched with delight several weeks later as Lahtil swayed up to Kahlil. Looking deep into his fascinated black eyes, she said, ''The Englishwoman makes good progress. I believe she will be ready to perform the handkerchief dance for the master upon his return. For her reward she has asked to go to the *souq*. I, too, would enjoy the outing. May we go?''

There was nothing subservient in Lahtil's manner now. The slanted dark eyes were sultry with the knowledge of what she had to offer, and the way Kahlil stared down at Lahtil told Tory that he seemed much aware of it as well.

He swallowed. ''Perhaps it can be arranged. Soon we will

go.'' He waved a dismissing hand, but Lahtil stepped closer until her robes brushed his tunic.

"Tomorrow? Please?'' She raised one little hand as if to touch his face. She let it float back to her side, keeping her eyes on him all the while, as if, with the least encouragement, she might touch him.

He stumbled, so hastily did he back away. "Yes, yes, tomorrow,'' he croaked, retreating to the door. Lahtil turned away, missing the fascinated look he sent after her, but Tory saw it. She smiled.

Becky, who sat next to her, shook her head at Tory's glee. "What hornet's nest are you stirring up, Tory? Don't make Lahtil discontent with her lot. The men will think her wanton for being so familiar.''

"Or I'll help her gain what she wants most: Kahlil. Since he won't take the initiative, she must.''

Becky wailed, "Tory, what are you going to do?'' When Tory remained silent, Becky rubbed her forehead. "Oh, God, I'd hoped this mess would teach you that the world doesn't always dance to your tune. When will you ever learn?''

Tory stiffened. "I am well aware of my folly. But I can't help my men until I escape. If I can help Lahtil and Kahlil, perhaps that will be a small recompense for my selfishness.''

Becky sighed. "Forgive me, child. I shouldn't take my nervousness out on you. I'm just worried about what will happen to us when Sinan returns.''

Aren't we all? Tory thought wryly. She patted Becky's hand in forgiveness, not realizing Lahtil had returned from her stroll about the courtyard until she spoke.

"Fear not, *señora*. Tory will please him by taking her rightful place in the harem. Have you not seen her dance?''

Becky looked incredulously at Tory's averted head. "Is this true, Tory? Are you resigned to your, er, place?''

Tory nibbled at her lip. She'd deliberately let the Arab girl believe she intended to fulfill Sinan's desires so Lahtil would have less compunction about encouraging Kahlil. She'd have to answer carefully.

"Let's just say I'm discovering there is more to enjoy here than I thought, and that I have much yet to learn,'' she answered. The oblique response pleased neither woman, but Tory avoided further questions by leaping to her feet. "Come! I'm starved.

And I want to hear all about the *souq*. We did get permission to go, did we not?"

Lahtil was diverted, but Tory knew Becky wouldn't let the matter rest. Indeed, that evening after Lahtil had retired, Becky remained in Tory's room.

Tory tried to evade the issue by climbing on a chest to peek out the high window at the sunset. She was confused about herself, so how could she tell Becky a truth she didn't know? She sighed, mourning the passing of the day into night's dark realms. Tomorrow she hoped to set her plans in motion. It would be too late then to turn back.

A singsong wail floated on the scented breeze as the muezzin called the faithful to evening prayer. Tory cocked her head to listen, no longer startled by the five-time daily ritual. She knew Kahlil and the other devout guards would be kneeling, facing Mecca on their prayer rugs, foreheads to the ground as they said their prayers. What a land of paradoxes Algiers was! The Koran stressed charity and brotherly love among Moslems, yet it also taught the philosophy of claiming an eye for an eye and a tooth for a tooth. Even Englishmen, who'd fought a bloody civil war over religious differences, were rarely so intolerant.

Islam decreed that a man should be brave and just, but the most powerful people in this land, the Turks, preyed on the weak, persecuted the helpless, and considered themselves good Moslems nevertheless. Still, they had a rigid code of honor of their own that Tory was just beginning to understand. Tory wished she had friends as faithful and loyal to her as Kahlil was to Sinan. Children were treated lovingly, and women were respected—provided they submitted to their men.

Tory jumped off the chest. This inactivity was making her melancholy. She had no choice. Escape was even more imperative now that the chains of her bondage were metamorphosing to silken cords, binding her in a way of life as foreign to her as it was distasteful.

It *was* distasteful, Tory told herself fiercely. Somehow the claim grew less truthful with every passing day, a fact that frightened her more than her captivity. Tory had read tales of men who became so used to imprisonment that the outer world loomed more fearsome than their small but familiarly comforting cage. She would not let that happen to her. She was doing the right thing by trying to escape. Of course she was.

So, when Becky asked, "What bumble broth are you brewing now?" Tory turned to her with a reckless smile.

"I'm planning our escape."

Becky gave a small gasp and collapsed on a cushion on the floor, wailing, "Tory, why must you always be so stubborn? We have about as much chance of escape as . . . as—"

Tory tilted her chin. "Men have escaped from Barbary before. Why can't we? Surely it is easier to escape from a lightly guarded harem than from a fortified bagnio?"

Knowing it was useless to argue, Becky sighed. "Tell me your plan. I'll listen, mind you, but that's all unless I'm convinced we have a real chance."

Tory sat down and lowered her voice to a whisper. Becky frowned at first, then looked intrigued, and finally excited. "By heaven, it might work. But what if Kahlil watches you too closely while you make your purchases at the market?"

Tory smiled slowly. "Kahlil will have eyes for only one person, unless I much mistake the matter. Besides, you can help keep him distracted."

"Well, it's worth an attempt, I'll grant you that. But Tory, how will you know what to buy?"

"I've asked Jarrod about the native plants. I shall find a dealer who speaks Spanish; he will tell me the proper dosage."

"But you might use too much, or not enough."

"I know, but what else can we do?"

Becky said steadily, "We can leave *before* Sinan returns."

Rising, Tory went to check the ostrich egg, ostensibly to see if her precious rubies were still safe. Not even to herself could she admit she didn't want Becky to see her face. "I can't leave Kahlil and Lahtil to take the brunt of Sinan's rage. Besides, how will we get out of this harem? You know Kahlil always locks us in here."

Becky walked around to lift Tory's averted chin. "Good reasons, certainly. But I suspect you have another one as well."

What Tory intended as a scornful laugh somehow came out high and nervous. "Don't be ridiculous. Of course I don't want to see him one more time."

"The truth will out, my dear?" Becky teased gently.

Tory flushed, yawning to avoid more questions. "Well, that's enough talk. We'd best be rested for tomorrow. Good night, Becky. Pray for us. If ever we needed God's blessing, it's now."

Becky accepted the rebuff, but her plump face looked drawn as she nodded and left Tory to her doubtful rest.

Many leagues away, Sinan's rest was even less certain. The xebec had fewer comforts than most American ships, and his captain's bunk was barely wide enough to accommodate his broad shoulders. But it wasn't the hard mattress that kept him awake; it was the same worry that had nagged him since he left Algiers: Something was wrong. The instincts he'd honed in years of merchant sailing had grown even keener in the last two years. Instinctively, he knew one of his new men was not to be trusted. The sailor watched him too closely, asked too many questions. He had the look of an informant all over him, and a not very subtle one at that. The question was, who had planted him aboard the *Scorpion*? Ahmet, who was still furious at the demotion visited on him by the *ta'ifa*? Hassan? Or any one of a half-score other men with reason to hate him? Something else bothered him, too. The feeling that some peril lay ahead—a danger that would have disastrous consequences if he didn't face it . . .

And that danger had Tory at its center. Tory. Just the sound of her name on his lips inflamed him. He burned hotter when he visualized her as he'd last seen her, tousled hair glittering in the candlelight like hammered copper as she slept, tempting lips parted, breasts pressing against her blouse as if begging to be free. Thank God she'd been asleep when he'd planted that maudlin kiss on her brow. Even now he didn't understand what had made him feel that disconcerting rush of tenderness.

But the other feelings . . . those he understood very well. And he needed to master this desire, not only because of who and what she was but because he couldn't afford to be distracted now, when he was so close to gaining what, a couple of years ago, he'd allowed himself to be captured for. A few more nightly journeys would give him time to finish making the maps. If only he could be certain that the dey's brother had Helen . . .

Sinan shifted, but even worry didn't chase the image of Tory away. He'd hoped these weeks at sea would help him forget her. Instead, she grew more desirable with every league he put between them. He'd been too long without a woman, he decided. When he returned, he'd take Lahtil. He'd hesitated to despoil her obvious innocence, but hell, she was ready and willing to fulfill the role she'd been taught from birth.

Distraction came at last in the sound he'd been expecting. He braced himself. The creaking of the door to his cabin was his only warning before stealthy footsteps approached his bunk. The moon shining through the porthole gleamed off the intruder's knife. Sinan forced himself to lie still until the last possible moment. The knife arced and began its descent.

He caught the man's wrist and twisted, pleased to feel the pop of muscles as he wrenched the attacker's hand aside and came to his feet in one fluid motion. The attacker staggered, dropping the knife and pulling himself and Sinan off balance. They fell, Sinan on the bottom. The intruder bared blackened teeth, spat in Sinan's eyes, and whipped another knife from beneath his robes with his uninjured hand. Sinan reached out blindly, tossing his head to clear his eyesight. There was a grunt when his fist connected with soft nasal bone, but the man wouldn't give up.

He kneed Sinan in the ribs and fought to raise the knife, but Sinan again caught his hand. With one of the attacker's wrists already sprained, both men knew the battle would be over quickly, but still the man persisted. What had he done to inspire such fanaticism? Sinan wondered.

"Damn you, who sent you?" Sinan hissed.

"*Chitann*, infidel, to send you to your kin!" With a last heave, the Arab elbowed Sinan in the throat. Sinan's grip slipped as he coughed, and the Arab wriggled free. Snarling, the assassin lifted the knife.

Before it could descend, however, another set of steps ran into the cabin. When the attacker whirled to face the new intruder, he was met by a sword in his belly. The knife fell from his hand as his blood and entrails spewed forth. He was dead before he hit the floor.

Coughing, cradling his sore throat, Sinan stumbled over to the oil lamp. His mouth tightened when he saw his attacker's sightless eyes. He sent a grateful look at Omar, his second officer, who was wiping his bloodied sword on the corpse. "Too bad you had to kill him. Now we'll never discover who sent him."

A grunt spoke volumes for Omar's disgust as he searched the body. Finding nothing, he straightened. "The spying jackal deserved to die. I knew he planned something."

Sinan sighed and clapped Omar on the shoulder. "I'm grateful, friend. Question the men and see if they'll admit to knowledge of this man and why he came among us."

Omar nodded and smiled wickedly. "Kahlil will be furious that he was not the one to protect you."

Sinan laughed. Omar and Kahlil were like brothers, though fiercely competitive ones. Sinan said feelingly, "Kahlil's task is not without perils. The Englishwoman will not be a compliant concubine."

Tactfully, Omar made no response to that, though masculine sympathy for his comrade lit his dark eyes.

"This voyage has been a disaster," Sinan grumbled, pulling off his boots to prepare for bed in earnest this time. "I've never seen so many protected vessels in one trip, though I'd wager a number of the passes were purchased from favored nations. Our stores are too low to go farther. Tomorrow we'll return to Algiers, though I hate to go back without a prize. Our investors and the dey will not be pleased. Four weeks wasted!"

"Praise Allah," Omar sighed. "The men have been complaining. They are long since ready to return."

"They are always ready to return. Barbarossa would be disappointed in his brethren's stamina," Sinan said dryly.

Omar retorted, "Barbarossa did not put to sea for weeks on end in his galleys, Sinan Reis. A man starts to lose his lust for fortune when he forgets what he's fighting for." After sheathing his sword, Omar lifted the corpse, heaved it over his shoulder, and departed. Shortly afterward, there came a splash and a muttered verse from the Koran. Then all was as still as before.

Sinan lay back down, ruefully admitting he, too, would be glad to go back to Algiers. Important though it was to keep the dey pleased with his performance, he felt an urgent need to return. He was sure that the assassin was connected to Tory in some way. He couldn't rationally explain his certainty, but he'd learned to trust his gut instincts; they'd saved him many a time in the past two years.

So what did that say about him, he wondered as he drifted off to sleep, when every instinct he possessed bade him take Tory while he had the chance?

PART II

"One ounce of honor is worth more than one
quintal of gold. Do not allow anyone to use you
as a toy. In the land where your pride suffers,
quit it although its walls be built of rubies."

—Desert Saying

Chapter 5

Tory grimaced at Lahtil. "How can you bear to walk around swaddled like a babe?"

Lahtil finished attaching her heavy black veil and pulled her headdress down until only her dark, mysterious eyes were visible. "You will grow used to it. It is better than enduring the stares of men."

Tory looked at herself in the mirror and giggled. "Well, our virtue is safe enough. They can stare all they like, but if we stir passion dressed this way, the men of Algiers have a predilection for draperies." Tory turned to her friend and asked curiously, "Has Kahlil ever seen your face?"

Night-dark eyes veiled themselves until nothing of life could be seen in Lahtil's black robes. Her voice, however, quivered when she replied, "Yes, once. The master called Kahlil to his chamber to confer privately. When I went in to serve him coffee at the usual time, Kahlil was there. I turned to leave, but the master bade me stay.

"And did Kahlil watch you?" Tory probed gently.

Lahtil nodded.

"Did Sinan notice?"

"He . . . is more relaxed in his customs than my former master, but I cannot tell you if he noticed, or minded. I was aware only of Kahlil."

Tory smiled at the revealing statement. Yes, she was doing the honorable thing in awaiting Sinan's return. If she could help Lahtil and Kahlil, she'd make something worthwhile from her stay in Barbary.

"Well, shall we go? I can't wait to get out of this house." Gaily, Tory took Lahtil's arm.

They met Becky, similarly attired, on the way to the harem doors.

"Good morning, *señora*. Are you looking forward to our visit to the *souq*?"

"Indeed I am, Lahtil. Have we been given leave to purchase anything?"

"*Sí*, Kahlil will give us a few sequins apiece, and he will allow Tory to purchase clothes."

Tory covered a sigh of relief by knocking on the heavy double doors. A key turned. The doors swung slowly outward. Kahlil stood in the opening, nodding to all, but looking only at Lahtil. When they reached the courtyard, Kahlil jerked his head and two turbaned guards followed them out the front door.

Tory was so glad to be outside she barely noticed that one of the guards was Ali. Had she seen his eyes, she might not have been so unconcerned about her appearance. But Tory knew nothing in those first heady moments except blissful liberty.

A dawn rain had washed away the accumulated filth in the gutters. Brilliant white balconies nearly met overhead, interweaving with patches of pristine sky in a heavenly patchwork quilt. A nondescript brown bird perched on an adjacent gate burst into sweet song, adding its paean to the new day. The serpentine streets were speckled with shadow as clouds drifted overhead on lazy summer winds. Tory drank in every precious sight.

She started when first she saw the imprint. She craned her neck as they passed it, only to spy another a few houses down. She slowed her pace to drop back with Lahtil. She gestured at the painted hand that seemed to cup the wall protectively. "What is that, Lahtil?"

Lahtil looked. "That represents the hand of Fatima, daughter of the Prophet. Legend says she marked the flags of the faithful with her hand, which she'd dipped in the enemy's blood. Good Moslems hope her sign will bring peace upon their household."

Tory returned to reality with a thud. Lahtil's pride as she explained the gruesome legend was a vivid reminder to Tory of what she'd almost forgotten: Charming, courteous, and wise though these people were, they were also, in many ways, as savage as their Roman, Vandal, and bedouin ancestors.

Tory eyed the graceful imprint speculatively, seeing a way to turn this custom to her advantage. Sinan's house had no such mark. Yet . . .

As they neared the market, the street became crowded. Aquiline-faced Moors strode by, their arrogance exceeded only by that of the uniformed Turks, whose swaggers were as bold as their fierce mustachios. Yet one mean-looking fellow wore a flower in his turban and carried a bouquet to his wife or sweet-heart, Tory supposed. Would she ever understand these people? This Turk was sensitive enough to enjoy flowers and even to wear them, yet she didn't doubt for an instant his skill with the scimitar swaying at his side.

Jews, wearing black silk turbans wound about triangular caps, shrank into doorways to cede passage to Turks and Moors. Tory watched with horror as the Turkish Janissary wearing the flower shoved a Jew against a wall and snatched his embroidered sash away. Tory awaited a cry of outrage, but none came. The Jew looked furious, but he walked on without a word. He received a sympathetic look from a couple of other Jews, but no one commented.

The pecking order was more firmly established here than anywhere she'd ever been, Tory reflected. Even a duke back home would not have dreamed of stealing a commoner's possessions without so much as a by-your-leave. Fascinated but wary, Tory walked on.

Artisans, wearing red caps atop shaved heads, hairy legs bare, led loaded, braying donkeys to market. A few women, veiled from head to toe, trudged in the wake of their men. Tory stared at them, wondering about their lives, until she was diverted.

A half-dozen men attired in long, full-sleeved *gambours* and blousy trousers strode by. It was their faces Tory stared at, however—their *veiled* faces. For a moment, Tory wondered if they were tall women dressed as men. Why else would blue veils shroud forehead, nose, and chin? But no, they moved with long strides that were boldly masculine, their economy of movement at once graceful and arrogant, riveting even among the crowd. One of them caught her eyes and stared directly into them, erasing Tory's last doubt. That gleam of interest and fierce pride was wholly masculine. Tory averted her head.

"Who are those men, Lahtil?" she whispered.

Lahtil looked and turned back hastily. "The scourge of the desert, the Tuareg. Raiders who rob or exact tribute from caravans traveling through the Sahara. They are far out of their territory. They must have come to Algiers to trade." Lahtil's tone was a blend of fear and contempt.

Tory digested this information, struck once more by the paradox of this land. Here, robbers walked with the haughty dignity of dukes and marquesses back home; the ruler of this odd country had himself been a crossing sweeper, according to Lahtil, yet he wielded a power unmatched by George III himself. Here, consequence was decreed less by birth than by status. Here, the strong were respected, the weak spat upon. Tory told herself grimly that she would do well to remember that.

Finally the press of humanity, Tory among them, emerged onto the broadest, straightest street in the city. Tory looked eagerly up and down. Lahtil had explained that the market was held on this street, which was abutted by two of the city's busiest gates: Bab Azoun and Bab-el-Oued. Tory's heart pounded as she craned her neck, looking for Bab-el-Oued. That gate, she knew, led to the north, the coast—and freedom.

Kahlil intercepted her peek. "The market is more interesting than the gates. You have three sequins. I'll examine your purchases and decide whether to allow you to keep them."

Tory itched to slap the superior look off his face, but she only snatched the gold coins out of his hand and flounced away. Soon, however, she forgot her anger, her discomfort, and even, briefly, her purpose, in the market's enchantment. Consequently, at first she didn't notice Ali's stocky figure hovering behind her like a malignant shadow.

The cobbled street was lined with food displays—dates, figs, spices, wheat, barley, coarse breads, melons, sweetmeats. Carts and blankets were spread with wares: carpets, leopard and lion skins, woolen cloaks and blankets, ostrich feathers, metal goods, silks and cottons. The air was permeated by aromas, piquant and foul, sweet and sour; loud cries and soft in Arabic, Turkish, Italian, Spanish, and dialects in between. The sounds and scents fermented into a mixture as heady as fine wine.

At first Tory just listened and enjoyed. But, enchanted as she was, she watched for an herb dealer. She passed an ancient man, his face as brown and wrinkled as a mastiff's, chanting a tale in Arabic. She mingled in his audience, wishing she could understand him. When he stared ahead without blinking, she realized he was blind. She longed to toss one of her precious sequins into the pottery bowl at his feet, but she didn't dare. Reluctantly, she walked on, ignoring the vendors' cries.

She almost missed the small cart; it was overshadowed by a large carpet display. A swirl of rusty white robe caught the corner of her eye as she passed. She hastened to the vendor, an old man with a long, razor-thin nose matched by keen dark eyes. His virulent blue cart held tiny racks on which sat small bowls of leaves and powders. Tory wasn't certain if the rank smells emanated from the herbs or from the old man, but she hadn't time to be squeamish.

She glanced behind her. Ali was fingering a carpet several paces away; Lahtil was holding a bolt of silk up to the sun; Kahlil was guarding Lahtil, but he caught Tory's glance and took a step toward her. Becky intercepted him, saying something.

Whirling back around, Tory asked in her slowest, clearest Spanish, "Do you have a tasteless, harmless powder to induce sleep?"

The old man looked at her uncomprehendingly.

Tory sighed, tapping her foot in vexation. She clasped her hands together then put them to her cheek and inclined her head as if resting on a pillow. She yawned widely.

Bobbing his head, the ancient pointed at a bowl and yawned in return. Tory was so excited he'd understood her she failed to notice Ali's watchful gaze. She pinched two fingers together to indicate she wanted a small amount.

The vendor nodded again, his red cap falling over one ear. He straightened it impatiently, took a small woven sack from the stack beside him and half filled it with the fine powder, babbling something. It was Tory's turn to stare uncomprehendingly until he held out his other hand and repeated his words. Smiling, she offered him one of her sequins.

His mouth dropped open. He snatched the coin and bowed deeply, giving her the sack.

Pocketing it, she held out her hand and tapped it. He stared as if he'd suddenly gone blind. Tory's mouth tightened, but she couldn't afford to make a scene. She patted the sack in her pocket and, pinching two fingers together, held up one finger with the other hand.

The old man frowned. Tory raised her two pinched fingers to her veiled mouth and made a loud gulping sound, then spread her hands and shrugged. The old man grinned, revealing precisely four blackened teeth. He eyed Tory up and down, as if gauging her weight, then held up two fingers, bringing his other hand, fingers pinched, to his mouth twice and swallowing.

Tired but elated, Tory nodded and turned away. One major purchase down, three more to go. Tory wandered to an artist's display. When Lahtil joined her, several garments slung over her arm, Tory turned to her and said, "I'd like to paint, Lahtil. Would you help me purchase brushes and paints?"

Lahtil nodded and discoursed with the artist, a beanpole of a man with a long, thin beard. Tory pointed to several brushes and small pots of paint. She sighed her relief when Lahtil paid for the items for her and gave her change.

Tucking the bundle under her arm, Tory asked, "Where are the horses sold? I've heard so much about North African horseflesh that I want to see them."

Kahlil, hovering at Lahtil's side, said shortly, "I'll show you the captain's fine stallion."

"I would enjoy that, but I'd also like to see the buying and selling," Tory interjected sweetly.

When Kahlil's face remained stony, Lahtil cajoled, "I, too, would like to see them. Please, Kahlil?"

Kahlil's expression softened as he stared into her upturned, pleading eyes. "Very well, little chicken. But only for a moment. And first we must purchase clothes. Sinan was explicit about how he wants his favorite attired."

With a mocking bow he ordered Tory to precede him. She sniffed, biting her lip to stifle a retort, but she stepped in the direction he indicated. They stopped at a wall where stacks of bright, soft garments were folded and draped. Kahlil sorted through them himself, grunting his approval or scorn. He arched an eyebrow at Tory, waiting for her to take an interest, but she had no intention of dressing to please Sinan. She tapped a bored foot.

Kahlil shrugged. A devilish gleam in his eyes, he held up several garments to Tory, then paid for them himself. Tory was looking about for the only garments she was interested in purchasing, so she didn't notice how ephemeral the materials were. She spied her goal and took a step in that direction, but Kahlil spoke to her sharply.

Grimacing, Tory stayed where she was, but she caught Becky's arm and pressed her last sequin into her friend's hand. "Go to that vendor and buy me a turban, a shirt, pantaloons, and sandals," she whispered urgently.

Tory drew Kahlil's attention by stepping up to admire an embroidered pair of slippers. "These are very nice. May I have them?" When he nodded, she picked up a soft cotton nightdress and stroked it. However, she was not so busy keeping him occupied that she didn't notice how Ali wandered after Becky. She watched him inching toward her as if to eavesdrop. Tory gnawed at her lip, but there was nothing she could do except pray he wouldn't tell Kahlil. Dammit, why was he so interested in their purchases?

When Becky came back, the garments hidden under her robe, Tory smiled at Kahlil. "I've spent enough of the master's money. Shall we go to see the horses now?"

Ali sneered at her innocent tone. She glared at him, vowing to watch him carefully. This slimy asp would strike a deathblow to their plans unless they were very, very careful.

When they reached the end of the street, Tory saw that one side was lined with tethered donkeys, the other with horses—but horses such as Tory had never seen.

She ran an experienced eye over them. They had the traits of the pure Arabian: small heads, deep, powerful chests, and strong necks. They were not large horses, but, as they daintily nibbled at their feed, they seemed descended from Pegasus himself, powerful enough to wing their way up to the sky.

An Arab in a striped headdress and white *haik* led a creamy white animal before a row of men attired in Western dress. Tory heard him saying in Spanish, "Orion is spirited but gentle. He will breed for you many fine stallions . . ."

Tory turned to Kahlil pleadingly. "Please, may I speak to the owner? I breed horses at home, and I'd like to discover what regimen gives them such lovely coats."

Before he could voice the refusal she saw trembling on his lips, Tory said rashly, "Please, if you let me, I promise to dance obediently for the master when he returns."

Kahlil hesitated, then nodded. "For a moment."

He made as if to follow her, but Becky stumbled, howled, and fell on her backside into a display, sending baskets flying. The vendor descended on her, screeching in Arabic, and Kahlil had to turn to appease him.

Tory sent a hard look at Ali. This time he didn't even bother to turn away. But at least he wasn't close enough to hear.

Hurrying to the owner of the horse, Tory interrupted, "Please, I'd like a word with you." He stopped his spiel and looked at her in astonishment. The Europeans did likewise.

Tory ignored their muttering and stepped closer to the Arab. "I want to purchase two of your horses," she whispered. "Today. Now. The ones with the greatest speed and stamina."

The Arab recovered swiftly. "Woman, spare me your pranks. You could have little money."

Riled at his scorn, Tory dipped into her cloak. She cupped

her hand to her chest so only he could see, then opened it. He blinked, dazzled by the blinding red sparks. Courtesy fell over him like a blanket. He excused himself to the other men. They eyed them curiously, but wandered off. "Hafez Gibran, at your service." The trader bowed. "Whom do I address?"

"My name is unimportant. Show me your finest horseflesh," Tory ordered in her most imperious tone.

The trader respectfully held up the leading rein of the cream horse. "Orion is the swiftest I have."

Bending, Tory ran her hands over the muscular legs. She patted the arched neck and looked into the alert dark eyes. Indeed, he would do nicely, and his name was appropriate—Orion, hunter of the heavens.

Tory glanced over her shoulder straight into Ali's eyes. She swallowed, but whirled back around. Kahlil, at least, was still occupied.

"Quickly, show me your strongest remaining animal."

Hafez indicated a showy gray that skittered away from his hand. "This one is strong as well."

The stallion's withers shrank from her light touch. He was barely broken, and his legs had a delicate look that bothered her. She shook her head decisively and pointed at a nondescript but powerful bay.

"I will take Orion and that bay."

The Arab's assumed respect became genuine. Curiosity gleamed in his eyes. "Are they for you?"

"That's no concern of yours. Come every day to the house of Sinan Reis, commander of the xebec *Scorpion*. When you see Fatima's hand painted at the entrance, take both horses, saddled and bridled, outside the gate of Bab-el-Oued in the early evening. You may have to wait." She handed him the two rubies.

The Arab's curiosity was replaced by craftiness at the urgency Tory couldn't disguise. His hand tightened around the stones. "That will cost more."

Tory stiffened. "Those two rubies are worth far more than two horses, even such fine ones, as you well know."

"Perhaps. But if the woman of Sinan Reis is making an assignation, it could mean trouble for me if it's discovered where you bought the animals."

Tory gritted her teeth, but she had no choice. She took the last precious ruby from her pocket and looked down at it. It was the size of a robin's egg and had the deep, blood-red fire found only in the finest of stones. Forgive me, Great-great-grand-mama, she said to herself. She made as if to drop it in the Arab's avaricious hand, but at the last minute she snatched it back. She made sure, however, that he got a good look at its size and quality.

"You can buy a small herd of horses with this one stone alone," she taunted, pocketing the ruby and patting it. "*After* you meet me. You get the last stone on delivery."

Gibran looked furious for a moment, then gave a grudging laugh. "As you have decreed, beautiful bargainer. I will meet you on the beach, in the first stand of brush beyond the fortresses."

The commotion behind her was abating. Leaning close to the Arab, she fixed him with a glare. "I'm making these purchases as a birthday surprise for my master. If you are not waiting with the horses when and where we agreed, I'll tell him of your rapacity. He and the dey will not be pleased."

Meeting her glinting eyes, he nodded silently.

When Kahlil said over her shoulder, "Come, woman, we go," Tory smiled up at him brightly.

To the trader, she gushed, "Thank you so much. I'm certain my own horses will soon look as healthy when I use your concoction." With a last warning look, she retreated. Kahlil led her off so quickly that she didn't see Ali step up to Gibran and slip a coin into that ever-ready palm.

Looking harassed, Kahlil herded his charges, pausing a few steps later to appraise their purchases. He raised an eyebrow at Tory's paints and Becky's books. "Perhaps our goods are not to your liking?"

Tory and Becky tried not to shift guiltily under the clandestine weight under their cloaks. "I but saved some coin for another visit," Tory muttered.

Kahlil looked sardonic, but said nothing. They set off again. Tory looked around for Ali, frowning when she couldn't spy him. Where had he gone? Before she could worry long about the matter, Becky walked up to Tory and peeked at her inquiringly. Tory inclined her head.

"Praise God," Becky whispered. "At least I didn't bruise my privates to no purpose." She rubbed her bottom.

Tory giggled. "I'm grateful for the help, but couldn't you have found a less . . . physical way to distract him?"

"My brother always said I had a bottom like a trooper. I guess I just proved it." Becky sighed lugubriously.

Tory whooped, her merry laugh ringing over the market's cacophony. One of those who turned to look for the source of the pleasing sound was a tall man dressed in silk robes and *kaffiyeh*. His dark gray eyes lit with a strange fire when he spied Tory. He approached.

"So, the Western jewel is still with us. Did our ambitious Hawk cheat the sultan of his prize?" he said in Arabic. Kahlil stiffened and turned to face the intruder.

Tory, too, turned to look, wondering why that melodic voice sounded vaguely familiar. Gray eyes delved into hers, darkening to charcoal at her direct gaze. Tory swallowed and took an instinctive step backwards. She glanced at Kahlil's set face and wondered what this arrogant Arab had said.

When Kahlil didn't answer, Hassan continued in Arabic, "He's been gone a goodly time. Could it be Allah has lost patience with this unbeliever who dares to command a ship sailing under the Koran's banner?"

"It is not for us to know the will of Allah," Kahlil countered smoothly, "only to obey His laws. Sinan has taken up the sword to defend and profit us, as a brother should. Since he is our brother, should we not allow him the time he seeks to study our ways? The banner of Islam is not to be carried lightly. He takes instruction from an *imam*, as all Algiers knows. I find that admirable."

Stepping closer to Kahlil, Hassan jeered, "Empty words to excuse an empty man. He has had over six moons to study. He is using the dey for some sinister purpose of his own, and, most loyal friend of the Hawk, I will know what it is."

Kahlil clutched the hilt of his scimitar at the threat. "And what, most ignoble Sheikh Hassan, is your purpose? Do you think to steal something that is not yours by impugning Sinan? You espouse the Koran with words, he with action. Is it you Allah will bless, or this 'unbeliever'?"

When Hassan whitened with anger, Kahlil pressed his point more keenly. "Your appetite for Christian women is well known. In fact, I have heard men of your own tribe mutter at your . . . habits. Such pursuit of material gain and earthly pleasure would not please Allah, either."

Hassan took another furious step forward, then clenched his fists and paused. Offering the ultimate insult—overt lust for an-

other's woman—he leered at Tory. His eyes dropped to her swaddled figure as if he would tear the veils away.

He turned back, allowing Kahlil to see the covetous, determined look in his eyes. "My purpose is my own affair. But you
can give the Hawk a message: I shall be watching him." In an
angry whoosh of robes, Hassan whirled away.

Kahlil was tempted to follow and challenge the insult, but his
responsibility lay with the woman. Harshly, Kahlil ordered the
group forward.

On they went. They were too far away to see when a stocky
Turk, who had watched from a distance, approached Sheikh
Hassan.

Sinan's heart pounded as the *Scorpion* anchored beneath the
mole. He told himself he was nervous about meeting the dey,
but the figure lurking in his thoughts was softly curved, pale,
and smooth rather than swarthy and bearded. He'd returned
empty-handed before, but never had his hands been cold and his
brow beaded with sweat.

No, he might as well admit it—the lady hellion had worked
him up into such a lather that he was fractious as a rutting stallion. After six weeks of tossing in his narrow bunk, he feared
one look at her would be enough to make him cast honor, caution, and even pride to the winds and spread her beneath him
where she belonged. . . . Sinan angrily straightened his finest
coat, a wide-sleeved *gambour*. By damn, he'd never been rattled
by a woman, he scolded himself, and he was too old to start
now.

But even as he climbed into the quarter boat to head for shore,
something deep within him knew another, more fearsome longing: to touch her hand and look into her eyes, to share his
thoughts with her. No more. This fear had kept him at sea so
long; this craven *djinn* rode him still.

The dey's audience chamber was crowded and noisy. However, when his presence was noted, a heavy silence descended
as, one by one, the men turned to look at him. Only then did
Sinan notice Sheikh Hassan standing by the dey. By the look of
things, Sinan reflected, he'd returned not a moment too soon.

Ignoring Hassan, Sinan made his obeisance to the dey, kissing
the plump, bejeweled hand. "Effendi, forgive my intrusion, but
I wanted to speak with you about my voyage."

"Was it successful?" Mustapha leaned forward.

Sinan straightened and crossed his arms over his chest. "We captured no prizes. But we were successful in ridding ourselves of vermin. One question remains, however: Who infested the *Scorpion* with an informer? Once, when we were in pursuit of a Maltese vessel, this man clumsily loosed our mainsail. By the time we had it secured again, the vessel was beyond our reach. It would almost seem someone hopes to keep me from adding to your treasury . . ."

Only Hassan and the dey could hear him. Sinan watched Hassan through lazy-lidded eyes as he let his words trail away, but the sheikh's expression did not change.

Mustapha watched Sinan study Hassan. Abruptly, he waved a commanding hand. "I wish to speak with Sinan alone, Hassan. We can continue this conversation later."

Hassan bowed and retreated, but he turned at the door to look at Sinan. Cool green eyes held smoldering gray for a long, tense moment. Then Hassan whirled and was gone. The other men in the room left at Mustapha's command until only the two ever-present Turkish guards at the door remained. They were too far away to hear, and they were so much a part of the dey's life that Sinan took them as much for granted as Mustapha did. Four of Mustapha's predecessors had been assassinated just within the last century, and the tiger dey had no intention of joining their rank. Sinan knew it was a measure of the dey's trust in him that he was allowed to keep his sword in Mustapha's presence.

At Mustapha's command, Sinan sat next to him on a large cushion. "Thank you, effendi. I regret my news is poor, but, under the circumstances, I'm relieved to be here at all. The informer made an attempt on my life."

The diversion worked. Mustapha frowned and put aside his recriminations. "Do you know who sent him?"

"Unfortunately, I do not. My own guard dispatched him a little too efficiently."

"Which is much to be preferred over incompetence," Mustapha pointed out.

Sinan grinned at the feeling in Mustapha's voice. "Indeed, I'll not argue with that." His smile faded. "I suspect I know who sent him."

Mustapha's eyes narrowed. "Yes? Who?"

"Our illustrious Sheikh Hassan." Sinan watched Mustapha closely. When he showed no surprise at the revelation, Sinan nodded. "It was as I thought. He came to you today to implicate me in some misdeed. What tales is he spreading about me?"

As if debating how much to relate, Mustapha twisted a huge sapphire ring on his finger. When he turned back to Sinan, his plump features were worried. "No tales, Sinan. Such makes him dangerous, for his plaint is Allah's truth. And it is a protest I hear ever more frequently from others."

Knowing what was coming, Sinan braced himself.

Mustapha sighed. "You are my most able reis, Sinan. For that reason, and that reason alone have I been so liberal with you. But even I cannot defy my troops and advisers indefinitely. You know enough of our history to understand that." Mustapha looked at him sternly.

Sinan nodded, for he did understand. The dey of Algiers was a ruler of absolute authority only so long as he wielded it well; if he was judged weak, or if he ceased to bring economic prosperity to the regency, then his absolute authority would become dissolute dithering. After that, it would be only a matter of time, and usually a short time at that, before someone stronger wrested the reins of power from his hands by guile or, more often, by force.

Mustapha continued grimly, "Some of my advisers are even doubting my devoutness because I allow you to command. You've had long enough, Sinan. You must decide what is more important to you—your position here or your boyhood religion. If you are to remain a reis, you must embrace the Koran. Studying is no longer enough now you've made such a powerful enemy."

Restlessly, Sinan rose to pace. He had to have more time! Did he dare pretend to renounce the faith that had been his bedrock since childhood? He cringed from the mere idea. But he would have no choice unless he could very quickly finish what he had come to do. And now he had to contend with Tory as well. She and her crew had complicated matters greatly.

Striding back to the dey, he bowed deeply. "I understand, effendi. I appreciate your patience. May I have one more moon? If I am unable to renounce my faith by then, I will give up the *Scorpion*."

Mustapha hesitated, then nodded. "One more moon." A chiding smile replaced his grim look. "And remember, Sinan, Allah or God is one divinity. Christ and Mohammed are both prophets we mere mortals do well to honor."

Sinan bowed his head in acknowledgment, even as he thought,

Not quite. Christ did not believe in exacting an eye for an eye and a tooth for a tooth.

"Effendi, how many of the Englishwoman's crew have been ransomed?" Sinan asked idly, sitting beside the dey, as invited.

"Most of them. And they brought a tidy sum. Your last capture has enriched the treasury more than those of all the other reis combined."

"Are they held at Bagnio Baleck?"

"Indeed. Why do you ask?"

Shrugging, Sinan let an embarrassed look descend over him. He cleared his throat. "Uh, the woman has asked me what happened to her crew. She will be pleased so many have been ransomed."

The dey's suspicious gleam was replaced by a lascivious smile. "Ah, the woman. She has pleased you, obviously."

Sinan's flush was genuine this time, as were his words. " 'Pleased' is not the right word. She has frustrated, aroused, and astounded me . . . but I have certainly not found her boring."

"Some men find the capriciousness of Christian women exciting." Mustapha nodded wisely. "I am not one of them, praise Allah, though I wish I could say the same of my brother." Mustapha broke off abruptly, as if regretting his frankness.

Sinan's eyes dropped. Here was the best hint yet. "I have heard he has several Christian women in his harem. Has he not found them pleasing?"

To his frustration, Mustapha clammed up, saying only, "It is not seemly to discuss another man's harem. Now, Sinan—have you any proof Hassan hired the assassin?"

"None, effendi."

"Then I can do nothing," Mustapha sighed. "However, if you were to embrace the Koran and bring me proof . . ."

Sinan agreed, rising, "I am well aware that I need proof. I know you cannot afford to antagonize Hassan. His tribe is too powerful. Now is not a good time for you to have to quell a rebellion. Nor can the treasury afford the loss of taxes. But I have made a few inquiries of my own. Hassan has offended many of his elders with his . . . loose morals. They are said to be muttering that his blood has been thinned by his half-French mother's. Nor do they like his treatment of the women in his harem or his intrigues. He has enraged the Tuaregs by kidnapping the sister of one of their chiefs. He has troubles of his own.

It's my opinion he'll end up stewed in a broth of his own making.''

"You could be right, Sinan." The dey lifted a stubby finger in warning. "See you are not the spice in that broth. I will expect your answer a moon hence. And if you hold to your faith, Sinan, I cannot promise to protect you. You may find yourself lucky to be in chains again. Keep that in mind as you weigh your choices."

"I understand, effendi. *Bilhana!* And Allah be with you until we meet again." Sinan kissed the dey's hand and backed out of the room, bowing.

The dey's fervent, "*Bilshifa!* I will remember you in my prayers," rang in Sinan's ears long after he'd gone. But soon his steps kept pace with his heartbeat. Then he was running, all his former nervousness and fear obliterated under the rush of blood inspired by one thought—Tory.

Tory's tongue circled her upper lip as she tried once more to paint a perfect hand. And, once more, the result looked like a deformed gorilla's palm. She threw the brush across the room.

"Blast!" she cried. "Why didn't I pay more attention to all those drawing lessons Greaty insisted I have?"

Becky looked up from hemming the pantaloons they'd purchased. "And so I asked you, at the time."

Retrieving the brush, Tory gritted her teeth and set to work again. She didn't notice Becky's surprised, approving look at her perseverance.

"You know, Tory, this sojourn in Barbary could be the best thing that's ever happened to you, if we make it out safely." When Tory snapped her head up in a glare, Becky continued serenely, "You've changed, m'dear. And, for the most part, changed for the better. You've learned that the world does not—indeed, should not—always suit your whims. Some things you have to accept and make the best of. Patience is not something you had much of two months ago."

Struck by the abigail's insight, Tory sat back on her heels. "Indeed, I believe you're right, Becky. Lahtil has made me realize much. She's had such an unhappy life, yet I've known few people sweeter or more accepting of their lot. She's *too* accepting, I believe, but I admit I need a measure of that fatalism. It's not so bad being a woman, after all." With a grim tightening of her mouth, Tory amended, "At least, it won't be, after I escape."

Becky secreted the trousers in the bottom of the chest, beneath filmy night robes. Then she approached her charge to hug her. "Our danger has been worth it, for that reason alone. It's a pity Sinan is not respectable. He'd be perfect for you, Tory."

A blank look replaced Tory's thoughtful frown. She bent over her painting again, saying nothing.

Becky sighed, but said only, "I'm famished, as usual. This heat keeps me hungry all the time. I'm going to fetch Lahtil and see if we can dine on the patio. It will be cooler there."

When Becky had gone, Tory rose and methodically put away her paints and brushes. She wadded up her pitiful attempts and threw them in the corner. She wandered around the room, but soon her feet took her to the chest. Almost against her will, she drew out the filmy dancing costume Kahlil had purchased for her. She'd been appalled at the briefness of the garments when she'd had a chance to examine them, but now, as she appraised them, she flushed.

Slowly, compulsively, Tory held the brief tunic and sheer, blousy trousers against herself. Would she dare to wear them for Sinan? Tory stared at her pink face in the mirror, only to shut her eyes at what she saw there. He was a pirate, *a pirate*, *a pirate*! she told herself, but the sensitive core of her body heeded her not. She wanted to wear these garments for him; wanted to dance like Salome for him. But when the dance was done, would it be her head or his served up on a platter? The churning in her gut did not abate. Tory kept her eyes shut in an effort to deny the feelings she couldn't yet face.

Thus, the deep, husky voice stunned her when it said over her shoulder, "Hello, my Amazon. The garments are lovely, but they will be more beautiful yet on your silken form. Will you wear them for me?"

Tory's eyes flew open, and there he was. Surely taller, more handsome, and far more disturbing than she'd remembered. Holding her gaze in the mirror, he approached, a gleam in his eyes that sent a shiver up her spine. But a shiver—of what?

Chapter 6

Tory felt as if she'd awakened from a six-week slumber to find herself in Eden, blessed beyond measure. Birds caroled, the wind sang to the beat of her thrumming heart and her every pore tingled with sensuality. Where the grayness of uncertainty had been, all was now vivid, renascent green. Sinan's return rejuvenated her like the joyous, life-giving green of a Saharan oasis, or like snowdrops defying winter's greedy clutch. Tory's lips parted to speak his name; she dropped the clothes to run where her instincts urged her. Before she could move, an errant sunbeam glanced off the dagger at his waist.

Tory froze, confused, as he hoarsely called her name and held out his arms. *Run to him!* her heart cried, but her eyes remained on that dagger. Symbol of all he was, reminder of how she had come here, warning that he was not the promise of home and happiness those welcoming arms made him seem.

She turned away, mumbling, "Welcome back, Sinan."

Sinan's arms dropped. His giddy joy at seeing her again faded. So, she had not missed him these interminable weeks, as he had her. It was true: Lady Victoria Alicia Grenville cared for no one but herself. Yet the admonition didn't ring true any longer. Her eyes had held something when she first saw him . . . And something as basic to him as blood and bone, stronger than pride, bade him test her.

"Tory," he pleaded, "look at me."

Slowly she turned, her arms crossed over her bosom. His heart pounding, he strolled up to her, pulled her arms down, and drew her to his chest. "Come, this is no proper greeting. Has Lahtil taught you nothing?"

Green eyes locked with blue. Both were aware they'd passed an important milestone in their relationship—but both feared to mark it.

Tory finally had to close her eyes to the gaze that probed her very soul. But her body remained painfully aware of the bone and sinew of him. How well they fit together, as naturally as bolt and latch, kettle and lid, one part indispensable to the other. Oh, God, she couldn't bear it. If he didn't release her soon, she'd throw her arms about him and prove how much she'd missed him. But she had more than herself to think of. Becky. Her crew. Greaty, who must be frantic by now.

Sinan sighed. So he'd imagined that look because he'd wanted so much to see it. Outraged pride and nagging disappointment gave him strength to release her. Immediately she turned away to put the dancing costume in the chest. His instincts, which had been attuned to her from the very beginning, warned him that she had retreated from him again. He clenched his hands against the need to embrace her until she had no room for false barriers, but his reason had returned. With it came caution. He mustn't forget who she was. They were from different worlds, the pair of them. After all, had she not disdained him and his country four years ago? Now, when and if she discovered who he was, she'd have double reason to hate him.

He walked away, forcing himself to put mental and physical distance between them. He couldn't afford to lose his head, especially now. Too many people depended on him. Lady Victoria Alicia Grenville, Lady Victoria Alicia Grenville . . . Even her name sounded aristocratic, aloof, arrogant. The heat in his body receded, leaving him sober and strangely melancholy. The cost of honor had never bothered him before, but he'd never paid such a high price. He paused when his boot struck something that crackled. He bent, picked up the wad of paper, and smoothed it out. He frowned at the crude outline of a hand. What the devil?

Tory turned from straightening the already neat chest, intending to throw out a light comment to dissipate the tension, but she froze when she saw what he held. Why the deuce hadn't she thrown her scrawls away? She bit her lip as, one by one, he picked up the drawings to scrutinize them.

Puzzled eyes met hers. "I didn't know you liked to draw. But why are they all the same? And a hand is rather a peculiar subject to choose, isn't it?"

"When we went to the market, I saw the hand of Fatima painted on several houses. I wanted to see if I could match its compelling grace." Tory smiled ruefully. "As you can see, I could not. I'd best stick to chairs and tables and linear objects in future."

Shrugging, Sinan dropped the papers and dusted his hands on

his pantaloons, watching her closely without appearing to. Her bright smile seemed strained. Why would she be nervous about the drawings? "Have you been so bored, then? Did you follow my instructions while I was away?" He wasn't sure whether to be glad or sorry when the old haughty look brought her chin up.

"Yes, master," Tory droned, bobbing her head. "My garments are suitably brief, my dance appropriately suggestive for a . . ." But she couldn't say it.

Sinan had no such trouble. "A concubine?" he taunted, stepping close to tilt that proud chin higher. "Your dress may be appropriate, but your manners are not. Welcome me as a concubine should." He pulled her limp arms around his neck. She didn't struggle when he kissed her deeply, aggressively, all lusting male now rather than the protector who'd seemed to greet her. She found this Sinan much easier to resist. Her mouth ached when he at last lifted his head to glare down at her.

Grunting in disgust, he pushed her away. "Bah! You've learned nothing. Kahlil will catch my tongue for his inability to discipline you." He turned away, as if indifferent to her reproachful look. Only he knew how his gut lurched with self-disgust. But he had no choice. If acting the role of master was his best defense against her, then he had to play it to the hilt. She'd fight enslavement like the wildcat she was, thus subjugating his own need to cherish her.

Since his logic was no comfort to either his conscience or his feelings, he was more brutal than he intended when he turned at the door to sneer, "You, my lady hellion, are not the only woman in my harem. It's past time, I think, to sample the charms of a woman who knows how to be one." To his astonishment, a soft hand covered his before he could turn the knob.

An even softer voice said, "Perhaps women need to be treated as such. Are you man enough to make a woman of me, Sinan Reis?"

Sinan turned his head in disbelief. But there she stood, no hostility apparent now. From the top of her burnished head to the tips of her slippered feet, she was seductive Woman challenging Man. For a moment, he fancied he saw an apple in her outstretched hand.

His craven *djinn* wailed a warning just in time to halt the hand reaching out to her. He blinked and, ludicrously, saw himself being served up like a pig on a platter, that same apple in his mouth. *Danger!* his instincts shrieked as he stared into the beckoning depths of her eyes. Get away or drown.

Groping for the doorknob, he muttered an incoherent excuse and beat a hasty retreat. Tory's delighted giggles trailed his flight until he was safely outside the seraglio. Hell's bells, who was prisoner here? With that thought as comfort, he went in search of Kahlil.

In her chamber, Tory collapsed on the divan, weak with laughter. Never had she seen such fascinated horror on a man's face. It was certain he did not know how to react when the tables were turned, she thought, laughing to herself. He'd looked at her as if she'd suddenly grown two heads when she invited him to make a woman of her. She'd certainly succeeded in distracting him from Lahtil. Perhaps she'd handled him wrong from the beginning. Men enjoyed the hunt; how did they like being the prey? The smile on Tory's face would have made Sinan break into a sweat, had he seen it.

Downstairs, Sinan found Kahlil chastising Ali. "Keep a respectful tongue in your head. Ahmet deserved more than demotion for challenging the captain's authority. You're a fool to believe him, no matter how long you've been friends. Our captain is a good man, Moslem or not. Ahmet, the womanizer, drunkard, and boaster, is not a shining star in Allah's firmament."

Sinan's lips tightened as he listened. Thank God he had not been observed returning. It was time to scotch this rumor spreading even among his own men. He sauntered over to the two men, answering Kahlil's glad greeting with a nod, but never taking his eyes from Ali's sullen features.

"If you've a grievance, Ali, spit it out."

Ali hesitated, then snarled, "The last one who did so was punished."

"Ahmet took up arms against me, Ali. Was I supposed to stand still and let him strike me down? How can I maintain authority if my own men flout it?"

Ali muttered something beneath his breath. Kahlil, who stood near him, looked shocked.

Only rigid control kept Sinan calm. "Speak up, Ali. I will not retaliate if your charge is fair."

Bracing his feet, Ali snapped, "An infidel should not have such authority over true believers."

"Even if his authority is granted by the dey?"

Fear replaced the scorn in Ali's dark eyes at the challenge. He backed up a step, then bowed his head. "I mean no offense, Sinan Reis."

Kahlil watched Ali march back to the bench beside the entrance before he turned to Sinan. "You should release him from service, Sinan. He's no longer to be trusted."

"Better a snake in open view than one hiding in the grass to strike the unwary."

"Perhaps . . . unless the snake is hungry to sink his fangs into the bosom of the family."

Frowning, Sinan turned to look at his most trusted lieutenant. "What are you hinting at, Kahlil?"

"Ali harbors lust for your woman, Sinan. He has several reasons to wish you ill now."

A chill ran down Sinan's spine and lurched into his gut. "Has he harmed Tory?"

"No, of course not. But, given opportunity, he will."

Sinan's eyes fixed on Ali with an inimical glare that reminded Kahlil of a lion he had once seen defending his pride from another male.

"He'll not be given an opportunity," Sinan murmured with deadly certainty. "Will you help me watch him?"

"Of course. But there is another who is far more dangerous."

Warily, Sinan bobbed his head toward the stairs. "Let's go to my chamber where we can be private."

After they had settled on plump cushions on the floor, Sinan demanded, "What happened in my absence? Was the woman hard to manage?"

"Not as difficult as she hoped to be. But she, too, bears watching. For such a one, she capitulated too easily to your commands. Your favorite is trouble, Sinan. She draws the vultures down upon you."

"I, too, find something different about her. I will be on my guard. But I deduce she is not the one you warn me of."

Kahlil shook his head. He leaned forward to emphasize his words. "When I took the women to the *souq*, we were confronted by Sheikh Hassan. He, too, lusts after the Englishwoman. He bade me give you a warning: He suspects your quick rise to reis and will be watching you. And, Sinan, I fear he must feel confident of defeating you, for he didn't even pretend to hide his greed for your woman."

The tingling at the back of Sinan's neck grew to an ache at

Kahlil's words. He was certain now who had hired the assassin, and he even knew the reason. Hassan had committed violence before to win a woman he wanted. Sinan's heart pounded harder at the thought of Tory's danger. If his vigilance wavered, Tory would pay the price. The summer was almost over. Soon Hassan would take his tribe into the vast wastes of the Sahara—where Western women had before disappeared without trace.

Kahlil looked curiously at his grim captain. He sensed the concern was not for himself, but for the woman. Kahlil wondered at the relationship between the pair, but such was none of his affair. Just as Lahtil was none of his affair, he reminded himself scornfully, but that did not prevent him from thinking of her. And worse.

Clearing his throat of the sudden lump, Kahlil queried, "And how was the voyage?" The two men were discussing the attempt on Sinan's life when a tap came at the door.

After Sinan called for entrance, Lahtil entered with refreshments. Kahlil averted his head.

Sinan frowned and looked at Lahtil. Her face was veiled, so why did Kahlil seem afraid to look at her? This was not the first time he'd acted oddly in her presence. Nor was it the first time Lahtil had looked at Kahlil's bent head with such intensity.

When she met Sinan's eyes, her own gaze dropped. "Welcome home, master," she said huskily.

Accepting a cup of sherbet, Sinan replied, "Thank you, Lahtil. I understand you coaxed Tory into following my instructions?"

Lahtil's slanted eyes twinkled before she veiled them with her long, thick lashes. "With Kahlil's help, master. Tory will dance for you tonight."

Heat disturbed Sinan's groin, and he wondered vaguely if he dared to let her dance. The Tory he'd returned to was subtly different from the Tory he'd left. He was not certain how, but whatever the change was, it fogged his wits and tormented his senses. He glanced up at Lahtil to question her, but froze with his cup halfway to his mouth.

Kahlil had been forced to lift his head to accept a cup from the tray Lahtil offered. They stared at each other with a look Sinan recognized—pure, unadulterated sensual longing.

When Kahlil's hand brushed Lahtil's arm as he picked up the cup, he jerked back, spilling sherbet on his tunic. With a cry of distress, Lahtil set the tray down and used the end of her sash to swipe at the stain on his broad chest. Kahlil rose as if scalded. Strangling out an excuse, he left.

Lahtil looked as if she might cry for a moment, but she picked up the tray and asked dully, "Is there anything else you need, master?"

Yes, Sinan longed to retort. Several bottles of wine and a whore, to relieve this cursed ache. Sighing, he dismissed her. When she was gone, he set his cup down and rose to pace. Weren't things complicated enough without this new problem? If the decision had been his alone, he would have given Lahtil to Kahlil without hesitation. How cruel of him even to have considered taking the girl's innocence! But the dey would be highly offended if Sinan rejected his gift.

Besides, Kahlil was a proud man, a Moslem to his toes. He'd be humiliated and offended if Sinan gave him the woman he believed he had no right to claim. Furthermore, Lahtil served as a buffer between him and Tory, something he needed more than ever now. Sinan sat down, crossed his ankles, and propped his elbows on his knees. What an imbroglio! What the devil would happen next?

When he at last girded himself for another encounter with Tory, his first sight of her did indeed seem inspired by the devil— with Tory as his handmaiden. The breath left Sinan's lungs in a whoosh. He stood to hard, taut attention, in every way. For such an odalisque as she did many a man dream of.

She reclined on her side on the divan, nibbling at a bunch of grapes. Her attire—or lack thereof—consisted of filmy blue pantaloons, a minute aqua vest corseting her abundant bosom, and a cream underblouse in a hue so close to her skin color that she seemed naked. A richly wrought girdle embroidered with silver thread and inset with pearls and jade cinched her impossibly narrow waist. A circlet of jade, pearls, and tiny silver bells adorned her forehead; her wrists jingled pleasantly with bracelets, and one slim leg was accented by an anklet of tiny silver bells. Her toenails were painted a shockingly bright peach.

When she turned her head to look at him, the heaviness in his loins became an iron ache that riveted him in place. He couldn't move. He didn't dare go forward; he hadn't the strength to retreat. So he could only stare into mysterious, kohl-accented eyes. Tory had always been beautiful, but now she was temptation personified, Venus and Astarte in one flesh sent to torment him.

And was she as dangerous withal? Was the invitation he read there real, or had she some devious plan in mind?

Calm deliberation grew harder every moment when his body urged him to do nothing but feel. The needs that had taunted him since he captured her were becoming so painful that he was almost beyond the point of caring whether she trapped him. Of what meaning were such paltry values as reason, right and wrong? Of what use was his own safety if he went mad trying to secure it?

Grasping at something, anything, to distract him, he croaked, "Have you supped yet? I'm famished." But his eyes were on the creamy skin of her bosom as he spoke.

"I'm finishing now. I intended to fix you a plate after my dance, but if you're hungry, come eat some grapes with me." She beckoned him nearer.

So Eve must have looked when she lured Adam to his downfall, Sinan mused with what little rational mind he had left. He, who'd come unscathed through over two years of slavery, had fought countless battles, and even now straddled a thin line of danger, was too frightened to move a step. If he did, she would not rise until she was his; if she became his, he feared he'd never let her go. And he could not keep the Lady Victoria Alicia Grenville a prisoner forever.

He didn't move a muscle.

She plucked a grape, raised it to her mouth, and bit into it with delicate white teeth. She chewed slowly, swallowed, then circled her lips with her tongue, doubling his torment. Unconsciously he duplicated the movement. He closed his eyes to shut out the pleasing picture. And she did please him. God, how she pleased him, he thought despairingly.

Sinan was too rattled to notice the observer to this wordless, heated exchange. Lahtil's bleak look softened to one of pride as she glanced from her pupil to her master. Tonight her presence would not be needed as Tory learned what it meant to be a woman. Lahtil's dark eyes closed in envy as another, very different image swam before her, but she opened them and banished all thoughts but those of duty. One remaining task and all would be perfect for the man she respected and the woman she'd come to love. She slipped around Sinan, noting with amusement that he didn't even hear her leave. She walked to the harem entrance and made a soft request of the guard.

She would not have been so satisfied had she read her pupil's mind.

Tory's heart tried to leap from her breast as she lay still under Sinan's burning gaze. Could she go through with this? Yes, he deserved to be treated to some of his own medicine, but she had not bargained on her own reaction to those molten green eyes. If she danced for him, would she be initiated by fire into an ancient rite for which she still was not ready? When Lahtil left, she knew she hadn't long to decide. She shoved the grapes aside and sat up. Her eyes went from Sinan to her own all-too-revealed body and then to the silk handkerchiefs Lahtil had left on the table.

They seemed to burn her fingers when she tucked them in her girdle. She had to dance for him, she told herself. Dressed as she was, Sinan would be suspicious if she refused to dance now. Her escape, and Lahtil's future happiness, awaited only her courage. Good reasons both, but, as Tory rose, deep down she knew she had to dance for an even more vital reason.

The music began, rising from below to nudge her conscience. This land, this music and, most of all, this man were in her blood. Her joy at his return left no more room for self-deception. She *had* to dance or bid good-bye to the only world she had ever known. Seductive as he made that sacrifice seem, she would not give up her chance for freedom without a fight. There, in England, Tory knew she would not be interested in a crude pirate. Grenvilles were meant for better things.

It would be a betrayal of all she knew if she didn't make one last attempt to escape him. Defiance was an ineffective weapon against him, but she knew now the awesome power he himself had told her of. It was her only hope.

So dance for him she would, with all the fire and eroticism this land incited in her soul. She knew she courted danger. She needed not only to manipulate Sinan but to control her own primitive impulses as well. But she was a Grenville, ever in command of herself. This would not be so very different from flirting in London drawing rooms. Instead of fluttering a fan or her eyelashes, she would use her body to tantalize. And when her dance was done, she would, with a laugh, hold him off. She'd entice and promise, but not deliver. He'd be so eager to win her favors that he would not suspect her plans for escape, and he would listen when she pleaded for Lahtil.

Then, after she'd bent him to *her* will for a change, she would know the courage of her convictions once again. A man she could rule was not a man she could respect. Without respect, there would be no desire. There was no danger involved. None whatever.

Tory glided up to Sinan's rigid figure. "Come, master, sit. I will dance for you." She took his hand to lead him to the divan, wondering at his stiff, almost clumsy movements, and at why he set a cushion in his lap. She kicked the rug aside, not seeing his pained look as he watched the gentle sway of her hips as her unbound hair flowed like a warm red tide past her waist.

Taking a deep breath, Tory turned to face him. She tilted her head and closed her eyes, letting the rhythm of quaita, drum, and cymbal flow through her body like a narcotic. She began swaying in reply, arms only at first; then shoulders, waist, and hips joined the languorous thrum. Tiny bells jingled as she moved.

Tory's hands fluttered to her waist and removed each handkerchief. Slowly, erotically, in time to her padding feet, she ran them over and around each arm, her neck, her waist. Finally, she placed them inside her blouse to warm them against her breasts. She pulled them out with her teeth, leaving her mark in the soft material before letting them flutter to her feet. Shimmying from the waist, keeping time with the music, she bent to move the handkerchiefs several feet apart, parallel to one another. Straightening, she idly danced about them and between them, tantalizing with her power to dance to the line of love, cross it, or avoid it at her whim, thus eschewing a lover's entanglements.

Gradually, she was transformed from the coquette to the wanton eager to fulfill her promise. Her movements quickened. With a sultry rotation of the hips, she inched one foot over the line and then, slowly, slowly, the other. Quickly she whirled and bent to push the handkerchiefs beneath her girdle until they hung from either side of her waist, accenting the feminine triangle. She pushed her hands through the material to invite gifts; then, with a flourish, she released the corner of each. They spilled to the floor as an offering of what she, too, had to give. Clasping her hands above her head, she swayed, bells and bracelets tinkling as she tossed her head and undulated her hips.

Sweat polished her skin to mother-of-pearl, tempting the man who sat transfixed, chest heaving, hands pressing the silk cushion into his intolerably aching groin. Oh, God, would this siren

song never end? He felt his doom drawing nearer with every
flick of her hips, for he knew that when she finished he would
have to take her, no matter how honorable, logical, or expedient
it might be to leave her alone. She was no virgin, as he'd suspected. No innocent could be so seductive. His arguments with
himself were feeble voices drowned by the roar of his blood. No
matter the consequences, she would be his.

And finish she did, after letting one of the handkerchiefs slide
down her body. It circled each breast with an erotic drift and
flicked once between her legs before she kissed it ardently.
Kneeling, she offered him the kerchief, her hair sweeping past
her hips to the floor. Thus she selected him as her lover as the
music faded to a subtle, dreamy close like the peace after lovers'
union.

Shaking, Sinan took the handkerchief. Inhaling her scent, he
kissed it and tucked it in his belt. "Thank you, my houri. You
need have no fear I will return this to you any time soon." He
knew the meaning behind the dance. If her chosen lover returned
her token, he signified his ending of their liaison. As proof that
such a gesture would be long in coming, he tossed the pillow
aside and let her see what she'd done to him.

Her eyes widened, but he was intent on lifting her into his arms.
Tory lay still against him, knowing she had to allow him a kiss.
But her plans could not account for her own reactions . . . The
searing mouth that took hers melted her icy reserve. The hands
roaming her spine and lower to arch her into him scattered her
plans before the sirocco of his passion. Her mouth quivered,
then opened to the famished thrust of his tongue. Her arms encircled his neck, her fingers delving into his soft hair.

The heart-pounding exertion of the dance now found an echo
of another kind. Vaguely, she knew she should draw away. In a
minute she would. In a minute . . . Drunk on the wine of his
mouth, she didn't protest when he laid her back on the divan
and unbuttoned her vest, kissing her deeply all the while. She
lay quiescent when he removed her girdle and pulled the blouse
free. Even when he inched it up past her waist, her naval, higher,
higher, she was barely aware of the cool air on her overheated
skin. But when she felt the warmth of his hands cupping her
breasts, her eyes flew open. There was something she was supposed to remember to do. What was it?

His mouth left hers to nibble the throbbing vein in her neck,
crossing her collarbone to push the material away from his goal.

When his mobile lips closed over the aching, turgid tip of one breast, her back arched in shock. Memory returned in a cathartic rush that brought her to herself again. She squirmed beneath him, trying to push him away.

"Be still, you little witch," he muttered against her breast. When she still struggled, he groaned, took her hand and pressed it to his rigid hunger. He mistook her gasp for passion. His blood gushed so at the touch that he didn't notice her relief when he let her go to jerk off the blouse.

He straddled her then, holding her arms above her head to stare down at her exposed torso. He took no note of her trembling, for it matched his own. His eyes riveted on the pink-tipped mounds, he didn't see her scared face. "Tory, Tory, I've wanted you forever. I'll die if I don't have you," he sighed, his face contorted with desire so acute it was pain.

He released her to tear his coat and shirt off, never taking his eyes from the most beautiful breasts he'd ever seen. When her hands pushed at his chest, he flattened them and rubbed them around. When she tried to pull them away, he led them to his belt and ordered hoarsely, "Come, my houri, finish what your dance began. You need not pretend to struggle to whet my appetite. I am starved for you."

He would have brought her hands to him again, but she cried, "No!" in such panic that he at last looked at her. What he saw in her face shocked him back to his senses.

There was passion there, but fear and pleading, too. "Please, Sinan, not now. Not this way. Can I not know you better first?"

His body tightened in rejection. His eyes dropped to the fleshy temptations, then lower to the feminine triangle so scantily covered and, he could have sworn, so ready to receive him. What game did she play now?

Almost he ignored her. If he went another day, another hour, another minute without her, this heaviness in his loins would sink him to perdition. He gritted his teeth, warring between desire such as he had never known and the chivalry instilled in him at his father's knee.

Tory's quavered plea, "Please, Sinan, all I ask for is more time," decided him.

His groin howling with pain, he forced himself to move. He tossed her blouse at her and bit off, "Cover yourself." He flung on his own clothes, then turned to look at her.

Dressed again, she stood behind the divan, watching him

warily. He took several deep breaths to clear his brain, then he stared at her as if she were a specimen and he a doctor assigned to carve her up to further his knowledge.

"What did you and Lahtil do while I was gone?" he queried softly.

"Very little. She taught me to dance, and we became friends. Kahlil took us to the market one day."

Sinan's eyes narrowed to jagged shards of glass, slicing into her. "And who taught you how to play the whore? And a cheating whore at that."

Tory's head reared up. "A whore is paid," she spat. "You stole my ship, my jewels and crew, and now you want to steal the one thing I have left to give. And you accuse me of being a cheat? You, a pirate, a scoundrel, a—"

Sardonic applause interrupted her tirade. "You do that so very well. I had no idea ladies were taught to tread the boards. First warrior, then virago, seductress a few minutes past, and now your best performance of all."

Tory frowned. "What performance?"

"The threatened virgin."

Flushing, Tory retorted, "Your vanity is boundless. I danced at your instruction, but I don't seem to have pleased you. Does it not occur to you that I'm not acting? Perhaps *you* don't please *me.*" Green eyes raked over her so slowly she had to steel herself not to back away.

"You please me, all right. And I, sweet seductress, please you."

Tory gnashed her teeth in frustration. "Why won't you believe that I just don't want you?" Tory knew she was endangering all her careful plans, but she felt raw, betrayed by that most fickle of allies—her own body. Her only defense was attack against the man who had incited that betrayal. She had to convince him she didn't lie, even if she knew she did. Thus, she stood her ground until he rounded the divan like a lion hungry to mate.

He stalked her retreat, backing her up against the wall. He put one hand beside her head; the other forayed down her body, between her breasts. Tory gritted her teeth and accepted the caress that trailed lower, lower, until he burrowed gently between her thighs. She gasped and tried to push him away, but he wouldn't allow it.

"This is how I know you lie." She felt the betraying moisture, too. She closed her eyes in shame, but she couldn't ignore his soft, satisfied purr.

"The body doesn't lie, Tory. Are you trying to fool me or yourself?" Pushing her legs apart, he settled that complementing, erect maleness in nature's sweet depression. Even through the layers of clothing, they both groaned at the contact.

Rocking gently into her, he buried his lips beneath her ear and growled, "So why, sweet torment, do you deny us both?"

Tory's knees threatened to buckle as his easy rhythm quickened, stroking the secret places she didn't quite understand. She stared up into the forest-green eyes of a man aroused to the limits of his control. What had he asked her? She struggled to remember, but it seemed as unimportant as her earlier need to escape. The moisture at the juncture of her thighs spread in syncopation to the stinging tautness of her womanhood, oozing to meet each urgent, sliding stroke.

Sinan saw the unfocused look in her eyes, felt the moisture spreading, and knew he should stop. He'd meant to torment her as she had tormented him, but his body was exacting its own revenge. He couldn't stop. He had to give her a taste of what she denied them, and God help him, he had to find relief for the pressure in his loins, no matter how quick and unsatisfying.

He nudged her legs farther apart and arched the cradle of her hips upward until he could feel her throbbing against him. He rested his forehead against hers to block out the arousing, dazed look in her eyes. Her arms crept around his middle to bring him nearer. It took every ounce of control he possessed to keep himself from stripping her pantaloons away and opening his own to take here there, against the wall. He wanted to thrust deep within that silken cavern, plunge into her again and again, and force her to admit how much she wanted him. It would be so easy. Such a flimsy barrier stood in his way . . .

But angry as he was, he couldn't begin their sexual relationship so crudely. She was experienced, yes, but she was still an aristocrat, and she would not appreciate being taken like a whore. So, lifting her chin, he took her mouth, rotating his hips faster. He felt the indrawn breath, the rush of wetness. When she arched her back against the wall and convulsed, he lifted one of her legs over his waist and pushed the tiny bit into her the clothing barrier would allow. His moisture joined hers.

The warm, pulsing spurts pressed so intimately close that, when they were done, she couldn't tell whose moisture was whose. Replete, stunned, she didn't care. Her legs sagged, and only the weight of him pinning her to the wall kept her upright.

Their breath slowed. He drew away to look at her. She looked back.

This, then, was the instinct that had started wars, duels, and dynasties; the need that assured the continuation of humanity and the immorality of man. What a curse and a blessing it was! For the first time, Tory understood the power of the weapon she wielded. Understood, too, that it was a two-edged sword that could as easily turn on her as protect her.

As passion faded and reason returned, she was horrified at her earlier complacency. She had a power over Sinan, true, but he had an equal power over her. She could not manipulate him, at least not sensually, without pulling her own strings. As she looked at him, she wondered if she would ever be the same again. Perhaps the world she had known was lost to her already.

For the first time, she contemplated not what she had given up, but what she had gained . . .

Sinan didn't try to read her quick-changing expressions. Her revelation was a humiliation to him. He was too disgusted at that moment to care about her feelings. Never had he lost control of himself in such a way. He stepped back and looked down at the stain on the front of his pantaloons, and he was ashamed. He was thirty-one years old, not a callow boy. He resented the woman who made him act like one.

He watched coldly as she sagged a bit before standing upright. "Do you still expect me to believe you don't want me, little virgin?"

His sneering emphasis on the last words cast a shadow over Tory's dawning revelation of how it could be between them. She clenched her hands to suppress a poignant rush of regret. "Believe what you like, as you always do. I'm but your slave. My feelings and opinions count for naught." She went to the chest to take off her jewelry.

Large, ungentle hands caught her shoulders and whirled her to face him. "Ah, but your feelings do count. This is not the end for us, Tory. It's the beginning. And I expect my lovers to participate fully." When she stared woodenly ahead, he pushed her chin up. "I'll make you admit what you feel if I have to keep you here forever."

She looked at him then, and he quivered as if struck when she taunted, "And what do you feel for me, mighty reis? Can you face that?"

Tit for tat, he thought wryly. That was indeed the central question. Since he couldn't answer it, he ignored it. Releasing her, he went to the door, where he turned. "Enjoy your rest. After tonight, you'll seldom sleep alone. I'll not return to sea for several weeks. Tomorrow your training as a good, obedient slave begins in earnest." He blew her a mocking kiss and exited.

Tory ripped off her garments, feeling suddenly soiled. Nothing had changed. She could no more manipulate him than she could move the Rock of Gibraltar. She should have fled while she had the chance. Now Sinan would watch her like the hawk they called him. Her dancing had inflamed him, all right, but it had not made him one whit more malleable, as she had hoped. Could she escape in time?

As Tory removed her pantaloons, she smelled his scent still on her. She quivered. For one brief, traitorous instant, the thought taunted her—*do I want to escape?*

Sinan's thoughts were as chaotic as he kept the scheduled meeting with Terence. Fiend seize it, he wished he'd never had the idea to come to Algiers. He'd accomplished only part of what he'd come to do. Now, with the complication of Tory and her crew, it became increasingly likely that only dire action would help him finish the rest. Helen, he thought despairingly, I'll find you even if I have to risk everything to do it. And it may well come to that.

Grimly, he entered the metalworker's hut. Terence was polishing an urn. His ready grin of greeting died at the look on his friend's face. He rose. "What news have you, man? It must be bad by the look of you."

"The dey has given me an ultimatum: Embrace the Koran within the next month or lose all privileges. My sources have told me nothing about Helen. If she's not with the dey's brother, I don't know where else to look."

Terence put a sympathetic hand on his friend's shoulder. "I'd help if I could, but things are becoming critical in Tripoli. If the Bashaw continues his demands, I fear it may indeed come to war. My presence will be needed more than ever then."

"Good!" Beau exclaimed savagely. "I'd welcome an honest fight instead of this havey-cavey slinking about."

A worried look shadowed Terence's mellow brown eyes. There

was a leashed fury about Beau, almost a desperation, and Terence sensed it involved more than Helen. "You're not telling me something. Is it a problem with the woman?"

Beau whirled away to stride up and down the limited space. "Hell, yes! She's stirred up a hornet's nest. I'd give my eyeteeth to be rid of her." But somehow, Beau refused to meet Terence's eyes.

Terence smothered a smile. He knew the symptoms when a woman was sticking in a man's craw, and Beau displayed all of them. "I'll take her with me to Tripoli disguised as my woman, if you like. I can smuggle her back to England from there." He wasn't surprised when Beau growled a refusal.

"No! I brought her in, I'll get her out, especially since I'll probably have to leave soon myself." Beau drew a rolled parchment from his cloak and handed it to Terence. "Tell me what you think of this." He watched as Terence spread it out on the table.

"As a safeguard, I'm drawing two maps of Algerine armaments. It's as close to scale as I can make it, but I'm no cartographer. Still, it should be roughly accurate and up to date when I'm finished with it."

Terence appraised the map, then nodded approvingly. "This should lend weight to our contention that these pirates respect only force."

They talked a moment longer. Then Terence shook Beau's hand. "My prayers go with you. I have every faith you'll triumph in the end. Over everything."

Beau knew Terence well enough to understand the oblique reference to Tory. "Then you have more faith than I, my friend. God go with you."

Beau hurried back to the house, pausing only to appraise one of the signs of the hand of Fatima. Tory's scrawlings seemed more inexplicable than ever. Surely she couldn't be planning an escape? She had no money, nothing to bargain with, and how on earth could she use this ancient Muslim superstition to her advantage?

Beau walked on, his head aching. One thing, at least, was clear: Tory would be his before they left. That wanton dance had settled it. She'd thought to tease him like the London coquette he'd so disliked four years ago. This time, however, she'd misjudged her man. He was no fop to worship at her feet.

As long as he'd had any doubts remaining about her virtue,

he'd been honor bound to leave her be no matter how much she deserved to be taught the dangers of toying with a man's passions. But no innocent could have danced so. He had no qualms about taking what she'd given to others. After that last contretemps in her chamber, she deserved it; more, she wanted it almost as much as he did. After he'd satisfied himself in that silken flesh, this obsession with her would end. It would have to end, for once she discovered his identity . . . He didn't finish the thought.

Chapter 7

From the rooftop balcony, Tory watched the dawn. Like all else in this exotic land, sunrise came not by half-measures. Here the sun was no shy, colorless virgin as she was in England, rising misty and pale; here she swept over the horizon like a coquette bedecked in glorious robes of crimson, pink, orange, and gold. Her warm smile beamed off whitewashed houses, minarets, and in the distance the Casbah.

"No matter where I go, or how this ends, I'll always remember the beauty of this land," Tory said to Lahtil.

"Hmm," Lahtil agreed absently, her thoughts obviously elsewhere. "Did the master enjoy your dance?"

Tory blushed. During the long, restless night, she'd wondered that herself. "I . . . think so. But I do, frankly, find him hard to understand." Tory squirmed as she remembered the erotic end to that dance. But even their bitter parting couldn't tarnish that memory.

"How was it, Tory? Did he hurt you?"

Tory didn't pretend to misunderstand. "We did not end the night as you suppose, Lahtil."

"You danced the handkerchief dance for the master, choosing him as your lover and he left you to spend the night alone?" Lahtil asked in outrage.

"By my choice. I am still not ready to give myself to any man." But Tory turned her head away as she spoke. She'd been ready, for some time, to do exactly that.

Lahtil's pretty face grew worried. "The master will be furious with you, and with me, for not teaching you obedience."

Tory took Lahtil's hands and said earnestly, "The master won't blame you. Besides, I had good reason for acting as I did. In fact, I hope to help you and Kahlil, not just myself." At Lahtil's questioning look, Tory elaborated, "I want you to know, Lahtil, that I'll do what I can to persuade the master to free you. Once he realizes how much you and Kahlil care for each other, he'll let you go, I warrant."

White to the lips, Lahtil sputtered, "Tory, n-no. If the master learns of my feelings he'll beat me, or perhaps even sell me. I could bear the first, but not the second, for I'd never see Kahlil again."

"Nonsense! Sinan is not so cruel as that. If he's handled correctly, he can be made to understand—"

"And you, I apprehend, intend to do the handling? How edifying. And what a refreshing change in your behavior."

Anger crackled beneath the silky tones like buckram. Tory dropped Lahtil's hands and turned. Sinan was dressed in riding breeches and tall boots. A cotton shirt stuck to his damp chest from his early ride. He tapped a riding quirt against his leg, betraying a leashed impatience that bade her be wary. But, as usual, Tory was more inclined to attack than retreat.

"I danced as gracefully as I could. I regret that you found me lacking." Tory's honey-coated barb struck home in his darkening face.

"You would have aroused a statue, and well you know it. But I, my sweet, am no statue." He spanned the space between them in two strides, lifted one of her hands to his fresh-shaven cheek, and rubbed it around. "I feel, I breathe," he bent to blow in her ear, smiling when she shivered. He took her other hand then locked them both behind her back. Still smiling, he said hoarsely, "I desire. No, m'dear, I'm no statue. I'm a man, as you will learn very shortly."

Pausing only to attach her veil, he pushed Tory down the stairs ahead of him, out the harem to the courtyard. The guards lolling about looked at them curiously.

Beau ordered a staring Kahlil, "See we're not disturbed for any reason." He proceeded, tugging Tory with him.

When she realized their direction, she dug in her heels. "No!" She was ignored. She went limp, but he just hefted her and draped her over his shoulder as if she weighed nothing at all.

She beat her fists against his back. "Bastard! Pirate! Let me go! You have no right to treat me thus!" All she got for her troubles was a slap on the behind.

"I've every right. You're my slave, remember? And dammit, woman, it's past time you learned the dangers of trifling with a man's feelings."

An angry boot shoved open the bath door. He deposited Tory summarily on a stone bench, mocking, "Damme, but you're heavy. It's time you put those lush curves to use. Let me show you how . . ." He reached out.

Tory was so furious she literally saw red. Dodging him, she dashed into the bathing chamber to grab a ladle. He was in hot pursuit, but she had time for a blow on one powerful arm. He barely winced. Tory found the ladle jerked out of her hand and sent flying, her person hauled against a fathom-plus of enraged male.

Teeth gritted, he snarled, "That's it. I'll tame you to my hand if I have to beat you three times a day."

Tory refused to cringe. *She* was the one wronged. Flinging back her head, she cried, "Then do it! Prove your brutality like the cowardly pirate you are. But muscles are the only advantage you have over me. You can shout your triumph from the roof-tops, but you'll still be a braying mule, pathetically bragging of your virility."

Sinan's rage cooled. Indeed, the little witch was right. These years in North Africa had borne out his belief that manhood had little to do with physical strength. Bending such a woman to his will required more subtle methods.

With grudging admiration, he released her, stepped back and executed a deep, mocking bow. "The braying ass will not lay a hand on you. That would be brutish and cowardly, as you so rightly state. But let us judge the depth of your bravery as well. Before this day is out, you will want me as I wanted you last night. Before this day is out, I will mind you more of a stallion than an ass, and you will feel yourself a mare eager to be ridden." Casually he unbuttoned his shirt.

Tory blushed at his deliberate crudeness. He'd never looked at her so: covetously, possessively, as if he owned her in truth and would prove it. Tory swallowed the urge to beg for the beating instead. He must never know how susceptible she was to him. She backed up a step, eyeing the door.

Shaking his head, Sinan chided, "No escape this time, fair

enemy. You brought things to this pass, not I, by symbolically selecting me for your lover last night. Pirate or no, I'll not disappoint a lady.'' He removed his boots and socks, then began unbuttoning his breeches. When Tory whirled away, he paused. His expression softened. He dropped his hands and went up behind her to knead her shoulders.

"Come, sweet, there's naught to fear. I'll be as gentle as any of your lovers.'' He bent his head to nibble her neck, missing Tory's frown.

When she tried to turn, he allowed it, but pulled her into an ardent embrace before she could speak. Tory stiffened under the pliant dexterity of his lips. He was so practiced, so certain she'd bend to his will. Only offended pride gave Tory strength enough to keep her lips and mind closed to the pleasure he wrung from her contrary body.

Sinan took a punitive nip at her mouth before backing up a step to gibe, "The citadel is well fortified this day, but I don't think it will stand before a long siege.'' Holding her eyes, he unbuttoned her vest.

Every nerve tensed as she prepared to run from him, but she knew she would not get two steps. Tory forced herself to stand still as he dropped the vest carelessly on the bench. But when he untied her sash, her instincts won. She bolted.

A large hand caught her and whirled her, toplike, free of the sash, then caught her long hair. Now she didn't even have hands to defend herself, for she had to hold her pantaloons up.

Prying her hands loose, he lifted her arms about his neck. "Come, love, bathe with me. That's all I ask. We'll go no further unless you wish it, I promise.'' He knelt to pull off her slippers, then tugged the pantaloons down past her knees and over her ankles, lifting her feet to ease them free. Her long blouse fell well past her hips, but the filmy material hid little from the roving eyes of the man still kneeling at her feet. A supplicant he was not, however.

He ran appreciative hands down one perfect long leg. "I can't wait until these are wrapped around me,'' he said huskily. His lips started at her ankle and coasted up her leg, but when he tried to slip his head under the blouse, she pulled away.

Sinan took a deep breath and stood, his eyes raking over her. The thin silk clung to every lissome curve in the bath's humidity. The indentation of her waist begged for the clasp of his hands; the hardening nipples of her breasts called for the touch of his lips. Looking lower, Sinan groaned at the sight of the barely visible auburn triangle. He had to bite his lip until it whitened to restrain his need to take her now, without delay. Forcing his eyes to her face, he saw she was not ready. He retreated to the antechamber and returned with a huge linen towel.

"Here, Tory, take off your blouse and wrap yourself in this. I will do the same in the other chamber."

Tory took the towel with a trembling hand, sighing with relief when he left her alone. For a craven moment, she looked about for an escape. Finding none, she straightened to her full height. Very well, he had her well and truly cornered this time. She no longer feared rape. His insufferable pride would never seek such bitter victory. He wanted her unconditional surrender; nay, he wanted her willing participation in her own defeat. He would have neither. Since he had the advantage in strength and, God help her, in her own weak response to him, she had only guile with which to defend herself. She'd gird it about her loins like a chastity belt, keeping the key buried in the mind that told her all depended on her cunning.

When Sinan returned, he was surprised to see Tory wrapped in the towel, calmly awaiting him. Her white, scared look was gone. Instead, her eyes glittered with feminine appreciation as they ran down his chest, paused on the brief towel he'd wrapped around his loins, then appraised each muscled leg. Even as his body surged in hot reply, his neck hairs stood on end. She'd given in too easily . . .

Tory scooped up her clothes and took his hand to lead him into the antechamber. She tossed the garments on a bench against the wall and pushed him down on the central bench, ordering, "Lie down, please, if you want to see what else Lahtil taught me while you were away."

He lay back, but eyed her suspiciously. "If this is some ruse to escape, it won't work. I'll catch you before you reach the door. Besides, I wouldn't recommend you wander about in your present attire. Some of my men have already expressed an interest in you."

An enigmatic smile curving her lips, Tory tugged on his elbow until he turned over and rested his cheek on folded forearms. "You have my word as a lady that I will not leave this chamber until you allow it." She went to a recessed alcove in the wall. It was packed with scented oils, perfumes, powders and soaps. Tory hesitated over a sandalwood oil, then veered to a different pot. A wicked gleam in her eye, she picked it up and returned to his side. She scooped out a gob and rubbed the half-set oil between her palms.

Ignoring the wary green eye cocked on her, she pressed her palms on his shoulderblades, smiling when he flinched. She spread her hands in tiny, ever-widening circles until his back glistened with oil. Then she began to knead, starting at the base of his spine, working her way up to the back of his neck, where she concentrated. Gradually, he grew pliant.

Strangely, as he relaxed, she grew tense. Even lying down, he was so big and strong that she felt dwarfed. To have all this male pride vulnerable beneath her hands made her feel like a cheat. What she planned to do to him was . . . not nice. But what choice had she? It was obvious he'd never willingly let her go, at least not until she was ruined. And responding to him would mean ruination, no matter how much her body proclaimed otherwise. Her kneading hands softened from professionalism to a womanly caress.

This was to be her last night with him. Surely she could indulge herself? Dreamily, she traced the muscles across his back. What would it have been like to have these wide shoulders above her blocking out light, danger, the world itself, as they created their own universe together?

The muscles under her hands bunched as Sinan stretched luxuriously. "Ah, my houri, you've learned well. But come, let me rub you down as well." She pushed him back down.

"No, I still need to do your legs." She wet her palms with more oil. He sighed and subsided. Tory's eyes burned a little even when she reminded herself he was a pirate. Somehow, now, when they had so little time left together, she no longer cared. Pirate or no, he was the most appealing man she'd ever met; it pained her to use him as she must.

She cleared her throat, rubbing the oil into his legs. "What is the Arabic custom in disposing of slaves who have served one well?"

"That depends upon the master. A few earn their freedom. Others are given so many privileges that they're content with their lot. Why do you ask?" he asked drowsily.

"What if a woman who has served her master well and never been taken to bed by him comes to care for another man?" She felt his tension return.

"Such behavior is not countenanced. Why do you ask?"

This was her last chance to help Lahtil. Tory took a deep breath. "Because, while Lahtil is very loyal to you, against her will she has come to care for Kahlil. And from the way he looks at her, I believe he returns her feelings."

Sinan swung his legs around and sat up. "Has she asked you to plead for her?"

She met his eyes steadily and shook her head. "No. In fact, she was afraid you would punish her if you knew."

"You didn't agree?"

Again she shook her head. "No. An arrogant beast you might be—short-tempered, rude, and brash—but you are just. You'd never punish someone for such a reason."

Ridiculously, Sinan felt ten feet tall. Such a litany of dubious virtues was little to crow about, but, under the circumstances, her trust was high praise indeed. A tight spot in his chest loosened in delight and surprise that she was so unselfishly trying to help Lahtil. Had she really changed from the vain coquette he'd despised in London four years ago? He patted the bench beside him. "Come, sit."

When Tory sat beside him, he took her hand. "I know of their feelings, but the resolution of this dilemma is not simple. The dey will be outraged if I give her to Kahlil. I also fear Kahlil's pride would never let him accept her as a gift. He'd consider it an affront to his loyalty to me and his creed as a Moslem to never covet another's woman. But if we can think of some way round these problems, I'll gladly give her to him. I'm interested in bedding only one woman."

Tory looked away from his sensual stare, but the thumb stroking her palm was not as easy to avoid. "What if you tell Kahlil that I resent Lahtil and demand that you sell her?" she asked. "Perhaps you could ask Kahlil if he knows a man who would desire to buy her for his harem. Then Kahlil could buy her with no insult to his pride."

After contemplating her idea for a long moment, Sinan nodded. "It makes sound sense. And from Kahlil's impression of you, he'll not doubt the truth of it. Nor will the dey."

Tory blushed at his teasing look, retorting, "But Kahlil's impression of you may change."

"Because I would let you hound Lahtil away?"

At Tory's nod, Sinan lifted her chin. Gazing deep into her eyes, he said throatily, "Ah, but Kahlil already knows you've bewitched me. He'll think the worse of you, but nothing less of me.''

Sinan brought her hand to his mouth. His lips hovered over it. He frowned and sniffed it instead. ''You little witch! Scent me with roses, would you?'' He lifted the pot threateningly over her head.

Her merry laughter rang out, and that curious little expansion in his chest grew at the sound. How rarely she laughed. He set the pot down and watched her with such intensity that her laughter died. '' 'Equal to the gods seems to me that man who sits facing you and hears you nearby sweetly speaking and softly laughing,' '' he quoted Sappho, easing her down on the bench. He mistook her fleeting grimace and moved his weight to her side instead of on top of her, where he longed to be.

In truth, his weight bothered her not. To the contrary, she longed to have him crush her into the bench until she had no breath for thought. She stared at him, knowing she'd never understand him, nor ever forget him. Why would a pirate know Greek poetry, or use it to woo a woman who was, after all, nothing but his slave? And dear God, why was he so sweet to her now, when she needed to be strongest? She turned her head away to hide her incipient tears.

Sinan kissed the nape of her neck, but she wriggled away and rose. ''Do you promise me, on your word of honor, that you'll offer Lahtil to Kahlil?'' Her voice was muffled, strained.

Standing, Sinan ground out, ''I have said I'll do it, and so I will.''

Squaring her shoulders, she turned to face him. ''Thank you, Sinan. You have my gratitude and my respect.''

''And what if that's not enough? What if I want more? Far more?'' He took several strides toward her, but she didn't back away.

''Then perhaps I can give it.'' When he cupped her face in his hands, she met his eyes bravely. ''Later, please? These stone benches are hardly comfortable. Tonight, after we sup. I'll dance for you again, if you wish.''

Sinan shook his head once, to clear it, then croaked, ''What did you say?''

Tory had to smile at his eagerness. He reminded her of Jarrod waiting for the treats of Turkish delight she sneaked him. She repeated, ''Tonight, after we sup, you will get what you want.''

But she couldn't sustain that hungry stare any longer. Her gaze dropped.

"Thank you, milady." He brought her hands to his lips and kissed them, knuckles, palms, and then wrists. "I promise it will be something you want as well."

So she feared, Tory reflected grimly. She slipped her hands away. "Well, shall we go? I long to see the stables. Jarrod said you'd take me when you returned."

"And so I will, sweet." A gentle hand on her shoulder halted her. "After we bathe."

"Bathe?" Tory squeaked. "You said we'd wait—"

"We will. As you said, these benches leave a lot to be desired. But I can't leave here smelling like a rose bower, and since you're responsible, it's only fair that you help cleanse me." He was leading Tory into the bathing chamber as he spoke. He turned up the spigots until steam rose in misty clouds.

When he took a sponge, dipped it in the water, and turned to her, she flinched, but he merely handed it to her. She scrubbed his broad chest quickly, then flung the sponge back in the water.

He raised an eyebrow. "Why such a hurry? You're not finished." He turned his bronzed back to her. Looking over his shoulder he said, "And don't be so hasty this time. Touching is the best part of bathing with someone else."

Tory bit her lip and eyed his back as if it were ridged with glass. Her hand shook when she sponged his gleaming flesh, slowly this time. She swiped the residue away with her other hand, rubbing, savoring. She had no choice, she told herself. He would grow suspicious if she seemed reluctant. Thus, when it came time to wash his legs, she bent to her task with enjoyment. Up and down she rubbed, from ankle to calf to knee, where she stopped. When she gave the other leg the same treatment, Sinan urged her hand higher.

"Come, do the job right." He quivered when her hand inched under the towel to his outer thigh.

Before Tory realized what was happening, he'd jerked his towel off and pulled her hand up to his inner leg. She was presented with a view of the backs of his long, powerful legs soaring like flying buttresses into firm, curved buttocks. She felt an almost uncontrollable urge to plant a love nip on that tempting, rounded flesh. Shocked at herself, she jerked her hand away from where Sinan was trying to urge it and stood.

Agitated, forgetting she wore a towel, Tory ladled a dipper of warm water and poured it over herself. She gasped when the water-weighted towel slid to her waist. She dropped the ladle and caught the towel before it fell. When she would have pulled it up, he turned and caught her hands, pulling her close.

"No, sweet. Remember the delights of anticipation? Experience them with me. When you come to me tonight, you'll want me as desperately as I've wanted you from the first."

Tory barely heard him over her pounding heart, but she felt him—oh, how she felt him. She couldn't see that intrinsically male part of him, but she felt it burning into her abdomen through the sopping towel. She was torn between curiosity and fear that what she'd overheard grooms referring to as a "weapon" would both look like one and be used as such. So she stayed where she was, allowing Sinan to admire her exposed torso. That, at least, was something he'd seen before and was unlikely to rouse him further.

How naive she was. Sinan looked down at the bounty he now held in his hands and longed to fall on her like a starved man. Instead, he forced himself to cup those full, firm fruits gently. He titillated her for long, luxurious moments, stroking, fondling. He watched her face, smiling when she flushed to match her nipples.

Only then did he give her the touch she craved. He courted each point with his thumb, once, twice, then flirted about them, making them pay full notice. Her eyes fluttered shut.

Dying to taste her, Sinan lifted her and sat her on the edge of the basin then arched her up to his hungry mouth. She gasped at the first touch, squirming until the towel slipped farther, barely holding at her hips. Neither of them noticed, for each knew only the pleasure of mouth to flesh, softness encasing hardness, and, lower, an emptiness aching to be filled by the boldness so eager to oblige. Sinan suckled one breast at his leisure, thoroughly, then turned his attention to the other. When he caught the pinnacle of the white mound between his teeth and pulled gently, she arched against him, crying out.

The towel gave up the losing battle and slipped to the floor. *That* caught Sinan's attention. Chest heaving in tempo with hers, he took a half-step back and allowed her to slip down. "Come, love, stand and let me look my fill." His voice was low, shaking.

Tory was so far gone that it never occurred to her not to obey. Swaying, she opened pleasure-drugged eyes. A small frown wrinkled her brow at where his attention was riveted. She glanced down. Humiliation froze the rivulets of fire in her veins. She moved her hands to cover herself.

"No, don't! I've dreamed of this too long . . ."

His hoarse entreaty struck Tory in every quivering nerve. Instincts as old as woman took possession of her. Her hands dropped. She stood erect. For minutes then, they stared at each other through the wisps of steam. Water beaded on their skin, glittering as the diffused light cast rainbows about them.

Starting at Tory's feet, Sinan ran his gaze up the delectable legs that flared into full, softly curved hips. He lingered at the auburn thatch joining her legs, shuddering as a drop of water fell to glitter on the floor like a gem of passion. He forced himself to move on, to her small waist and the luscious, thrusting breasts, finally to her face. He frowned. In contrast to him, she stared at only one place . . .

A tremor shook Tory as her curiosity was satisfied with a vengeance. So this was what made a man . . . Tory eyed the long blade arching upward to his belly like a scimitar. No one who'd bred as many horses as she had could doubt that awesome length's purpose in nature's scheme; however, it would not be Sinan's belly it would slash . . .

Concerned, he took several strides toward her. "Tory? What's wrong?"

Still she watched him. When he drew her hand to his arousal, she flinched and tried to pull away, but he forced her fingers around the pulsing shaft. "See, sweet, there's nothing to fear. I'm a man like any other." This time he let her go, watching in puzzlement as she fled.

Her hand tingled as she dressed, as if the feel of him was branded forever into her skin. So soft, but so hard, all at once. Like his will: velvet-sheathed steel. She'd almost let him seduce her into forgetting that, but thank God she'd remembered in time. How dare he treat her like a harlot! What reason had he to think her loose? The more she thought on it, the more furious she grew. When he came into the antechamber to dress, she turned away and buttoned her vest.

Sinan ignored the aching that seemed to worsen by the hour, his eyes intent on Tory's stiff back. What on earth had he done to offend her? Why had she changed so quickly from passion to icy rejection? When they were dressed, he caught her face between his hands.

"If I touch you in a way you don't like, Tory, you've but to tell me. Women are different, and different things please them."

How dare he quote poetry to her one minute, then compare her to his whores the next. Tory fumed. The soft yearning dissolved along with the reprimands of her conscience. He deserved what she was going to do to him. And more.

"Indeed, and you'll find out soon enough what pleases me," Tory agreed sweetly. She attached her veil. "Shall we go to the stables?"

Sinan watched her sashay to the door, the back of his neck prickling again. Dammit, why did he of a sudden feel like the prey rather than the hunter? As he held the door for Tory, her flowing dress and regal bearing made him fancy her as Diana, a bow over one shoulder. Would he play the role of Actaeon, dying for his temerity in gazing upon the naked goddess? No matter how he scolded himself, his uneasiness did not abate.

When they entered the courtyard, a small whirlwind threw himself on Sinan. "Oh, Sinan, Sinan, I am so glad to see you back safe."

"Did you ever doubt it? And where have you been?"

Jarrod shrugged. "About. I came as soon as I heard you'd returned."

Sinan ruffled his hair. "I am flattered that you rate me above your other adventures. What has it been this time? Begging in the marketplace? Translating for some merchant?"

"Translating. I have earned more than usual, Sinan." A grimy hand offered several coins, but Sinan waved them away.

"Enough, Jarrod. I've told you over and over you owe me nothing. Keep your money. You may need it if I ever fall out of favor."

Jarrod looked worried as he watched Sinan walk away. "Something is wrong," the boy told Tory. "It's said in the *souq* that Sinan is in disfavor for returning with no prize."

A frown crinkled Tory's brow, but she smoothed it away. "His next voyage will doubtless end more favorably—for him, that is." Tory made no attempt to disguise her bitterness. She looked at Sinan, who was talking seriously to Kahlil; then she turned to Jarrod and took his hands.

Bending to his level, she whispered urgently, "I need your help, Jarrod. Can you get paints from somewhere and paint the hand of Fatima next to the front door?" Tory had originally planned to wheedle Kahlil into letting her do the painting, but now that Sinan was back she didn't dare ask. He'd be too suspicious. Jarrod was her only hope.

Jarrod looked bewildered. "Yes, there are paints in the storeroom. But why do you want me to do this? Has the master converted to Islam?"

"No, this is just, er, a treat for Lahtil. She loves the custom, and I want to surprise her. It need stay on only long enough for me to show it to her. Then we'll paint over it."

"But, Tory, it could be seen and misinterpreted."

"What could one day hurt?" Tory asked in genuine bewilderment. "It's not so different from a welcome sign over the door, is it?"

Jarrod opened his mouth to argue, but Tory put a finger over his lips when Sinan started toward them. "Please, Jarrod, this is important to me. No harm can come of it in a day, surely."

This was the first request she'd ever made of him. Sighing, he nodded. He was rewarded with a brilliant smile and a peck on the cheek.

"Thank you, Jarrod. What a man you will be. I envy the lucky woman you choose," Tory said sincerely.

Sinan arrived in time to catch this remark. He scowled at the pair. Dammit, why did she charm everyone but him? He took her arm more roughly than he had intended.

"Come, my dear, let us proceed to the stables."

Tory glared at him, but said a sweet good-bye to Jarrod.

Sinan wondered at their exchanged stare, but he had more important matters on his mind. Kahlil threw a glare at Tory as they passed.

"Yes, I've told him," Sinan answered Tory's questioning look. "He doesn't feel charitable toward you at the moment. He'll buy Lahtil when he collects the sum we agreed upon." He shut the outer door behind them.

Tory sighed in relief. "Thank you, Sinan. You are a man of your word." She looked curiously about as they entered the small stable. It was dim after the brilliant sunshine, but she could make out two stalls.

"And are you, milady, a woman of yours?" Sinan pushed her gently against the wall next to the stable door. "I've kept my promise to you, but you've yet to fulfill yours to me."

Tory's laugh sounded false to her own ears. "What would you have me do? Spread myself for you in the hay?"

"That sounds interesting, but too hasty for what I have in

mind. Perhaps later. Just keep your word to me. I've waited for you long enough, Tory. I'll not wait another day.'' He muttered the last words into her throat, nuzzling hotly.

Tory eased away from him. ''Tonight, as we have agreed. Now, what is this handsome fellow's name?'' She patted the powerful black stallion.

''Eclipse. He's one of my proudest acquisitions. He cost me the sum of one entire capture, but he was worth every sequin.'' Sinan accepted the change of topic. He had to get a grip on himself or he'd fall on her tonight with little patience and less finesse.

''He reminds me of one of my prime bloods back home. I've had offers from the Prince of Wales himself for him, but I'll never sell him. He's bred some fine foals.''

''You sound quite knowledgeable. How is it that a lady knows so much of horses?''

Finding no condemnation in Sinan's interested gaze, Tory relaxed. ''Because I've bred them since I was small. My family's stables are renowned throughout England. I'd officially set up a stud if my grandmother would allow it.''

Her voice was so wistful that Sinan wondered yet again if he'd misjudged her. A longing to breed horses was a peculiar one for a London flirt. Had she changed since her capture, or had he misjudged her four years ago?

''And why will she not allow it?''

''Such occupation is not 'proper' for a lady. You'd never know what a hoyden she was in her own youth from her behavior today. She thinks to mold me into the image of what she should have been. She'll not succeed.''

Sinan turned her gently to him at the grim determination in her voice. ''Is that why you left England?''

''Partly. My grandmother was trying to force me into marriage with a man I detest.''

''And who is that?'' Beau asked idly, his thumb rubbing her delicate cheekbone.

''Baron Cedric Howard.'' Tory caught the flicker in Sinan's eyes before he dropped his hand and turned away. ''Do you know him?'' she asked incredulously.

''Of course not. How could I?'' He drew her to the other stall and began listing the virtues of the bay mare snuffing into her hay.

But Tory wasn't listening. She'd been too involved in their

battle of wills of late to unravel the mystery of his identity, but now her old curiosity was stimulated. He had lied to her just now. Somehow, incredible as it seemed, he either knew Cedric or knew of him. Her head whirled with the implications of that. He spoke faultless English, knew British history well, and quoted Greek poetry as naturally as a scholar. Conversely, he wielded a knife and sword as adeptly as any pirate and seemed to enjoy the respect he had earned with those abilities. Yet he was gentle with Lahtil and kind to an orphaned boy. Nor had he used her, Tory reflected, as any other pirate surely would have.

Try as she might, Tory could think of no culture that fostered men of such complexity. He was neither pirate nor gentleman, neither Arab nor Westerner; he was an amalgam of all. She longed to stay with him and solve his mystery.

Tory watched him gesture with finely shaped hands as he described the equestrian abilities of the Berber horsemen he'd purchased the mare from. And she admitted, finally, that nothing would ever be the same again. Even if she succeeded in escaping him, she'd be bound tightly in memories. The London dandies would seem more insipid than ever. If she left him, she'd never know the mysteries of the flesh, or the pain and joy of childbirth, or the comfort of growing old next to a shoulder strong enough to lean on even after it stooped. He had spoiled her for other men.

Blinking her blurring eyes, Tory castigated herself, Yes, and you might know all those things if you stayed, but at what price? Justice, honor, and self-respect were not idle values to Tory. She'd been instilled with pride in her ancient heritage since she was old enough to toddle. Even if she longed passionately to betray those values by willingly becoming a pirate's mistress, she could not. She would hate herself; eventually, she would hate him.

And what if he offered her marriage? Tory bit her lip to stifle an hysterical giggle. She visualized the announcement in *The Times*: "Lady Victoria Alicia Grenville to wed Sinan Reis, most honorable pirate captain of the dey of Algiers, family unknown." Any offspring would indeed have a proud heritage to live up to. Their father could show the boys how to ravage the seas as efficiently as he did, and she could train the girls to be model concubines. Gorge rose in Tory's throat.

Sinan stopped in midsentence when Tory coughed. For the first time since he began speaking he looked at her. The white, anguished features drew a gasp from him. "Tory, what is it? Are you ill?"

When he drew her into a gentle embrace, Tory slumped against him, too weak to deny herself. One last time his heart would beat against hers, one last memory to warm her during all the long, empty nights of her life. For she had no choice. She had to leave this very night. But, oh, it hurt, she cried inwardly, burrowing into the rock-solid muscles of his chest. Almost she turned to him and said, Take me to bed. Leave me no choice. Lock me in the harem and stay with me forever.

Her lips longed to open, but two images kept them closed: the portrait gallery at the ancestral mansion, painting after painting glaring at her in disapproval; and Greaty's small, proud figure serving tea in the salon with all the aplomb of the duchess she was. Defeated, she closed her eyes. She blanked her mind of everything but this last bittersweet pleasure of being held by the one man she couldn't have, the one man she . . . loved?

She thought her heart would break when he pressed his lips gently to her hair and whispered, "What is it, love? Come, share your thoughts with me. I want to know you in every sense, not just the biblical one."

Unable to bear more, Tory pulled away. "I've a headache. Please let me retire until this evening."

Sinan wondered why his bold Tory seemed so listless of a sudden. "Of course, Tory. I'll escort you."

"No! I want to rest—alone, for now." Tory hurried out of the stable into the house.

Frowning, Sinan followed, watching her climb the stairs. When she shut the harem doors, he locked them. For good measure, he ordered a guard to stand watch. She was acting peculiar, and he would not risk her escape. Not now. Not when this gut-deep ache was about to end. He hardened at the thought, but forced himself to turn away. He had business to attend to.

Thirty minutes later, he leaned against the arch of the coffee-house across from the home of the dey's brother. Sipping a tiny cup of thick coffee, he chatted with the other men, surveying Saud's house. On a side wall, he saw a grilled fan-shaped window. If the house was laid out in typical fashion, that should be the harem—but would Helen be there? If so, would she still be the woman he'd loved all his life? Or would she be changed beyond all recognition by the trials of the past three years? No matter how successful he and Terence were, if he failed on this part of his mission, he'd never forgive himself. Desperate measures might be all that could save Helen now. . . .

After a long bout of weeping, Tory cradled a pillow, feeling calmer. It was all very simple, really. Muddled emotions must not sway cold logic. It was nonsensical to think she could love a pirate. Her plans were made, and she had no choice but to follow through on them.

Tory rose and went to the chest, where she collected the tiny fabric sack and several paintbrushes. She emptied the sack into a small pot and set it on top of the chest, where it blended innocuously with her other cosmetics. With sewing scissors she snipped the horsehairs off the brushes, then tossed the denuded sticks behind the chest and stacked the tiny bundles of horsehair carefully on top of the pantaloons and shirt she would wear to make her escape.

Then, calmly, she dressed in her dancing costume and went in search of Becky.

Becky blinked, then sat up on the divan when she saw the dancing costume. "Tory!" she exclaimed, scandalized. "Surely you won't let the captain see you in that . . . that . . ."

Tory wondered wryly how Becky would react if she knew how very little—nothing, in fact—Sinan had seen her in. "It's necessary. He must have other things on his mind tonight."

Surveying the revealed curves, Becky snapped, "He'll certainly have other 'things' on his mind. Is it what you intend?" Becky regretted her sharp words when Tory turned away, shoulders hunched.

Becky rose to stroke Tory's shining hair. "Listen to me, the proper abigail. We're not in London now, but the old instincts die hard. It's best we leave tonight, as you say, before it's too late." Becky frowned when Tory still wouldn't look at her. "Or is it already too late?" She lifted Tory's chin.

Tory muttered, "My virtue, such as it is, is still intact, if that's what you mean."

"No, I don't doubt that. I admit when we were captured, I thought all was lost. I never dreamed a captain of the most ruthless Barbary regency could show such restraint. I know now Sinan will never take you against your will." Becky hesitated, but the questions had to be asked. "But is it against your will any longer? Do you really want to escape?" Becky wanted to cry at the despair in Tory's glimmering eyes.

"How can you ask that? Do you think I can betray every value I cherish by giving myself to a pirate?"

"I'm not asking about your loyalty, Tory. I want to understand the yearnings of your heart," Becky corrected gently.

Tory pressed her hands to her cheeks. "What would you have me say?" she cried. "That I long to stay with him in whatever capacity he wants me? That I long to lie with him and bear his children?" Tory flung her hands down and straightened. "No, Becky, my heart's yearnings will bring me only despair. Let's speak no more such foolishness. Make ready. We must leave before dusk, when the gate closes."

Becky tried on the garments, adjusting them until Tory was satisfied, but all the while the abigail worried. She'd cared for Tory from birth. She'd been there when Tory laughed gleefully at her first step, and when she wept for weeks after her kitten was trampled. Tory did everything with vigor; when she rode to hounds, she was in the lead, and the first in on the kill; when she gave a house party, she oversaw every detail, from the lowliest flower arrangement to the music for the orchestra; when she made friends, she made friends for life, standing beside them through joy, strife, wealth, and poverty.

Thus, Becky feared, when Tory loved, she'd do it wholeheartedly, like her grandmother. If Tory had done the unthinkable and given her heart to a pirate, what future could she have in England? It would matter little in the end whether she arrived with her virtue intact; people would believe the worst anyway. Tory already lived on the edge of society's approval for having refused to conform. Now even her grandmother's wealth would not save her from ostracism. Becky knew intuitively what Tory would do—she'd bury herself in the country and devote herself to her beloved horses. What a fate for one of such beauty and generosity of spirit. Surely being the beloved of a talented, just man was preferable to that, even if he was a pirate. Becky knew instinctively that Sinan would cherish Tory as she deserved. God, why couldn't he be English, or even American, Becky thought despairingly. Anyone, anything, but a corsair.

So did Becky and Tory struggle with their own private demons, each dreading the day's waning. When the sun was lowering in the sky, Tory bestirred herself.

She didn't see Becky's agonized expression or realize that Becky had changed her clothes and made a request of the harem guard. At his grudging nod, Becky descended.

Tory had little time, she knew, as she knocked on Lahtil's door, but she was glad. Her emotions were too fragile to withstand a long visit. So, when Lahtil answered, giving her a welcoming smile, Tory blurted, "Lahtil, I only have a moment, but I want you to know the master understands about you and Kahlil. He has agreed to sell you to Kahlil, who waits only to collect the funds."

Lahtil lit up like a bonfire. Tory blinked, squelched her envy, and hurried on, "It's scant repayment for your friendship. I'll always cherish this time with you." Tory returned Lahtil's shy hug fiercely. Both women smiled a little shakily when they drew apart.

"Come, Tory, let us talk more. There must be something I can do to repay you." She held the door wide in invitation.

Tory shook her head. "No, the master arrives soon to sup with me. I wish you every happiness, dear friend." Tory whirled and hurried to her room.

Lahtil peered after her, wondering at the emotion in Tory's voice, but then she smiled and hugged herself, her normal curiosity muted by joy. Soon, soon, she would belong to Kahlil. Smiling dreamily, she closed her door.

When Sinan returned, he was too engrossed to notice the hand painted next to his door. He paused in the middle of the courtyard, surprised to see Becky huddled with Jarrod. He walked up to the pair. They started apart guiltily. "Why aren't you in your quarters, Becky? It's late."

Becky flashed a shaky smile. "I came down to give Jarrod a treat." She handed the boy a piece of Turkish delight.

Biting into it, Jarrod smiled nervously under his mentor's eagle eye. Sinan scented a plot, but he was in no mood for delays. By damn, *nothing* would distract him from Tory this time.

"Whatever you say, madam. Shall I escort you back to your chamber?" Becky put her hand on his arm with a last warning look at Jarrod.

Sinan didn't miss the exchange. "I don't know what you're plotting with Jarrod, but he's loyal to me. No bribery of candy will change that." Sinan smiled pleasantly when Becky stumbled on the bottom step.

She flushed, wondering what he'd say if he knew it was not him she betrayed. It was too late to wonder if she'd done right. Jarrod knew. He would barely give her and Tory time to get out of the house before alerting everyone. Becky was too nervous to notice the dark eyes watching their retreat. They settled like cold, hard stones on Jarrod's narrow back.

Becky didn't know whether to be glad or sorry when Sinan dismissed the guard at the harem entrance.

"You may retire. There's no need for a guard this night." Sinan locked the doors behind them like a man intending to stay awhile.

Becky's heart lurched at that decisiveness. Tonight, then, would tell the tale. One way or the other, Tory's fate would be decided, and then there really would be no turning back. Stifling her doubts about her own part in that fate, Becky retreated to her room and readied herself.

When he stood at her door, Sinan straightened his shoulders and smoothed one hand over his hair. His heart already thrummed in anticipation, and he hadn't even seen her yet. He knocked and entered. Tory stood, back propped against the chest, ankles crossed, staring through the grilled window at the tiny patch of blue sky.

How sad she seemed, Sinan thought. Like a caged bird longing for freedom. Yet when she turned to him, there was joy in her eyes. She took a step, then shyly stopped as his eyes swept over her.

Had there ever been a more beautiful woman, he wondered, or a dancer who filled her costume so perfectly? His eyes paused on the white skin heaving up and down at her bosom. Elation thrilled him when he realized she was as excited as he. He held out an imperious hand. "Come. It is time. Fulfill your promise to me."

Mesmerized by those hot, compelling green eyes, Tory took two steps toward him before she caught herself. "Do you not want me to dance for you?"

A singularly masculine smile curved the handsome mouth that she longed, more than ever, to feel against hers. "No. I want only one thing: to feel you under me and around me."

Tory shivered as his explicit words were accompanied by an even more explicit look. Her frantic pulse settled lower, in the pit of her belly. She skirted him and went to the tray she had had sent up. She was filling a plate with couscous when a firm but gentle hand on hers made her set it down.

Sinan drew one of her hands around his strong neck, and tucked the other behind his back. "My body needs the sustenance of yours, vixen, not food," he said. "Let me show you how very hungry I am . . .'' Warm lips settled over hers, stifling her protest. They brushed softly, and Tory was defenseless. Her lips trembled and she opened her mouth like a bird giving voice to a song that could no longer be stilled.

''Sinan, Sinan,'' she moaned against his hair when his mouth traveled lower to seek her satiny cleavage. His flicking tongue singed her skin, her inhibitions, her very will, and she knew it not when her vest opened to his urgent hands. He kissed her, demanding the response she gladly gave. He tugged her blouse out of her pantaloons and thrust his hands beneath it. They sighed when he cupped her full, aching breasts.

Tory ignored the inward warning to stop. She had to touch him, feel him against her one last time. It was little enough solace for the lonely years ahead. So when he slipped her blouse up over her head, she let him, pushing his coat off his shoulders and pulling at his shirt with clumsy hands. Then he, too, was bare from the waist up, the brassy sunlight burnishing his skin, gilding the soft hair to dark gold strands. Tory ran her hands over his chest, then bent to plant a kiss on one flat male nipple.

Groaning, he lifted her against him until she felt him thrusting boldly into her abdomen. Wrapping his arms around her back, he arched her upward until he had free access to the nipples pouting for his lips. He closed his mouth over one, teasing with lips and tongue until she was limp and sighing, her head thrown back, her hair streaming over his arms. He feasted like a hungry babe at first one breast, then the other. But there was nothing childlike in his expertise, or in her response to it. When he set her down, her breasts were moist and flushed, her lips eager for his. Even the iron rod caught between them didn't frighten her— until he urged her to the bed.

His eyes scorched her torso. ''You burn me up, love. Come, warm me in your furnace, let me fill you with my fire.'' He whispered even more erotic words against the tender cord in her neck.

Tory's knees barely supported her. She longed to collapse onto the bed and wish the world well lost. She almost succumbed. But then the sunlight glinted off something he had removed and set next to the bed before embracing her. A knife, a jeweled, pretty thing, but a weapon nonetheless. Symbol of all that he was, reminder of why she couldn't give in to this painful need.

A soft hand covered his when he tried to open her girdle. He barely heard her words—''Wait, Sinan, let us drink first''—over the pounding of his heart. She pushed him down on the bed. He grabbed for her, but the passion boiling through his veins made him clumsy.

She evaded him and went to the chest, where she'd set the tea tray. He levered himself up against the pillows, watching as she added honey to his cup, as he liked, and stirred it. She added a pinch of something else, hesitated, then added two more, and stirred again. He was too busy enjoying the bouncing of her breasts as she moved, the supple, sun-dappled skin, to note that she added only one pinch to her own tea, dipping into only one pot, instead of two, as she had for his.

Smiling, she carried the tray to the bed and set it down next to the knife on the table. Handing him one cup, she took the other. The scents of mint and honey tickled his nose, but he scarcely noticed. He drank so quickly the liquid burned his tongue.

He allowed her two whole sips before he took the cup away with a muttered "Enough. You can drink a pot later, but now . . ." He caught her wrist and pulled her down atop him. He sighed with pleasure at the silky weight of her bare breasts. He caught her face between his hands to kiss her passionately, his tongue thrusting keep into her mouth to explore every crevice. He unfastened her girdle, tossed it beside the bed, and reached 'or the pantaloons.

"Lift," he ordered huskily into her mouth, feeling suddenly too weak to move her.

She lifted only her head. His heavy eyes opened and stared into hers. He blinked at what he saw there. Such sadness. Regret and despair. What was wrong? he wondered vaguely, yawning. Languid warmth oozed through him. Suddenly, he had to fight to stay awake. He tried to focus on her face, but she retreated in a cloud, floating away from his need to hold her. Blinking again, he got one last, haunting glimpse of those turquoise eyes. Watching. Waiting. The truth burst upon him then.

He whispered, "Do you hate me so?"

His head fell limply to the side, and the dey's warning rang in his roaring ears: "See she doesn't poison you with your own tea . . ." Then he knew nothing.

Chapter 8

Silence descended on the room, but it was not a peaceful one. It was a tomblike dearth of life and joy, the silence of betrayal. Tory stared down at Sinan with brimming eyes. Telling herself she had no reason to feel like a traitor didn't lessen her anguish. He was so still. What if she'd given him too much? She'd lessened the dosage beyond what the herb-seller had suggested to be sure she didn't harm him, but if the man had been mistaken . . .

A sob catching in her throat, she flung herself next to him and put her head on his chest. She slumped when his heart thumped in her ear, then gathered herself to move, but the effort was beyond her. Now, when he was asleep, she could allow herself the tender good-bye her heart yearned for. She rested her head in nature's hollow between chest and arm, tilting her head back to look at him. She ran her finger over his long curling eyelashes, down the straight blade of a nose, to the full mouth that said so much about his character: strong, sensual, but gentle, too. How could she bear to leave him? He was the only man for her; if she left him, she would condemn herself to loneliness.

Her tears puddled on his chest and ran down his side, staining the fine cotton sheet. Agonize though she did, the truth was she was doomed to unhappiness if she stayed and doomed to unhappiness if she went. At least if she escaped, she'd have a chance of saving her crew. She'd put Greaty's mind at rest, and she'd have the dubious pleasure of keeping her body and her pride intact. If she stayed, she'd have physical and perhaps emotional joy—until the first baby was born. Could she bear to watch the last descendant of the Grenville line become a pirate, a tool of tyranny?

"No," she whispered abjectly. Far better to leave now than to face that calamity. She inhaled deeply and rose, lingering over Sinan to plant a soft kiss on his lips. Then she turned away to add his jeweled dagger to her cache.

She pulled on pantaloons and shirt, stuffed her hair under the turban, then slipped her feet into sandals of the type worn by Algerine men and practiced her walk. She lengthened her stride, making a conscious effort to keep her hips still.

She removed the pot and smeared the brown paint on her face, throat, hands, ankles, and feet until every exposed inch of skin was light brown. She faltered momentarily. What if the paint permanently stained or scarred her face?

She gritted her teeth and proceeded. It was too late now to worry about that. Besides, she reflected bleakly, her looks didn't matter anymore. She fanned her face, then took the stacks of horsehair, dipped the ends in honey and held them against her upper lip to make a drooping mustache. When it was set, she fetched her tiny hoard and the last ruby. Sticking the dagger in her belt, she gathered a water flask and a small sack of provisions. Lastly, she removed the harem door key from Sinan's cloak. She did not look again at the still figure on the bed.

The key snicked in the lock; then her steps retreated. The sounds seemed to rouse the sleeping man, for he stirred, one long arm reaching out. He grabbed the pillow and, with a sigh of relief, subsided, his cheek against it. The glowering sun dyed the tiny tears drying on his chest to crimson drops.

The guards at the door were tired, but they straightened as two figures approached. The squatty Andalusian woman who did the laundry waddled toward them in her black robes, accompanied by her son, who was half Turkish, half Spanish. Each carried a basket of clothes. The old woman scolded her son for his slowness.

The laundress's shrewish temper was a standing joke among the guards. They dug one another in the ribs at the long-suffering look on the young man's face. As they neared, her son lost his temper. "Enough! If I am so slow, next time you can make two trips and carry the clothes alone."

The guards nodded approvingly at his sharp tone. A mother deserved respect, but she was a mere woman, after all. No woman should be allowed to dominate a man, even a young man who was but half Turkish.

When they would have passed with only a nod, the guard who spoke Spanish lifted a staying hand and conferred with the other guard, who had been on duty all day. He caught the young man's arm to keep him from exiting. "Why do you leave so late? Don't you usually come in the morning?"

He nodded. "*Si*, but she was sick today, and I had to help

her.'' Keeping his eyes respectfully lowered, he whispered, ''They say the plague has come again, so don't touch her as she passes.''

The guard blanched and jerked his hand away. He flung open the door. ''*Out!* Leave the clothes outside when you bring them back. Don't come again until you've recovered.''

The heavy door slammed behind them. Tory and Becky leaned against each other for a weak moment, then hastened north toward the gate of Bab-el-Oued. Tory loaded their supplies into one basket and discarded the other, but Becky insisted on carrying it. She pulled her veil over her face and dropped three steps behind Tory's swagger.

Twilight was almost upon them. Algiers at dusk was a pretty scene. Voices drifted from walled gardens; the sweet scent of jasmine mingled with the aromas of coffee, roasting lamb, and bubbling couscous. Overhead the moon pointed a long, curved finger at the star glittering on the horizon as if to say, ''See, look at what you're leaving.''

And with every step, she distanced herself from Sinan. Tory forced herself to widen that gap, for it was too late to go back. Even now they approached the gate.

Becky cast worried glances behind them as the gate loomed up. Where was Jarrod? Why hadn't he alerted the household? She barely listened as Tory argued with the gatekeeper, who said it was too late to let them out.

''It's not dark yet! Here, I'll pay twice the usual toll,'' Tory snapped.

The swarthy Biskran sent an avid glance at the coins she held, looked about, then snatched them. He unbarred the massive gate stretching twice a man's length above their heads and grunted, ''Come!''

Tory plunged into the short, vaulted tunnel that had been cut through the thick city wall. She returned when Becky didn't follow.

''Becky? Come, we must hurry.''

Becky turned from looking down the street. She followed, her steps leaden. The Biskran shoved past them, opened the second, smaller gate, and stood aside. Tory emerged first, then Becky. The gate clanged shut behind them.

Ignoring Becky's protest, Tory took the basket. With one last look at the wall towering above her head, signifying protection and imprisonment, she took the journey one step at a time, pausing only when she was well away. A sandy beach sloped to the sea. Allah's evening canvas was even lovelier than usual, his vivid painting of purple, magenta, and gold reflecting off the indigo mirror of the sea, but Tory took no notice. She cast a wary eye at the Fort of Twenty-four Hours, which guarded this vulnerable northwest sector of Algiers. She saw flickering lights, heard muted noises, but there was no sign of pursuit.

Glancing once at the Turkish and Moorish cemeteries rising ghostly white on the coastal hills, she shivered and walked on. She had too much to fear of the living to be spooked by the dead. They walked until they came to the band of scrub and eucalyptus where the trader had promised to meet them. Tory's hand shook as she switched the basket from one hip to the other. She squinted into the gloom. Was that a shadow? Tension drained away as she saw Gibran waiting patiently with the horses.

Tossing the basket on the ground, she went boldly up to him. "The reis will be pleased at your honor. Here is your final payment." Gibran turned the huge ruby over in his palm, savoring its cool, hard weight. Then he looked at the figure before him and bowed.

"Tell the reis I hope he enjoys his gift."

Tory wondered at his sardonic tone, but before she could question him, he melted into the trees. She frowned at his haste. She heard hoofbeats retreating, then a piercing whistle.

Was that the jingle of harness? Tory froze in the act of tying their provisions to the saddle. She listened, but all she heard was the surf and the wind. She was imagining things.

She turned to Becky, who hadn't said a word since they'd left the city, and laced her hands together to help her mount. "I'm sorry, but we'll have to ride astride. It shouldn't be far to a fishing village. All we have to do is follow the coastline. Surely a fisherman will take us the short distance to Majorca for the money we have left."

Becky settled in the saddle with a grunt, pulling her robes down over her legs as far as they would go. "I've never been on a horse in my life. By heaven I hope this will be the last time."

Even through her misery, Tory had to smile at Becky's disgust. She vaulted easily onto her own mount, soothing him when he danced sideways. At first it seemed strange to ride astride, but she decided she liked the greater security and freedom of movement, even in the odd saddle. It had a high pommel and cantle and no crupper. She shifted her weight to one side, but it seemed stable enough. She looked at Becky's awkward seat and knew they would not get two steps this way.

She urged her skittish horse next to the bay and plucked the reins out of Becky's limp hands. "Just hold on. I don't think we've far to go."

Looping the reins around one hand, she urged Orion forward with her knees. At first the ride was peaceful. Tory inhaled the salty air, savoring the first freedom she'd known in long months. Stars were rising in multitudes now, and the quarter-moon allowed just enough light for her to see the path. The tide drowned out other noises, nor was she expecting pursuit.

Thus, when it came, she was unprepared. She heard the tramping hooves first. She glanced over her shoulder. Out of nowhere, it seemed, a half-dozen riders topped the rise behind them, cloaks flapping in the breeze like vulturine wings.

Shouting, "Hold tight!" to Becky, Tory kneed her mount. The stallion had been chafing at his chain bit and he set to a gallop with a will. Tory had chosen their mounts well, but leading Becky's horse slowed them down, and the pursuing horsemen were closing the gap with frightening speed.

Becky recognized the problem. "Go, Tory. Leave me!"

Tory ignored her tug on the reins and bent over Orion's neck, urging him to greater speed. He tried with all the valiance of his great Arabian heart to deliver, but the bay was tiring, and the footing was treacherous. The bay stumbled, and Becky lurched sideways before grimly pulling herself back into the saddle. The near-disaster cost them precious time. The victorious whoops of their pursuers were right behind them now. Tory knew there was only one thing left to do. She dropped Becky's reins and pulled Orion to a rearing halt.

Whirling like a tigress at bay, she urged her mount between the pursuers and Becky. She pulled Sinan's dagger from her sash. The tip caught a flash of starfire, matching the deadly glitter in Tory's eyes as they were surrounded. She eyed the grinning circle of male faces, pausing on two. Her last hope died.

Hassan and Ali stared at her with almost identical expressions of lust, leering at the way her seat delineated the smooth lines of her thighs. When Hassan urged his mount forward, Tory reared her head up, clutched the knife, and braced herself to meet him . . .

● ● ●

Sinan groaned and flung an arm over his aching head. He smacked his tongue against the roof of his foul-tasting mouth. At first he knew only vaguely that something was amiss, but soon the silence of the room rang in his head like a warning bell. He forced his eyes open—to the sight of the cup sitting beside his bed. Memory rushed back. Tory had drugged him! He sat up, grunting as his head tried to disengage itself from his shoulders.

A cursory glance at the gaping chest—drawers open, clothes hanging over the side, her dancing costume heaped on the floor— told him all. He rose and wobbled to the door. He slumped against it in momentary despair when it wouldn't open. Then rage came to his aid, rushing through his veins and sweeping out the dregs of the drug.

Damn her, damn her seductive body and her lying eyes; she would pay for this. Just please, oh, please, dear Lord, he begged silently, keep her safe. The conflicting nature of the two thoughts didn't occur to him as he drew back a boot and kicked the door with all his might.

Downstairs, the guards were seeking the source of the strange tapping noise that had been bothering them for the last hour. It had an echoing, diffused sound that was hard to pinpoint. Finally, one guard put his ear to the bath door. He flung the door open. There was Jarrod, tied to the antechamber bench, tapping one hard-soled sandal frantically against the stone floor. The guard rushed forward and pulled the gag from his mouth.

"The master is asleep in the harem. We must wake him! Quick. His lady is in danger!"

At that moment, a mighty crash shook the upper story. The guards did the unthinkable then. They unlocked the harem door and peeked inside the forbidden sanctum. They gaped as Sinan, bare-chested and bristling with rage, shoved the broken door back against its hinges and stepped around it, leaving it sagging to one side.

"Have my horse saddled immediately!" he snapped. "Include provisions for a week." He strode into his room and pulled on a clean shirt, pausing when he realized his knife was gone. The little fool! She knew nothing of how to use a knife.

Visions of Tory, her throat slit with his own knife, tormented him, but he forced himself to continue preparations. He had to find her, quickly! He stuffed a heavy purse of sequins into his cloak and tossed an extra burnoose and *haik* over his shoulder. Night was just falling, so he couldn't have been asleep long. He wondered for a moment why she'd given him such a mild dose; then he shrugged the thought away as unimportant. She'd betrayed him, mocked him, and manipulated him for the last time.

He would find her if he had to dig Algeria apart grain of sand by grain of sand. Then, by God, he'd stamp her as his possession in the age-old way until she'd never contemplate leaving him again. To his past reservations and quibbles he gave not a thought. No woman was going to make a fool of him, as she had done, without suffering retribution. No lady could act the wanton as she did; he was through treating her as one, tossing night after night in his cold bed in reward for his gallantry.

His angry thoughts were interrupted by Jarrod. "Sinan, Tory is in danger. Ali overheard Becky telling me of their plans. He tied me up and escaped to warn Hassan. I fear he was waiting for them once they reached the beach."

Icy fear froze Sinan's rage. "How do you know this?"

"Becky wanted me to know their plans because of the danger," Jarrod lied, as he had promised Becky he would. He shared her belief that the captain was meant for Tory, but he also agreed that Sinan and Tory had to arrive at the same conclusion on their own. "Ali told me his plans for less noble reasons." He hesitated, as if fearful to continue, then said in a rush, "He wants you to know that he has been spying for Hassan for days, waiting for the chance to snatch Tory. He's known of her plans for escape since she went to the *souq*. He made a bargain with Hassan . . ." Jarrod's voice trailed away.

"Go on, Jarrod," Sinan commanded harshly.

In a pained whisper, Jarrod finished, "Hassan has promised to give Tory to Ali when he is finished with her."

A snarl of rage rang in the chamber, a sound so feral that Jarrod backed an instinctive pace away from its source. "Tory and Becky went to Bab-el-Oued only a little over an hour ago. If you hurry, you may be in time to save her," Jarrod babbled, hoping to soften Sinan's frightening expression.

"Oh, I'll catch them. And may Allah have mercy on Ali and Hassan, for I'll have none." His movements measured and deadly of purpose, Sinan picked up a brace of pistols, strapped on his sword, stuck a spare knife in his belt, and slung a pouch of shot over his shoulder.

"How is Tory dressed, Jarrod?"

"Becky said she'd be dressed as a man, with a false mustache. Becky is wearing black robes."

Sinan nodded and turned, but paused to clap Jarrod on the shoulder. "Thank you. I owe you a great debt, which I swear to repay." With a swirl of cloak, he was gone.

Tightening her sweaty grip on the knife, Tory grunted, "Come no nearer, stranger. Let my mother and me go on our way in peace. We've nothing of value." Tory prayed, but Ali's presence gave her little reason to hope. They obviously awaited her. That fiend of a horse trader had betrayed them.

"So cheaply you rate yourself, Englishwoman. What a pretty boy you make," Hassan taunted in reply.

So the ruse was useless. Tory paled beneath the paint, but she wasn't defeated yet. "I know many things the women in your land are kept ignorant of, Sheikh Hassan. You'd be wise not to see how manlike I can be."

Hassan threw back his head and laughed. "What a spirited little cat!" He leaned forward in his saddle. "Will I feel your claws, my kitten? We will spend many long, delicious days— and nights—exploring those differences. Come, now, put the knife down. Even if you know how to use it, of what good is it against so many of us?"

"I cannot kill all of you, true," Tory conceded calmly. She leaned forward to emphasize her own words. "But I can do you enough damage before they stop me to make you wish you were dead." Tory slashed the air in the direction of his crotch, laughing throatily when he urged his mount backwards. "I breed horses at home, you know. Geldings are so much easier to manage than stallions."

Rage had made her rash. Too rash, she soon discovered, when the horsemen, at Hassan's order, fanned out in a circle around them and gradually closed the ring. One grabbed a struggling Becky and flung her before him across his horse, swatting her on the rear until her writhing stopped.

Tory desperately turned Orion this way and that, stabbing the air with the knife, but there were too many of them. Her mouth set grimly. Very well, if she was to be captured, Hassan would not go unscathed. She ignored the men closing in behind her and concentrated all her energies on the dark, purposeful features of the shiekh. When he reached out to jerk the reins from her hands, she was ready for him.

She struck like a cobra, smiling in satisfaction when he drew back with a screech and sucked the deep gash in his hand. He looked at her, and his expression made her blood congeal. He gave a curt command to his men. Grumbling, they backed off.

"Since the Hawk has denied me the pleasure of your virgin blood, and since you have had the foolishness to draw mine, I have no choice but to repay your impudence in kind." He drew his sword and urged his mount forward.

Tory backed Orion, but the bedouins formed a wall behind her. She could burst past Hassan, but what of Becky? Defeated, Tory sheathed the knife, sat erect, and waited for the first slash. Perhaps it was best this way, after all. It was a better end than what he had planned for her.

The sheikh's white teeth glittered in a rapacious smile. "Ah, how foolishly brave for a woman. But I'm not ready to let you die—yet." He eased his mount alongside hers and pushed her cloak aside with the tip of his sword. He slashed off the single button holding her shirt closed.

Tory dropped her reins to clutch the gaping material. An icy-hot flash of pain stung the back of her hand. Dully, she watched blood drip from the shallow gash.

Smiling, Hassan sheathed his sword and lifted his hand to rub his wound against hers. Disgusted, she tried to pull away, but he caught her wrists in one hand and pulled them away from her bosom. To her horror, he bent his head and licked their combined blood away from her upper breast.

She swallowed her nausea, barely hearing his "Thus our fluids mix for the first time, woman. I cannot wait until we pause to rest, for then they shall mix again and again." He forced her chin up. "But first I've a need to feel your tongue. You shall soothe the damage you did me, cat, as your first lesson in obedience."

Releasing her, he held his long, well-shaped hand out to her. Tory knew what he wanted her to do, but no power on earth, not even the threat of violent rape or death, could force her to put lips and tongue on that dark, commanding hand in a mockery of a caress. Teeth? That was another matter . . .

His nostrils flared with his growing lust when she obediently bent her head, her hair tumbling out of the loose turban. She opened her mouth, her breath stirring the back of his hand, making him shiver. Suddenly her jaws gaped open, and she clamped her teeth down on his wound with the ferocity of a lioness. He howled, boxing her ear, but she bit harder. Her growls of satisfaction made him break out in a sweat. His face whitening with fear as much as pain, he drew his sword with his free hand and whacked the hilt against the side of her head.

Tory sagged, falling, falling. She was unconscious before she hit the ground, but a smile of savage triumph lingered on her lips as darkness claimed her.

Only by invoking the dey's authority was Sinan able to rouse the gatekeeper and get out of the city. He'd wasted another precious hour by the time the gate clanged shut behind him. He galloped out onto the beach, fearing what he would see. He was torn between relief and despair when he found nothing but trampled sand. Two horses could not have disturbed the earth so much. Hassan must indeed have her. He closed his eyes, so enervated by fear that he swayed. He knew how Tory reacted to captivity. And his treatment of her had been gentle compared to what Hassan would mete out.

By sheer willpower, Sinan forced away the horrible visions of her lying beaten and violated. He took a deep, calming breath as he did before every battle. He couldn't afford the luxury of fear or even the guilt that gnawed at him for not having set her mind at ease by revealing his identity. He had to focus his energies on two ends: finding her and getting them all out alive.

He dismounted, squatted over the tracks, and tried to gauge how many men Hassan had with him. He guessed a good half-dozen. He mounted and followed the marks, but when they turned south into the fertile plain, he lost them.

Sinan drew Eclipse to a halt, his mind working over the problem. He could wait until morning and hope to pick up their trail by questioning vineyard and orchard hands along the way, but he doubted Hassan would stop for the night, and so there would be no witnesses now, when he needed them most. Hassan knew he would be in pursuit and doubtless planned to get far away as quickly as possible.

He could hope to track them by following the most logical route through the Atlas Mountains to the outskirts of the Sahara, where Hassan would meet the rest of his tribe; or he could obey his instincts, gamble that he knew where they were headed and ride there hell-for-leather. Traveling alone, on one of the swiftest horses in North Africa, only a couple of hours behind them, he should have a good chance of arriving before them and laying a trap.

Hands firm on the reins, chin set in granite, he turned south and urged Eclipse into an easy, ground-eating lope.

Darkness, pain, thirst, and hunger greeted Tory like hobgoblins when she awoke, after a fashion. She was tied, face downward, on her loping horse. She groaned, only to realize she was gagged. Tears fell. For several weak moments, she was too miserable to care if anyone saw or heard that she was beaten. Dear God, why was it every time she reached out for freedom that she brought disaster to herself and everyone else with her? She looked frantically about for Becky. She finally spied the abigail's black robes. At least Hassan had allowed her to ride upright.

Relieved, Tory rested her cheek on Orion's side. Soon the powerful, rhythmic motions of the stallion's muscles soothed her, gradually infusing her with a measure of his strength. Dammit, she might be trussed like a chicken awaiting slaughter, but Hassan's greedy teeth would not find her plump and tender. She'd be as tough as boot leather, gagging him until he sought better sustenance elsewhere. Had she not kept a fierce Barbary reis at bay for months?

She ignored the facts: She had held Sinan off only because he was too fine a man to enjoy rape, and Hassan was vastly different in nature. Bravado aside, courage was all that kept her from hysteria. She sensed Hassan wanted to see her groveling at his feet. She'd do anything to deny him that pleasure, even if she had to enrage him into killing her.

Closing her eyes, she wiped her mind clean of all but the resolve handed down to her by twenty generations of Grenvilles. She had to conserve her strength; she'd soon have need of all of it.

Her first test came when they paused at a stream to water the tired horses. Hassan didn't bother to untie her hands. He hauled her down and propped her against a tree trunk, then ungagged her and thrust a smelly goatskin to her lips. She longed to spit the lukewarm water in his taunting face, but thirst was making her giddy and she needed alertness above all else. She drank until he took the skin away.

Capping it, he swung it back over his shoulder and squatted next to her. "I hope you're enjoying your ride, my fine lady. Shall I adjust your saddle?"

The false solicitousness made her yearn to tear his eyes out, but she kept her gaze lowered and remained silent. Letting him think her beaten could be their only hope. Her head lolled forward as she appeared to doze.

"Pshaw!" He stood in disgust and nudged her contemptuously with a boot. "You're as weak as the rest of your kind. Doubtless I'll tire of you soon." He gave a curt order that she be allowed to ride astride and mounted his own horse.

He didn't see the rising sun giving Tory's eyes a fiendish glow before long lashes shielded them. A stocky bedouin slit her ankle bonds and hauled her to her feet.

Tory bit down a groan of agony as sensation returned to her feet. She would have fallen if the Arab, with a snort of contempt, hadn't picked her up and thrown her in the saddle.

Hassan joked to his men, who broke out in raucous laughter. Tory threw him a look of such hatred that his eyebrows rose. A gleam of interest returned to his eyes. "Ah, so you've some fight left in you, have you? Good. Soon, little toy, we shall see how much. In a week or so, we'll reach our destination. Then you'll become invisible, one more inconsequential grain of sand in the desert instead of the English aristocrat you think yourself."

"Why the haste, Shiekh Hassan? Do you fear the Hawk will swoop down on you?" Tory goaded in her turn.

Hassan's mount, a strong, swift gray, shifted under the sudden tug on its reins. "Let him come. Even if he brings his men, they'll have no chance against us. City-dwellers are women compared to men of the desert."

A harsh cough caught Tory's attention. She looked at Becky, who shook her head slightly. Tory's open mouth snapped closed. She nodded slightly in gratitude for the reminder, pinned a chagrined look on her face, and bowed her shoulders. They proceeded up the tortuous trail.

In other circumstances, Tory would have enjoyed the hasty trip. Even the grueling pace, the days of riding with only an occasional hour to rest, wouldn't have bothered her if she'd had something besides rape and quite possibly death to look forward to at the end of it.

The fertile strip of the Mitidja, with its lush vineyards, orchards, and olive groves had long since been tamed and utilized by man, but now they traversed the first range of the Atlas. They emerged on the High Plateaus where even the dey's hand seldom reached. Here customs were ancient and people lived bounded only by the laws of Allah and tribe. These sedentary and seminomadic Algerians were as intransigent as the mountains they lived in, Jarrod had told her.

The scenery was spectacular. The writhing path wound through slopes barren of trees, but occasionally they traversed tableland lush with native and cultivated grasses. Soon the terrain roughened again, and torrents rushed through the valley with such fury that Tory could hear the sound of the water far below. When she rounded yet another bend she gasped in delight. A waterfall thundered down a limestone cliff to marry with the river, water thrusting into water to give birth to villages clinging to the slopes.

On they trudged, rising as they reached the Saharan Atlas, traveling through gorges, around bend after bend of gradually more austere landscape. Forest ceded to shrub-dotted slopes interspersed with herds of goats and flocks of sheep. As the sun lowered on another day, fear returned to Tory. The numbing pace had saved her so far, but soon they'd have to pause for a full night's rest. She could feel her mount stumbling with weariness. They hadn't eaten all day and she was faint with hunger, but she would gladly have gone on when Hassan raised a hand and ordered a halt.

They were on a straight stretch protected by huge boulders on either side. Tory watched as Hassan's men made a careful survey of the area and reported back to him. He looked about, then nodded and dismounted. It was obvious he feared attack. Tory tried to take comfort from that, but she sensed it was not Sinan he feared. The implications of that were beyond her. She was simply too weary to care who captured her. Whether she was Sinan's captive or Hassan's or someone else's she would still be a prisoner.

When Hassan lifted her from her saddle, she didn't struggle. She stumbled over to a boulder and sat down. They ate hard bread, figs, dates, and dried meat. The food was not fresh, but it tasted like manna to Tory. She felt somewhat refreshed when she finished, but her face was beginning to pain her. The exposure to the sun and the effects of the paint had combined to irritate her skin. When Hassan handed her a goatskin, she took several drafts. He took the skin from her, poured some water on a rag, lifted her chin, and scrubbed her face. She moaned in pain and tried to turn away, but he ignored her discomfort and ripped away the straggling remains of her fake mustache.

"You deserve a beating for daring to pretend to be a man.

You are nothing but a foolish woman, as you shall learn before I am finished with you.''

After that, Tory would have let him flail her skin off flake by flake rather than protest again. He rubbed for a few more moments, then tossed the rag away in disgust.

He caught the point of her chin between two fingers and bent to taunt, ''It's useless. Perhaps you are stained for life. If you have ruined your beauty, I shall sell you south as a domestic slave.''

His cruelty brought stiffness back to Tory's backbone. This barbarian wasn't fit to serve tea to her, a Grenville, much less threaten her with servitude. Tory surged to her feet, fury giving her strength.

''Anything is better than enduring the touch of your filthy hands!'' Tory turned away, but he spun her back around.

When she met his furious glare steadily, a nasty smile curved his mouth. ''Ah, that's better. Come, my cat, it's time you showed me your claws. When you cry out with pleasure you will not think my hands so dirty.''

He shoved her ahead of him up the path to an encircling group of boulders where a mat lay ready.

Tory struggled, now that she knew what he intended, but he caught her hands and brought them up behind her back until she groaned and fell to her knees. Tory tried to scramble up, but he blocked the narrow gap and casually, insolently, threw back his cloak, opened his pantaloons, and bared his stiffening length.

Shuddering in disgust, Tory closed her eyes, sick in body, mind, and heart at the thought of what was to come. Becky cried a protest from beyond the encircling boulders. Tory's eyes opened. There was a loud crack, then silence. Tory's eyes narrowed to glittering slits of light. Long lashes doused them.

She fell back on the blanket, parted her legs, and lifted her arms. ''Come, master, I yield,'' she said huskily. She arched one arm above her head as she stretched, pressing her full breasts against her shirt.

Gray eyes fixed on that display, Hassan dropped down beside her and reached out to rip her shirt away. Tory's slowly reaching hand gripped a rock just as his hands connected. The material tore in concert with his guttural hiss as she whipped the rock up to bash it against his head.

Since he was so close to her, he felt the movement in time to dodge, and she only managed a glancing blow. He caught her wrist in one hand and squeezed until she dropped the rock, then clasped her neck in his hands to choke the life out of her. At first Tory tried to pull away, but his strong hands tightened until her head began to whirl. Her struggles grew weaker, but then her eyes opened and stared directly into his. With her last strength, she tilted her head slightly to give him better leverage. And she smiled, a ghastly, strained smile, but a smile nonetheless.

The pressure at her throat eased as the world narrowed to a tiny pinpoint of light. Through her ringing ears, Tory caught his words: "Woman, you will not escape so easily. When you are broken to my hand, then will I kill you."

Her struggling senses gave up the battle. She fainted, not even feeling the kick with which he tried to rouse her.

When next she woke, she was tied hand and foot, belly down over her horse. And so she stayed throughout the last day of the trip. By the time the sun set, Tory was in agony. She bit her lip until it was as raw as the rest of her to keep silent. She knew she'd get no mercy; she would not give Hassan the satisfaction of pleading for it.

They halted at last next to a river. Tory was hauled down from the saddle, untied, then propped back up. She sagged over the pommel, too weak to sit up.

Hassan sneered in disgust but mounted behind her and snarled, "We've reached Biskra. Another day's ride and we meet my people. You will say nothing as we enter the town, or your friend's throat will be slit." He twisted her head around to force her to look at Becky.

She, too, sat before an Arab, who grinned at Tory and displayed a long, curved dagger. Tory nodded. She watched dully as they entered the city that would be a land of no return for her.

Chapter 9

Biskra was likened to a desert port by Algerians for good reason: From its position at the foot of the Great Atlas, it gave an intimidating view of the Sahara stretching infinitely east, west, and south. Here, Biskra seemed to say, there is plenty from my river, shade under my palms, goods in my bazaar, and company from my people. There, a short distance away, is emptiness: scorching sand, danger, and death. Stay awhile, enjoy my bounty.

It was an invitation Tory longed to accept. Other women had disappeared into the Sahara, but the fact that she would be neither the first nor the last only deepened her despair.

Biskra seemed to be a series of villages stretching for several miles. Tent *douars* ringed the outskirts. As they passed through rows of palms, mud huts gave way to white-walled buildings. Burnoosed men herded sheep or goats before them to market. One Arab thundered through the streets on a fine horse, brandishing a sword and laughing as people and animals scrambled away.

When they reached the *souq*, Tory saw several blue-veiled men. Their matching indigo turbans were banded with white about the forehead. Tory recalled that Lahtil had called them Tuaregs, members of a fierce Saharan tribe.

She was toying with the idea of calling out when Hassan stiffened. He, too, stared at the Tuaregs before averting his head and cantering his stallion past them. Tory felt him relax only when they were lost in the crowd. Tory peered about for some sign of Sinan, but she saw nothing unusual.

Some of the women bartering at the *souq* were veiled, but the Berber women were bare-faced, displaying tattooed chins and foreheads. Their palms were red with henna. They stood beside men trading honey, wax, and hides. Tory caught a handsome Arab youth staring at her.

Hassan squeezed her waist warningly. "Say not a word if you value your friend's life." Casually, as if threatening murder were commonplace to him, he gestured toward Becky.

The sun winked off the dagger half hidden in Becky's robes. Tory nodded in wordless acquiescence. As long as he held Becky, she didn't dare attempt escape. He knew it, damn his barbaric soul.

"So, Englishwoman, you begin to understand that here I am master. See that you remember it until we reach my tribe, and I may let you both live."

His sneering arrogance grated on Tory, but she was too exhausted to care. Let him gloat, she thought. If the only way out for her was death, she'd meet it at her own hand rather than become his toy.

They stooped at a house adjacent to the crowded market. Tory was too listless to notice the tall Arab, *kaffiyeh* pulled over his face, following them. When they stopped, the Arab dismounted, tied his black to a low wall, and leaned against it. Hassan hauled her out of the saddle and shoved her roughly into the broiling hut.

· The watching Arab stiffened. A tanned hand reflexively reached for the gun at his belt, clenched, then fell back to his side. He straightened and melted into the crowd.

On entering the hut, Hassan shouted. A wizened little woman appeared, her face covered with tattoos. Large copper earrings dangled from her ears, and her skinny body was garbed in a cotton *haik* belted by a rope. The crone acknowledged Hassan's orders with a gap-toothed grin.

"Clean yourself. The door will be watched and your friend will remain in the saddle with Solah. If you try to escape or call for help, she will be killed." Hassan forced Tory's face to his by pulling her hair. "Upon my return, see your manners match your dress as my slave. If you once again raise a hand to me, I will cut it off."

When Tory closed her eyes, he smiled and embraced her roughly, ignoring her impotent struggles. "When I'm deep inside you, Englishwoman, you'll admit me to be your master." She turned her head away from his kiss, so he nipped her neck, then released her. The door closed behind him.

Tory rubbed her neck, her stomach churning. When the old woman pushed her into a tiny room and indicated she strip, Tory balked. "No!"

But "no" meant no more to this woman than it had to any other person in this accursed land. Muttering, the crone picked up a thong. With the desert woman's strength, she tied Tory's hands behind her back and proceeded to cut her clothes away. She gasped at Tory's pale glory, rubbing a pearly shoulder as if expecting her hand to come away white.

Dipping a sponge in cool, soapy water, she began to wash. Tory struggled until the gentle massage began to relax her. What difference did it make? Hassan would strip her himself if she didn't obey, and if she ached less, perhaps she could think more clearly. Thus she stood docile until the old woman began to scrub her sore face and neck. The paint on her hands and feet had faded, and the rest had come off in the washing, but the facial residue was more stubborn.

Tory averted her head, protesting, but the ancient scrubbed vigorously, to no avail. The woman flung the sponge in the bowl and helped Tory dress in pantaloons, filmy blouse, and long, richly embroidered blue tunic with full sleeves. After brushing the tangled red hair, the crone bound a silk covering about Tory's head and secured it with silver buckles. Finally, she fastened silver anklets around Tory's ankles and bracelets on her wrists, then slid Tory's feet into leather slippers.

She led her charge to a tiny mirror on the wall. What little Tory could see in the wavery glass pleased her. Her fine dress couldn't disguise her brown, cracked face, bruised throat and fatigue-shadowed eyes. Tory was unaware of the way the clinging garments accented her lush curves. She forced herself to consume the nasty paste and cloudy water the crone offered.

The sun was sinking, but the tiny house was still unbearably hot when Hassan returned. He stopped short. Tory slept on her side on a carpet. His eyes smoldering, he took a long step toward her, glanced out at the crimson horizon, cursed, and shook Tory roughly awake. He lifted her to her feet and shoved her outside.

Foggy with tiredness, Tory barely noticed when he threw an enveloping *haik* over her possessively. The fiery arch of the sun, half above, half beneath the horizon, made her blink. Hassan's men swarmed about, loading provisions on camels, tying the horses on leads, shouting to one another. Tory barely had time to notice Becky's drooping figure atop a sullen camel before she, too, was hefted on a hulking brute. Tory struggled when Hassan tied her hands to the pommel. She held on as best she could when she was jarred forward, backward and forward again as the beast lumbered to its feet. Mounting his own camel, Hassan took her leads. Off they started, winding through the town.

Tory knew this was her last chance. She looked frantically about, but saw few pedestrians at this dinner hour, and they paid the common sight of a caravan no heed. She opened her mouth to call for help anyway, but the watching Ali, riding next to her, pulled his pistol from his belt and pointed it at Becky's back. Tory swallowed the cry and threw him a look of hatred.

So she began her trek into the Sahara, the bleak landscape a match for her soul. Scrub-dotted hills smoothed to flat wastes as they descended from Biskra. Forever the barren, scorched land undulated, infinite and forbidding as the realms of hell, and with every step, Tory went deeper into perdition. The monotony was broken only by ridges rearing out of the unforgiving earth. Soon cracked soil conceded to sugary sand. Swish, swish, went the camel's steps, but Tory was too desperate to find the rhythmic sway soothing.

For most of that night they rode. Tory wondered, when she was capable of coherent thought, why Hassan hurried so, sometimes glancing over his shoulder. As if now, more than ever, he feared pursuit. Why? He'd won. If Sinan was to overtake them, he would have done so by now.

Tired though she was, Tory drew the logical conclusion. Hassan feared someone else. Someone who threatened him more the deeper into the desert they traveled. Tory sensed Hassan was trying to reach the meeting place of his clan—and reinforcements. It was late August, still too early for all his tribe to gather . . . unless he'd summoned them early out of fear.

Hope flickered in her heart until she realized she'd be in the same position—slave to a man's whims—regardless of who held her. She was naught but a female receptacle, even to Sinan. These primitive bedouins would be no different, no matter which tribe captured her.

Tears threatened as she thought of Sinan. Had he even tried to find her? She'd left little trace, true, but perhaps he was so angry he was glad to be rid of her. Tory focused on Becky's swaying back, but the sight of that proud little spine bent with weariness pained her further. There was nothing to do now but endure. However, the next time they stopped, she'd try to reach Becky after the camp slept. If she could incapacitate Hassan when he tried to take her, they might have a chance to steal a couple of camels and get back to Biskra before they were caught.

But, Tory resolved, if all else failed, rather than endure the enslavement Hassan planned, she'd die. With his mean temper, it shouldn't be difficult to incite him to murder. But first, she vowed, he'd regret laying hands on her. Galvanized by even such a bleak purpose, Tory worked at her bindings.

Eos yawned in the east when they finally stopped. Tory gave up trying to work free and watched as Hassan sent two men before and behind them to scout. She looked about. Eerie shadows danced on the gentle dunes about them like desert spirits defying the approaching day. The stars overhead glowed with a luster she had never seen, as if offering comfort to the harsh land below. It was cold, amazingly cold considering how hot it had been at sunset.

And all about them was silence, silence such as Tory had never heard. No trees rustled, for there were none; no water burbled; few creatures cried in the night. Most who thrived in the harsh climate were silent slitherers or burrowers.

In happier times, when life had been a great adventure, before she learned what danger her impetuosity could visit upon her and those she loved, Tory might have seen a strange beauty to the landscape. Now the terrain was a bleak reminder of her isolation.

When Hassan ordered her camel to kneel and slashed through her bonds, she didn't struggle. Watching dully as his men hobbled the animals, she deduced that they hoped to foil thievery. While Hassan listened to the scouts' reports, Tory tried to reach Becky, but he grabbed a fistful of *haik* and pulled her up short. After a final curt order, he caught Tory's arm and dragged her to the black tent set up for his use. Ali watched them go, his eyes hotly envious.

Hassan secured the tent flap behind them. He turned to her, his civilized veneer stripped away. She saw him then as he really was: a man who had been reared to think himself superior to other men, a lord to lowly women. She was a possession, like the red carpet spread at his feet, the guttering lantern making their shadows dance grotesquely, and the wooden bowl containing dates and figs awaiting his hunger.

The appalling idea of being any man's possession infused strength into Tory's sapped limbs. Turning away from his lustful stare, she casually surveyed the tent. "Why did we travel through the night? Whom do you fear?"

Hassan's muscular body stiffened. "I fear no one, woman, as you will learn soon enough."

"Not even the Tuareg?" Judging by his flexing jaw, Tory knew her blind shot had landed dead center.

"Caution and fear are not the same. Once I reach my tribe, the Tuareg will not dare attack us. And my scouts tell me we are not being followed, so I was apparently not seen in Biskra." Hassan crossed his arms and boasted, "Do you know why they hate me? Because I took some of their women on a raid after they had stolen my camels and my favorite stallion. We sold the females when we were finished with them. Most women, unfortunately, lack spirit enough to interest me for long. Come, Englishwoman, show me you are different.'' He advanced, his handsome features ruthless. For too long he had waited to have her. Nothing would stop him now.

Nothing but Tory, strengthened by the invisible Grenville legion cheering her on. Arching her fingers into claws, Tory said softly, ''If it's spirit you want, I'll gladly oblige. You've threatened me with beating, rape, dismemberment, and death. Carry through your threats, for I promise on my word as a Grenville I will never submit to you. If you force me, somehow I'll avenge my honor.''

Hassan eyed her proudly tilted head with something akin to admiration, for revenge, at least, he understood. ''I am warned, lovely cat. I will be on my guard. But I did not risk the dey's wrath or bring you here on a whim. You are a thirst I must quench inside your lovely body.''

Tory backed away until the tent's rough wool scratched her back. Frantically, she looked about. Nothing except . . . Tory ducked Hassan's grab and reached for the lamp. But her long headdress was her undoing. Hassan caught it, wrapped it around his hand, and pulled her into his arms. Tory scratched, bit, but he forced her hands behind her back and ripped off her *haik*. When Tory kicked him, he snarled, dumped her on the red rug, threw his weapons in the corner of the tent and himself atop her.

His lust had grown until it was a fever in his blood, rushing to fill his groin to bursting. He ripped her tunic open, too intent on baring her breasts to notice her slow reach for the lantern.

As she felt the cool dawn air strike her exposed bosom, her fingers closed on the lamp handle. Tory shuddered when Hassan's hot lips fastened on her breast. Uncaring if she set them both afire, she dumped the oil on the rug and tried to hit him.

He knocked the lantern away. The oil ignited and tried to consume the rug, but the fibers were damp, and the flames flickered out. Cruel hands released her only to go for her face, but Tory was able to dodge the wild blows in the darkness.

Bellowing like a lusting bull, Hassan fumbled at his clothes, then ripped at her pantaloons. ''Daughter of *Chitann*! You call me master, beginning now!''

Tory tried desperately to shove his heavy body away, but her strength was no match for his. Her searching hands felt nothing but sand. Her pantaloons tore. God, deliver me, she prayed silently, tears coming to her eyes.

In answer, a howl pierced the dawn quiet. Hassan went still. Panting with rage and lust, he raised his head to listen.

Then came a cry from one of his own men, "*Razzia!* Tuareg!" The warning ended in a gurgling choke. Hassan rose to his knees and scrabbled in the dark for the knife and sword.

He straightened his clothes, grabbed the weapons, and charged out of the tent. Thanks welling from her heart to her lips, Tory straightened her own clothes and followed, praying she and Becky could escape in the confusion.

A nightmarish scene straight from an El Greco masterpiece met her eyes. Light and dark, shadow and luminosity, battled in one grotesque epic. White-robed bedouins were locked in mortal combat with black- and blue-robed Tuaregs. Some warriors used swords, others knives and lances. Two men already lay fallen, one Tuareg, one Arab—a life for a life, in the Moslem way.

This was no thieving raid, Tory sensed, but the most ruthless *razzia* of all—the dawn raid of revenge. The breaking day and the pure desert air outlined the warriors with a clarity as stark as the challenge they faced: life or death.

Tory glimpsed Ali battling a tall Arab in white robes and *kaffiyeh* before their duel took them behind a tent. She slunk around the edge of the *douar*. To her horror, she spied Becky, bound and lying near the feet of Hassan and a fierce Tuareg, who were fighting near the horses. Tory picked up a fallen knife and crawled on her knees toward Becky.

Ever after she would remember that journey on sludgy sand as the longest of her life. Grunting men labored all about her, steel clanging against steel. As Tory reached Becky and sliced her bonds, a hoarse moan sounded above them. A last gasp for life gurgled in the Tuareg's throat before he fell face down across the two women, blood from the hole in his chest gushing over them both.

Becky and Tory screamed and pushed the lifeless form away. A victorious Hassan grabbed Tory by the hair. He pushed her across the bare back of the horse he'd unhobbled before being set upon. Tory kicked out at him. He staggered back, giving her time to slither off the horse.

Shouting to Becky, "Saddle two horses!" Tory turned to meet Hassan. Just then, Ali and his adversary rounded a tent, distracting her. The sun burst over the horizon, baring the strong, determined face of the man who had lived in Tory's heart for days without number. No longer did she deny her joy at the sight of it.

Tory's elated "Sinan!" made Hassan turn in time to see Sinan knock Ali's scimitar away and bury his sword in Ali's chest. A stunned look on his face, the Turk blinked at his former captain, coughed up blood, and sank to the ground. Sinan sheathed his sword and turned, his face lighting up at sight of Tory. Calling her name, he ran toward her.

Taking advantage of Tory's shock, Hassan grabbed her about the neck, snatched the knife from her hand, and held her before him as a shield. Sinan froze, his features icing over with rage.

The battle was abating, for the Arabs were hopelessly outnumbered. No sooner did they dispatch one Tuareg then another rose to take his place. Only two of Hassan's men still stood. They threw down their weapons at the sight of Hassan's cowardly act, watching expressionlessly as their chief used a woman to shield him. Their loyalty to Hassan had been tested many times: in his unseemly profiteering and consorting with that scoundrel of a dey; in his avaricious use of women. Still, they had remained loyal to the son of the sheikh they and their fathers before them had revered—until now.

For at last Hassan's true worth could no longer be doubted. He had committed the sin no bedouin could stomach in his leader—cowardice. He had not only tried to escape in the thick of the fighting, he now used a woman as a shield to avoid facing in fair combat the man he had stolen her from.

The Tuaregs tensed as if debating whether to charge Hassan, but they looked from Sinan's stiff face to the woman to the dune behind Hassan, and hesitated. Muttering among themselves, they tied up their two prisoners and clustered in a group to wait. Becky, shaking so much she could no longer stand, slumped to the ground, her moving lips soundlessly praying for Tory's safety.

Hassan taunted Sinan, "So, you are worthy of your name, eh, infidel? The Hawk has once again snatched his prey. But to seize me, you must come through the woman. I would enjoy killing her, for she's been nothing but trouble to me." Hassan punctuated his warning with a flick of the knife. A tiny dot of blood appeared at the base of Tory's neck.

Sinan took an enraged step forward before he caught himself. God, to lose her now, when she was within feet of him, would send him mad. Taking a deep breath, Sinan said calmly, "Perhaps I yearn for your blood more than your leavings, coward.

Your death would bring me more than pleasure: With you gone, there will be little interest in persecuting me.'' Sinan glanced behind Hassan. Then, his eyes as dewy cool as mint, he looked back at the sheikh.

A bead of sweat dribbled down Hassan's brow despite the cool air. He tested Sinan's words by opening Tory's torn blouse. Baring one firm breast, he fondled it in full view of the watching men. He smiled when Sinan flinched. ''A brave front, Hawk, but it is this woman you want above all else. Come, will you be bolder if I tell you I have not yet tasted her? She guards her body like a wildcat. Regrettably, I have felt only her claws, though I'm certain, given time, she would have purred beneath me. Do you still reject my leavings?''

Sinan swayed under the vast surge of relief. A tender smile encouraged Tory before he looked at Hassan again. ''Yes, she's brave and strong and far too good for you, Hassan. Release her, and you may live. Harm her, and I will kill you if Ismail doesn't.''

A nervous tic jerked in Hassan's cheek at this mention of the Tuareg chieftain. He surveyed the watching Tuaregs, but their veils were affixed and he could not tell if his archenemy was present. Hassan tightened his grip on the knife and lied boldly, ''You don't frighten me with your threats. Why do you not admit we are at an impasse? Let me mount my horse and leave. I will send the woman back to you unharmed.''

''Certainly you will,'' Sinan snorted. Out of the corner of his eye, he saw a shadow blocking out the sun behind Hassan's back and quickly added, ''You have nowhere to turn to now, for once word of your attempt to flee reaches your tribe, your own people will spit upon you.''

Tory's ears roared, and her body ached from holding itself stiffly away from the blade. She wished more than ever she spoke Arabic. Why did Sinan not abuse this monster as he deserved? Tory considered slamming her foot down on Hassan's, but she knew her slipper would do little damage to his red moroccan leather-covered toes. Bodily and emotionally abused, she had to fight to stay upright.

Hassan saw the watching Tuaregs staring behind him just as he caught the stealthy sound of movement. He was distracted enough to give Tory precious room to move her head. Everything happened at once then.

Shouting in English, "Tory, duck!" Sinan dived for Hassan's legs.

Tory complied weakly, becoming a deadweight on Hassan's arm. He threw her on the ground to block Sinan and turned to face his new assailant. A mounted Tuareg filled Hassan's vision, his turban bluer than the pristine Saharan sky behind him. His upraised arm was menacing and powerful as a genie's as he poised to strike. Hassan's last sight was the arcing lance.

For the first and final time was Hassan aware of his own mortality. Allah allotted him only that second of regret before the lance impaled his chest, the tip exiting through his back. The knife dropped from Hassan's limp hand. His riven corpse collapsed, blood pooling around it, oozing into the thirsty sand. Blank gray eyes stared into the brilliant morning sun. Hassan's two living men muttered a quick prayer.

A victorious cry broke from Ismail and was joined by his brothers. The ancient hatred between Tuareg and Arab had been fueled by vengeance. Blood lust satisfied until the next raid, the Tuaregs' joy resounded from dune to dune.

Becky flinched away from the savage sounds. But she watched with a very different emotion as Sinan lifted Tory to cradle her across his knees and rock her back and forth. Gently, he drew her bodice closed, then rested one hand on her chest as if verifying her flesh and blood reality.

"Tory, Tory, Tory," he whispered, tears glistening in his vividly green eyes. He ripped off his *kaffiyeh* to dab at the scratches on Tory's throat and the blood splashed on her tunic, scolding unsteadily, "Woman, when you recover from that fiend's abuse, I may beat you myself. My heart still pounds with fear that I'd find you, only to see you killed before my eyes."

Tory placed a shy hand over his heart. The frantic thumping invigorated her weary, aching body. He cared about her, despite everything! He'd followed her, risked his life to save her. The love singing in her heart was no longer a melancholy dirge. It was as joyful as Handel's "Hallelujah Chorus," echoing against the rafters of her being with poignant resonance. This man was meant for her. She'd deny it no longer.

She cradled his lean cheek in her palm, her eyes lit from within and without by an unearthly radiance. "Oh, Sinan, I'm so glad you came for me. I know now I should never have left you. Please take me back. Give me another chance, and I'll make you so happy you'll never turn from me to another."

Sinan's heart lurched between happiness and fear. Was it gratitude that made her speak so? Afraid to hear more, he swooped on her mouth, gentling his ardor when she flinched. He soothed her cracked lips with a tender lick and drew away, his eyes promising more, much more.

"We have much to talk about, sweet, but I want you to sit in the shade while I speak to Ismail. Without his help, I never could have found you or gotten you away."

Tory nodded, leaning on him as he helped her to a tent. She sat in the opening so she could watch. Becky threw herself down beside her and caught her in a glad clasp. Tory hugged her back, whispering, "I'm so glad you're safe, Becky. I never would have forgiven myself if anything had happened to you."

"God answered our prayers by bringing Sinan to us, love. If not for him . . ."

Tory shivered at Becky's pregnant pause. Reaction set in. The tears burst, healing like a salt bath, stinging but beneficial. Stroking Tory's hair, Becky indulged in a few tears of her own.

A short distance away, Sinan gravely offered his hand to Ismail. The Tuareg hesitated, then indulged the Westerner in his odd custom. They conducted their conversation in a combination of the Berber Sinan spoke and the Spanish Ismail knew from his caravan dealings.

"I will thank Allah in my noon prayers for sending you to me, Sinan Reis. Never before have I welcomed the help of a city-dweller, but you fought almost as well and bravely as my own men. I thank you, and my tribe thanks you."

"It is I who must thank you, Ismail. You knew what route Hassan would follow, and I would have been hopelessly outnumbered even had I been able to track them. I will not forget our bargain. I will begin at the *besistan* in Algiers and continue searching until I find some trace of your sister. She will be brought back for you if at all possible."

Ismail's steady black eyes searched the pale Western face for veracity, but finally he nodded. "I believe you, Sinan Reis. You go with your women now?"

"Yes, if you've no objection. I left abruptly, and I've much to see to in Algiers."

"Take three of the horses," Ismail offered magnanimously, not seeming to realize that he generously bestowed upon them their own mounts.

Hiding a smile, Sinan bowed. "You have my gratitude. We

will leave soon so as to travel some before the midday heat. Again, my thanks, and I will send a messenger as soon as I have word of your sister. You will ask your tribesmen to give him safe passage?''

Ismail's dark eyes glinted. ''We sometimes allow such, even without tribute, but give him this.'' Ismail pulled a tiny silver *feisha*, a hand dangling on a leather thong, from his cloak pocket. He stroked it once, then handed it to Sinan. ''It was my sister's. He who bears it will have safe passage through all our territory.''

Sinan pocketed the charm. ''So be it.'' When Ismail turned away to help his men begin the grim job of sorting bodies— Hassan's men for burial, his own to be taken back to their tribe and buried with the honor due them for having died nobly in battle—Sinan halted him. ''What will you do with Hassan's body, Ismail?''

The dark eyes went as cold as a Sahara night. ''We will take his head for a trophy and leave the rest of him for the ants. Even that is too noble an end for the jackal.''

Over two years in Barbary had still not hardened Sinan to the harsh, swift justice of this land. He shivered, but said only, ''Health and happiness, Ismail.''

''And to you, Sinan Reis.''

When Sinan arrived at the tent, he found Tory sleeping in Becky's arms.

The abigail looked up at him regretfully. ''Poor mite, she's had little enough sleep these past hellish days. Can we not let her be?''

''I wish we could, Becky, but if we don't start soon, we'll have to travel in the heat of the afternoon. We'll take it slow, but I'd like to be in Biskra sometime tomorrow. She can sleep until we're loaded.'' Sinan made to turn away, but he inched back around as if compelled. His strong face was more hesitant than Becky had ever seen it when he asked, ''Was she really glad to see *me*, Becky, or was she just relieved to be rescued?''

Becky looked over Tory's shoulder to the heat even now beginning to shimmer over the parched earth. Sinan had earned the truth. ''She would have been grateful to any liberator, but it was you she wanted to see more than anyone else, Sinan.'' Now, why did that bring such an odd look to his face? Becky wondered. A look between pleasure and pain, as if his heart rejoiced but his mind scolded him for a fool.

When he would have walked off, Becky asked, ''What happened after we left? I told Jarrod to alert you to our escape, but you didn't follow us until it was too late."

Their voices roused Tory enough for her to hear Becky's question and Sinan's answer.

"Ali tied Jarrod in the bathhouse, and I was unconscious from Tory's sleeping powder for a good hour," Sinan growled. He stalked to the horses.

Sleepiness flown, Tory straightened and looked reproachfully at Becky. "Why didn't you tell me you thought I should stay, instead of warning Jarrod without my knowledge?"

"Because I knew you wouldn't heed me. You were acting emotionally, not rationally, Tory. My counsel to wait would only have made you angry."

Tory gave a disgruntled snort and lay back to grumble, "How have you learned so much of human nature, Becky?"

"I'm not so wise, love. I just know you very well, as I should, since I rocked you in your cradle." Becky smiled.

Tory pillowed her cheek on her arms and watched Sinan saddle their horses. "He's angry with me, isn't he, Becky?"

"So it would seem. Do you really blame him?"

"No. I would be angry if he had deceived me so."

"Don't worry about it, Tory. He'll come 'round."

What then? Tory wanted to ask, but she knew Becky had no more answers than she did. One thing was clear enough: Uncertain future or not, she wanted to go back with Sinan and grab whatever fleeting happiness fate granted them.

For, despite everything, he made her happy. Just watching him work was a pleasure. How gracefully he moved. A supple sway from the waist as he hefted a saddle in place, an economical movement of arms and hands, and the job was done. Did he do everything as efficiently, whether he was saddling a horse or subduing a woman? The thought rankled, for she had never thought to be any man's lapdog.

This man, least of all. From that first stare as he hovered in the rigging of the *Scorpion*, he had challenged her, and Tory had never refused a challenge. He delighted in goading her, then frightening or seducing her out of her temper. Sometimes it seemed he played a Machiavellian game with her in which she knew neither the stakes nor the rules. She knew not why he had come after her or why he was so remote now. As if he felt the intensity of her stare, he turned to glance at her, only to quickly swing back around.

Anger she could understand, but not this avoidance of her very glance. After that first spontaneous greeting, he had not seemed glad to see her. Could it be he had another reason for saving her? Something more in keeping with his calling than with the hero her romantic instincts painted him? Tory rubbed her goose-fleshed skin at the thought that he was a true heir of Barbarossa after all.

The worry receded, for, though Tory racked her brain, she could see no advantage to him in saving her other than the obvious one—to win her favors. Still, he must desire her mightily to take such risks. Something didn't quite fit, but Tory was too tired and relieved to beg trouble anymore. All her schemes and worries had landed her in one scrape after another. For once in her life, she would live one day at a time. She owed Sinan that life, and she knew what he'd ask for in exchange. Did she still have the strength to deny him—and herself—again?

Tory's weary body found no rest on the journey back to Biskra, her mind no solace. When they paused at noon to rest, she was fractious enough to force a confrontation with the man who still ignored her. Aggressively, she stalked to where he watered the horses.

"If you've a grievance with me, please spit it out. My horse has been more company this day than you have."

He started, but didn't look at her when he replied, "Now is not the time and place for this discussion. It can wait until we return to Algiers."

Had Tory been less tired, she might have caught the strained tone, the clenching of his hand on Orion's mane, but all she wanted at the moment was to bridge the distance between them. She seized his arm and turned him to face her, exploding, "No, now! I'll be mad long before we—"

Her words stirred up a tempest. Sinan gave a strangled snarl and flung the precious leather water pouch aside, too enraged to care when it spilled part of its contents..Hurrying forward, Becky grabbed it up, capped it, then watched this inevitable confrontation with rueful eyes.

Large, angry hands caught Tory's shoulders and shook her once, twice, Sinan growling all the while, "You deserve no less! How do you think it was for me, living for days on end with the knowledge that you were Hassan's latest toy? My constant companions on that hellish ride through the mountains were questions: Is she still alive? How many times and how brutally has he raped her? Will he give her to his men or keep her for himself?''

Tory, quiescent now under the rough hands, stared up into his blazing eyes. She grappled with the significance of this deep, welling anger and, more telling, a torment similar to her own.

"I even blamed myself for making you run," he went on. "I asked myself if I was too rough. I should have given you more time." He released her at last, stepped back, and crossed his arms over his heaving chest. He closed his eyes until his breathing had quieted. When he opened them again, Tory quailed under the green eyes that had never been more ruthless.

"But I blame myself no further, Lady Victoria Alicia Grenville.''

Why did he say her name so distastefully, as if it galled him?

"My duties to you are discharged. You've your 'virtue' intact. When we return, you can go to Majorca or Spain or wherever you desire.''

Tory swayed with shock. He would send her away? Why? It didn't make sense for him to go to such trouble to fetch her only to send her away. She blinked, focusing on his unyielding features, too upset to ponder why the escape she'd long sought was now a threat rather than a promise. . . .

"You may go back to your balls, routs, and dandies with my blessing. May they have more joy of you than I did.'' When he would have turned away to finish his chores, a small voice stopped him. Tory the Terror would have disdained its tone.

"And what if I don't want to go? What if I want to stay with you as your—your mistress?" She stumbled only a little over the word. Instinct warned her that if she was to make amends, she must do so now.

At that, Sinan met her pleading eyes. "Then, my lady, I would bid you welcome, and I would cherish you as you were meant to be cherished." The softening green eyes hardened to jade again as he finished, "But the decision is yours, and yours alone. Go or stay. It's up to you." And he turned back to setting up camp to wait out the heat.

Becky patted Tory's white cheek. "There, dear, at least now you don't have to live in suspense any longer.''

"What will I do?" Tory wailed.

"Follow your heart, Tory. Forget that Grenville pride and remember who you are above all—a woman.''

"Are you advising me to become a pirate's mistress?" Tory asked incredulously.

Becky winced. "I wouldn't put it so crudely. A mistress bestows her favors out of greed, not love. You've no need of Sinan's possessions. You've a great need of his attentions."

"Slippers by the fire and the patter of little feet?" Tory gibed.

"No, a strong shoulder to lean on, a keen, intelligent mind to interest you, and a will to match your own," Becky countered. "Traits you've never found in any of your London beaux, and probably never will." Becky smiled ruefully. "Of course, if your grandmother ever finds out what I'm advising you, I'll never work in England again. But then, I don't doubt that if she'd been given the same choice with her Gerald, she'd have opted for anything to stay with him. Think on it, Tory." And Becky went to sit under a shading outcrop, leaving Tory to her thoughts.

Becky was right, she knew. Greaty had loved her husband Gerald in a way that was mocked, reviled, and envied by their friends. She would have sacrificed everything to be with him. The loving example set by her grandparents, the only parents she'd ever known, had been impossible to equal in any of her own potential matches. Tory had never felt more than mild affection for any of her suitors. But what she felt for Sinan was in no way mild.

He confused her, thrilled her, infuriated her, made her happy and sad all at once. Was this love, this great need to be with him and make him happy? Tory didn't know. But she'd little time to decide.

She had even less time than she supposed. They were bone weary upon reaching Biskra the next day, so their reflexes were slow when the accident occurred.

Orion and Eclipse had clashed from the beginning, so Tory and Sinan had ridden with Becky's calmer bay between them, but they relaxed their vigilance upon reaching Biskra late that afternoon. An unattended mare whickered at the stream where they paused. Orion's nostrils flared. Eclipse jibbed closer to the mare, jolting Tory as she dismounted. She fell to the ground near Eclipse's stamping feet.

Becky hopped off her bay and rounded Orion's hindquarters to help pull Tory away. Orion, his competitive instincts aroused, sensed the movement behind him and lashed back with his hindquarters. One powerful hoof caught Becky's leg. There was the sickening crunch of snapping bone. Becky howled as the blow knocked her backwards.

Sinan turned from helping Tory up, too late to prevent Becky from being injured. He shouted, "Get Eclipse away!" and rushed to Becky's side.

Tory complied, tying the snorting stallion firmly to a tree, then ran back to Becky, who was now lying supine, one leg bent at an odd angle.

While Sinan rushed off to find a doctor, Tory held Becky's hand, tears in her eyes at the abigail's pain-filled groan. Becky joked weakly, "If that's not irony for you: I survive a pirate attack, a kidnapping, and a bedouin raid unscathed, only to fall victim to a randy horse."

That Becky spoke so unusually bluntly was an indication of her pain, but Tory played along. "It's just like you to be difficult," she scolded unsteadily. She draped her cape over Becky, hoping Sinan would hurry.

"How will I be able to accompany you back now?" Becky's worried question ended on a moan.

"I'll not leave you, you silly pea-goose." Tory turned to Sinan and the tall, very thin Arab with him. She watched, frowning, as the doctor removed the cloak and examined his patient. In a high, whining voice he gave an order. Looking grim, Sinan nodded and disappeared, soon returning with a door he had obviously filched from someone's house.

He knelt to smile reassuringly at Becky. "We've got to get you out of the street. Hold tight to Tory's hand, and I'll lift you onto this door as gently as possible." Gentle though he was, Becky fainted when he moved her.

Tory was relieved she wasn't conscious to feel the long walk to the Arab's home, Sinan at one end of the makeshift stretcher, the doctor at the other. By the time the leg was set and wrapped, Biskra's trees were set aflame by a sullen Sol angry at its sinking. Tory sat vigilant over Becky until she awoke. With a reassuring nod to Tory, the physician retreated to his chamber to give them privacy.

Her color was better, and when she asked for food and drink, Tory knew she'd be all right. The three of them ate together, the silence growing heavier as each avoided the one subject that had to be broached.

Finally Becky banged her plate down on the low table beside her divan. "We all know I can't travel those mountain passes in this condition. I know you need to get back, Sinan. I suggest you take Tory with you.''

A raised hand silenced Tory's objections. "Don't argue with me, Tory. I'm useless as your chaperon now, as we both know. This will give you and Sinan a chance to settle things between you. I'll be fine here.''

Tory's hesitant gaze met Sinan's probing one. He nodded at the wordless question. "Arab medicine is in some ways leagues ahead of our own, Tory. I've paid the doctor handsomely. We can send for Becky as soon as the leg partially knits. But the choice is yours.''

Sinan turned away to stare out the window at the dark street. Much as he longed to beg her to come back with him, he would not. Becky needed rest, and Tory couldn't help with that. He needed her more than the abigail did, but he was through with these frustrating games. He would not plead, coerce, or even charm. She would make this decision of her own free will. If there was to be nothing else between them, he wanted to know it now, while he still had a chance to recover from this emotional debacle.

Tory hesitated.

Becky urged, "Go, Tory. You know how you are in a sick-room. You'd drive me to distraction.''

In the steady gray eyes that had always looked at her with love, Tory read Becky's true wish: "Here's your chance at happiness, love. Don't throw it away out of misplaced guilt. I want you to go.''

Biting her lip, Tory agreed, "If it's what you want, Becky, I'll go.''

Sinan turned at that. He clasped his hands behind his back and said softly, "No, Tory, it has to be what you want. If you meant those words you spoke to me so sweetly, then come with me in full knowledge of what's to be. If you've changed your mind, then stay. For both our sakes.''

The choice was bare now, and Tory could not dress it up as anything other than what it was—a decision to give herself to him or to sever their tenuous bond now, cleanly, ruthlessly. For an instant, Greaty's face haunted Tory, reproaching her for what she was about to do. But even the legendary Grenville honor was chaff before the whirlwind of needs this man agitated.

Bowing her head, she sealed her fate. "I'll come, Sinan.''

Becky sighed in relief.

Sinan took a joyful stride toward Tory, but caught himself and said evenly, ''I'm glad, Tory. I'll see to purchasing provisions. We'll leave at dawn.'' He hurried out to beg, borrow, or steal food for them even if he had to roust every market seller to do it.

A curious peace descended over Tory. It was odd to feel so right at promising to give herself to a man out of wedlock, and he a pirate to boot. But a lifetime's credo could not make her regret her decision. Things had gone too far. If she left him now, without testing this affinity between them, she'd grow bitter with regret. Perhaps she committed a crime against the society she'd been raised to revere, but denying her heart's yearning would be a more heinous crime against nature. For he did fill her heart. If Tory had doubted before that she loved him, she doubted no longer. Nothing that felt so right could be wrong, no matter what society said.

Tory sensed, in that moment, that she truly became a woman, with all the responsibilities and joys thereof. She'd earn pain too, perhaps; but at least she'd have memories to sweeten the hurt, instead of the gnawing ache of regret for battles unwon and even unfought. Bone deep, she knew she was doing the right thing.

A few weeks later, she would hate herself for this certainty . . .

PART III

❦

"Come fill the cup, and in the fire of Spring
Your winter-garment of repentance fling;
The bird of Time has but a little way
To flutter—and the bird is on the Wing."

—*THE RUBAIYAT*,
Omar Khayyam

Chapter 10

Dawn swept a trembling, luminescent curtain over the land when Tory and Sinan departed Biskra. Its mystic red-gold light heightened Tory's fatalism. Yes, she wanted to go with Sinan, but to gladly become a pirate's mistress? What would come of this betrayal of all Greaty had raised her to be?

Soon after leaving Biskra, they came to a spectacular gorge rearing out of the desert like a medieval stone castle. Phantasmagoric spires, pinnacles, buttresses, and gargoyles had been winnowed into the red sandstone by gritty sands. Surely no Gothic architect could have competed with nature's grand design, Tory thought.

Sinan paused to let her look her fill. "Impressive, isn't it? The Arabs call this Foum-es-Sahara—Mouth of the Sahara. You can see why."

The contrast between mountain and desert was indeed striking. They followed the track winding up the mountain. Far below, a river rushed through a ravine.

On they rode as the sun sank behind hulking mountain walls. When they bedded down at night, Sinan seemed sensitive to her confusion and exhaustion, for he merely kissed her and slept at her side on his own mat. They continued the grueling pace for several days, speaking little.

Tory wondered what he brooded about. Soon he would expect her to deliver what she'd promised so many times. Womanlike, Tory felt torn. Part of her yearned to surrender at last to his virility, to give him the ultimate gift she had never thought to bestow outside marriage. But another part cringed from that intimacy. She'd feel physical pain, she knew, but it would be quickly over, whereas the emotional wounds she invited could scar her indelibly.

Now she had a chance, a slim chance assuredly, of forgetting him someday, when she was back in her elegant, cynical world. If she opened her body to him as she'd opened her mind, she would inevitably open . . . Tory sat straighter. It was already too late. Denying the truth would serve no purpose.

She loved him.

There, she'd admitted it. The earth didn't open to swallow her up, nor did the seas boil, nor the sun fall from the sky. But the inner cataclysm she felt rocked the foundations of her existence. It no longer seemed wrong to give herself to a man out of wedlock; the pirate who had stolen her possessions and now her heart was still the most honorable man she'd ever known; this land of her captivity was becoming more home to her than London's rowdy, dirty streets.

She hadn't even sense enough to regret her downfall. She *wanted* to give her virginity to him. He had no need to steal her jewels or ships. She'd happily share all she owned with him, nay, even give up every shilling to stay with him. For what he had taught her was beyond price: that there was great good and great folly beyond England; that pride in self became arrogance unless it was tempered by compassion; that the wealth her society coveted availed her nothing in adversity, indeed, could cause a seductive poverty of spirit replenishable only by moral fiber.

Tory smiled wryly, picturing Greaty's face as if she were privy to her thoughts. How horrified she'd be to find her willful granddaughter maudlin with love for a pirate. The vision of Greaty's outrage was so vivid that Tory's smile faded.

For Greaty's sake, she forced herself to take a clear, cold look at the facts. What did she really know of Sinan, after all? Not even his nationality. He could have a wife, or several wives, tucked away in some corner of the globe. Out of infatuation was she endowing him with qualities he didn't have? After all, he'd proved how ruthless he could be. Would he use her body as he'd used her possessions, then cast her aside? Unwillingly, she recalled her first impression that he had a grievance against her. Was he motivated by more than desire?

Desperate for reassurance, compelled as the moon in its cycle around the earth, she looked at him. His brown hair's gold-tipped ends ruffled in the brisk mountain breeze. Alert eyes scanned the rocky cliffs above them. The noon sun sought every fluid line and angle of his body and found no flaw. Physically, he was undeniably magnificent, but Tory had known handsome men before who left her cold.

No, his outward beauty went deep into the bone, sinew, and

impulse of him. He had a confident love of life Tory had seldom seen in her acquaintances. The men she knew spent their days trying to keep boredom at bay, never happy with themselves or their accumulating possessions. Somehow Tory knew Sinan would be happy no matter what he did. Be he pirate, lord, or even street sweeper, he'd make the most of his talents. Such harmony devolved only from inner peace.

The niggling doubts receded. He was what he seemed: an honorable man trapped in a dishonorable profession. A handsome, wonderful man who desired her greatly, even if he didn't love her. Yet.

A tender smile curved her lips. Yes, he'd taught her much, but he had much to learn, too. She would be no compliant mistress. Seductive, stimulating, and, she hoped, fascinating, but never submissive. He had freed her of convention, taunting and tempting her into womanhood; it was only right that he be chief recipient of her new gifts.

Serene at last, Tory lifted her head to look about. They were traveling along a river now, having left the rough track. "Where are we going?"

"You'll see soon enough," came the terse reply.

Tory glanced at Sinan. Just when she had resolved to charm him, he became his most exasperating. How was she to . . . Tory's ire ended on a gasp.

Their gradual descent had led them to a small valley. It seemed a shining topaz set in an austere silver crown of jagged mountains. The land sloped down to the river galloping merrily along its course. The water nourished the ripe golden grain growing to its edge. Reapers labored, sheathing stalks to take to mill and market. In the distance, Tory saw a shepherd boy limned against the sky and grass by his white *haik* and tall staff. His flock of sheep dotted the grasses like tufts of white yarn on a pastoral loom.

Sinan halted his mount on the rim of the slope, smiling at her enchanted expression. "Do you like my surprise?"

"Indeed I do. But why have we stopped here? I thought you needed to get back." She looked nervously about. "Is it safe for us alone here? What if some of Hassan's tribe—"

"After his cowardice, his tribe will feel no need to avenge him. These mountain-dwellers will not be hostile if we leave them alone. I've camped here before. It's safe enough." His tone softened. "You need to rest before we go on. There's a sheltered glade not far from here that will be an excellent place to set up camp.'' He watched her closely for resistance, but she smiled into his eyes.

Inching her mount closer to him, she picked up his hand and whispered into it, ''Lead on, my master.''

He pulled his hand away and turned Eclipse so abruptly that the stallion snorted. Surreptitiously, he rubbed his palm against his thigh, but that only spread the tingling throughout his body. He'd won her submission at last. Why did it seem like a Pyrrhic victory?

Because he had won it by guile, he answered himself. She believed she was giving herself to a pirate. She'd be furious if she knew his true identity, and that she'd really had little to fear from him all along. Worse, if she discovered his intent to humble her, she'd never forgive him. His mouth curled at the irony of his position: She accepted him as a pirate; she would revile him as he really was, a patriot of the country she scorned.

The only honorable thing to do, he acknowledged wearily, was to tell her the truth. But he knew just as surely that he would not. The sweetness she had at last let him taste would sour, and he'd never feel her writhing under him in desire.

He shifted in his saddle, telling himself he had no reason to feel guilty. If he told the truth, she might betray him in her anger. Besides, why shouldn't he sample what others had tasted? His reward for risking his life to save her had been sleepless nights and a painful, constant ache. She wanted him. Her very presence proved that.

No, they'd gone too far. For some obscure reason, only Tory could give him surcease. He had to have her now, whether it brought disaster to all of them, whether she hated him ever after, whether he grew to love . . . He welcomed the interruption as they reached the glade he remembered from a trip he'd made a year ago.

An overhanging cliff formed a snug hollow so close to the river that moss crept up its sides. Vines heavy with flowers grew in wild abandon down the cliff, falling over the hollow almost to the ground. The river broke off here into a tiny tributary that gurgled over rapids, falling into a lovely pool that was shielded by cliffs and trees.

Tory's delight with the spot was obvious. Dismounting, Sinan held his arms up to her.

She looked at him. He looked back. Their mutual uncertainty

dwindled as the power of that exchange made them that most rare and lovely of things: lovers first in spirit before their bodies even touched. Thoughts of self faded in a lovely new day rife with possibilities. Sinan forgot his gnawing desire in the longing to hold her close to his heart. Tory forgot her virginal fears, needing only to cradle him in her arms until the earth crumbled and the stars died. There was nothing they could not do together, no battle they couldn't win together.

Lifting her down, Sinan whispered shakily, "Come, love, let me tend you and make you comfortable." He wanted nothing in life more than he wanted to bury himself in her and hear her sweet cries, but first he had to soothe her poor face. They'd been unable to wash the paint off, but he had one more remedy to try.

Tory cupped his proud head in her hands. "Just being with you makes me happy." She tried to slip her arms around his neck, but he stopped her with gentle pressure on her wrists.

Swallowing the lump in his throat, Sinan unwrapped her headdress, took off her tunic, and led her to the water's edge. He folded her filmy blouse away from her throat, freezing when he saw the blue-black marks.

"Did Hassan do this?"

Tory kissed his chin to assuage the pain in his voice. "Yes, but the bruises no longer hurt. They'll fade soon enough."

"You'll have to tell me everything that happened . . . later." His voice softened on the last word.

"Yes," Tory agreed fervently. "Later."

At his suggestion, Tory sat on the riverbank, content just to watch him. However, when he bent, scooped up a double handful of mud, and came back to her with the oozing mess, her eyes widened. She scrambled to her feet. "What are you doing?"

"I'm going to give you a mud pack. It's an ancient cosmetic trick that might work. We must get that paint off, sweet, before it damages your face."

Tory's eyes softened. Ah, he was so much man, and that part that made him so spoke eloquently of his desire, yet he still put her comfort first. Touched beyond words, Tory lifted her face and closed her eyes.

She groaned when the cool mud soothed her dry, burning skin. When he had smoothed it over her face and throat, he rinsed his hands and led her to a grassy spot in the sun.

"We'll wash it off when it's dry. I'll set up camp while you rest." He folded a blanket under her head for a pillow, then hurried away, flushed, to unload the horses and pack donkey he'd purchased in Biskra.

Tory closed her eyes. She listened to the babbling stream, the sighing wind, and the cackling birds, and never had she known a greater peace. An hour later, she snapped awake from a doze. Groggily she looked around for Sinan, forgetting her mud pack.

The tethered horses and donkey cropped grass. A fire awaited, ringed with stones, kindling gathered. And there he sat, a good ten feet away, arms wrapped around his knees as if he had to force himself not to touch her. He felt her glance, looked at her, then hastily away.

Tory smiled slowly, unaware of her ghastly aspect. For once, he let her set the pace; for once, he went too slowly for her. He was much too far away . . .

Propping herself up on an elbow, she called huskily, "Come, Sinan, you didn't bring me here to leave me roasting in the sun." She bent one leg at the knee and thrust her breasts forward in what she imagined was a seductive pose.

Indeed, she got Sinan's attention. Hot green eyes swept longingly over her body, but his expression changed when he appraised her face. His lips quivered. He coughed and looked away.

Tory was puzzled. "Shyness from *you*, Sinan? Surely not. Have I done aught to offend you?"

Sinan looked at her again, teasing, "Nay, Tory. Perhaps I'm overawed by the look of you, a Nubian princess taking her ease in the sun." He tried to still his mouth, then gave up the struggle. He threw back his lustrous head and roared, hearty chuckles resounding off the cliff walls. His eyes streaming, he looked at Tory, who had her head cocked to one side, bright eyes gleaming in the hideous mask. That set him off again.

Really, she decided, this was an odd way for a seduction to proceed! What was she to do, attack the man? Tory scratched irritably at her itching nose, then froze when she felt the mud crack under her fingers. She groaned as she realized she was acting the coquette with half of the riverbed stuck to her face.

"Why didn't you remind me?" she reproached on a gasp, leaping to her feet.

More laughter trailed her to the pool. She knelt and leaned over to see her face in the sweet, clear water. A gruesome visage greeted her, nose rearing like a snow-capped peak where she had scratched the mud away. She tried to stir up anger at Sinan for laughing at her, but she really couldn't blame him. A quiver grew into a smile and broadened into a grin when she saw the cracks at her cheeks, eyes, and jaw widen. Really, she was a picture! She bent to wash the mud away, then paused, her eyes gleaming like aquamarines set in an impish clay deity.

"Oh, Sinan," she trilled. "Can you help me wash this mess away?"

"As my Nubian princess commands," he agreed, putting his palms together and bowing.

Had he seen the gleam in Tory's eyes, he would have approached more warily, but she had her back to him. He knelt beside her just in time to get two generous handfuls of mud smack in the face.

"Ah, now we make a fitting pair," she crowed, scrambling on her knees away from him. "The Nubian prince and his princess!"

Two green eyes sizzled an opening through the mud dripping down Sinan's face. "And his witch, more like," he growled, pursuing her on his knees.

Tory was too busy laughing to realize he was forcing her to retreat to the stream. "You seemed so pleased with my mud pack I thought you might like to try one," she teased between giggles.

He brandished a handful of mud threateningly just as she realized she was cornered. When she held up her hands in supplication, he inched closer and agreed softly, "Shall I show you one of the things I'm eager to try?"

Strangely, he seemed to have forgotten all thoughts of vengeance. He rinsed his hand in the pool and advanced in earnest. Tory blinked as the playful gleam became an intent, hungry look. As she felt water wetting the tips of her slippers, he pounced, forcing her down on her back on the sloping bank until she trailed half in, half out of the water.

"What your lips taste like flavored with good Algerian mud, for example," he finished against her mouth. It was awkward at first, and hardly tasty, but the mud didn't hinder the play of their tongues. Tory cupped his head to slant her mouth more closely against his, returning the passioned dart and retreat, thrust and parry. But when their mouth moisture mingled with the mud, they drew apart. Grimacing, they washed the mud away.

Sinan turned her face from side to side. "The paint is gone," he sighed in relief. "And the burn is not too bad." He kissed her brow.

Tory felt suddenly shy at the look in his eyes when he drew back. She grabbed up her tunic to dry her face, tossed it aside, and said the first thing that came into her head. "Your kisses are always pleasing, Sinan, but that was the most earthy one yet."

The lips that had been full with passion a moment ago stretched into a delighted grin. "Tory, Tory, what a joy you are!" He pulled her against his broad, vibrating chest. They stayed like that for several moments, enjoying the sun on their hair, the warmth of body to body, skin to skin, where Tory had her face buried in his throat.

But soon Sinan's aching desire returned in full measure. Her breasts were so warm, so scantily covered by damp, filmy cloth. He clenched his hands on her shoulders to keep them where they were. Then he did something that would trouble him later: He gave her a last chance to change her mind. His body screamed a protest, but somehow he couldn't bear to take her, or even seduce her, without her total consent.

He put her away to look into the turquoise eyes that had such power over him. "I want you to know, Tory, that I yearn for you as I've never yearned for another woman. But I won't take you. I'll only gladly accept your favors." As he waited, he fancied the very earth stilled, the birds quieted, and the river paused in its course. He watched her face change from shyness, to acceptance, to . . . His heart leaped to his throat. Did he imagine her desire was tempered by a tenderness that answered his own?

But he didn't imagine her soft reply.

"Then accept, my pirate love. I am yours, as was meant to be. Savor your victory: I want you, I need you, I . . ." Her voice trailed away. She took his hand and led him to the bower he had prepared.

The thick moss, covered by a carpet, made a soft mattress. The flower-heavy vines shielding the cleft created a sensually dim and scented boudoir. Sinan stumbled into the cavity with her, so dazed he almost bumped his head before he remembered to duck.

He sat there, hands limp in his lap, watching her disrobe, wondering where his triumph was. Was not this the moment he had schemed for? Lady Victoria Alicia Grenville was not haughty now. She was warm, willing woman eager to share his bed. But no delirious joy shook him. Instead, the lump in his throat grew until he almost choked.

Never had he felt so low. He was a scoundrel, a lecher—a cheat. What right had he to violate such loveliness? He had little enough defense against her charms when she fought him, but the simple grace with which she disrobed now shook him to his boots. She wasn't coy, shy, or even seductive. She removed her clothes unhurriedly, smiling at him all the while as if she had pleased him thus many times before; as if he were her lover in truth.

She knelt before him after removing her jewelry, pulling her blouse off to bare her torso for his pleasure. Her sun-dappled breasts bounced gently as she stood to pull the pantaloons down her long, long legs, then kick them aside with a graceful flick that made him break out in a sweat. At last she sat, removed her slippers, tossed her hair behind her back, and curled her legs to one side, giving her body to his eyes and whatever else that pleased him.

She reminded him more than ever of Eve, primeval woman, both innocent and seductive in her beauty. But he was no Adam. Nay, he was the serpent, tempting her falsely for his own evil designs. Her scorn, even her treatment of Henry, no longer seemed to matter. He had won. She came to him willingly. If he took her as his body bade him, his vengeance—and her schooling—would be complete.

And when she learned the truth, she would hate him as much as he hated himself . . .

He couldn't do that to her, or to himself. Like the serpent, he'd slither out on his belly. Humbled, still swollen with desire, he forced himself to move.

Tory couldn't see his distraught expression, for his back was to the sun. When he moved, she thought at last he would embrace her. With a glad cry, she went to meet him, flinging herself against his chest.

And he was lost.

A tortured groan escaped him as her unbound breasts teased his chest. Perhaps even then he could have forced himself to behave honorably—if she hadn't buried her fingers in his hair and pulled his mouth down to hers. But the things her lips, moving from side to side, did to his, the agony of pleasure he felt when her tongue darted shyly into his mouth to coax his own into hers, scattered his thoughts into the dark realms of despair.

Where they belonged, was his last conscious thought. Then he knew nothing, felt nothing, but the taste, the touch, the temptation, of Tory.

When she tugged at his shirt, he helped her remove it. When his chest was bare, she pushed him down on the carpet and leaned over him to rub the muscles defined by soft whorls of honeyed fur. He wrapped handfuls of her hair about his fists, some primitive instinct clamoring to chain her to him, to enslave her as she, the concubine, had enslaved her master. With her hair brushed out of the way, her breasts hung ripe and savory for his tasting. He pulled her down to his famished mouth, sighing as he closed his lips over her, teasing her puckered flesh to greater eagerness.

It was Tory's turn to sigh. She arched her breast into his mouth with a passion that would later make her blush. She'd forgotten she was a lady giving herself to a pirate out of wedlock. She knew only she was woman; he was man. This give-and-take was both natural and right. When he turned his attention to her other breast, his heavy breathing warm on her flesh, she straddled his restless hips to fumble blindly.

She felt it against her, rearing up through his pantaloons so urgently she wondered he didn't slash through the material. His teeth made tiny, arousing nibbles at her breasts, his hands cupping each full, flushed fruit so he could sup the better. She tugged so hard that the drawstring tore. There, at last it was open. He raised his hips so she could shimmy the pantaloons down his legs.

She had to lift herself to help, and he groaned a protest, pulling her back down atop him to kick the garment away. He was bare then before her, big, beautiful, and brutally aroused.

This time, however, she felt no fear. She stilled his restless hands by placing them low on the hollows of her hips.

He froze, his breath wheezing, his eyes glued to her passion-flushed face as she eased away from him to look. When her fingers closed about him, light, tentative, curious, he leaped into her hand. She jerked away as if burned.

"No, Tory, feel me, please . . ." he entreated hoarsely. His thumbs began a slow, sensual circling of her delicate pelvic bones, widening and exploring up her throbbing abdomen, down to the edges of her auburn triangle.

Compelled, she cupped him in one hand, amazed that her fingers couldn't close about him. For a moment she hesitated.

Could she ever take him all? He arched upward when she thumbed the tip of that awesome length. Muttering a harsh, earthy curse, he flipped her over on her back.

"My turn," he growled, locking her wrists on either side of her head to melt her doubts and her body to mindless surrender.

He used his body to tempt her, rubbing his chest from side to side over hers, the hairs scraping with exquisite, frustrating friction against her throbbing breasts. He pulled his hips teasingly away when she tried to push her belly against his, only to bend one knee and press it gently into her own urgency, rubbing until she sobbed for breath, for release.

But he wouldn't give it. He couldn't bear to end this sweet torture, for then the world would intrude again . . . Still holding her hands, he scouted the hollows, curves, and hills he longed to conquer, his lips blazing a trail from her hip to her armpit, exploring her belly to stab her navel with his tongue. He turned her over to make the back of her ache as much as the front, nibbling from the hollow of her knee, up a shapely thigh to nip her full, dimpled buttocks. On he went, trailing his tongue up her shivering spine to kiss the back of her neck, blowing her hair aside to nibble at the lobe of her ear.

"Who is slave here, woman? What silken chains you wrap around me." He caught a handful of her hair, twisted it into a rope and bound it around his throat, chaining them together. "Thus could I stay with you, forever. Never let me go, Tory," he whispered into her ear with such raw emotion that she struggled frantically to free herself.

She had to touch him, had to . . . When at last he freed her hands, immediately she turned to latch on to him. Big, he was so big, she thought with what little coherency she had left. The swollen, throbbing proof of his need for her no longer gave her pause, so thoroughly had he aroused her. A strange transmutation had taken place within her, centering in the moist, yearning well of her womb. She wasn't Tory anymore, complete and happy in herself; she was Sinan's woman, aching with the need to belong to him. She held within the secrets of her body the mysteries of life, and she wanted to explore them with this man, and only this man. The primitive need to bond with him brought sweet words, pleading words, to her lips.

"Please, Sinan, come to me. Show me what to do."

Even through the drowning waves of passion, Sinan sensed something in her words he should attend to. He blinked his blurring eyes and tried to focus on her face, but Allah had blessed them too much. The cup of passion was full; there was nothing left to do but drink from it.

When Sinan hesitated over her, Tory's clamoring blood aroused age-old instincts. She was aching, empty, and she knew, big as he was, that she could sheathe him well. She spread her legs beneath him and pulled him into position.

So came his fall. That passioned little tug and beckoning wriggle of hips sent him over the edge. Gladly he went, giving up his earthbound pride, honor, and caution to tumble into the cosmos with her. No matter what followed, he knew with sudden clarity, he could do naught else. This joining had been inevitable, destined by the fates that had sent her on that voyage. She was his; he was hers. From this moment on, they would truly belong together as he knew, somehow, God had intended when he stayed the *Scorpion*'s course.

He caught her burning cheeks in his hands. At his husky urging, her heavy-lidded eyes opened obediently. Green eyes dived into liquid turquoise. His identity immersed itself in hers, hers in his, until they were no longer even man and woman, separate; they were one entity obeying the urges of their ancestors to meld into one beautiful, powerful life force. But he paused long enough to make sure she understood the importance of this moment. Later, after she knew the truth, she would never forget whom she belonged to . . .

"Understand this, Tory. In another moment, there will be no going back. When I take you, you become mine, mine and no other's. Not you, not your family or your position, nothing on this earth can change that."

Was ever possession sweeter? Tory wondered, staring up into green eyes fierce with desire as they staked their claim, fierce with something else even more poignant . . . Tory the Terror, who had never bowed to a man in her life, nodded once in agreement.

Her smile was a beautiful, fiery thing that warmed him, body and soul. "I understand, Sinan. Take what is yours."

A tremor shook him. Feeling he'd die if he had to wait another instant, he urged her thighs farther apart. He feared he'd explode as the inflamed head of him touched her moist heat.

He gritted his teeth and capped his surging desire. He nudged her, entering a tiny bit. He pressed harder when he didn't slide in as he should have, since she was well prepared. Still he encountered an obstruction that blocked his passage. Something was wrong, something he must think about, he thought vaguely.

Tory gave him no time to think. She writhed beneath him, her flesh glistening like a gilded idol's in the dappled sunlight, inviting him to plunder her treasures. When her hands went to his buttocks, kneading, pulling, pleading, he forgot the obstruction. He forgot who he was, why he should hesitate. There was only Tory and this inevitable moment.

He surged forward at the same instant she bowed her hips to urge him inward. The two pressures were enough. When he breached her, she cried out, in pain, in pleasure, in triumph. At last she was one with him, possessing him in the throbbing depths that had yearned for him weeks without end. Tory was so busy savoring his hard presence that she barely heard when he cried out, too—a very different cry.

"God, no!" cried the conscience that shamed him even as his body and heart savagely rejoiced. She had known no one before; she was his, his alone, as he had longed for her to be. The primitive exaltation was heady but brief, for he knew he deserved her not. She was a virgin, as pure in body as she was in heart. He'd taken despicable advantage of both. With a Herculean effort of control, he braced his hands to return to the cold reality he deserved.

Tory sensed the change in him. Once more she let her instincts guide her. Murmuring, "Oh, my love, you feel so good, warm and pulsing within me. Take me, show me how to please you." She moved her hands from his buttocks to the place where they were joined, raising her head in fascination.

The movement made her clench around him. It combined with her words and the touch of her hands to weaken his conscience by reasserting the body pushed beyond control. When she licked one male nipple, he hesitated no longer.

"So be it, my darling. Let us please each other. And to hell with tomorrow!" He caught her hands, kissed the palms, and brought them behind his neck. He lowered his head to kiss her with all the tenderness in his heart.

When she tried to push her hips up into him, he held her still, whispering, "Not yet. Wait until you adjust to me. I don't want to hurt you." He urged her legs a bit farther apart and forced himself to lie quiet in the arousing position. If it killed him, he'd make her initiation a memory to cherish in the years to come, no matter what happened.

But, as usual, she foiled his careful plans and noble intentions. Tory-like, she groaned, "Hurt be damned! Don't you understand you're about to send me mad? Show me what to do, damn you!" She gave an aggressive bump into him, sighing in pleasure when he slid deeper.

A sound half a laugh, half a cry of pain, escaped him. "Lady hellion, sweet torment, you're a woman like no other—my woman. Always."

The thought urged him on. He swooped down on her mouth and began a gentle bucking with tongue and manhood, thrusting, retreating in concert until she was throbbing above and below. The pain was chased away by fleet tremors that danced from him to her. Or from her to him? It didn't matter, she decided, twining her tongue around his. This mating was a coupling in the best sense of the word, requiring two joyful participants.

Tory's tension built with every rhythmic insertion of his hardness into her softness. Gradually, she caught the cadence and began to fling her hips upward every time he burrowed down. The steady surge and retreat, full and empty, was as irresistible as the tides. She was drowning, drowning . . .

She clutched his shoulders, afraid of the strange, building tautness possessing her even as he was. She tried to quicken their duet, to end it and own herself again, but he laughed softly and bent her knees against her chest. She was left helplessly open and receptive to his deep, deep exploration. He shifted his hips to move higher over her, rubbing against her, into her with long, slow strokes that left her impaled, possessed.

He watched her eyes drift closed, saw the clenching of her jaw, felt the trembling of her around and beneath him, and knew she was close. "That's it, love, feel me, us," he urged between pants. She had to hurry, for he couldn't last much longer. The feel of her, elastic yet tight, taking him so perfectly, was the culmination and fulfillment of many long, lonely nights. Too many times had he dreamed of seeing her thus: hair a glittering fall of copper leaves spread about them, cheeks flushed with passion, breasts as hard-tipped as the manhood she called to. He shut his eyes, for just looking at her made the pressure in his loins increase. He was bursting, bursting . . .

He could veil his eyes but not his senses. He smelled the scent of their sweat, touched the silk of her skin, felt the heated clasp of her womanhood. "Tory, Tory," he whispered, driving more urgently into her, primitive now in his need to hear those first sweet cries.

And hear them he did, but were they his or hers? They cared not as they reached the end—and the beginning—together. The budding in Tory's womb burst into full flower in time to bathe in Sinan's life-giving spray. Their cries united into a paean as he filled her, made her woman—his woman; and she possessed him, absorbing the essence of body and heart that made him man—her man.

The words that escaped Tory then were as natural a culmination as the warmth pulsing into her. They were right, glorious, inevitable, simple but devastating in their effect on their recipient: "I love you."

Sinan stiffened, his bodily ecstasy matched, nay, surpassed, by the joy filling his heart. She loved him! Praise God, she loved him! He slumped against her, spent, happy as Adam with his Eve in Eden. He opened his mouth against the hollow of her throat to echo the words back to her. But, as sensation faded, the world loomed up again, shadowing his sunny paradise in gloomy reality.

He loved her, aye, had loved her for weeks, but had been too much of a coward to admit it. Was her love for him steadfast enough to withstand the coming shock? What would she do once they left this sheltered valley and returned to Algiers? It would be only a matter of weeks then before she discovered the truth. Would it be best to admit his love, or would she later consider the confession as suspect as the rest of his conduct?

As he struggled with himself, Tory's sated body relaxed. She yawned. Her hands grew limp about his neck, then fell.

When he looked at her with torment in his eyes, she was not awake to see it. When a deep, husky voice murmured, "And I love you, my own," she didn't hear it. And when a solitary tear dripped from the handsome, guilty face above her own to glisten down her cheek and pool in the cleft of her breasts, she didn't feel it.

Chapter 11

Apollo lashed his chariot beyond the horizon, leaving the valley aglow in his fiery wake. Passion-hued skies made a colorful backdrop for the small rock-circled fire and the crimson carpet laid next to it. Copper plates and cups for two glittered in anticipation of a joyful dinner.

The cheery atmosphere was not shared by the dark figure of the man who stood slumped against a large boulder, a booted foot propped behind him. One large hand was clenched against his thigh as he stared unseeingly at the sunset.

This play of hearts, bodies, and minds was no longer a game. It had become, through his own foolish making, a battle of titanic proportions. The stakes were high: happiness or lifelong loneliness. This time, however, he didn't relish the challenge.

He'd never had less confidence than he had now, when he needed it most. Not when, as a stripling, he'd made his first sea voyage under a Spanish captain who knew nothing of his prominent family; not when, at the age of sixteen, he'd clumsily followed the widow Bennet's lead when she offered to make him a man; not even when he was led, beaten and chained, to meet the tiger dey.

The beliefs of a lifetime had been shaken by this fiery, beautiful woman. She forced him to face an aspect of his character that sickened him—his own hubris. He was far more guilty than Tory of all the sins he'd accused her of: more selfish than she, more susceptible to the wiles of the flesh, more flagrant in his disregard for truth. Her scorn of him and Henry had been but a convenient excuse for his actions. In truth, simple carnality had led him to this pass. He smiled wryly.

There was nothing simple about his need for Tory. She was more than a fever in his blood. She was vital to his essence, as perfect for him as if he'd taken clay and molded her to suit his lonely dreams. Thus had he been drawn to her and stood here now agonizing over what he'd done. Only she had tempted him to cast aside the code of ethics on which he prided himself.

Dress it up as he might, he had ruthlessly seduced a virgin, a lady born, using deceit to charm her.

Ah, but he paid his pound of flesh now. He, who had set out to humble her, felt as low as a peasant dreaming of a princess. She, the lady who had commanded respect and obedience all her life, had given herself to him joyously, asking nothing in return. Not freedom, not promises of fidelity, not even . . . he smote his thigh. He didn't deserve to be the man she loved. But he longed to be. Oh, how he longed to be. And, even as he berated himself, his primal instincts rejoiced, whether he'd purloined her offering or not. At least she'd never forget him now.

Sinan wondered if Tory had any idea how magnificently she'd routed him in their battle of wills. Her generosity had accomplished what her defiance had not. He could no longer deny she was the woman he'd awaited for thirty-one years. Never again would peace or happiness be his until she was his in God's eyes, the world's eyes—but most of all, in her own.

And she was the one woman on this earth with reason to hate him.

Should he tell her the truth now and pray he could convince her of his devotion before they left? Or should he woo her as ardently as his heart bade him during this respite before the devil demanded his due? Instinctively, he sensed it was too late to lay his heart at her feet as he longed to. Once she discovered his real identity, she'd consider his avowal part and parcel of his cold-blooded seduction, with no more meaning than the sallies bandied about by the London swells he'd first seen her surrounded by.

Sinan pulled the handkerchief from his pocket and ran it through his hands, remembering how she'd looked when she danced. Had he been forewarned then of this agony, would he have been strong enough to let her go before being singed like a moth in her loving flame?

He smiled sadly. No. Despite this agony of remorse and fear, despite the fact that she'd spoiled him for other women, and despite the knowledge that he might only have a few weeks of her to savor for the rest of his life, he had no regrets. She was meant to be his.

Calming strength flowed through him at the thought. She had wanted him, wanted him enough to become the mistress of a pirate in defiance of all she held dear. And her inexperience gave him an advantage: No woman ever forgot her first lover, particularly if her initiation was pleasurable. And Tory's had been. He had felt her spasms about him.

Sinan's hand unclenched. He straightened away from the rock with a look Tory would have recognized. Decisively, he shoved the handkerchief back into his pocket. Indeed, he had another advantage: He knew the powers of the flesh. He would use that power to woo her, in bed and out, until she felt so cherished she'd forgive him when she learned the truth. And, God willing, she would need him for the lifetime he yearned for.

His stride firm again, Sinan lit a small lantern and carried it with him into the hollow. When he saw her, his face softened with tenderness. One cheek pillowed on that astounding cloud of hair, long eyelashes brushing flushed cheeks, reddened mouth parted with her breathing, she was the picture of innocent yet seductive womanhood. Eve before the Fall. Mate of his body, beloved of his heart.

Ah, forgive me, love, he thought. If he hadn't been so vindictive, he might have realized that her boldness emanated not from experience but from courage and purity of heart. She'd stood up to the dey and to him not because she wasn't afraid, but because she was brave enough to defy them in spite of her fear.

She'd helped Lahtil blossom until Kahlil could scarce wait to pluck her. And she'd coaxed an independent, homeless urchin out of his shyness until he boldly faced the Turkish guards instead of scampering out of their way as he had in the past. In short, she was everything he'd ever wanted in a woman: strong, intelligent, willful, but feminine to her toes with all the intuition and compassion of the best of her sex. He would do anything, face anyone, defy the fates themselves to win her. As he might well have to . . .

Tory stirred. Yawning, she emerged slowly from the depths of sleep. Her eyes opened to the sight of Sinan's face, smiling as he had in her dreams. It was natural for her to open her arms to him, letting the blanket fall from her shoulders.

Thunking the lantern down, he hauled her into his arms, burying his warm lips in the graceful curve of her neck. He closed his eyes, hoping the tight clasp of his arms, the trembling of his body, conveyed his message.

Indeed, Tory wondered at the emotions emanating from him. He seemed . . . desperate to hold her. She tried to pull back to look at him, but he muttered something incoherent and held her still. Sighing, she relaxed.

For minutes they sat like that, silently savoring their closeness in an emotional bonding as moving as their earlier physical one. Finally Sinan cleared his throat and drew back. She folded the blanket across her breasts, flushing as she felt twinges in the secret places of her body. But she flung her long, tangled hair over her shoulder and peeped back at the man who had caused them.

Tory blinked at the suspicious moistness in his eyes. He turned up the lantern wick. When he looked at her again, she assumed she must have imagined it, for his gaze was steady and faintly amused.

"Love's Labour's Lost, my dear? Have I worn you out so? Or was it Much Ado about Nothing?" He dropped a wicked wink.

Tory's shyness receded at his attempt to put her at ease. How many men would so gently mock their own prowess? The fierce rush of love made her response shaky with sincerity. "Nay, my pirate lover. It was A Midsummer Night's Dream. The Tempest."

Something lovely, something fleeting, chased across his face, but before she could pinpoint the emotion, he drew her close, turning her cheek into the pounding hollow of his throat.

"Then it shall be As You Like It, my captive love," he whispered. "Now, and for as long as you'll have me." And All's Well That Ends Well, he prayed silently.

Putting her away from him, he said briskly, "Come, we need food. I have prepared a banquet for us, of sorts. Do you want to wash first or after?"

Her cheeks grew rosier. "First, I think."

His eyes dropped to the barely covered curves of her breasts, but he said evenly, "I will play lady's maid if you need help." He was relieved when Tory shook her head, for his body was reacting to her despite his efforts to control it. If he set hands upon that silken skin, it would be later still before they ate . . .

"I'll fetch the water and soap for you." He hurried away and returned with a steaming leather bucket of water, a bar of soap, and a chamois rag. Setting them down, he backed away. "I'll be waiting." Clumsily, he bumped his head on leaving the hollow.

Tory giggled at his earthy curse, her eyes soft. Her arrogant lover was as susceptible to her as she was to him. She'd felt his tension, seen the hunger of his look. Though her body still ached from his taking, she longed for him in return.

Dreamily, she soaped herself, washing off the traces of blood and something else that made her tingle in remembrance. She rinsed and relathered the rag, then rubbed it over her breasts, reliving the way he'd fondled and kissed them.

She wished suddenly for a mirror. Did she look more womanly now, with fuller lips and breasts? She felt more like a woman. Sinan's woman. Softly she repeated the words aloud.

How right they sounded. Married or no, pirate or no, she was glad at what had happened between them. Perhaps misery would be her lot in the future for having abandoned a lifetime's mores, but for now, she had no regrets. He was the only man she would ever love; she'd do whatever was necessary to win his love in return. She knew how susceptible men were to the pleasures of the flesh. How delightfully dangerous that she was so susceptible in return . . .

After drying herself with the blanket, she reached for her clothes, but donned only the sheer blouse and pantaloons. There was no one to see but Sinan. And she *wanted* him to look at her. She slid her feet into the slippers and combed her hair with her fingers. Taking a deep breath, she went out to meet her lover.

"If I didn't know better, I'd consider myself Lothario's latest conquest," he teased, walking to the crackling fire. She was too busy admiring the impromptu banquet—copper dishes reflecting back the rising stars, steaming bowls of rice and stew decoratively centered by a jug of wildflowers—to notice his start.

She raised an eyebrow when he busied himself filling two plates without answering. Was that a flush on his cheeks? Did he actually feel a little guilty for having taken her? She sat down next to him, letting her breast brush against his arm. He started and would have spilled one of the plates had she not steadied his hand with her own.

She leaned so close her breath tickled his ear. "Perhaps I should explicate the theory and say, dare I hope so?"

With a strangled groan, he slammed both plates down, shoved her back on the carpet, and lowered himself atop her. "Vixen, don't you know when a man is trying to show his gratitude for the precious gift you've given him? Now be quiet and let me woo you." He tried to push himself away, but Tory wrapped her arms about his neck and rotated her hips into his.

"Hawk, don't you know when a woman has no need of wooing? You've no need to win me. I'm already yours. By my choice. The happiest choice I've ever made, I think." Stunned green eyes delved into hers, probing for the truth of her words. Then an odd look darkened the brilliant green, like a cloud passing over the sun. He gave a little sigh that sounded remarkably like pain before he took her lips with famished hunger.

Tory's matching greed shattered the last of his control. The steaming dishes grew cold as their bodily hunger was surpassed by an emotional one. Trembling, they undressed each other, murmuring their pleasure as steely muscles met soft curves. The fire shed its rosy blessing upon them, flickering on ivory skin merging with bronze. Soon it was impossible to tell where she began and he ended.

Indeed, it was a tempest, an earthly Eden they created in sharing what God intended when He gave man his mate. Their soft cries broke in unison as the stars wheeled above them. Meteors zoomed down to earth to die a spectacular death, pulsing their last in a blaze of glory as if in sympathy with their human counterparts. Then came peace, a sated quiet where all else but this, and each other, was superfluous.

Back in reality, Tory yawned, "I'm starved, but too tired to eat. Shall we retire?"

"Nay, love, you'll need strength for what I have planned. Come, dress before you grow chilled in the night air. I'll reheat the food. All you have to do is eat."

Grumbling, Tory did as she was told. She revived with the first flavorful bite, however, and ate eagerly. When they'd eaten their fill, they cleaned the dishes together. Then, hand in hand, they retreated to the hollow. Sinan blew out the lantern, gathered her into his arms, and pulled the blanket over them.

He kissed Tory's brow. "Sleep, love." Tory needed no second urging, for never had she been warmer, wearier, or more content.

Long after Tory had dropped off, however, Sinan lay awake, staring into the darkness, wondering painfully if this was all he would ever have of her.

To Tory's surprise, Sinan seemed in no hurry to leave their secluded haven. She asked two days later when they would return, and Sinan turned away before answering tersely, "Soon enough. Let's enjoy this time together while we may."

Tory found the reply inexplicable, but she didn't question him further. These few halcyon days might haunt her in the months to come, but for now she merely savored the greatest happiness she'd ever known.

They shared everything: the little chores, the blanket at night, sometimes the same dishes, and, of course, their bodies. They confided thoughts, tastes, hopes, and found an unexpected empathy in the sharing. They both loved horses, exotic foods, fine wines, art, and Shakespeare. Strangely, they discovered even their values were similar.

One day when Tory was complaining about the tyranny of the dey, Sinan interrupted her tirade with a dry "At least he has some restraints on his power. It wouldn't take a bloody civil war to dethrone him. Merely a brief, ruthless rebellion by his own soldiers. He's selected by them and ousted by them. A far more democratic process than your own outmoded monarchy."

"The dey has no restraints on his power. He can wield life and death at a command. Our kings and queens are restrained by Parliament."

When Sinan looked skeptical, Tory continued more forcefully, "England has inequities of her own, I agree, but nothing compared to this land. When I return, I'll be far more patient with her ills than I have been in the past."

"*If* you return," Sinan corrected, running a gentle finger around her obstinate chin, "I suggest you go to one of the lower courts and watch some of the poor and powerless being tried for stealing food. Justice is sure and swift indeed—for them. But what happens to the reckless young macaronis who have killed watchmen in their pursuit of diversion? Usually, naught. If that's justice, I want no part of it."

"You prefer the dey's merciful wisdom, then?" Tory queried sarcastically. "Jarrod would find your claim as unbelievable as I do."

"Even Jarrod, an orphaned Jewish boy of the lowest rank in the land, can request an audience with the dey to relate his grievance. Can you see your George the Third granting a similar audience to a London guttersnipe?"

Tory could only give a grudging shrug at that. "Are you implying that Jarrod has only to present his case to the dey to have his inheritance given back to him?"

"No," Sinan sighed, "I'm suggesting no such thing. His father had too many creditors, and Jarrod has no proof of what happened. If he had, with my championship, he'd have a good chance of gaining justice from even the tiger dey. Islam decrees that recompense be paid to the family of one who is killed. At the very least, a harsh fine would be levied against the Turk who tried to cheat Jarrod's father. Do you believe the same would happen in your sainted England? Can you really imagine a chimneysweep challenging a duke and winning a farthing to compensate him for a similar loss? He'd never get his plaint past the lowest magistrate, much less to the king.''

Bringing her knees up to her chin, Tory wrapped her arms about her legs and stared broodingly into the fire. When she looked at him, the turquoise eyes were clear and direct. "No, I can't imagine it. In this instance, at least, I'll have to concede you're right. But greater access does not necessarily mean greater justice. Surely you don't claim that the dey is fair?''

"Based on his own sense of values, yes, in most instances.''

When she frowned in revulsion at the mere idea, he chuckled and put his arm about her. "It took me some time to reach that conclusion, Tory, so I don't expect you to be convinced any more easily. Shall we end this most engrossing discussion with the agreement that tyranny, whatever its form, is not to be tolerated? The dey, your king, and that upstart Napolean are all, in their ways, tyrants to be resisted. I just don't want you to make the usual arrogant English mistake of assuming that all virtue lies in that isolated isle, whilst the rest of the world is meritless.''

"That I can agree to, for I realized that truth long ago. But then, nowhere on earth are conditions for justice as close to ideal as we both hope for.''

"There is one place, Tory,'' Sinan countered softly.

"Where?'' Tory looked at him in surprise.

He hesitated, then drew her more closely under his arm. "One day, when you're ready to hear it, I'll tell you.''

Tory relaxed in the curve of his arm, her body comfortable but her mind buzzing with questions. Why did he delight in tantalizing her mind as much as her body?

So they both believed in justice to all regardless of social position. Surely that was an odd belief for a pirate to have? She was more curious than ever about him. What happy blend of circumstances had created him? Sometimes she'd wondered if he was a deserting seaman from England, so perfectly did he speak the language. Yet he'd spoken of "your king,'' as if he'd have no part of George III.

Perhaps he was Scandinavian. But surely he'd have at least a slight accent? She could discern none other than an occasional clipped inflection. Tory nibbled at her lip, but then she gave a mental shrug. It couldn't hurt to ask. After what they'd shared, surely he'd tell her some of his background.

Thus came the questions Sinan had been dreading. "Where were you born and raised? By what strange circumstances did you become a pirate? With your logical mind and values, you seem more like a barrister than a notorious Barbary reis." Tory felt him tense. She turned to look at him. She could see only his profile, but a muscle in his cheek flexed.

"I was captured over two years ago when I crewed on a Danish merchantman," he answered with a calm he didn't feel. Keep as much to the truth as possible, he warned himself. She'll have less to resent later. "Since I was not ransomed, my only way of bettering myself was to work my way up through the ranks. When I did, I discovered in myself not only an affinity for piracy but an enjoyment of it. My men are not savages, Tory. They but hungered for leadership. We never kill indiscriminately. A dead captive brings no ransom."

Tory was well aware that he had evaded most of her questions. Why was he so reluctant to tell her about himself? He gave her no more time to speculate.

Grinning lustily, he stood and swung her into his arms. "Enough talk, woman. I've a mind to explore some different issues with you." His eyes wickedly admired her breasts.

Tory crossed her arms, grimacing at him when he grunted and strained comically under her considerable weight. "Really, sir?" she said in her best Tory the Terror manner. "And what could those be?"

On arriving at the pool, calm, moon-silvered, and inviting, he lowered her to her feet with an exaggerated sigh of relief. "Why, but your athletic abilities, madam. On your English estate, you must have ridden to hounds—"

A regal nose lifted into the air as she said haughtily, "Sir, I'll not countenance your ribald innuendos. Tell me what you want of me and have done."

Her impish gleam belied her pose. Sinan knew she was in the mood to lead him a merry chase. Good. It would be a wonderful diversion.

He took two steps until he rubbed against her. He pressed one leg between hers and stroked softly, sensually. "What I want of you, vixen," he growled like a mating tiger as he stripped her, "is . . ." He grabbed two handfuls of supple, warm flesh and kneaded them until her eyes closed. Quickly then he threw off his own clothes and lifted her into his arms. She struggled, her eyes glinting at him in the moonlight.

Quelling her rebellion easily, he finished his portentous sentence. " . . . is to see how well you swim!" He smiled into her stunned face and leaped into the pool with his sensuous burden.

The night was balmy, but even so the shock of the water made them gasp. Sinan had chosen his spot well, for it was just shallow enough for his head to break water. When Tory squealed and hung on to him, he smiled, enjoying the slide of warm, silken skin in cool, satin water.

"Ah, what a pity," he teased. "You don't swim. How unfortunate. You've no choice but to hang on to me."

Tory wrapped her arms about his neck, flailing with her legs as if in fear before twining them about his. She leaned her head back in the water to plead breathlessly, "Don't let me go." She shifted, rubbing her breasts against his chest and wrapping her legs higher. She smiled inwardly when she felt him surge against her, but she stared innocently into his eyes, as if unaware of the response she'd elicited.

"I'll not let you go, hellion. That's a promise," he whispered, capturing her lips with his.

Somehow that promise had the sound of a vow, Tory thought. Another time, she might have pursued the subject, but now she was in the mood to pay him back in his own teasing coin. So she responded ardently, opening to the hot probe of his tongue, caressing his back before cupping his buttocks. He groaned and lifted her legs higher. When his swollen member pressed for entry, she made her move.

Sinan's only warning was the release of his mouth and a glimpse of impish blue eyes before he found his head rudely pushed below water, his arms empty, and his manhood throbbing in frustration. By the time he came up, sputtering, Tory was halfway across the pool, swimming with long, experienced strokes. For an instant, he was angry. Then he chuckled. He should have known better than to tease her and expect no retaliation. Pleasurably, he watched her, catching a flash of white thigh and shapely buttock moving in harmony. Her hair floated behind her like a gossamer rudder, seeming to add direction to each powerful stroke.

Couldn't swim indeed. The little witch. What other surprises did she have in store for him? Torn between amusement and exasperation, he watched her pull herself out of the water onto a large flat rock on the other side of the pool. She disported herself comfortably, lying on her side, one arm propped beneath her head, one knee bent. When she'd arranged herself to her satisfaction, she tossed her hair over her shoulder and smiled at him. Even across the pool, he could see the glint of her teeth and eyes in the bright moonlight.

"Come, seaman, take what you desire, if you dare," she called throatily.

"Ah, so you've read Homer, have you? Very well, my siren, sing me to my doom." He waded toward her.

Tory looked doubtful for a moment; then she shrugged, threw back her head, and sang. He went stock-still. His eyes glazed over. His mouth opened, he gasped for air, and then his hands went frantically to his ears. He shuddered when he still couldn't block the sound and stuck a forefinger in each ear. He rocked from side to side, keening.

A strangled laugh shook Tory at his mime of sudden madness, but she controlled herself and sang even more lustily. He trembled, and with a stifled groan, he sank beneath the water. Tory laughed until her sides ached. At first. But when he didn't rise above the water, she sat up.

"Sinan?" she called. When there was no answer, she scrambled to her feet and ran her eyes over the pool. "Sinan!" Not a ripple of water or a flash of bronze disturbed it. Her heart pounding, Tory dived into the water.

Something strong immediately clamped about her ankle. She struggled instinctively to get away before she recognized that touch. She went still. They broke water together. "Why you—" she began, but he silenced her in the way of a man with a maid. When she was pliant against him, he lifted his head.

Soft turquoise eyes peeped up at him, and he was so moved by them he was afraid of what she'd see in his own. So he ducked and whispered in her ear, "Ah, peace at last. You could indeed drive a man to madness with that voice."

Tory drew back to look at him quizzically, and he concluded, "What caterwauling! Your singing master must have been tone-deaf."

Her merry laughter rang with his in the cove in defiance of the fates gathering to bruise them. For now, all was joy and laughter and love as Tory admitted between giggles, "The poor man used to plug his ears with cotton before our lesson, but he still winced every time I opened my mouth. I knew I couldn't sing, but Greaty was convinced I only needed more training. I finally put a stop to it by singing at one of her soirees. Never has a salon emptied so fast, and never has a singing master been given his congé quicker or taken it more gladly.''

The look she slanted him was so vitally alive that he longed to snatch her into his arms and beg her to be his, now and always. All he did, however, was sigh forlornly. ''So I'm not to hear my siren again?''

Tory lifted a wicked eyebrow and said saucily, ''It was not my *voice* I intended to tempt you with, sir.''

His eyes opened wide at that. Then the glittering green was veiled by half-closed lids. Tory was still unsure of herself. Had she been too bold? Suddenly the look on his face made her nervous. She wondered the water didn't boil about them. He definitely had the look of a man done with talk . . .

Indeed, he advanced, backing her into shallower water step by step. ''So you thought to drive me mad with desire by baring your lovely body, eh?''

''I was just pl-playing, Sinan,'' Tory stammered. ''You've seen all I have to offer, so how could I drive you m-mad with desire?''

''What innocence! Shall I show you how very wrong you are, siren?''

The water was waist deep now. Covetous green eyes fixed on the lush curves agleam with water and moonlight. Tory felt her nipples harden despite her nervousness. Until now he'd been gentle with her, but had she teased him too far?

As if he read her mind, he purred, ''The mere look of you is a temptation to any man, hellion. But to flaunt your bountiful charms before your lover is a blatant invitation he most eagerly accepts.'' He lunged before the words were out, and Tory found herself held against a man who seemed maleness incarnate.

He cupped one breast and drew back to look at it cradled in his big, rough palm. ''Is this what you would use to tempt me?'' He bent and blew on the hard tip until it tightened in yearning for the touch of his mouth. He denied her, straightening to smooth a hand over her full buttocks.

''Or these? Or this?'' He brushed a taunting kiss over her mouth. His voice grew husky when he lifted one of her legs about his waist to run his hand from pink toes to dimpled hip.

"Or this? Or this?" He traced her supple back to the curve of her hips.

"Perhaps this, most of all?" He sighed, touching the spot both were most aware of.

Tory quivered when his hand gently searched the wet curls for the womanly treasure she longed now to bestow on him. Somehow the fact that neither could see what his hand did made it more arousing. The soft lap of water, the gentle moonlight, made magic of this moment and this place where it seemed Venus and Eros would appear to grant their blessing.

And Tory became as lost to that magic as Sinan. He'd never hurt her, even pushed to the limits of his control as he was. So carefully did he caress her, savoring the soft petals until she could barely stand on the one leg he allowed her. He made her so wild that she longed to cast aside all restraints and admit to the evocative image forming in her mind: he, the master gardener, pruning and planting the bower he had coaxed to full bloom.

Sinan savored her pink cheeks, her sighs. He wanted to drive her as wild as he was driven until she met him demand for demand. So he withdrew his touch, leaving her moaning with disappointment, and urged softly, "Come, lover, here I am. Deliver on your promises."

Dazed turquoise eyes opened. His strong face was awash with tenderness as soft as the moon dust gilding his hair, but she read something else, too. Desire. And need—a man's need to be wanted by his chosen lover. She understood. He wanted her to take the initiative, not just to respond, but to invite with action as she had in word and play.

Novice that she was, a part of Tory was yet horrified at her actions. When she merely responded to his overtures, she could tell herself she did so to please him. If she became the aggressor, she'd have to admit she had needs as basic as his.

It seemed he knew the choice he'd given her, for now he stood still, offering no further inducement. As he watched her, he knew it was still too soon to challenge her so. Before these weeks were up, she'd have to come to terms with this need as he had. But not yet. For now, this was enough.

"Very well, my shy siren. You win. You have tempted me beyond control. Come, drive me mad . . ." He lowered his mouth to sip of passion's wine with her and sup of love's fruits.

Soon the play of tongues, mouths, and hands was not enough

for either of them. Sinan lifted Tory's other leg about his waist and pressed his swollen manhood against her.

Tearing her mouth away, Tory gasped, "Here?"

The question was moot, for the long, silken slide was aided by their liquid boudoir. "You came to me by water. And where else to give a siren her due?" Sinan sighed against her neck, cupping her hips to push her downward on his pulsing shaft until she engulfed him fully. "You will find that water has de . . . lightful prop . . . erties."

Thus did Tory rediscover water's buoyancy in a highly unscientific manner, which Archimedes would have frowned upon. The liquid support made it easy for Sinan to lift and lower her at his will, filling and emptying her in concert with the surging rhythm of the pool. The sounds of their breathing, quickening in unison, were almost drowned out by the miniature tidal wave they created. It grew in urgency as they did, uplifting them, surrounding them with the gift of life and each other.

Sinan moaned, "Lean back farther, love." Tory obeyed blindly, twining her legs about his waist like a vine climbing for the sun. Indeed, though it was full dark, Tory felt the sun rising within her with each impassioned lunge. When she leaned back, he used to her advantage the greater access she'd given him. His strokes went long and smooth, lingering at the top to tease the throbbing center of her. She arched her back in ecstasy. With a husky murmuring of praise, he harvested the bounty of her breasts, nibbling and suckling in perfect, shocking counterpoint to the wicked movements of his hips.

Tory forgot herself then. She was no lady reared, but the woman she'd been born to be, and Sinan was her man. His sturdy legs supported her; his arms sheltered her. His manhood probed the depths of her being, reaching for the essence of all that made her woman. And when he found it, they reveled in it together, crying out as the sun rose full and glorious within them. Tory was bathed in its heat as Sinan's showering warmth filled her and fulfilled her.

Their sun set slowly, but left its glow behind. Tory cradled Sinan's head against her breasts as he nuzzled her in exhausted enjoyment, like a drowsy babe taking a last sip before sleeping. Tory stroked his hair, giggling at the foolish analogy. The proof of his virile manhood was still snuggled in her as if reluctant to leave.

Sinan drew back to look at her, smiling at her pleasured glow.

"And what are you laughing at, pray?" he mock-growled, letting her aching legs slip down at last. He took her hand to walk with her from the water.

"Why, I was thinking how sweetly you nuzzled me, like a babe. Then, realizing how foolish I was, I laughed. There's nothing babelike about you."

Instead of laughing with her as she expected, he grew silent. He dried her and helped her back into her clothes, but said not a word until he, too, was dressed. Then he took her hand, seated her near the fire and stirred up the coals, adding more wood. When flames leaped, he sat beside her.

"Tory," he said gravely, "you surely realize the possible consequences of our recent . . . enjoyment. How will you feel if you conceive my child?"

Tory stiffened and tried to pull her hand away, but he would not allow it. She turned her head to stare into the flames before answering dully, "I try not to think about it."

He turned her chin to make her face him. "It's a very real possibility, and one you must accept. Please don't ask me to deny us the joy we have found, for I cannot. And if you're honest, you will admit that you don't want me to."

She took a breath to disagree, then gave a helpless little shrug. It would be a lie to deny it, and they both knew it. "No, but neither do I want to bear a bastard to take up his father's trade."

Wincing, he released her to hug his knees. He broke a long silence with a whispered "And what if I told you I don't plan to be a pirate for much longer?"

She drew a quick breath, then scrambled on her knees to face him. "Oh, Sinan darling, do you do this for me?"

He opened his mouth to deny it, but snapped it shut. "Partly," he said instead. "But piracy's also no longer a practical way of life for me unless I agree to become a Moslem, which I will not. You must speak to no one of this, of course. My life could be forfeit if you do."

Some of Tory's joy receded. What did he hide? "But where will you go? Can you come back to England with me?"

"No, I could never be happy there. I hope you'll agree to come with me instead."

"But where? Who are you?" All her frustration rang in the two short sentences, but he gave her no relief.

"You'll find out soon enough. Now to bed, wench. To *sleep*.

You've worn me out with your insatiable appetite.'' She rose to the challenge as he had known she would.

"*My* insatiable appetite? You . . . rake! You're the one who wanted to explore my 'athletic' abilities!'' She leaped to her feet and turned away in a huff. Only later would she realize how easily he had diverted her.

Strong arms grabbed her from behind before she'd gone a step. "And most impressive those abilities are, too. For a while there I wondered if you'd studied acrobatics more assiduously than singing. What strong legs!''

Tory flushed from her hairline to her toes at the fervent appreciation in his voice, but he gave her no time for embarrassment. He lock-stepped her to the hollow and lay down beside her.

He kissed her brow chastely and pulled her into his arms, soothing her. "Come, sweet, don't be embarrassed,'' he cajoled. "You are perfect in every way. I'm but teasing. Your response is delicious, and I hope you will become even bolder.''

Sighing, Tory relaxed. Her puritan instincts still reared disapproving heads, but not as sternly as before. She was truly becoming decadent, she thought sleepily. She dozed off on the delicious thought that if she was to be led astray, at least she would enjoy every minute of it.

When her breathing was steady, Sinan allowed his guard to slip. Before blowing out the lantern, he drank her in with all the love he had to hide when she was awake. He put a hand on her warm, soft abdomen.

"Be fruitful, my love. And, God willing, you will never be able to hate the father of your babe.''

Chapter 12

Somehow Tory was not surprised when she awoke the next morning to find their snug little camp dismantled. She silently accepted the cup of Turkish coffee Sinan offered.

"Dress in comfortable clothes, Tory. We've stayed long enough. Too long, really. I've much to do in Algiers.''

Still she was silent. Sinan took the cup away and gathered her into his arms. He cradled her head in one big hand and kissed the two fat tears in her eyes. "I know, love, I don't want to leave, either. But we can have this joy again, as long as we're together."

This was the closest he'd come to a commitment. Was she more than an interlude for him? Tory opened her eyes and basked in the warm green gaze. Questions tumbled in her mind, but before she could voice them, he patted her head and turned away.

"Come, help me pack the last of our supplies," he tossed over his shoulder.

When mounted, they paused to look back at their lost utopia. The pool reflected puffy clouds floating overhead. Saplings at the water's edge dipped gracefully before the brisk breeze to trail supple arms in the water. The wildflowers climbing up the cliffs winked at them as if bidding them swiftly to return. And the hollow where Tory had given her virginity to the only man she would ever love was dark, quiet, as if it, too, mourned their departure.

It was Tory who faced forward and led the way up the trail, her back ramrod straight. With every step of that long, tiring journey, her sense of foreboding grew. The fate that awaited them, whatever it might be, could not possibly be as blissful as the one they'd left.

Sinan's thoughts were even gloomier, for he knew what they faced. If he delayed longer, he would be too late to meet with Terence, and he had to relay critical information to him in case he and Tory didn't make it out. However, it was the emotional storms brewing that concerned him most.

Perhaps the bonds they'd forged in the glen would be strong enough to bind them. He did his utmost to strengthen those bonds by ardently making her his each night. Passion fed on their mutual fears, growing greedier as they neared Algiers, as if both knew they had to store up memories for the scarcity to come. Tory's unease was based on instinct; Sinan's originated from cold, hard facts.

He made himself face them. It would be a formidable challenge to get them out, but first he had to complete the personal part of his mission. His mother would never forgive him, and he would never forgive himself, if he left without Helen. And now he had the further complication of Tory and her crew. If he lived to hear her recriminations, he'd get an earful when she learned the truth about him. Her emotions ran too deep to allow her to forgive such a deception easily. If she loved, she would do so passionately; if she hated, she'd do it well. And he'd given her good reason to hate him . . .

Thus neither rejoiced upon reaching Algiers. When they entered the house after stabling the horses, Kahlil, the only guard, greeted them effusively.

"I'm relieved to see you, Sinan. Was the woman harmed?"

"No, thank God." Sinan's half-smile embraced Tory in a way that made Kahlil's eyes narrow. "She was too much of a handful even for our lordly sheikh."

At Kahlil's questioning look, Sinan continued quietly, "The late sheikh. I joined the Tuaregs on a revenge raid and saw him spliced by their leader like the pig he was. He died quickly but not well. He tried to use Tory to shield him, but I got her away in time."

"And Ali?" Kahlil asked.

A smile as savage as any victorious Tuareg's claimed Sinan's face when he answered the question succinctly and laconically, "Dead. By my hand in a fight fairer than he deserved."

Before Kahlil could ask more questions, Tory interrupted, "Sinan, I want to bathe."

Nodding, Sinan gestured to his officer to unlock the harem doors. Kahlil did so, waited until she came out with fresh clothes, then relocked them.

Sinan himself guarded the bath door while he questioned his first officer. "Has the fury toward me quieted in my absence?"

"Yes, Sinan." But Kahlil did not seem pleased. "I am glad you did not have to kill Hassan yourself. It will make it easier for the dey to be lenient."

At Kahlil's gravity, Sinan braced himself. "Tell me the worst, man. What the devil has gone wrong now?"

"Your woman cajoled Jarrod into painting the hand of Fatima on your doorstep. It apparently signaled someone when she would make her escape. Jarrod forgot to paint over it after she disappeared. It stayed on your house for two days and nights before we noticed it. We whitewashed it, but those who saw it took it to mean that you'd decided to accept Allah as your God. The dey summoned me to question me about your whereabouts and to ask why you had not acquainted him of your decision to embrace the Koran." Kahlil spread his hands in a gesture of helplessness. "I . . . did not know what to say. I feared we'd lose face if I told him a lowly concubine had tricked us all and escaped, so I told him you'd explain upon your return.''

This was far worse than he'd expected. Sinan closed his eyes and leaned wearily against the bath door, his mind working frantically. Indeed, the dey would be furious at the disrespect shown all Moslems if he explained how that sign had appeared next to his door. And not only would he lose face in the dey's eyes but he could lose his head as well if it was discovered he had no intention of converting to Islam. What possible explanation could he give for the seeming disrespect? That a boy did it as a prank? He couldn't say that, for Jarrod would be immediately suspect. Punishment for his Jewish scorn of the ancient custom would be swift and sure.

The dey would be disappointed if he knew how easily Tory had outwitted him. Worse, he'd be suspicious at the way the hand was so swiftly painted over. Try as he might, Sinan could think of no satisfactory explanation for either its appearance or its disappearance.

The choice was grim: Tell the truth and hope Mustapha would still give him the time he'd promised; or leave now. But even if Mustapha kept their bargain, he'd be watching. The dey was a cautious man, with good reason. One whiff of betrayal, and he would be like a bloodhound on the scent. He'd order his guards to shadow his erstwhile favorite's every step. And that Sinan could not afford.

Which perforce left him only the latter option. Sinan opened his eyes to stare blindly over Kahlil's head. Perhaps that would be for the best, after all. His meeting with Terence tonight was propitious. As to his other reason for being here, the time had come for desperate measures. Another ten days with Tory would be bittersweet. It would probably sway her not at all in the end, but it would tilt him even further off balance. Besides, he would still have the voyage . . .

Most persuasive of all, his sea-roving instincts growled, *Escape now or you might not have a chance*. Sinan straightened.

''Go to the palace and get a work order for the Bagnio Balek. Tell them the *Scorpion* needs outfitting for her last voyage this season. They'll not question it when they hear of my return. Inform the harbormaster there will be a handsome bonus for him if all is in readiness by tomorrow night. I'll tell the Guardian Bashaw the same.''

Kahlil nodded, but paused to look at the man he respected

and liked, emotions warring in his black eyes. "You are leaving, are you not? You will not embrace the Koran."

Sinan smiled ruefully. "You are perceptive, as usual. Can I trust to your discretion, Kahlil? I know it's asking much, but if you don't help me, I may lose my head. Surely the prizes I've won for the dey will more than compensate him for the loss of the *Scorpion.* I would not turn to thievery if I had another choice. If you act betrayed, no one will suspect you were doing aught but following orders, as a loyal officer should."

"And I will be made to look the fool."

Since that was unarguable, Sinan did not respond for a moment. An idea germinated in the back of his mind. Sinan moved away from the door to stride up and down while he nurtured the seed to fruition. He whirled to face his first officer, but more, his friend.

"Kahlil, I've a proposition for you. In my other life, my family business has far-flung interests, but as yet we have no North African representative. Since I'll be unable to return here in future, I'd like you to work with us as our broker to open up trading contacts. Your share of the profits would be handsome."

Kahlil shook his head before Sinan could finish, his strong features affronted. "I will not accept charity, Sinan. I may help you out of friendship, but not for reward."

A rude noise greeted this high-flown sentiment. "Hell's bells, man, I'm *giving* you nothing. You'll work damned hard for every piaster. And with your contacts throughout the Mediterranean and your flair for leadership, you're the ideal person to help us."

"And who is 'us,' Sinan Reis? Is it not time you told me who you really are?"

"Yes, Sinan Reis, is it not time?" Tory, sweet-smelling but steely voiced, exited the bath to stare at him over her veil.

It was still too soon, Sinan told himself. Kahlil would have to know, but not Tory. Not yet. *Coward*, he mocked himself as he replied, "You'll know soon enough, Tory. Let's retire, and I'll explain what has happened." To Kahlil he said, "Well?"

Kahlil looked indecisive, but finally he nodded slowly. "I will do as you command. I could not live with your death on my conscience."

Tory gasped and looked sharply from one man to the other, but neither heeded her.

"As to the other," Kahlil went on, "I must think upon it."

"I understand, Kahlil, but in your deliberations, consider

Lahtil. My possessions will be confiscated, and it's too late to legitimize my sale of her to you. The dey may take her back and give her to another of his captains."

Kahlil paled. He said abruptly, "We must talk more, Sinan."

Placidly, Sinan agreed, "Yes, come to my chamber in a few hours and we'll make our plans final."

He took Tory's arm and escorted her up the stairs. They were barely out of earshot before she loosed a barrage of questions.

"Not now, love, I haven't time," he said evasively. Upon entering Tory's chamber, he silenced her in the way he liked best. When she was limp against him, he drew back to tease huskily, "Now, what was it you wanted to ask?"

She collected her scattered wits. "Why are you in danger?"

He explained, watching her features become pinched as she listened.

"You mean it's my fault that we have to flee?"

"Your plan was to your credit, my love, but much to my discredit. In all innocence, you've made our escape imperative. If all goes well, we'll be at sea by tomorrow night."

"But, Sinan, what of Becky? I can't leave her."

Sinan groaned and rubbed a weary hand across his brow. "My God, I'd forgotten about her." He thought for a moment, then dropped his hand. "If Kahlil accepts my plan, he can put her on a ship for England."

"And where, Sinan Reis, are we bound?"

But Sinan was walking to the door as if he hadn't heard. "Get some sleep, love." He winked, adding as he walked out, "I'll return in a few hours, so rest while you may."

Rest, Tory snorted to herself after his steps had retreated. He was the most exasperating, arrogant . . . It was just like him to dump a hornets' nest of worries in her lap and blithely bid her *rest*. Her mind whirled with so many questions she felt light-headed.

She ripped off her veil; it was one thing she'd miss not at all in her new life, wherever it might be. For amid this sea of uncertainty, Tory had one anchor to cling to: Wherever Sinan went, she went. Back in civilization, she could reassure Greaty and then ransom her crewmen by messenger. For she would not leave him, no matter who he was. She needed him, and one day soon he would have to admit he needed her. She didn't know what he'd fled from or to what, or even where, he would return. But she did know that whatever he'd done, she would stand by him.

She climbed into bed, comforted by the thought that for once in her life she was thinking unselfishly. She cared not if he lived in a mansion or a hut in the wilderness. She'd make either place a home for both of them. She would learn anything, dare anything, to win his proud, brave heart.

She drifted off to sleep on the thought, unaware that her resolve would soon be tested in a way she never envisioned.

Sinan looked in all directions before drawing the parchment from his cloak. He unrolled it, propped it against a low wall and sketched by the light of the moon. He was already far too late for his meeting with Terence, but this was his last chance to finish the map. He wished he had more solid information to dispatch as to what country would next lose favored status, but the dey had been closemouthed of late.

Dammit, it went against his grain to leave with his mission unfinished, but he had more to worry about now than his own skin. He stuck the finished map in his sash and hurried to the metalworker's hut. Terence opened the door at his scratch and motioned him inside.

"I'd almost given you up, man. Tales are flying fast and furious about you. Have you really renounced Christianity? Did you retrieve the Lady Victoria, or was her disappearance mere rumor?"

Again Sinan went into explanations.

Terence whistled when he finished. "I've never held to the view that women are naught but trouble, but you almost convince me. Indeed, your escape seems imperative. Do you mean to take her with you?"

"Of course." Sinan pretended not to see Terence's quirked eyebrow at his certainty. "But I need your help. If I'm to find Helen, it must be tomorrow. Do you think you can get into Saud's house as a pot-seller?"

"His kitchen, perhaps, but nowhere near his harem."

"Not you, agreed. But what of a young assistant?" Sinan went on in a low tone.

Terence's alert brown eyes narrowed in consideration. He nodded. "Yes, it might work. But even a small boy will be viewed suspiciously if he nears the harem. Now, if he happened to be chasing something. A monkey, perhaps . . ."

Grinning, Terence went to the rear of the hut, untied a leather thong, and came back carrying a small monkey, which promptly climbed onto his shoulder. "One of the advantages—or disadvantages, depending on one's point of view—in trading with these people is their odd idea of what constitutes currency. You see before you the price of one copper urn. Meet Aladdin."

"Does he come with a lamp?" Sinan asked dryly.

"No, but he's as mischievous as any self-respecting genie and just about as artful. He'll make a wonderful collaborator."

"Good. I'll send Jarrod at first light. Go while the household is awakening and the guards are less alert. I pray Helen is still an early riser. Send Jarrod back to my house with word. If she's there, I'll get her out if I have to mount a full-scale attack."

Terence tied the monkey back up and returned, his handsome bearded face worried. "Beau, don't you worry what will happen even if you do find Helen? These past years must have been rough on her. She'll not . . . have an easy time of it back home."

"What would you have me do? Leave her to be passed from Turk to Turk like a soiled garment?" Beau clenched his fists, his features tormented.

Terence sighed heavily. "Not at all. But you must prepare yourself for the possibility that she might want to stay. Three years is a long time."

"Bobby needs her. So do I. Anyone back home or elsewhere who scorns her will have me to deal with."

"Prejudice is too insidious to be dealt with in your usual inimitable way, Beau. Nothing will quiet the tattlemongers."

"Cochrans are no strangers to gossip. Besides, they'll be too busy speculating about my return to spare much thought to Helen."

"You've the right of it there, unfortunately." An odd inflection entered Terence's voice.

"What do you mean?"

"Somehow word of your mission has reached Congress. It's just as well you're leaving tomorrow, for your purpose here will not remain secret long. If some ambitious legislator takes it in his head to notify our consul—"

A thunderous frown shadowed Beau's face. "Who the hell told them?"

"That I don't know. I only heard about this from the last dispatch. Your father has ordered you home as soon as possible. For all our sakes, I hope you've had a chance to finish the maps. Have you discovered which country the dey will break treaty with next?"

"Not specifically, but he's becoming disgusted with England's arrogance, and he is leaning toward the French."

Terence groaned. "That news will make you a most unwelcome messenger. I needn't tell you that Congress is still furious with the French over the XYZ Affair. For once, I'm in agreement. Demanding a bribe indeed! Where's the map?"

Still steaming, Beau jerked the parchment from his sash and spread it open on the workbench. "I finished it just tonight, and I've had no chance to duplicate it yet. This is the only complete copy. Tell me, does Congress know about you as well?"

A sly smile curved Terence's thin lips. "Apparently not yet, and I mean to make good use of their ignorance while I may. I think they'll be glad I'm there soon enough. The Bashaw is still insulted by the niggardly terms he was offered compared with what Algiers got. We'll either have to pander to his greed or force him to be reasonable at sword point."

"I almost hope that happens. Then our presence here will have served a valid purpose. And at least then there will be no more argument over the need for a navy. I'll leave this complete map with you to send with the next dispatch. It will probably be safer. I'll take the incomplete map with me."

Brown eyes met green in grim concurrence. Both knew the odds Beau faced in getting away safely; there was no purpose in voicing them. Terence rolled the parchment up and secreted it in a tall copper jug.

Beau pulled another object from his pocket. "In getting Tory away, I made a deal with Ismail, a Tuareg leader, to seek his sister who was sold into slavery by Hassan. I will be forever in your debt if you can make inquiries about her. I would not impose so upon you if I had another choice, but neither Tory nor I would be alive without Ismail's help. I hate to leave without attempting to fulfill my promise to him."

Terence sighed, but he took the charm Beau handed him and listened to the description of the woman and her last known whereabouts. "I'll do what I can, Beau. I presume I'm to send this with a message if I discover news of his sister."

"Yes, the charm is a guarantee of safe passage through Tuareg territory. Thank you, Terence."

"I'll collect, old man, be assured." The two men grinned at each other, but Terence quickly sobered. "I don't need to tell you you go with my prayers. I don't envy you. Even if you somehow manage to get away, you've a dogfight awaiting you in

Philadelphia. And Jefferson can offer little help. As Republican Vice-President of a Federalist administration, he would just stir up more bad blood against you. And there's enough already between him and Adams.''

"With good reason. Jefferson's made no secret of his opinion of paying tribute to these rascals. But I'm not worried. I'm a private citizen; they cannot court-martial me.''

"Under those cursed Alien and Sedition Acts, private citizenship is no guarantee of immunity. I've heard some journalists have been arrested for 'arousing discontent with the government.' And I can't think of a more sterling example of inciting discontent with the government than what we're doing. You'll have a ticklish time of it, I fear.''

Beau waved an impatient hand. "I'll welcome a good open fight. It's past time the cowardice of this policy is laid bare for all to see.''

"Now, on that I heartily agree. Let us hope next year's election will prove others are as disenchanted as we.'' Terence held out his hand. "Good luck, Beau. I'll await Jarrod as you instruct, but then I must get back to Tripoli. I need to keep a close watch on events.''

"May you have more luck than I, my friend.'' Beau shook Terence's hand.

A rakish smile lit Terence's face. "You've not been completely unlucky, I suspect. You have said little about the Lady Victoria, except to definitively state your possession. I wonder why?''

Beau's flush was more revealing than his answer. "On that I'll not comment except to say that a brawl with Congress will be a skirmish compared to the full-fledged war that awaits me when Lady Victoria Alicia Grenville discovers who I am.''

"You've not told her?'' Terence blinked in consternation.

"Not yet. I intend to wait until we're at sea.''

"Where she can't betray you,'' Terence guessed.

"Where she can't run away,'' Beau contradicted flatly.

"Ah, caught at last, are you?''

"Aye.'' The one word, spoken with such feeling, abolished Terence's teasing grin.

"You've a battle royal on your hands, all right,'' Terence agreed at last. "But I've never known you to fail to win the lady you wooed.''

Beau drew his cloak about himself without answering, for he

certainly didn't feel so confident. "I must go, for I've much to do. Godspeed, Terence. Be careful."

"And you, Beau. Tell your father to keep me informed of events back home."

Beau nodded and exited. When he returned to his house, he found Kahlil awaiting him. Beau greeted the other two guards, then requested that Kahlil follow him to his room.

Once there, Beau and Kahlil sat down on cushions. "Have you made your decision yet?"

"If I agree to your offer," Kahlil answered cautiously, "how can I be of service to you, since my name will be mocked from Constantine to Oran?"

"If we handle this right, you'll end the hero rather than the fool." Beau explained the plan he'd perfected on his walk back.

Kahlil nodded thoughtfully. "Yes, it might work." He looked Beau straight in the eye. "I've always admired your intelligence, Sinan Reis, but only now do I understand how devious it is. You are a spy, are you not?"

Beau's mouth tightened. "One man's spy is another's patriot." If Kahlil helped him in this dangerous undertaking, he deserved to know the truth. Slipping his hand into his coat, Beau bowed from the waist. "Beaufort Avery Cochran, at your service. On a private mission to infiltrate the dey's band of corsairs to discover what nation is in favor and to determine the status of the regency's armaments."

"British?"

"American."

"With the intent of declaring war?"

"With the intent of protecting our Mediterranean shipping from threats of attack by some means other than bribery. If war becomes necessary, so be it." Kahlil frowningly digested this.

Beau pinned Kahlil with an austere gaze. "You came here from Constantinople, Kahlil. We both know your first loyalty is to the sultan and that the dey has no interest in furthering anyone's goals but his own. He pays only lip service to the sultan's firman. We have no quarrel with the sultan. It could be to both our countries' advantage to hasten Mustapha's defeat. You can use your new influence—with the assistance of the commissions you'll be earning as our broker—to see that a more loyal Turk is elected by the Janissaries."

When Kahlil seemed struck by this, Beau laid the last of his cards on the table. "Besides, this is the only way for you to win Lahtil and hope to keep her. She would make a lovely first wife."

Kahlil hesitated one more moment, then stuck his hand out to cement their bargain in the Western manner. "You were named the Hawk with good reason, my friend. I salute your keen vision."

"And I your practicality and courage. May our continuing association be as loyal as our friendship. Your next duty will be to travel to Biskra, escort Becky to the nearest port, and put her on a ship for London." Beau lowered his voice. "But for now this is what I need you to do. . . . "

It was almost dawn by the time Beau had rousted Jarrod, accepted the boy's relief at his and Tory's safe return, and explained how he needed his help.

Jarrod nodded silently, but his great dark eyes filled with tears. "You are leaving." It was a grim statement of fact, as if Jarrod had always known this day would come. He read the answer in Beau's compassionate eyes.

Jarrod's face set with fierce pride. His eyes dried as he seemed to pull within himself. "I will do as you command," he said formally. "God go with you." And he ran out before the words trembling on Beau's tongue could fall.

Slowly, Beau walked up to Tory's room. Jarrod would be bewildered and unhappy, at least at first, in America. But what would he have here? Nothing and no one to care for him.

And so Beau was faced with yet another complication by the time he stood over Tory. The long night he'd planned had dwindled into day. He watched his sleeping lady, his stomach tied in knots. The right thing to do, he knew, would be to wake her and warn her of what was coming, to tell her that, if he was caught, he might never see her again; that no matter what happened, he was humbled and honored to have known her; that he would carry her image with him to his grave.

There wasn't time. But inwardly he jeered at himself, Coward. You can face death by strangulation, beheading, or impalement, but you can't tell the woman you love that you regret the trick you've played on her.

The coming day didn't alarm him as much as the night, when, the battle won, the only enemy left would be that most deadly one—wounded pride. And his lady had a surfeit of it.

As if she sensed his presence, she stirred. Her eyes fluttered open and stared vaguely up at him in the candlelight. She sat up abruptly. "Why are you so late? What's amiss?"

"Nothing, dear. It's taken me this long to plan our escape." He sat down beside her. "Tory, it's almost dawn. I want to tell you what you must do. Pack a small satchel, and wear the dress and cape you arrived in. In my room, under the round carpet in the middle of the floor, you'll find a trapdoor. What's in it belongs to you. Make your good-byes to Lahtil this morning, for Kahlil will escort you to the *Scorpion* soon after. With a little luck, I'll be joining you later." He smiled faintly, but he looked at the hand he held as he spoke.

Tory frowned. His tension went beyond nervousness. What was he not telling her? Her old unease returned, but she tried to stifle it. He would never do anything to harm her. Would he?

"What are you going to do?"

"Accomplish at least one of the things I came here for, God willing."

"Would you quit talking in riddles!" She grabbed his arm. "You aren't going to leave me behind, are you?"

That startled him into looking at her. "Of course not," he shouted in exasperation.

Her worst fear quieted, Tory let him go, plumped her pillows, leaned back, and looked at him. "Then everything will be all right," she said simply. "I feel it here." She took his hand and brought it to her heart.

With a fervent "Pray God you're right," he snatched her to him and began to rock her back and forth. After a moment, she leaned into the circle of his arms to ask gravely, "What of Jarrod?"

"If he'll come, I want to take him with us."

Tory hugged him tightly for that. Ah, what a man he was! She swallowed back her tears, then set him away. "I might as well get started and enjoy my last Algerine dawn." She rose, blushing as he admired the lush curves revealed by her thin lawn nightgown.

Beau leaned against the wall with a negligence he didn't feel, staring at her. The rush of battle excitement didn't fortify him as it usually did, for this challenge could not be won by physical valor. Sword and pistol would avail him nothing. This crisis would have to be met with a moral rectitude that, at the moment, was beyond him. If Tory was unable to forgive him, as he feared, honor would demand he take her home to England. Had he courage to do it?

It was a question he couldn't answer. He straightened and went to the door, where he turned. "No matter what happens, Tory, know that what I've done was for . . . need of you. These few weeks together have been the happiest I've ever known. Don't spoil them, love. We deserve a chance together if you'll trust me. Try to remember that."

And he was gone, his words ringing in Tory's ears. Her strange sense of foreboding increased. No matter how she tried to banish it as she packed, it shadowed her like a brooding thundercloud massing to dump ruination upon her.

On that steamy late August morning, tempers were irritable throughout Algiers. The faithful sea breeze had deserted the city, leaving it exposed to the merciless heat of the hottest time of the year. So it was that, when Kahlil arrived very early at the palace, the sleepy secretary who finally answered his summons didn't dare wake the dey. He affixed his seal to the work order Kahlil requested for the Guardian Bashaw of the Bagnio Balek.

"His Excellency will be glad to hear of Sinan's return and of his eagerness to put to sea," the secretary said. "I will tell him that Sinan requests an audience for this evening. Why does he not come sooner? He surely knows His Excellency will welcome his decision to embrace the Koran. Nor will Sinan be blamed for Hassan's death, since the sheikh was killed by Tuaregs."

Kahlil shrugged. "Sinan has acted peculiarly since returning with that Christian she-cat. He bears close watching."

"I will tell His Excellency of your reservations, Kahlil." The secretary yawned. "Later."

"Forgive me for disturbing your rest, but Sinan Reis was most insistent that I put the English slaves to work on the *Scorpion*. He is indeed eager to return to sea." Kahlil nodded cordially. *"Bilshifa!"*

When Kahlil gave Beau the work order a short time later, he warned, "Make haste, for the dey will hear of my suspicions about you this very day."

Nodding, Beau straightened his most elegant silk *gambour* and *kaffiyeh*. "After Tory has packed and made her good-byes to Lahtil, escort her to the Marine Gate and tell the gatekeeper

I'm taking her to the slave market at Constantine. Assist her on board the *Scorpion*. Then take your station.''

Beau wheeled smartly and departed on his mission.

At about the same time, several blocks away, a bearded pot-seller and his young Jewish assistant scratched on Saud's door. A surly, sleepy guard answered. He would have slammed the door in their faces had not Terence stuck his foot in the jamb and said in harsh Turkish, ''Your master will not be pleased that the new pots he ordered were refused delivery.''

The door opened a crack. When Terence shrugged, heaved his sack over his back, and turned, the guard stopped him. ''I know nothing of these pots, but you can go around and talk to the cook.'' To Jarrod he said, ''Keep that monkey on a tight leash.'' Jarrod bobbed his head, shifting his own sack to his other arm so he could brace Aladdin tighter on his shoulder.

Watching the odd pair suspiciously, the guard shadowed their steps as they traversed the courtyard. Terence and Jarrod both glanced about. The house was laid out much like Sinan's. The living quarters and the harem were obviously up the stairs. As they passed the stone steps, Jarrod surreptitiously took a handful of chopped dates from his pocket and tossed them up the stairs. He caught his toe on a loose tile and stumbled. Yelping, he fell, pots clattering from his sack. Aladdin scampered from his slack grip. The hungry monkey, who had not been fed the night before, scurried up the stairs after the dates, chattering in delight.

The guard scowled and cuffed Jarrod. ''Clumsy fool! Fetch that filthy animal before he wakes the master.''

Jarrod rose and walked slowly toward Aladdin. When Terence began cursing fluently, catching the guard's attention with his acerbic opinion of his assistant, Jarrod tossed another handful of dates higher up the stairs. Two choice morsels landed on the second-story balcony.

Aladdin followed the trail of bait as if trained to do so. When Jarrod rounded the curve of the steps, his heart sank. There was surely the harem, but it was much more securely guarded than Sinan's. Two huge turbaned eunuchs scowled at him.

With a sickly grin, Jarrod gestured at the monkey and spoke in English in a singsong voice, as if calling the monkey, ''Helen . . . Helen Stoville, I am sent by your brother to find you. If you're in there, put a kerchief in the northeast window of the harem.''

Jarrod held his arms out to Aladdin. The monkey cocked his head, grunted in disgust at his empty hands, and ran up one guard's baggy pantaloons to perch on his shoulder and screech in his ear. The guard made the mistake of pulling Aladdin's tail. To Jarrod's delight, the monkey shrieked, bit the guard's hand, and scampered up the grille in the harem door to sit on the arched lintel. Eyes bright with ire, he shrewishly lectured the guard for his rudeness.

He was just out of reach, chittering loud enough to wake half of Algiers. When the other guard, with a disgusted look at his comrade, who was sucking his bleeding hand, drew his scimitar, Jarrod gasped in genuine alarm and ran forward.

"No! I can get him down."

"Then do so before I silence this demon in a monkey's skin," the eunuch growled back.

Jarrod inched closer, using his singsong voice again, "Miss Helen, Miss Helen, come out if you're in there so I can see you." He repeated the words with every step until he was finally close enough to rise on tiptoe and see inside the harem corridor. The guards stood aside when he reached into his pocket for a date. He held it up to tempt Aladdin down, peering inside the harem.

He saw curious, yawning women attaching their veils, some even shockingly bare-faced, peeking out of their rooms to see what the commotion was. Most were attired in sheer night rails or kaftans, but it would be years before Jarrod would do more than blush at such a sight. His inventory was impersonal and hurried. Dark hair, red hair, brown, but no blond . . . Wait! A small fair head rounded one door at the end of the corridor. A sweet, winsome face looked straight at him.

Aladdin leaped into his arms and reached greedily for the date, so Jarrod had to back away, but he resumed chanting in his singsong voice, "Miss Helen, Miss Helen, your brother will rescue you today. Leave a kerchief in the northeast window to signal as soon as you're ready."

Bowing an apology, Jarrod gripped Aladdin's collar firmly and retraced his steps. Below, Terence was tapping an impatient foot. He grabbed Jarrod's arm, scolding, "That's the last time you bring that animal with you. Get rid of it or I find myself a new assistant!"

He shoved Jarrod's sack at him, gathered his own and said curtly to the guard, "We will return at a more auspicious time. I apologize for the trouble this *djinn* has caused."

Hastily they exited. Cursing, the guard slammed the door. Around the corner, Terence asked out of the side of his mouth, "Was she there?"

"I glimpsed a woman who fits Miss Helen's description. I know she heard my instructions. We'll soon discover if it was she."

The Bagnio Balek, the largest prison in Algiers, was located in the center of the city. It was a grim oblong building with two upper galleries supported by squat stone pillars. Swaggering arrogantly, Beau rapped on the door with the hilt of his dagger. The portal swung open to reveal the Guardian Bashaw sitting on a stone bench inside the antechamber smoking his water pipe. His Turkish guards lounged beside him. They were armed with swords, pistols, and cudgels; the chains, halters, and handcuffs hanging ready on the walls attested to the grim purpose of this gloomy, smelly hell-hole.

Beau nodded politely and pulled the work order from his cloak with a flourish. "The *Scorpion* must be readied for sea today. I want the English prisoners escorted to the Marine Gate and put to work immediately."

The Bashaw pulled his pipe from his mouth, burped, and said, "Why must you have the English prisoners? They are already committed to work elsewhere today." He stuffed the order in his tunic after reading it.

"Because the work I want done is too menial for my own men." Beau sniffed. "And I want to see how they have progressed under your loving care. I did capture them, after all."

The Bashaw guffawed. He ordered one of the hovering guards, "Tell Estevez to bring the English Nazranis here. They work at the harbor today."

Ten minutes later, the shuffling of feet was heard. A baker's dozen men emerged into the antechamber, rubbing their eyes. Sleep was a precious commodity in the bagnio, and only those fortunate enough to have coin to purchase a bunk had much of it. The rest slept in the halls on stone floors. Beau appraised the tired, ragged group of men as they sullenly answered their roll call. He swallowed his compassion, for the Bashaw would respect only the arrogance of a favored reis. Beau had been imprisoned here, and he knew what rigors they'd faced.

They'd not yet noticed him standing in the shadows. They looked thin and weary, but at least they were not chained, and they walked as if they had not recently tasted the bastinado.

perhaps they would be strong enough. If they were to survive what lay ahead, they'd have to be.

He moved forward when the roll call was done. McAllister, face shaggy with a brown beard, turned his head. His eyes fired with outrage and hatred. He took a furious step forward.

The corporal, Estevez, saw the look on his face and cuffed him in the jaw. "Keep a respectful look about you. You work for Sinan Reis today."

McAllister hawked and spat at Sinan's feet. His face changed not a whit when Estevez cuffed him again, harder. "I'll not work for ye, ye scoundrel," McAllister growled in English. "What hae ye done wi' the Lady Victoria?"

Beau crossed his arms over his chest and looked stern. "I see you've not whipped the insolence out of them yet," he said in Turkish to the Bashaw.

When the Bashaw lifted his hand to have McAllister taken away, Beau strode up to McAllister and looked him eye to eye. "That won't be necessary. I'll teach this dog some manners before I return him, that I promise you."

Before McAllister could make another rash comment, Beau wheeled and opened the bagnio door himself. He jerked his head, and, pushed by Estevez, the men filed past him. Each cast him an angry, resentful look, but McAllister did more.

In a voice harsh with menace, he warned, "Ye'll not always hae the upper hand. Ye'll regret yet what ye done tae us an' our mistress."

Beau pretended not to hear. After thanking the Guardian Bashaw, he exited, watching the prisoners march to the Marine Gate under escort. This would be one hell of a voyage, he thought ruefully. *If* they ever made it out of the mole.

The sun was full up by the time he reached the house. Beau nodded in answer to Kahlil's questioning look.

"So far, so good. Is Jarrod back?" At Kahlil's nod, Beau looked to where he pointed.

Tory was on her knees beside Jarrod, speaking to him earnestly. Steadfastly the boy stared over her head, but Beau could read his tension.

He approached the pair and heard Tory say, "But Jarrod, Sinan would love to have you with him. He told me so."

"Indeed I did, Jarrod. You'd be a great help to me if you'd come."

Tory rose, looking at him in relief, but Jarrod stared at his feet. "You say so only out of kindness. What do I know of your world?"

Beau knew better than to pull the stiff little body into his arms, as he wanted to. Instead, he tapped one finger thoughtfully on his cheek. "People are people wherever you go, and I've never known a boy who knows them better than you do. With your knowledge of languages and business, I can train you to work in my father's shipping office. In fact, you'd be doing me a favor. I won't have to seek an assistant when I go home."

Tory looked sharply at him. So his father owned a shipping company . . . She was almost disappointed. If he'd been poor, her devotion would have had more meaning.

Finally Jarrod looked up, a flicker of hope in his eyes. "Truly?"

"Truly." Beau offered his hand. "Shall we shake to seal our bargain?"

Solemnly Jarrod put his hand into Beau's. Beau leaned close to whisper, "Thank you for what you did for me. In a moment, you must tell me what you learned."

After they shook hands, Beau escorted Tory to the stairs. "Have you packed? Said good-bye to Lahtil?"

"We breakfasted together, but I haven't told her yet. Sinan . . ."

"No more questions now, Tory. Tonight I'll answer everything, I promise. Just do as I've asked. We'll lunch together, and then you must board the *Scorpion* and wait. Becky will be sent home, don't worry."

With a disgruntled look, Tory went up the stairs. She glanced under the trapdoor as Sinan had ordered, gasped, and drew out her jewels. He'd filched them from his comrades, not for his own gain but to keep them safe for her. Even when she'd spat and scratched at him like a wildcat, he'd been considerate.

Tory put the jewels in her cloak, wiped her eyes, and went to conclude the hardest of her chores. She found Lahtil just leaving her room.

"Good morning again, Tory." She smiled. "Has the master returned?"

Tory nodded. She led Lahtil back into her chamber, where she drew her down to a cushion. "Lahtil, Sinan and I are leaving this very night, if all goes well."

The pretty smile faded. "Oh, Tory, I'll miss you so," Lahtil whispered.

"I'll miss you more, I warrant. You're the best friend I've ever had." The two women embraced fiercely.

Tory drew back to look at her. "Perhaps you and Kahlil can visit us."

"Am I still to be sold to him?" Lahtil caught her bottom lip between white teeth and held her breath.

"I think the master has a plan that will allow Kahlil to ask for you as a reward from the dey." Tory went on to explain, briefly, what Sinan had told her.

Downstairs, Beau hastened back to Jarrod. "Did you accomplish your mission this morning?"

"Yes, Sinan Reis. I saw a tall, pretty, fair-haired woman. I believe she heard my message, as you instructed."

This time Beau couldn't resist a quick hug. "Thank you, my boy. You relieve me mightily. Of course, it might not be Helen, but my gut tells me it is. I'll go to Saud's house late this afternoon. If the guards follow their usual procedure, they'll play dice at dusk. Then is my best chance."

"But what can you do alone, Sinan? Let me come."

"No." Beau shook his head adamantly. "I must do this alone. I need you to help guard my lady. I also want you to lead Orion and Eclipse aboard the *Scorpion*. Tell the gatekeeper I plan to sell them to a buyer in Morocco. Here's some money for the toll."

Jarrod pocketed the coins.

Beau put a hand on the boy's thin but wiry shoulder and looked down at him sternly. "If I do not make it to the ship by sunset, you are to persuade Tory to sail without me." He smiled faintly. "I'm certain my new crew will be only too eager to go. It's Tory I'm worried about. If necessary, lock her in my cabin. Do you understand?"

"Yes, Sinan Reis."

"Good. I know I can depend on you. Pack what belongings you need and be ready to leave after luncheon."

At Beau's insistence, Kahlil ignored protocol and sat down to a gay luncheon with Tory, Lahtil, Beau, and Jarrod. Each knew this would be the first and last time they sat so companionably, and the knowledge gave a special tang to the burghal and piquancy to the sherbet.

At the meal's end, Beau lifted his glass in a toast. "To our future happiness and prosperity."

Each drank wholeheartedly to that. When they put their cups

down and looked at him, Beau stood. "Come, sirs and madams, to your posts."

Jarrod went to the stables; Tory hugged Lahtil a last time and let Kahlil escort her to the door. She paused to look up at Sinan. "Thank you for my jewels," she said huskily.

He smiled the smile that had never failed to move her, even in the beginning. "It's little enough, but all I could save without rousing suspicion." He kissed her hand. "You're not to worry about Becky, now. Kahlil will fetch her as soon as he can get away and put her on a ship for England. I've sent a messenger to tell her we're leaving. He takes funds enough for her to buy passage if for some reason Kahlil cannot reach her. She'll be fine."

When he released her hand, she cradled it against his cheek. She could ransom her men as soon as she got away, so all her worries were appeased. Except the greatest one . . .

"Please be careful," she said. "When will you join us?"

"By sunset." He hesitated, then added, "If I should not be there by then, go without me." He put his fingers over her lips when she would have protested. "It won't help me for you to be taken again. Go back to England, and I'll come for you when I can."

When her lips trembled under his fingers, he removed his hand to give her a gentle kiss. "Don't cry, love. Nothing under heaven or on earth can keep me from you, now I've found you. Not even your own pride."

While she was puzzling over this cryptic comment, Beau looked at Kahlil over her head. "Return quickly so we can set the last wheel in motion."

He kissed Tory's forehead. "You've a surprise awaiting you aboard ship. Remember me when you see it."

Tory's last glimpse of Algiers passed in a haze of tears, but she mourned it not. Her thoughts and mind, indeed, her heart, were left with the dynamic man who was about to embark on a last mysterious mission. Instinctively, she knew he'd made light of the danger. Her heart thrummed with fear for him.

When they reached the Marine Gate, Tory roused enough to hear Kahlil's response to the gatekeeper's query as to their destination. "Sinan Reis is taking this woman to sell her in Constantine. She must board his ship."

Shock rippled through Tory. For one horrible instant she wondered if it was true as they passed through the gate, Jarrod following, leading the horses after paying his toll.

She scolded herself. Sinan had proved time and time again that he was honorable. She had no reason to doubt him now. She told herself that over and over, but always at the back of her mind beat the doubt, *Then why won't he tell you who he is?*

However, when they boarded the *Scorpion*, all else was wiped from her head. "McAllister," she whispered.

Then, "McAllister!" She flew to him, and he, his strong face sagging with relief, for once forgot his Scottish reserve. He caught her in his arms. For one heady moment they were not mistress and employee but two compatriots overjoyed to see each other.

"Lass, it's that glad I am t' see ye." He set her away, an embarrassed flush reddening his face. "Has that divil harmed ye?"

It was Tory's turn to blush. "I'm fine, Captain McAllister." She looked him over. "I wish your captivity had been as pleasant."

"I've had worse. I'll be fine, lass. Noo, why are ye come?"

Tory looked over to the two bagnio guards who were watching suspiciously. McAllister saw them watching and went back to mending a sail. With a final salute to Tory, Kahlil returned to shore, taking Omar with him. Tory leaned against the mast and started talking in a low voice. Under cover of the sail, she passed McAllister the small pistol Sinan had given her.

Kahlil had been muttering resentfully about Sinan for the past couple of days, so none of the guards were surprised when the confrontation occurred late that afternoon. Kahlil had just returned to the house when Sinan ordered him harshly, "Come here. I want to speak with you." He turned on his heel and strode to the rear of the courtyard.

The other guards strained to hear, but could not. Sinan's gestures grew more angry, Kahlil's posture more hostile, until finally Sinan exploded, "How dare you question my actions? I'm accountable to no one!"

"Not even His Excellency? It's time he was told of your odd behavior," Kahlil threatened back.

There was an expectant hush; then Sinan drew back a fist and hit his officer in the jaw. Kahlil snapped his head back under the blow and crumpled against the wall. His head sagged on his chest.

Sinan leaned over, apparently to see if he was conscious, but he whispered, ''Send word to me of the dey's reaction when you can. We'll send you further instructions as to what to do after you resign. Allah be with you and Lahtil.''

Then, scowling, Sinan stalked past his shocked guards and out the door. He carried only his weapons, the clothes he wore, a money pouch, and the map. At last he'd conclude his mission. One way or the other . . .

To his profound relief, he saw a kerchief hanging from the northeast window of the harem. He'd sensed she was here, but it was comforting to have proof at last. Frowning, he appraised the house that was as well fortified as the Bastille. It was to be the hard way. He pulled his pistols from his belt and loaded them.

Omar slapped Kahlil's cheeks until he groaned and opened his eyes. ''Why did you quarrel with Sinan Reis?''

Kahlil came alert at the question. He leaped to his feet, but swayed back against the wall. He held his hand out to Omar. ''Help me get to the dey. I must warn him.''

''Warn him of what?''

''If I'm to accuse my captain of treason, I must go to the dey first. Quickly, there's not a moment to lose.''

Somehow, the walk to the dey was anything but quick as Kahlil stumbled every other step. But his mind moved with agility around the best words to use. The dey would be furious that the warning came so late, but Sinan had given him the means to appease that anger. The cache of sequins and jewels, some earned even when Sinan was still a captive, should soothe Mustapha considerably. And he should look with favor upon the man who so honestly delivered it. Surely he would want to reward Kahlil with the meager price of one female slave?

Saud's three guards were dicing when the rap came at the door. One of them got up, grumbling, to answer it. He frowned when he saw Sinan Reis standing outside, his cloak drawn closely about him despite the heat.

''Yes?'' he asked politely, unwilling to offend this favored corsair.

''I have a message for Saud from the dey.''

"Saud is not here. You can leave it with me."

Sinan shook his head. "I'm to deliver it personally." He barged in and sat down on a bench. "I'll wait."

Scowling, the guard slammed the door and sat back down to his coffee, eyeing the arrogant corsair with disfavor. When Sinan leaned back at his ease and looked bored, the guards relaxed and returned to their game.

When they were arguing over a point, Sinan whipped a pistol from his cloak. "If you value your lives, you'll very quietly bind one another." He tossed some cords at their feet, then leveled a second pistol on them.

They looked stunned, then furious. One enterprising fellow peered up the stairway and opened his mouth—to find it filled with the business end of Sinan's pistol.

Icily determined green eyes froze the sound in his throat. Sinan held his second pistol on the other two, gesturing with it impatiently. One guard reluctantly began tying up the other. When he finished, Sinan removed the pistol barrel from his captive's mouth and prodded him in the chest with it. "Tie up your comrade."

The guard obeyed shakily, too frightened now for further boldness. When he was done, Beau pulled his hands behind him and tied him up; then he gagged all of the guards with their sashes and heaved them to their feet. He shoved them inside a storeroom and quickly trussed them together to a pillar in the middle of a cleared space.

He saluted them mockingly. "Have a peaceful rest." He closed the door and stole up the stairs, blessing the heat that had caught the household napping. As Jarrod had said, two eunuchs were on guard, but one was dozing and the other was mopping his sweating forehead, looking bored.

Sinan hesitated. He could use his dagger to silence the man who was awake, and he could knock the other one out. But he hated to kill indiscriminately. The poor devils had hardship enough to live with as it was. Even in the stress of the moment, Sinan shook his head in commiseration. No, boldness had carried him this far. Perhaps it would carry him a little farther. He belted his pistols and drew his cloak over them.

Whistling, he rounded the corner. The more alert eunuch stiffened. He rose to his imposing height, his hand reaching for his scimitar. "By whose permission do you enter here?" he demanded in outrage. He recognized Sinan, but this corsair had no right to approach another's harem. His hand tightened warily about the hilt of his weapon.

Sinan took a few steps closer before pausing. He looked about in confusion, then clapped his hand to his forehead. "I came to see Saud. I'm sorry, I didn't mean to invade his harem." A lusty grin stretched his face. He walked another step closer, almost within striking distance.

"Still, now I'm here, can I have one peek?" He strained to see beyond the shadowy grille.

The eunuch was pulling at his sword when Beau knocked him out with his pistol butt. He quickly did the same to the sleeping guard, who never knew what hit him.

He rapped on the harem door, calling softly, "Helen, Helen, come quickly. It's Beau." He waited. No response.

He searched in the eunuch's pocket for the key, found it, and unlocked the harem doors, entering without a second thought. "Helen," he called urgently. One woman peered around a door at him. She was scandalously clad in a sheer kaftan and little else. Beau spared her an appreciative glance before she slammed the door, squealing an alarm. He proceeded down the corridor, his heart drumming. Finally, when he got no response except gasps and squeaks from dark-haired lovelies, he resorted to opening the doors. One languid beauty sprawled on a plush divan raked him with an appreciative glance. He blew her a cheeky kiss and continued down the corridor.

He found Helen in the last room—bound and gagged. Quickly he freed her and drew her into his arms. "Ah, Helen, I thought I'd never see you again," he sighed into her rose-scented hair. His arms tightened. Something good had come of this debacle after all.

She burst into tears, clutching at him with trembling fingers. "Oh, Beau, I'm so glad to see you! How is Bobby?"

"I'm sorry, little sister, but we've no time. Come."

He wrapped her cloak about her and attached her veil, averting his eyes from her revealing costume, and hustled her down the corridor. When a red-haired houri tried to block their path, he shoved her out of the way without a qualm. She landed on her backside, screeching abuse.

Beau quickly slammed the door behind them, locked it, and tossed the key into the shadows. That should keep the eunuchs busy for a few moments when they awoke to check their precious charges for harm.

''That red-headed witch tied me up,'' Helen explained as they hastened down the stairs. ''She saw me put the handkerchief in the window and suspected an escape attempt. She intended to tell Saud when he returned.'' She grimaced at him, and he glimpsed her old dry wit when she added, ''You've never experienced politics until you've lived in a harem. Congress is positively courteous in comparison. She's become Saud's favorite of late and will do anything to curry favor with him.''

They were out the door before Beau breathed easily. ''Walk as rapidly as you can without drawing attention,'' he warned out of the side of his mouth.

She obeyed despite the fact that the cobblestones bit through the thin soles of her slippers. They hurried more with every step until, by the time they approached the Marine Gate, they were running. Beau threw uneasy glances at the sun, lowering ominously in the sky. In another fifteen minutes, it would set.

He drew the proper toll from his pocket and offered it to the gatekeeper with a nonchalant ''I'm taking my new woman on a pleasure voyage.'' The gatekeeper arched an eyebrow, but if Sinan was man enough to service two at once . . . He accepted the fee with an envious sigh.

They had sighted the *Scorpion* when a vaguely familiar back loomed up ahead. The man turned.

Sinan groaned: Ahmet. Of all times . . .

Hatred burned in Ahmet's eyes as he looked at Beau. He eyed Helen's bracelet, from which dangled a telltale ram's head— Saud's symbol.

''At last you make a mistake, infidel,'' he crowed. ''To steal another's woman is a crime you cannot talk your way out of.''

Beau pushed Helen around Ahmet. ''Quickly, run to that dinghy and row for the *Scorpion.* '' He pointed to his ship. He could see Tory and McAllister standing at the rail, watching. Helen complied.

''Out of the way, Ahmet, or I'll do what I should have done long ago and end your miserable existence.'' Beau drew his pistol.

Ahmet scrambled out of the way, snarling, ''Go, infidel. The guns will kill you before you clear the mole.''

When Beau hastened around him, Ahmet kicked him in the knee. He fell, the pistol flying from his hand. Before he could pull his other, Ahmet was upon him.

Beau dodged the fist aiming for his nose. It grazed his cheek.

He slammed his own fist into Ahmet's Adam's apple, feeling savage satisfaction when the Arab choked. Using his knees, he flung Ahmet backwards, then leaped to his feet. Still prone, all Ahmet could do was grab.

He caught the end of Beau's sash, which had come undone in the hurried walk. Beau felt it give, but knew only the primitive need for escape. He leaped into a dinghy and literally rowed for his life.

Thus he didn't see the scroll Ahmet picked up and looked at narrowly. The Arab hurried back to the gate.

Beau was panting when he reached the *Scorpion* in time to assist Helen aboard. "Prepare to depart!" he yelled.

Every man aboard scrambled to get the *Scorpion* to sea despite their hatred of the man who had given the order. Their necks were stuck out just as far as his.

However, Tory had other thoughts on her mind. She thanked God for sparing him, but THIS was his last mission? She clasped her hands behind her back to hide their trembling, looking from the fair head to the brown one. "Who is this woman, Sinan Reis?" She emphasized his title, her eyes steady on his. "More to the point, who are you?"

When Beau didn't answer, Helen took pity on this lovely woman who looked so frightened. Thinking to reassure, she removed her veil to reveal classically beautiful features. With a loving look at Beau's rigid figure, she answered, "My rescuer, Beaufort Avery Cochran. My—"

But the words were snatched from Helen's mouth by the harbor guns' first blast. It shook the *Scorpion* from port to starboard and from stern to bow, though they were too close under the mole for it to land. But Tory felt it not. She was debilitated under the impact of that name.

Her face drained of every vestige of color as she looked into the pleading eyes of the man she loved. Only pride kept her upright under the waves of unbearable pain.

"Beaufort Avery Cochran," she repeated dully.

It was a name she recognized.

PART IV

"Let every soul look upon the morrow for the
deed it has performed."

—THE KORAN, 59:18

Chapter 13

Beau took a step toward her, but she didn't back away. She looked down her regal nose at him and said tonelessly, "You egotistical bastard. Humiliating me wasn't enough. You didn't just lust after my body. You lusted after my self-respect. Well, you've won. I hate myself."

The scent of panic wafted across the deck as the English seamen looked about them in bewilderment at the strange xebec, but Beau heeded it not. McAllister was left to give what orders he could, for Beau was blind to all but Tory's ashen face.

"No, Tory, it's not as you think. Let me explain . . ." He reached for her arm, but she flinched away. And then there was no time.

McAllister interrupted impatiently, "Ye must mon the helm since ye ken the harbor best. Get below, lassie. I ken not what this scoundrel's done t' ye, but he'll help us noo if he values his neck." McAllister stuck Beau's own gun in his ribs. Tory stumbled below, Helen following.

Thus Beau was forced to watch his worst nightmare come true. But duty, always cursed duty, forbade him to follow his instincts and pursue Tory. He glanced at the circle of ragged men who were scared, angry, and desperate for guidance.

Snarling his frustration, he whirled on McAllister and knocked the gun away. "Keep your impudent hands to yourself. Without my help you'd be rotting in the bagnio, you fool. If you want to live to see the sunrise, stand out of my way."

A menacing rumble answered him as the Englishmen banded about their captain, circling Beau like a school of sharks.

Propping his hands on his hips, Beau roared, "By the saints, if you don't obey, every man jack of you, I'll sit on my duff and let them blow us to perdition!"

The clustered men looked at one another in consternation. McAllister's pebbly brown eyes didn't soften, but he was a realist. "Aye, yer blood's as thin as ours." He rapped out of the side of his mouth to his erstwhile crew, "Hatches battened doon, gear clear for running.'' And, to Beau, ''What else would ye have us do?''

Beau relaxed a little. ''Where are the bagnio guards who escorted you to the ship?''

''Havin' a brisk evenin' swim.'' McAllister nodded to two figures flailing in the water near the mole.

That concern allayed, Beau turned to more pressing matters. One by one he fixed each sailor with a stern look. ''Men, I don't blame you for your resentment, considering our last encounter, but I assure you my neck is as precious to me as yours is to you. If we're to get out of this in one piece, you must obey me. Are you with me?'' When he got grudging nods, he cast a wary eye at the mole, then continued hastily, ''Built low and narrow for speed as she is, this vessel takes on a lot of water. The footing will be tricky when we get under way if you don't stay on the grating to the sides.'' Beau stomped the platform on which he stood. Another grating banded the opposite side of the *Scorpion*.

''In this fair wind we should be able to use the square sails, but be ready to switch to lateens if we lose the wind. Got it?'' Again, reluctant nods. ''Heave short,'' he ordered curtly. McAllister relayed the command, and two seamen began hauling in the anchor cable until there was scant slack on the line. As soon as the sheets were set for sailing, they could hoist the anchor and get under way with full control instead of bobbing about like a cork on a line, unfurled sails fighting against the anchor's tug.

Beau jerked his head at a group of men. ''You four, aloft. Loose all sails.'' When McAllister looked at him as if he'd run mad, Beau smiled dryly. ''Aye, it's a tricky anchorage, but I've navigated it many a time. We need all sail, for time is of the essence.'' He gazed piercingly at the remaining men.

''Do any of you have gunner experience?'' When two men nodded, he ordered, ''Run out the larboard guns. Fire only on my order.'' They scurried to obey. Only McAllister heard Beau's aside, ''Pray God we won't have to use them.''

Narrow-eyed, Beau watched the gunners load the guns from the muzzle, ramming first shot, then powder down the bore, then pouring more powder on the touchhole wick. Their movements were a mite jerky but became smoother as they worked. Beau nodded. They'd do.

Beau took the helm from a relieved crewman, ordering tersely, ''Go aloft and keep a sharp eye out for pursuit.''

McAllister handed the man the eyeglass he'd found in the captain's cabin and turned to glare at Beau. "And what am I t' do? Stand as figurehead?"

"You are mate, of course. The men will doubtless respond more readily to your commands than to mine. Set the fore and tops'ls." McAllister nodded, and his roar echoed across the deck.

McAllister relayed the next commands automatically, for xebec or his own late lamented *Defiant Lady*, getting under way proceeded about the same. "Break her out!" Up came the anchor. "Set all sail!"

The men waiting to raise the mainsails obeyed, and the *Scorpion* quivered as the wind took her. Under Beau's steady hand, she turned away from the mole.

McAllister sniffed at the smoothness with which Beau handled the tricky moment, but he turned a puzzled gaze on the mole, which was slowly receding behind them. Why were they not fired upon?

Beau grinned sardonically at his confusion. "Algerines are a practical lot. Without orders from the dey, they are reluctant to fire upon one of his most prized cruisers commanded by his favorite reis." Beau thought, Kahlil, my friend, may Allah bless you with many sons as fine as you are.

But Allah, it seemed, was not in a blessing mood, for simultaneous with the thought came a flash from shore and an angry roar. Shot whistled past, splashing so close it grazed their bowsprit. The *Scorpion* shook but went gamely on under Beau's steady guidance. Beau was dismayed and puzzled—until a thought occurred to him. He held the helm with one hand long enough to feel his sash, then grabbed the tiller again as he muttered a foul Arabic oath.

"Ahmet!" he said under his breath. The weasel had taken his map of the harbor defenses, and it was apparently proof enough for the gunnery commander that they were to be stopped at all costs. By God, the cost would not be theirs alone. They'd not sink without a fight!

Beau rapped to McAllister, "Bring the larboard guns to bear!" While McAllister was relaying the order, Beau trained an eagle eye on the lighthouse battery.

Even to someone who knew the defenses as well as he did, it was hard to pinpoint exactly where to shoot in the deepening gloom as the sun set below the horizon. The instant the next flash came, Beau heeled the vessel to bring her larboard guns as high as possible, putting her in good firing position but making her vulnerable to a broadside, and cried, ''Fire!''

The *Scorpion* bucked as her guns retorted to the blast that struck the tip of their mizzenmast. Splinters, smoke, and bits of shot rained down upon them, obscuring Beau's vision. Something hot grazed his cheek, but he barely felt it through his relief.

Praise God, they were trying to dismast them. The dey's men badly wanted him alive, it seemed, and the *Scorpion* unharmed. Fortune hadn't deserted them yet. The harbor had guns enough to make mincemeat of their light xebec, but finesse was not an Algerine strong suit. And darkness was upon them . . .

''Douse all lights!'' Beau commanded, tailing off, ''And pray for darkness and a fair wind.'' McAllister himself scrambled to obey.

Beau strained to see through the clearing smoke. His grin was savage as he beheld tiny figures frantically trying to put out the fire their blast had started. A loud explosion, blowing out more defenses as a magazine ignited, was music to Beau's ears. More angry shots came in rapid succession, but Beau didn't order a retaliatory blast. In this gloom, the flash would merely pinpoint their location, and they hadn't a prayer of disabling even part of the harbor's batteries. Darkness, speed, and silence were their best allies now.

''Secure the guns!'' he called softly. ''Bear off!'' McAllister gave the appropriate commands, and the *Scorpion*, wind on her beam, winged for the point and safety.

His instincts proved true as the blind shots went wild. Gleefully, the *Scorpion* sliced through the waves, water sluicing out of her scuppers as she flicked her tail like her namesake and presented only her narrow stern as target. Soon even the eastern battery's shots fell short.

Only the huge sixty-eight-pounders left to go at the southern tip of the mole, Beau thought. He glanced up. The night was cloudy, but fitfully so. So far Diana had kept her smile hidden, but if she beamed just as they rounded the mole . . .

He looked up. The men had fitted the mizzensails to the grazed mast, so they had almost full sail. Beau glanced at McAllister.

''Almost away, my surly friend, but just to be safe, let's sail to windward.'' McAllister nodded in agreement and bawled the necessary commands.

The *Scorpion* zigzagged a tortuous course into the wind. Tacking slowed their progress but made them a difficult target as the twenty-foot guns on the southern battery began firing in the logical way—in a line along their last known course.

Beau and McAllister both let out a breath of relief as, slowly, even that awesome firepower began to recede. Beau eased his sweaty grip on the tiller and prepared to turn it over to McAllister so he could go below, his thoughts flying to Tory.

Came a cry from the lookout, "Sail ho astern!"

Beau craned his neck and made out the ghostly gleam of sails bearing down abaft of them. At that moment, the moon emerged from the clouds, giving him a clear view of the ship. Beau groaned. The regency's proudest acquisition, the *Crescent*, a frigate bestowed so generously upon the dey by America's Congress, was in hot pursuit. And dammit, the wind was picking up.

"Brace the yards, smart now!" he yelled, gripping the tiller tight again. Even the men aloft heard his frantic bellow. They didn't wait for McAllister to relay the order, for they knew they hadn't a chance against the frigate. The men scrambled to turn every rag to the wind. Soon the wind was at their beam. Water foamed over the sides and through the grates as they picked up speed, but the frigate still gained on them by maneuvering likewise. Soon she was close enough to fire with her bow guns, but her shots went wide because the xebec presented such a narrow stern.

Beau debated quickly and silently. In this brisk wind, the *Crescent* would soon run them down. If they were to stand and fight, he preferred to choose the time and place. Besides, it had been his experience that the corsairs were ineffective campaigners. They preferred the direct approach—boarding and hand-to-hand combat. Since the *Crescent*'s crew outnumbered them and the frigate was swifter, he had no choice but to test his men's wits and skills against her.

What irony, Beau reflected sardonically, that he, an American patriot laboring for his country's cause in an Algerine xebec, should be outgunned by an American-built ship bestowed on the enemy by his own government. Praying the fates could not be so unkind, he turned to McAllister.

"Prepare to come about, McAllister." When the Scotsman looked at him askance, Beau growled, "Engaging them is our only hope. If we come about now, we'll be ready for them when they draw abeam. Aye, we don't have as many guns, but we've abler gunners. Let's see what stomach they have for a broadside. Ready the starboard guns.''

Looking grim, McAllister relayed the commands. When the sails were set, Beau yelled, ''Helm's alee!'' and put the tiller down. The *Scorpion* shuddered, sails flapping, as she turned in the eye of the wind, but then she caught the new tack and went gamely on. The moon allied itself with them for the moment, and they were able to perform the maneuver in the darkness. The *Crescent* gave another roar with her bow guns, but she was as blind as she was bold. Beau strained to see.

The *Crescent* was also running without lights, and he was fearing he'd have to guess when to fire when the moon peeked out. Beau gasped and shouted, ''Fire!'' for the frigate was almost past them. The *Scorpion* shook as her guns reported. Beau glimpsed their gunports hastily opening, but they were too late. The frigate took part of their broadside, but the ships shot past each other too fast for them to do more than stave in a few planks far above the waterline.

Angrily, bristling like a wolverine, the *Crescent* wore ship to pursue. The *Scorpion*, sails shortened for action, waited, gun ports bared like the teeth of a snarling fox cornered in its den. Indeed, guile and skill were their only chance against the frigate's brute strength.

McAllister and another crewman had left their posts to help man the guns, so they were ready with most ordnance when the *Crescent* drew abeam. To a man, they braced themselves, for this time the frigate was expecting them. Simultaneously the two ships fired. However, the *Scorpion*'s low hull made a smaller target, and the frigate's gunners were as ineffectual as Beau had suspected. All but two shots went wild. These slammed into the deck, damaging some rigging but injuring no one. Beau breathed a sigh of relief, for he hadn't a man to spare.

Their shot hit the frigate in several places just above the waterline. She began to draw in water. Bellowing orders, Beau veered sharply away as soon as they were past her.

They sailed a short distance and turned to position themselves for the next encounter. The moon passed in and out of clouds. They hadn't a hope of outrunning the frigate into darkness, so Beau didn't even contemplate it. But they had their advantages as well: At least the xebec was more maneuverable and, in a lighter wind, swifter.

Events bore him out as the frigate clumsily tried to follow their sharp turn and bring her guns to bear again, but she was too big to outpoint them, especially settling under water as she was. Angrily she lumbered after them.

Beau's ready gunners raked her with shot just above the waterline as they slightly misjudged the swell of the waves. This time the frigate was luckier, and two of her shots struck home. The *Scorpion*, too, began to draw, but not as badly.

Beau opened his mouth to give the order, but McAllister had already sent the lookout below to man the pumps. Beau peered at the frigate, which was turning clumsily after them. While their shots had taken their toll on the *Crescent*, another engagement could cripple them as well. He debated running for the open sea, but the frigate was still almost fully maneuverable. It would be best to end this now. He knew of only one way to do it without risking another broadside.

"Man the stern chasers," he ordered grimly. "Aim both guns for her mainmast. As you value your lives, men, don't miss. Fire when ready."

McAllister and the three other gunners exchanged a grim look, secured the larboard guns and silently readied the two small stern guns. One shot each would they be allowed before the frigate was in position for another broadside. They had to make them count.

Smoothly they loaded. Blowing on their matches, they watched the frigate approach, her sails luminescent under the watchful moon. The *Crescent*, swift and sure as good American know-how had made her, bore down to strike the killing blow.

From captain to able seaman, the *Scorpion*'s crew watched tensely as the gunners decided their fate. At the last possible moment, they touched wick to fuse.

Boom! the small cannons reported. This time Allah was generous. Both shots struck true. With a satisfying crack, the frigate's mainmast split and toppled to the deck. Screams sounded as the timber crushed human and inanimate matter impartially.

Beau took quick advantage. "Spread all sail, men! Let's get away while we may! Close all ports!" Each seaman obeyed eagerly. Slowly the distance between the two vessels grew.

The frigate tried to follow, but she was too crippled to match their speed. However, an enraged shout echoed over the water in a voice Beau recognized. "All the curses of hell upon you, infidel! May your daughters look like camels and your sons like women . . .''

The insults slowly faded into the night. Beau's face lit with unholy glee as he grabbed his speaking trumpet and shouted back, ''May your welcome be warm when you return to Algiers, Ahmet!''

But his smile quickly faded . . . Tory. Something told him the engagement past would be child's play compared to the battle to come. Turning the tiller over to a hand, Beau squared his shoulders. He turned to go below—and found his way blocked by McAllister.

''Ye're a gifted mariner, pirate or nae, and thankful I am. But ye've some explainin' t' do, laddie, before ye gang near the lass.'' A crewman had lit several lanterns, now they were safely away, so Beau's expression was clear.

Even the stout McAllister blinked at Beau's sudden fury. Cool as a cucumber he'd been throughout the battle. Why had he reached the limits of his patience now?

Indeed, Beau caught McAllister's tattered shirt in his fist and hauled the shorter man to his toes, growling, ''Not you, not the duchess, not even Tory herself will keep me from her. She became mine by her own choice, and I've never laid a hand on her in anger. That's all you need to know of our affairs.'' Beau let the Scotsman go in disgust.

McAllister calmly straightened his shirt and shook his head at his men, who growled at Beau's temerity. But he didn't budge from Beau's path, either. So this pirate knew of the duchess, did he? There was something odd going on here. For the mistress's sake, he needed to find out what.

Thus justifying his own curiosity, McAllister answered mildly, ''It's the mistress ye must convince. But t' get t' her, ye must go through me—after ye've told me who ye are.''

Beau's lip curled. ''A fearsome Barbary pirate, who just happened to risk his neck for your mistress—several times—and for the lives of your own worthy self and your scurvy crew.'' Beau sent a challenging look to the men encircling him.

'' 'Tis odd indeed. First ye capture us. Then ye free us and lead us t' victory against yer former comrades when ye could ha' well betrayed us. So I'll overlook yer rudeness if ye talk, laddie.'' McAllister glanced at his men, who were picking up belaying pins and edging nearer, ''Fast.''

Would he spend the rest of his life making explanations? Beau wondered bitterly, but he had too much respect for his body to see it beaten to a pulp. "I'm Beaufort Avery Cochran, son of Robert Cochran, American merchant. Sent by him and other interested persons to infiltrate the Algerian corsairs, curry favor with the dey, and glean information about Algerian fortifications and political plans."

McAllister and his men looked at one another uncertainly. Wild as the story seemed, it fit the facts. McAllister looked Beau up and down. Aye, he had about him the brash manner of an American. "Ha' ye any proof?"

"Unfortunately, the map I drew of the harbor fortifications was taken from me as I tried to reach the ship. My father will verify my story. If I live to see him." Beau glanced meaningfully at the few sailors who still watched him resentfully, pins bouncing against their palms.

"It so happens," he went on, "my father sent a message to me, asking me, at the duchess's behest, to intercept your mistress in her journey. To keep her safe." Beau's voice was dry at that, but then he leaned nearer McAllister and snapped, "Think, man. Don't you find it strange that we took your vessel without the loss of one life? I informed my men that if any one of you was killed, the killer would forfeit all share of the booty. And I risked everything to get the rest of you away. I felt . . . responsible, you see."

Even the angriest of the seamen looked thoughtful at Beau's obvious sincerity. The seafaring life was a hard one, requiring strong souls to lead it and stronger men to lead them. They recognized authority and truth when they heard it. One by one they put the belaying pins away and melted into the darkness to give the two captains privacy.

McAllister shook his head in admiration. "Ye're a braw lad, t' be sure. I believe ye. But what of yer treatment of the lady Tory? I sense a certain . . . familiarity in yer manners."

Only then did Beau's resolve seem to waver. "That I cannot excuse," he said at last. "Except with the explanation that she's all I've ever looked for in a woman. When I had a chance to win her, I took it. Fault me for that, as I do myself, but what's done is done. She's mine now and I'll not give her up."

McAllister, for all his stern demeanor, had fond memories of a flame-haired lassie in his own youth. She'd married another when he would not give up his wandering ways. Deep down he knew he'd made the right choice, but at times, as now, he wondered. Watching the myriad emotions play across Beau's strong face, McAllister sighed. For lost youth, for hot heads, for the feeling that made the world go 'round.

He had only one question left. "Are yer intentions honorable?"

That, at least, was easy for Beau to answer. "Yes. If she'll have me."

When Beau's regard did not waver, McAllister stepped aside and offered his hand. "That's good enough for me, laddie. Good luck t' ye." He dropped a slow wink. "And invite me t' the first christenin'."

Beau shook his hand firmly, wishing he were as confident. He went below, his steps steadier than his nerves.

McAllister strolled about the deck, looking at the stars. He wondered if his long-ago love ever gazed and remembered, as he did. Then, like the practical Scotsman he was, he went briskly about assigning duties to the men.

As they left the harbor, Tory hurried below and took the only cabin with a lock. She stiffened as she realized whose it was, but right now privacy was imperative, so she smothered her revulsion, jerked the quilt from the bunk, and sat down in a chair. Her instincts proved true, for Helen came knocking at the door shortly after.

When Tory ignored her entreaties she went away. For minutes, Tory was in such a stupor that she barely heeded the blasts shaking the ship's timbers, landing uncomfortably close. Once she wished, absently, that they'd land nearer and spare her the necessity to think ever again.

Her eyes focused vaguely on the Spartan cabin: narrow bunk with sea chests at one end, table and four chairs and a built-in cabinet against the wall containing charts and nautical instruments. Sinan's cabin.

No, she corrected herself dully, Beaufort Avery Cochran's cabin. And the pain that swamped her was so numbing that she barely recognized McAllister's voice.

"Lassie, douse the light. Milady, do ye hear me?"

Tory stumbled over to blow out the lantern, then groped her way back to the chair and cocooned herself in the blanket. But no matter how she tried to pretend, she wasn't in her mother's womb any longer, innocent, unknowing.

And the friendly darkness became a beast engulfing her in

memories. She went down, down to his belly where all she had suffered to become was consumed by the bitter bile of the truth she'd labored to learn. How well she remembered the name Beaufort Avery Cochran . . .

That April of 1795, Tory was to attend her first masked ball during her debut season. At seventeen, she considered such an event exciting, even when her grandmother insisted that she attend. For once, their wishes agreed. At last she'd be able to wear the costume she'd found in the attics.

When dressed, she turned this way and that, appraising herself in her glass. What ancestress had been so daring? she wondered. She'd have to hold her cloak tightly about herself, else Greaty would never let her out of the house. Becky was hard enough to convince.

"I'm no green girl, Becky, and I've heard other ladies wear far more revealing costumes," she said into Becky's protests.

"Other *married* ladies, miss mule." Becky frowned at the tall, voluptuous Queen Boadicea Tory made.

Diaphanous golden silk swathed every pronounced curve. Two gold discs, stiffened with buckram, were lavishly embroidered to look like breastplates. They glittered with every breath Tory took, embellishing the bosom that, even at seventeen, was impressive. A gilded chain cinched her waist; her regal braids were accented by a savage gilded crown inset with glass cabochon rubies. When Tory put on the brief gilded mask, each side winging up and down her cheekbones but barely covering her eyes, she could have been the Icenian queen herself, come back to haunt the Roman descendants of the men who had dared to steal her kingdom.

Becky shook her head. "Some Roman centurion is like to carry you off, dressed that way."

"Pooh!" Tory scoffed. "The lily-livered dandies I've met wouldn't be so bold." Tory was enjoying her first season, but she was beginning to find her suitors' adulation a trial. She'd soon realized their fulsome but innocuous compliments were seldom sincere and always self serving. She began to watch their eyes, raking over her or appraising her jewels, rather than listen to what they said. She meant nothing to them beyond the two purposes society allowed women. To those with pockets to let, she was golden security; to those with wealth, she was a well-bred filly being groomed as a brood mare.

She'd be neither. She would wed only if she found a man she could respect who would respect her in return, not because of her name, her appearance, or her fortune but because of her character. If she was being unreasonable, well, surely that was one of the prerogatives of her position. Of what use were her wealth and status if they forced her to become as much a man's servant as any tenant's wife?

Her grandmother, as stubborn and single-minded as her granddaughter, dismissed such foolish notions. Greaty badly wanted an heir, if not of the Grenville name, at least of the Grenville blood. The title had passed to a cousin several times removed when the duke died, for there were no direct male heirs. Only Westland itself had been entailed, however. The mines, the ships, the Indies estates, remained in Greaty's hands. To pass to Tory. And her heir.

So her grandmother rode roughshod over Tory's proclamation that she wanted to wed for love, as Greaty herself had. "Sentimental drivel! My marriage was arranged by my father as you well know."

Clarissa, dowager duchess of Westmont, was short, plump, and round of face, but imposing withal. Perhaps it was the arrogance in the set of her stubborn chin, or the intelligence in her sharp hazel eyes, but she was seldom treated with anything but respect. By anyone, that is, but her recalcitrant granddaughter.

"And you were in love with Grandfather before your wedding trip began."

"So? If you'd respect my judgment as I respected my father's, you might experience the same. But no, you insist on choosing your own husband. Well, miss, then choose. That's all I ask. I'll not say you nay as long as he's respectable."

"And potently healthy."

Greaty reddened at Tory's plain speaking. "I've given you too much freedom, gal. I never should have allowed you to breed horses. You need a husband to bridle those wild impulses."

"And such a stable you've given me to select from." Their argument went on as their arguments always did: each set in her own opinion, neither really listening or crediting the other with valid concerns. Had Greaty been less insistent, Tory might not have balked; had Tory been more amenable, Greaty might not have pushed so hard. But despite their deep love for each other, the conflict between them grew apace with every soiree and musicale.

Mindful of this conversation on the night of the masked ball, Tory tried to look objectively upon the costumed men begging the favor of a dance. She adored her grandmother, who'd been the constant in her young life since the tragic death of her parents when she was a child. She also knew that ultimately she would have to wed. But as she danced until her feet ached, and as she parried one inane comment after another, she couldn't delude herself, even for Greaty's sake. Pirates, courtiers, kings, and jesters these "noblemen" could pretend to be, but inside they were foppish, excruciating bores. She would be miserable married to any of them, and she'd make them miserabie in return.

She prettily excused herself to her next partner and retreated to a corner, but her golden gown blazed under the thousands of candles, drawing brightly winged males to her flame. Tory cursed her impulse to wear the costume.

Her skin crawled with the sensation of the male eyes attached like leeches to the salient parts of her anatomy. To assuage her discomfort, Tory played her usual game, mentally classifying her suitors into two groups: those who lusted for her fortune, and those who lusted for her person.

One man straddled both categories. Baron Cedric Howard was the son of one of Greaty's closest friends. His title was old, his estates as healthy as his thirty-five-year-old body. Still, his wealth was paltry compared to hers, and by the way he looked at her she knew he wanted more than her possessions. At first, she'd found him maturely attractive, with his tall, muscular physique, black hair, and blacker eyes. He'd been a rakehell in his youth, but since returning from the Continent, not a whisper of scandal had attached to his name.

Greaty approved his suit. "Reformed rakes make exemplary husbands, Tory. You need a strong man. Give him a chance."

She'd flirted with him, testing him as she did each of her suitors, to find that though he had more wit than most, he held her in no greater respect. Besides, something about him bothered her. A certain coldness deep in his eyes, perhaps, that never warmed even when he smiled. Thus, she kept him at bay as she did all her suitors, with a bright smile, a flutter of her fan, and a light remark. However, the tactics were not to work that night. It began when she was surrounded by her usual bevy. Someone asked, "Is it true your grandmother has brought two guests to the ball—Colonials, no less?"

Tory frowned. Greaty had not mentioned guests to her. More tiresome suitors, probably. Tory affected a yawn to disguise her irritation. "I certainly trust not. I daresay they'd step on my toes and dribble their wine." Like the rest of these graceless fops, she thought to herself, but her comments were taken as witty derision of American manners.

Cedric chuckled louder than any. "Fear not, ma'am, I'll keep the boors at bay. The Americans will get short shrift here."

Smiling sweetly behind her mask, Tory cooed, "How gallant of you to wish to protect me. I fear I'd swoon if I were touched by a Colonial reeking of his fields or fish market." Her foot tapped the floor impatiently, but none of her entourage seemed to catch her sarcasm. Tory would not discover until too late that Greaty had arrived in time to hear every word from the shadowed doorway where she stood between two tall men.

More hearty laughter sounded. Cedric bowed. "I would be honored to act as your champion, for whatever reason."

You pompous ass, Tory thought, I don't need your protection. She'd become adept at society's game of conversational backbiting, but suddenly she could bear no more. Perhaps because was tired, perhaps because she wearied of feeling like a meaty bone being eyed by a pack of mongrels, she decided honesty would make a refreshing change.

Her head tilted to an imperious angle. "My poor little heart is thrilled to have so strong a protector, even from so inconsequential a danger. I'll sleep more soundly this night." Even the dullest-witted of her suitors caught the sarcasm that time. They looked uncertainly from her to the baron's reddening face. But Howard recovered quickly.

Bowing from the waist, he purred, "I am gratified that I have set your fears to rest. Members of the fair sex deserve to be cherished and nurtured like the fragile flowers they are, is that not so, gentlemen?"

Put the little woman in her place for daring to criticize the big, strong man, Tory thought. She leaned forward to emphasize her point, then wished she hadn't when every man's eyes lowered to the glittering enticement of her breasts. Her response was a little harsher than she'd intended.

"But some flowers are hardier than others, would you not agree, gentlemen?" Again, concurring nods as ten pairs of eyes reluctantly returned to her face. Tory had an attentive audience when she concluded haughtily, "Some of the loveliest flourish best when left alone but die from a surfeit of attention. Colonial or English blueblood, a bore is still a bore." Rising as regally as Boadicea herself, she sauntered away from them, leaving them buzzing at her rudeness.

Tory sought privacy in the rose arbor in the gardens. A brilliant moon gave a romantic touch to the artistically arranged benches. Tory's enjoyment was spoiled soon enough, however.

Cedric said smoothly over her shoulder, "It's not like you to hide, m'dear. Are you ashamed of yourself?" He sat down on the stone bench next to her.

"Can't you see I want to be alone?"

"Do you? Or do you merely want me to pursue you?"

A long arm draped about her shoulders. Tory stiffened, but she sensed he was excited by her challenging remarks and would welcome the chance to prove how fragile she really was. She was too far from the house to be heard if she screamed, and her pride revolted at the idea. She could handle him herself.

Thus, when he lowered his mouth over hers, she allowed him the kiss. His breath quickened, and he inched a hand up from her waist. With a laugh, Tory caught it, teasing, "Really, Cedric, you'll muss my costume." He tried to kiss her again, but she turned her face away. "Later, when I know you better. We'd best return if we don't want to cause talk. You go first."

He took the bait and swaggered off. Tory was reluctantly rising when she heard loud voices. She walked out of the arbor to investigate.

Some distance away, Cedric stood on the ballroom steps, facing a man with his back to her. He was farther from the light, so all she caught was a tall figure garbed in a black domino. She heard Cedric say, "How dare you spy on us, sir? Gaping at your betters, you Colonial lout?"

Tory gasped when the man with his back to her stuffed the words back into Cedric's mouth with his fist. With a muttered comment she couldn't hear, he stalked into the ballroom. Tory hurried forward in time to see his sun-tipped brown hair before he disappeared inside.

Only when she reached the steps did she notice the third man, helping Cedric to his feet. He dusted off Cedric's jacket. "Forgive my friend, sir. He's most sensitive to British criticism. He lost four brothers in our War for Independence. Truly we did not mean to spy on you. We only wanted to see the gardens.''

''If it were possible to call Cochran out without having Lady Victoria's name bandied about, I'd do so, sir. If he insults me again I'll do so anyway,'' Cedric snarled.

Wondering who Cochran was and why she was involved, Tory walked up to the two men. The stranger turned. He had an open, likable face capped with brown hair, but his bow was short. ''Henry Stoville, ma'am. Forgive the intrusion.'' He retreated.

Tory blushed when she realized what had happened. The Americans must have seen Cedric embracing her. Worse, she'd seemed willing. She glowered at Cedric, who was rubbing his bruised mouth. Without a word, she flounced past him into the ballroom.

She didn't see the angry man again that night, but she caught his friend watching her curiously. When he approached to ask her for the last dance, she accepted.

Tory found that this American had a ready wit and kind heart. He relaxed after they'd talked, as if realizing she'd not sought Cedric's attentions. When he asked to call upon her, she assented.

That night, Greaty came to her room. ''Well, miss, what have you to say for yourself? Why were you so rude to your admirers? The one night I want you to behave yourself and make a good impression—'' Greaty bit her lip and turned away, as if regretting her hasty words.

Tory's eyes narrowed. Wrapping her robe about her, she rose from the chair before her cozy fire and faced her grandmother. ''And why, pray, did you want me to make a good impression?''

''It hardly matters now, since you've given him such a disgust for you. I wanted to introduce you to the son of an American merchant we do business with. I've known the boy for years, and I was most impressed when I saw him again. He's come to England to further their connections. You never saw him, but we heard every word of your conversation with Cedric. What did you mean by seeming so contemptuous of Americans? I know full well you've often admired their spunk.''

Tory sighed, for the first time a bit ashamed of herself. It was a wonder Stoville even asked to dance with her. ''I didn't mean it the way it sounded. I was trying to put Cedric in his place, not insult your guests. But it serves you right if you were embarrassed. You shouldn't spring such a surprise on me.''

Greaty stiffened. ''The only thing that embarrassed me was to have to claim you as my granddaughter. Well, no matter now. Beau Cochran is not a man to push himself where he's not wanted. I doubt either of us will see him again any time soon.'' She stalked out the door.

Tory grinned. How royally she'd sabotaged Greaty's match-making without even knowing it! The arrogant American not only thought her a snob but thought her a woman of loose morals as well. Thank heavens Greaty didn't know about *that*. Here was one unwanted suitor she would not have to contend with.

However, Cochran was a name that came up often over the next weeks. Her friends were agog over the charms of the handsome American, who was rumored to be heir to a large fortune. Even the men, with the exception of Cedric, seemed impressed. The more Tory heard him raved about, the warier she became. She took care that their paths never crossed. Henry Stoville, at least, accepted her explanation of her seeming rudeness readily enough.

''I believe you, Tory. And if your suitors that night are any sample, I can't blame you for using whatever means necessary to keep them in their place. Beau, however, is not so forgiving. I asked him to come with me to meet you and he nearly bit my head off.''

Tory sniffed, her distaste for Cochran's arrogance growing. ''That suits me fine, Henry. Shall we ride?'' She soon had even more reason to dislike Cochran . . .

One day she raved to Henry about the fine gray stallion she'd discovered. The next day, when she sent her manager to purchase it, the animal had been sold—to Beaufort Avery Cochran. Tory furiously took Henry to task.

He'd shrugged sheepishly. ''I didn't realize Beau would buy it or I would not have mentioned it to him.''

''Why does he dislike me so?''

''He says you represent all the things we Americans fought against: arrogance, conceit, power, and selfishness. I've tried to explain you're not at all like you seemed that first night, but he won't believe me.''

Henry looked away, alerting Tory to more calumny. ''Well, what else does he suspect me of? Being a murderess?''

''He . . . disapproves of our friendship.''

That was the last straw. Tory's distaste for Cochran turned into outright animosity. How dare he condemn her unheard, without even meeting her face to face? From that time on, she cultivated her friendship with Henry. At first she did so to spite Cochran, but soon she found, to her surprise, that she was genuinely attracted to Henry.

He was different from any man she'd known: witty but kind, gentle but strong, and always considerate. Somewhat to her regret, the attraction never deepened. She liked him, yes, and admired his fine qualities, but deep down she knew he, too, considered her a weak woman in need of protection. Not even to herself could Tory admit that beneath her independent aspect ran a streak of romanticism a mile wide. She wouldn't, couldn't marry unless she found what Greaty had known: love. Foolish dreams, perhaps, for someone in her position, but ones she couldn't dismiss. She knew Henry Stoville didn't figure in them, but since she enjoyed his company, she sought it.

For three weeks Tory and Henry did everything together. Fate threw him in her path even when they had not arranged to meet. Once, as she exited a Bond Street milliner's, she saw him across the street with Cochran. They were too far away for her to see Cochran's face, which was shadowed by his hat, but she recognized his tall, muscular build and glimpsed honey-brown hair. Henry crossed to speak with her, but Cochran stayed where he was, watching them with stiff disapproval. Tory flirted more strenuously than usual with Henry.

At the end of that conversation, he kissed her hand and begged an audience with her to discuss a serious matter upon his return from Bristol in a week. Mystified, but conscious of Cochran's glare from across the street, she agreed sweetly.

The letter came the next day. It was in a strong, unfamiliar masculine hand. When she read it, she almost choked with rage.

"Madam," it said, "since an appeal to your heart is pointless, I appeal to your Honor as a Lady. Henry is near promised to my sister. The affection between them is real and of long standing. Nevertheless, if you truly care for him, then forget that I have written. If you but toy with his heart, then consider how strained the business relationship between our families will become if Henry spurns my sister because of your spurious affections." There was no ending other than the bold, dark name: Cochran.

The bounder! How dare he presume to lecture her! Besides, Henry's feelings were his own concern. He'd never hinted at anything stronger than friendship. However, a week later, Tory discovered how wrong she was.

Tears came to her eyes as he bent on one knee before her to deliver an impassioned speech. He waited, looking at her expectantly, and only then did Tory realize she'd inadvertently encouraged him by letting him squire her about as she had let no other man. Her lips shaking with distress, she rose and went to the bay window facing the street. She groped for words to make her refusal as painless as possible, but no matter what she said, she knew she'd hurt him.

She wiped her tears away and pasted a bright smile on her face before turning to face him. "Sir, you honor me highly. I value your friendship beyond words. These three weeks spent with you were among the most enjoyable in my life."

When his face lit with hope, she realized such roundaboutation was more cruel than kind and finished hastily, "But I cannot marry you. We should not suit."

His face whitened. Slowly, he rose. "You think yourself too good for me. It's because I'm American."

Tory shook her head violently. "Nay, truly! I'm . . . just not ready to wed." To her own ears, the excuse sounded lame. If only she'd had some warning, she could have prepared herself. Guiltily, she recalled Cochran's letter. But why was she to heed the advice of a man who despised her?

Henry slammed his hat back on his head and stalked to the door, where he turned. "All London knows your grandmother is urging you to wed. You need not lie to me, ma'am. Why in God's name did you encourage me if you had no feelings for me?"

"I . . . did not mean to give you false hope, Henry. I but wanted a friend and truly had no idea of your . . . regard."

But he had already opened the door. He took one step out, then paused to look back and say softly, with a bitterness that ate at Tory's soul, "Beau was right about you. Would to God I'd listened to him." He slammed the door and retreated. Tory knew she'd never see him again.

Tears streamed down her face, both for him and herself, for he'd truly been her best friend since childhood. How had things become such a coil? She moped about the house for the next week, torn between relief and sadness when she heard Cochran and Henry had departed for America.

As the pain faded, resolve took its place. She'd allowed Henry to come too close, to share too many of her thoughts and true feelings. As long as Greaty wouldn't let her retreat to the country and her horses, she'd have to make certain she didn't make the same mistake again.

And so began the behavior that earned her the sobriquet Tory the Terror. She flirted with every male who made advances, but never favored any of them with more than a pretty smile. She never danced more than once with any gentleman, never allowed more than a touch of the hand. Soon it was whispered she was as heartless as she was lovely.

Greaty reacted by introducing more persistent suitors. To keep them at bay, Tory became even more outrageous. She began to gallop in Hyde Park at the fashionable hour and walk the streets without an escort. She even let an occasional curse pass her lips at gatherings. Two years later, she'd earned a fast reputation. She cackled to herself when she heard the gossip, for it was her determination to avoid entanglements that made her seem to encourage them. Let them think what they liked. She'd make Greaty's life so miserable that she'd be forced to send her to the country.

However, Greaty was made of sterner stuff. She was not a woman to turn away from Tory's open declaration of war. That last season was more grim than gay, for both of them. In the midst of it, the dowager duchess delivered her ultimatum: Tory would wed her most loyal suitor, Baron Cedric Howard, or be disinherited. Sure of her upper hand now, Greaty set the date and put the announcement in the papers.

So Tory had been driven to her last act of rebellion. Taking all her jewels and the first portion of her mother's bequest, she fled in her new yacht. To freedom at last . . .

An ugly, bitter laugh rang in the tiny cabin. Freedom. It was but a chimera. Every time she reached for it, she awoke to a living nightmare. This time, at least, she had no one to blame but herself.

From the beginning, she'd suspected Cochran was not what he seemed. She'd even sensed he knew her, but she'd deliberately stifled her misgivings because she was so attracted to him. She might as well experience what she'd be condemned for, she'd told herself.

"You naive fool," she sneered. So masterfully had he seduced her that she'd thought herself the instigator of their tawdry tryst. She'd all but begged him to take her, then reveled in her own humiliation. She was surprised he'd wanted to sully himself in her flesh. He must have longed to humiliate her very badly. How had he managed to hide his contempt?

Well, done was done. He'd used her, as she'd used him. He was nothing but a stud, she tried to tell herself. Men were not the only ones who lusted. Now her curiosity was satisfied, she had no reason to see him again. Yes, that was it. She'd stay locked in this cabin until kingdom come if need be.

Never to see him again . . . Tears burned her eyes, but she gritted her teeth. She would not cry over him. He wasn't worth it. He stirred her heart not at all. He was a blackguard. She didn't love him. She *didn't*.

But painful images flashed though her mind: his gentle possession, his back arching as he spent himself within her; his green eyes stroking her as tenderly as his hands after he saved her from Hassan; his laughter echoing with hers as they sported in their pond. And finally, his obscure plea before they left Algiers: ''No matter what happens, know that what I've done was for need of you. We deserve a chance together if you'll trust me. Trust me. Trust me . . .''

The words echoed in her mind until their clamor drowned out everything but the urgent need to admit the truth. This man, this pirate, this rude American, this liar, cheat, and thief was the only man she would ever love. She loved him, but God, how she hated him, too, for making her admit it even now in the ache of betrayal.

She would nurture her hatred, feed it with resentment, until it crushed her foolish heart. For there was no future for them. They'd had all the happiness God had allowed them. It was time to face reality now. And make the best of it as she had always done.

She realized at last that the ship was quiet. Soon he would come. One last time she would face him. And never, never, would he know how he'd hurt her.

When the knock came, she rose, smoothed her dress and her expression, and went calmly to the door.

Chapter 14

Wiping his sweaty palms on his pantaloons, Beau waited. Would she give him a chance to explain? Dear Lord, show me the right words, he prayed. I've hurt her. Let me make amends.

His turmoil was hidden when Tory opened the door to his knock. They stared at each other. Her face was whiter than he'd ever seen it, but composed. Too composed. She looked at him as if she didn't know him. His heart thudded harder. She would not make it easy for him.

But then nothing easily won was worth having . . . The old saw revitalized him. He'd win this wonderful woman back to his side. Not even her own stubborn pride would stop him.

His warmest smile quirked his lips. "Greetings, milady. We are safe and have but to decide our destination. May we talk?" This time his smile had no effect. She remained frozen, one arm blocking the doorway.

He barely recognized her voice, so stiff was it. "We've naught to discuss. Our destination is clear: England, posthaste. If that's all . . ."

He put his palm flat on the door when she would have closed it in his face. "No, that is not all," he said grimly. He didn't make the mistake of trying to charm her again. Instead he challenged, "It's past time for plain talk. I need to return to America, and I want you with me. We can dock in Spain, book passage for just the two of us, and send McAllister on to your grandmother with news of your safety."

When a disdainful curl of her lip was her only answer he lost his patience. "Air your grievances to me. Heap retribution upon my head. Fly at me with your fists and nails. I deserve all, I admit. But do not shut me out, for I cannot bear it."

"*You* cannot bear it! You insufferable bastard, I . . ." She took a deep, shaky breath and drew herself to her full height. Her voice was calm again when she finished, "I fear you will have to bear it, sir. I have nothing to say to you. Any relationship we might have had ended with my knowledge of your true identity.''

But her brief outburst was telling. He glimpsed her hidden anguish. Though it twisted his gut with regret, it also gave him hope. Despite everything, she was still not indifferent. This time, when she tried to close the door in his face, he wedged his boot in the gap. He shoved the door inexorably open with his shoulder despite her opposite pressure.

A frustrated groan escaped Tory. As usual, he'd brook no opposition. Damn him, damn him. Abruptly, she released the door, stepping nimbly aside as he came flying into the room. He stumbled over a chair and fell to the floor.

Tory propped her shoulders against the bulkhead, crossed her arms, and sneered, ''Most appropriate. Now slither out the same way.''

Beau stood and straightened his clothes. ''No, my dear, I'm not the snake in your paradise. I'm your Adam. I'll make you admit it if I have to sail us around the world a dozen times.'' His face set, he advanced.

The pain hammering at Tory's composed facade beat one small hole, then a gap. When he reached out those long, strong arms she'd dreamed of leaning on for always, the facade fell. If he touched her, she'd shatter into bits . . .

''*No!*'' she croaked with such horror that he froze. The hurt was at last bare for him to see, in her eyes, in the hands spread to ward him off. It slashed through him like a saber, leaving a raw wound on his heart. He forgot all but a need to comfort and reached out again.

She ducked under his arms and ran to the other side of the cabin to cower behind the table. His proud love, cowering? No, God, I didn't do this to her. I *didn't*. He pleaded hoarsely, ''Tory, you've naught to fear from me. I'd cut off my arm if I could undo the wrong I've done you. Please, please try to understand that I didn't intend to hurt you. I misunderstood so many of your actions, both four years ago and after your capture. What I realize now was courage seemed arrogance; what was innocence seemed mockery. It was unforgivable of me to judge you so unfairly, but even you must admit I had cause.'' Was she even listening? She trembled like one with palsy as she stared down at her hands clenched about the table edge.

''Nor, when I took you to Algiers, did I intend to . . . know you. You were not only a lady, you were unwilling, and I've never taken an unwilling woman in my life.'' Finally she looked at him. He winced at the tears in her eyes.

"But that's what I cannot forgive," she cried. "Don't you see? If you'd raped me, I could hold my head high. But I gladly bestowed my honor on a pirate, thinking he would nevertheless guard it well. Instead I discover that man despised me. But did he take his revenge by a beating from which I could recover with my body and my self-respect intact? No, he was much more subtle. He took all I had to give, changing my fear to desire, my hate to . . ." She broke off.

He took an eager step forward. "To what?"

Tory hesitated, then gave a little shrug as if deciding the truth didn't matter now. "To love," she whispered with ineffable sadness.

His heart sang with joy, but the notes were discordant, for he knew she would not have made the admission if she still loved him.

Indeed, she continued, "More fool I. You wanted only to avenge yourself in my body. My . . . silly dreams meant nothing to you."

"Tory, that's not true . . ."

"You're like all the others, using me for your own ends. No, you're worse than they. At least they don't pretend to be something they're not."

"But I had no choice—"

"One word, Sinan." She paused to take a breath—part gasp, part sob, but pure anguish—as she realized what she'd said. "Oh, I forget, Beaufort Avery Cochran. One word is all it would have taken to reassure me. Would it have cost you so much? It would have saved me such grief and terror if I had known who you were long ago." She took another breath and would have continued, but a fist smashed down on the table. She jumped and finally looked at him. Really looked at him.

And wished she hadn't.

Her sanity depended on keeping him at arm's length, regarding him as the heartless villain he was. But the man who stared at her with such burning regret was no devil. He was human, with all the attendant flaws and virtues. He was so dear to her. She wanted to bury her head in his chest and cry with him. But she dared not forgive him. He didn't care for her. She had to put him out of her life.

Assured of her attention, Beau straightened, braced his feet and began the most critical speech of his life. "You are well versed in history. I was on a mission commissioned privately. Secrecy not only ensured my safety from the dey but was vital to avert a scandal back home. *No one* knew my purpose, not until the very end. And at first I knew little of you and, frankly, trusted you less. You know why. I couldn't rely on you. Not then."

When her mouth twisted bitterly, he sighed. "Yes, you're right, even had the danger been less, in the beginning I wouldn't have told you the truth because I wanted to humble you. I won't lie to you about that, for I'll have no more lies between us. But I know now you're a big enough woman to understand and, mayhap, to forgive." He waved a hand to indicate she sit. When she had done so, he knelt before her and took her hands. She gasped and tried to pull away, but he kept her gentle prisoner.

"Nay, love, let me touch you. See? I don't burn or contaminate." He stared at her so intensely that her struggles ceased. Her wide, tear-washed turquoise eyes met his. Guarded, hostile, but at least she looked at him.

Beau kept his voice even with an effort. "Do you know what happened to Henry Stoville?"

"No, I have often wondered," she admitted.

"Well, wonder no longer. He was killed in a corsair battle almost three years ago. He captained a voyage that should have been mine."

Restlessly, Beau stood and paced up and down, unaware of her gasp. "He was different after we returned from England four years ago. He was bitter. Cynical. But my sister loved him still, and they wed despite my urgings to wait until Henry had recovered from his feelings for you. The marriage was not . . . happy. They left their infant son with my parents and voyaged to the Mediterranean in an attempt to settle their differences. Henry was killed. I blame myself for that. I knew the dangers. I never should have let them go."

He whirled to face her, concluding harshly, "But I blame you for his unhappiness. Why in the name of heaven did you encourage his affection, then reject him so cruelly? He said you mocked him and lied to him."

Stung, she retorted, "It's not true, but I'll not defend myself to you. Think what you like, as you always do. Now I'll appease your conscience and admit you had some justification for not telling me who you were. But that changes nothing. Indeed, you should have left me strictly alone instead of . . . tormenting me.''

"So I told myself, madam. But you forget one thing.''

Tory lifted her head warily at the urbane rejoinder.

"Your effect on me.''

Shakily, Tory rose to get away from him. Away from the look in his eyes. Away from the things it made her feel.

He pursued her, step by step, forcing her to back away. His deep, sensual rasp brought her skin out in gooseflesh. "I've likened you to a siren more than once, and so you've affected me. You tempted me beyond my control, my dear. Honor, right, wrong, justice, even reason—all were nothing compared to the desire you aroused in me. I had to have you, even knowing you'd hate me later, when you learned the truth.''

"Well, you've 'had' me, sir, so leave me be,'' she burst out in panic at the look he raked over her. Never again could she allow him the liberties his eyes took, or herself the liberty to enjoy them. "Any wrong I did you has been more than avenged. Let us leave it at that.''

Tory tried to dash away, but he imprisoned her by putting one palm flat on the bulkhead on either side of her head, reminding her vividly of their first meeting. She didn't want to think about that, or where it led, so she closed her eyes to shut out the sight of his face. But she couldn't block the sound of his voice.

"I can't leave it at that. Fate threw us together, Tory. I feel in my heart that God is not finished with us yet.'' Gently he put one hand over her left breast. Her eyes flashed open as he bent his head to whisper, "Listen to me, and to this. For both our sakes.''

His eyes, those green, green eyes, Eden-sent, hell-bent, transfixed her. He was truly a snake, she thought with a logical remnant of her brain. A magnificent king cobra, twining about her body and mind, mesmerizing with his unblinking stare. His mouth opened. The tip of his tongue flickered out to lick her lips. She let her head fall back, baring herself to him and the ecstatic death awaiting her.

For it would mean her death to belong to him again. The death of Victoria Alicia Grenville, the woman she'd only recently come to know and love. She'd be consumed if she allowed him into her body and heart again. When she felt his teeth sink gently into her neck, she knew she couldn't allow it. She could never be his victim again. The transitory ecstasy he offered was not worth so high a price as self-respect.

With a mighty effort of will, she put both hands on his shoulders and shoved him away. She froze his reaching arms with an icy, "No, Mr. Cochran. You've had all the sport of me you're going to. You've made your explanation. I accept your apology, such as it was. Now please, take me home."

Her voice was the cold, proud voice he'd first heard four years ago; her face, though paler, was the same exquisite, determined face. But those eyes. God, those eyes would follow him through the seven seas, into his very dreams. Vulnerable, entreating, so sad they swayed him as nothing else could have done. Aye, she needed her home, and familiar things about her. Perhaps there she could find it in her heart to forgive him.

"As you wish." Bowing, he captured her resisting hand to kiss the palm. "To England, lady mine." He let her go, warning, "This is not the end of it. No, my stubborn love. This is a new beginning."

But when the door closed behind him, it had a final-sounding click to Tory's ears. She told herself she was glad. Once she reached England, he would have no more power over her senses, as his perfidy had cost him his power over her heart. By the time she slept, she almost believed the repeated words. Almost.

Helen, McAllister, and Jarrod watched Beau measure the dimensions of the small dining hall pacing up and down. Winking at Helen, McAllister whispered, "He'll live to a hale and hearty age, lass, though I fear this illness ha' nae cure."

When Beau turned a fierce glare on him, McAllister blinked innocently. He pointed with his knife to Beau's untouched plate. "Fevers of the brain sometimes take well t' nourishment. Eat."

"Humph! Since the men voted you captain, of what use am I?" Beau kicked at an unoffending table leg, then winced.

Jarrod giggled, but sobered under Beau's glower.

"Don't you need to see to the horses?" Beau snarled.

"They've had their morning ration, sir." Jarrod stuffed a bit of dried meat into his mouth and chewed in hurt silence.

"Beau, quit snapping at the boy. I wish you'd find something to do. You're making the entire crew nervous, including me." Helen's reproof was ignored. After a harried glance at her, Beau returned to pacing.

McAllister's lips twitched as he pushed his own plate aside.

He nodded at Beau's stiff back, put one hand on his heart, pointed a forefinger at his temple and made a twirling motion. Helen and Jarrod giggled. Beau whirled in time to catch McAllister in the act.

Growling like a starved wolf, he leaped to the table and pulled the captain up by his lapels. "Crazy, am I?"

"As a rabid dog. And just aboot as vicious. For two weeks we've put up wi' yer growlin' and groanin'. If ye persist in this behavior, I'll let the men throw ye overboard the next time we make landfall. Wi' my blessin'."

"And mine," Helen said clearly.

Beau released McAllister to stare at his cabin boy. "You, too, Brutus?"

Jarrod paled. "No, Beau. I'll never betray you."

Sighing, Beau patted Jarrod's shoulder and muttered, "Forgive me, lad. That was totally uncalled for." At Jarrod's tart nod, Beau smiled. It was a fleeting, pale thing in contrast to his old, cocky grin, but it was the first that had crossed his lips in the two weeks since they'd sailed.

He tweaked Jarrod's ear. "I know you better than that. Instead of helping push me overboard, you'd dive in on my heels."

"Beau, you know we're but teasing, but you are about to send us mad. She won't talk to any of us willingly, so perhaps it's time you forced the issue." Helen took his arm to stare up at him with loving exasperation.

"That's sound council, laddie. Once ye let the Lady Tory get the bit in her teeth, she'll run till she drops. That one respects nothin' but a strong hand on the reins and a stout pair of thighs to curb her."

Beau raised an eyebrow at the implication. "Are you suggesting what I think you are, McAllister?"

McAllister shrugged, but the gleam in his eye was that of a man intimately familiar with some of the world's roughest ports—and the women who waited there. "I'm but sayin' if ye want t' win the Lady Tory, ye'd best use all yer weapons. Patience hasna worked. Now I must take the night watch. Best of luck, laddie." He ushered Jarrod out with him.

Helen said softly, "Beau, I didn't live almost three years in a harem and remain the innocent I used to be. There is so much to life I didn't know. In an odd way, I'm grateful to Saud. He made the grief at Henry's death much easier to bear. First in hatred, then in a strange respect."

Putting his arm about her, Beau said, "I wish I could have found you sooner. But don't worry about that. It's all over. Now you can go home."

"Can I? Can I ever really go home again? It won't be the same to me. Because I'm not the same person who left. And I'm not so naive as to expect the same reception as if I'd never been a concubine."

"No one will dare say it to your face, my dear. Besides, if you've been sullied, may every woman be so fortunate. You were never so lovely four years ago. You were an unhappy, petulant girl. Now you're a woman."

Helen dropped her head on his chest. "I pray you're right, Beau. For Bobby's sake. He is truly well?"

For the dozenth time, Beau reassured her, "He was an active, normal child when I left, and Father has said nothing otherwise in any of the dispatches. I'm certain he's well. He'll probably be a rare handful when we get back. You know how Mother and Father dote on their only grandchild."

Helen pulled away to ask gravely, "When do we return?"

"I'll put you on a ship when we reach London. But I can't return yet." He let her go to lean a broad shoulder against the bulkhead and brood into space.

"What if she doesn't forgive you, Beau?" Helen knew the whole story now. Though she sympathized with Beau, she understood Tory's feelings.

A large hand clenched at the possibility. "She will. She has to."

Helen went to the door. "I pray you're right. But I can tell you, as a woman well versed in harem politics, that nothing gives a woman greater pleasure than to feel desired by a man she cares for. Passion leaves little room for subterfuge."

Left to his thoughts, Beau gritted, "Dammit, what am I to do?" Surely not what McAllister advised. Yet desperate straits required desperate measures. No matter how many times he knocked on Tory's cabin door—*his* cabin door, he reminded himself irritably—she refused to answer. Helen and McAllister had no better luck. Tory would allow only Jarrod to see her, and she refused to discuss Beau.

"Tell him to leave me be. It's too late for aught else."

Unhappily, Jarrod took the message to Beau, who waited in the companionway. Beau slammed a fist against the bulkhead. "Damn her! May her pride warm her at night."

He wouldn't have been so furious had he seen Tory standing, her ear to the door, her fist in her mouth to keep herself from calling him back as he stormed away.

Jarrod hastily backed out of his path, and the basket of trash he carried spilled to the floor. Beau paused to help clean up the mess. His eyes narrowed on several bloodstained, wadded rags. He picked one up and looked inquiringly at Jarrod. The boy's blush was all the answer he needed.

He threw the rag down and stomped to the deck. He harshly dismissed one of the sailors who was climbing into the rigging to change a sail, and took his place. The familiar task took little effort and less thought, but he had neither to spare at the moment. All his energies were concentrated on surviving the pain coursing through him.

So, God hadn't answered his prayers. Tory was not pregnant. There had been little chance she would be after their two weeks together, but he had hoped nonetheless. If children were planted in pleasure rather than in some biological act, Tory should be carrying triplets, now. Instead, those heady days and nights had not borne fruit. He'd have no pregnancy to use against her as a last, desperate measure.

That had been a fortnight ago, Beau remembered now, staring gloomily at the opposite bulkhead. He took the handkerchief from his pocket and pulled it through his hands, remembering silken flesh. Did he dare follow McAllister's and Helen's advice—and his own instincts? What if she hated him even more afterward? As things stood, she'd never relent anyway, so what did he have to lose? Nothing. And he stood to gain a great deal.

He allowed himself the luxury of picturing the red-haired, green-eyed son or daughter he could beget this very evening. His eyes softened. He longed for a child from Tory, not merely to chain her to his side but to link them, now and always.

Even if she refused to wed him, he would cherish the child, he told himself recklessly. She was the only woman he wanted as the mother of his children. And what a bold, bright, beautiful child it would be! Living, breathing proof of their physical and emotional bond.

Most persuasive of all, if she carried his child, how could she deny her feelings for its father?

He straightened away from the wall, his heart light for the first time in two weeks. But his conscience chided him. Did he justify satisfying this intolerable need by pretending it was for Tory's benefit? He paused with his hand on the knob to search his soul, but the hesitation was brief. If he didn't truly believe that he was the man for Tory and she the woman for him, he'd leave her be. Now she gave him no choice but to prove it to her.

Stuffing the kerchief back in his pocket, he went out on deck. McAllister had bought something that would aid him when they stopped in Gibraltar to take on supplies. And, knowing that canny Scot, he'd gladly lend it to this enterprise.

That evening, when Jarrod brought her dinner, Tory was surprised to see a dusty bottle sitting next to the plate of potatoes and roasted pork. "What's this, Jarrod?"

He set the tray down on the table. "Compliments of the captain, mistress. He thought it might end your sleeplessness."

Tory looked at him sharply. "How does McAllister know I'm having trouble sleeping?"

"His cabin is nearby. We've all heard your steps in the night. This is the finest Spanish brandy." As he talked, Jarrod was opening the bottle. The rich bouquet tickled Tory's nose as he poured a small glass.

She sipped obediently. Her eyes opened wide as the brew steamed a passage to her empty stomach and sent tendrils of warmth throughout her body. She'd had brandy before, but she had forgotten its potency. Still, after the sting faded, it gave her a lovely, relaxed feeling. Lord knows, her nerves needed relaxing. But she was just bored. She didn't regret rejecting Beau in the slightest. And she didn't need this ancient panacea to comfort her, either.

Nevertheless, when Jarrod went to recap the bottle and retreat, she put her hand on his arm.

"Leave it, Jarrod. I'll have another glass later."

His gaze dropped. He agreed blandly, "Yes, mistress."

Tory snapped, "Quit calling me mistress!"

"But you are a lady, the captain's chosen woman. It is not fitting for me to call you by your name."

"Poppycock! I'm no one's 'chosen,' least of all that . . . that . . . pirate's."

Jarrod shrugged. "If you say so, mistress." He left before Tory could vent more frustration.

Somehow the only sensible thing to do was to pour herself another glass. A nightcap seemed appropriate after dinner. She glanced at the door. Oh, yes, she'd forgotten to lock it. She would do so when she finished this glass of brandy. Warmth seeped through her with every sip. For the first time in two weeks, she didn't feel on the verge of tears. What a marvelous restorative brandy was! She poured herself another glass of bottled warmth, feeling happier by the minute.

Somewhere between her fourth and fifth glass she forgot all about locking the door . . .

The bottle was half empty when firm footsteps entered her sanctum. She peered at the intruder through a contented haze. Ah, Sinan. Just the man she wanted to see. Now what was it she wanted to ask him? She frowned, trying to remember. Something had bothered her for days.

Beau looked from the bottle, to Tory's limp hand cradling a full glass, to her face. When she smiled welcome, he knew just how far gone she was. His body, which had been growing hard in anticipation, wilted. Dammit, he'd intended her to nibble the bait, not swallow it hook, line, and sinker!

"Ah, my favorite corsair!" She straightened from her slumping posture and weaved to her feet. She grabbed the side of the table to steady herself against the suddenly rough pitch of the ship and raised her glass to him in a drunken toast. "Brave, fierce, and lusty raider of the Mediterranean, I salute you." She drank deeply, only to stare in bewilderment when the glass was snatched from her hand and slammed down on the table.

"You've had enough," a deep, familiar voice growled above her head.

Tory straightened with offended dignity. "Are you implying, sir, that I'm drunk?" She spoke slowly and distinctly.

"As a skunk," he sighed, pushing tendrils of hair back from her flushed face with a tenderness that should have troubled her, but didn't.

"Well, you're right. And it feels won-der-ful!" She stepped away from him to dance about the room. At least, she thought she danced. Beau thought she resembled a pregnant elephant leading a stampede.

"Wait until tomorrow," he said dryly. When she stumbled against the bunk and almost fell to the floor, he caught her. They looked at each other.

Tory blinked at the intensity of that green stare. He'd looked at her just so when he united their bodies for the first time. Possessively, hungrily, as if he couldn't get enough of her.

Defenses down, she basked under that look. Oh, yes, that was it . . .

He sat her down on the bunk, knelt, and removed her shoes, then lifted her skirts to roll down her stockings. As if he couldn't help himself, he molded the long length of her leg with his hands, shaping, caressing. Savoring.

Her voice, husky with drink and something else that made his heart somersault, asked solemnly, "Was I a good lover?"

His hands clenched on the smooth curve of her thigh. "The best I ever had." He cleared his throat. "Why do you ask?" He began unbuttoning her dress, hoping she wouldn't notice how his hands trembled.

She didn't, for her thoughts had turned inward. She opened her mouth to admit she wanted him to remember her and gasped instead when he tugged the dress over her head, then worked on her petticoat. What was she doing? What was he doing? Everything came back to her in a rush. This wasn't Sinan, her first lover. This was Cochran, the man who'd taken her in lustful revenge.

She tried to shrink away from him. "No! Go away!"

"Shh. I'll never hurt you again," he soothed, easing her petticoat down to her waist. He lifted her hips and pulled it off. For a forbidden instant, he cradled her, shuddering at the luxury. It would be so easy to pull off her chemise and leave her bare and vulnerable. But he couldn't take advantage of her in this state. Nor did he want her to use drink to justify her reaction to him.

Every straining muscle crying protest, he tucked her in bed. "Sleep, love. And soon, very soon, I'll show you what I think of you as a lover."

Her drowsy eyes fluttered open. "How wonderful," she sighed, cradling his hand against her cheek.

He smiled sadly, for he knew she was unaware of what she said. As she drifted off to sleep, he kept vigil at her side. Protecting her from the world—or himself?

The next morning Tory woke to the sound of moans. Who was making that infernal noise? she wondered irritably, intending to bury her head in the pillow. The moans grew louder as she moved and her head seemed to crack in two.

Gingerly, she felt it. She was only slightly relieved to find it in one piece. She had a sudden, more basic need to worry about first. Slowly, inch by inch, she lifted her head from the pillow. She was almost sitting when an explosion rocked the cabin.

"Oww . . ." Her wail bounced off the walls and reverberated inside her skull as the door slammed back. She buried her head in her hands, taking deep breaths until the pain receded enough for her to open one eye.

The sight of Cochran, grinning from ear to ear, did nothing for her spirits, her temper, or her nausea. "Do you always open a door that way?"

"Only when my hands are full. Your breakfast, my lady." He slapped a tray of steaming coffee, hot bread, fruit, and honey on the table.

Tory turned an interesting shade of chartreuse and looked hastily away. "Most considerate of you," she gritted, bloodshot eyes narrowed on his innocent face. She suspected he had a very good notion of how she felt this morning. His motives in bringing her breakfast were not philanthropic, but she was in too much pain to survive an argument.

"Now be a good fellow and leave me alone." She went back to the ordeal of trying to rise. She threw the covers back, forgetting she wore but a chemise.

Beau, however, was very aware of that fact. He clasped his hands behind his back and said lightly, "You're right. From the signs, I infer that I need to leave to prepare your marker. I'll have the carpenter begin immediately on R.I.P."

The initials struck a chord in Tory's memory, but she didn't care at the moment. One foot groped for the floor.

"Rest in peace," Beau teased.

"Death sounds pretty good right now," Tory whispered as she swung her hips around and stood.

She swayed so that Beau took pity on her. He caught her before she fell. "I'll tease you no more, love. Just don't ever use drink again to escape me or what I make you feel. Now, what is it you want to do?"

"Relieve myself. It's a chore I've been doing on my own for a good many years and hope to manage for a good many more. Now, take your hands off me and get out!" Tory winced when her voice rose, but she was too unnerved at his touch and her inability to remember last night to soften her tone.

A heavy silence descended. Tory was braving herself to look at him when he led her to the chamber pot and helped her sit down. "Five minutes. I'll be back," he said grimly.

Tory tensed, waiting for him to bang the door, but he snicked it shut. A few minutes later, she rose, feeling slightly better.

She grabbed the first robe she came to in the chest, but her hands paused as she recognized the azure material she'd worn such an age ago. Why had he kept it? She had little time to ponder the thought. She hastily drew the garment on when his footsteps returned, reasoning scant covering was better than none.

She was wrong. Beau stopped as though poleaxed when he entered the cabin. His gut lurched with the memories inspired by that wispy blue veil. She drew the garment tight, tying the ribbons, but that only accented her full bosom. Even pale and drawn, hair on end, she was desirable. More than desirable, for that Victoria was a lovely memory cherished by the heart that loved Tory now. Beau yearned for them both.

Uneasy at the look in his eyes, Tory sat down at the table and cut off a tiny chunk of bread. She nibbled, trying to work up her courage. Finally she blurted, "What happened last night?"

He hid his slow, pleased grin. He sat down across from her, booted feet stretched out before him. "How could you forget last night?" he mumbled reproachfully. "Ah, what a woman you were. What grace, what responsiveness." He picked up her hand to kiss her fingertips, his bright head bent in homage.

Tory jerked her hand away. "I don't believe you. Even drunk, I wouldn't have let you . . . I wouldn't have—"

"The term you're looking for is 'fucked'," he said in the hard voice of a man hurt but too proud to show it.

Tory choked on her last bite of bread. When the fit passed, she cradled her aching head in one hand and glared at him with hatred. "You low-born bastard, that's all I ever was or ever could be to you, isn't it?"

He leaned across the table to skewer her with keen, angry green eyes. "No, my high-born lady. I said that was the term *you* were looking for."

When she frowned in confusion, he moved his chair next to hers, stuck his face into hers, and gritted, "There are two kinds of copulation. One satisfies a biological need as basic as hunger or thirst. The other fulfills both that urge and the emotional need for closeness with a chosen lover. Which we had last night, which we had in the mountains, and which we will have again I leave you to decide. The difference between the two is but a state of mind."

He calmly poured himself a cup of coffee, then stood and moved to the door. She fumed, unable to believe he'd leave her to puzzle over the incredible statement. How dare he pretend *she* was the one to decide whether they loved, or . . . or . . . Even in her thoughts she couldn't say the word. But crude as it was, she knew it defined what he'd done to her and would do again if she allowed him to.

"You're not only a bastard, you're a liar! I remember now. You didn't do anything last night but put me to bed."

The broad back paused at the door; then he turned to face her. Tory sensed she wouldn't like his answer, but she flung up her head in defiance when he drawled, "It's not what I did. It's what you said." When she didn't pursue the subject, he raised a taunting eyebrow, shrugged, and made to turn.

"Oh, very well! What did I say?"

"You, Lady Victoria Alicia Grenville, were concerned at what kind of lover you'd been," he taunted. When she reddened, his eyes focused on her with deadly purpose.

So did a hawk look at its prey before it swooped, she thought vaguely. She wanted to run, but she could only sit and wait for his talons to close.

"An odd preoccupation for a woman who cares naught for her lover. This is an interesting subject we must pursue. When you've recovered from your . . . indisposition."

Tory leaped to her feet, too frantic to notice the arrows impaling her skull. "No! Never again will I let you touch me!"

"Ah, but you will. Deny it as you like, but your brandy-soaked brain was more honest last night than your hypocritical little morals are now. Why don't you admit the truth, Tory? You want me. Your body says so, your mind says so." His voice softened to a purr. "Your heart says so, if you'll listen to it." He took a great stride toward her, but when she clamped her hands over her ears and shook her head, the light left his eyes.

Wearily, he set the cup down and straightened. "Expect me tomorrow for dinner. I'll be staying the night, Tory. Not man nor beast will stop me."

She jerked her hands down to clench them at her sides. "And me? Don't I have the right to stop you?" she cried.

"If you really want to stop me, you will. But you won't want to, my stubborn love. You've but one thing left to settle. Which kind of coupling will we have—a fucking or a loving? It's up to you, Tory."

The door closed behind him, but his words rang in her ears long after. She hated him! She hated his arrogance, his presumption, his boldness, she told herself fiercely. Most of all she hated him for being right. For she knew even better than he did that, for reasons she couldn't admit, she'd never be able to resist him. She'd gladly open her body for his use.

She couldn't bear it. She must stop him somehow. If only they weren't at sea. But where could she run on the ship? The lock wouldn't keep him out. There had to be some way to protect herself. She looked vaguely about the chest. If he'd kept her robe, he might have kept something else, too. She lifted the lid of the chest.

The next evening, Tory felt recovered and in fighting fettle. When Jarrod knocked with her dinner, Tory sent him away. There was a pause, then a worried, "But, mistress, the master is joining you to sup. Please, let me in."

"Go away! I'm . . . unwell. I don't feel like eating. Tell the master not to come." Came a heavy sigh, then retreating steps.

Tory's stomach growled, but she ignored it. She'd been too nervous to eat lunch, and now she'd get no dinner, but she would gladly suffer hunger pangs if it would keep Cochran out. He could not know her headache was gone. Surely he'd be considerate, as he had been in the past? To be sure, she pushed a chair under the knob of the bolted door. Then she sat down to wait.

Expected though they were, she tensed when the steps came. She watched the doorknob turn one way, the other. There was a silence, a forbidding lull before the storm, then a foot crashed against the lock. The bolt split from the frame, but the door held because of the chair. Another kick, and the chair legs snapped like dry kindling. The door crashed back.

He'd washed his hair and dressed in a burgundy cutaway jacket, tight buff pantaloons, and Hessians. It was the first time she'd seen him in Western formal attire. At any other time, he would have made her mouth water. Instead, the look on his face dried it with fear. On shaking knees Tory rose to meet him, holding her small pistol in her skirts.

"Why are you here?" she demanded boldly.

He slammed the door behind him and kicked the chest in front of it to keep it closed. Then he turned. He raked her prim figure, muslin dress buttoned to the neck, with his eyes. His mouth curled to match his mocking look.

"You know why. The time for pretense is past, Tory. You still want me. You virtually admitted as much last night. Since your mind won't listen to me, perhaps your body will." And he advanced with the air of a man determined to exercise his rights. As if he had any over her.

Anger at his presumption steadied her. "Stop right there, corsair!" Her hand whipped the pistol up.

He went still. Then he shook his head ruefully. "Tory, this is like an encore performance. Haven't we been through this farce before?"

"No, Sinan Reis, alias Beaufort Avery Cochran, alias rat." Her mouth smiled sweetly, but her eyes were cold as Arctic seas when she finished, "There's one big difference. You see, this time the gun is loaded. I checked."

"Really? How thorough of you. I believe my line is, 'Take your revenge. It's the only way you'll be free of me until I've taken what I want.' " He took one slow step forward. Another. His voice was deep with an emotion that tore at her fragile composure. "But there's another difference as well. This time," he whispered, his eyes holding hers as he advanced, "you want me, too."

Tory's hand jerked with shock when he leaned against the pistol barrel and dared, "Pull the trigger, lady mine. For only death will end my power over you, and yours over me. Do you remember what you told me when you came to me that first time in the mountains? I'll never forget. You said, 'Take what is yours.' Well, I'm taking back what you gave me. The only way you'll be free of me is by killing me." His voice softened still more as he finished simply, "Life has no meaning to me if you won't be there to share it."

A strangled cry escaped Tory. Oh, God, his eyes, his body, his voice, his words. How could she resist him, and his passion? But she didn't dare believe him. Barely aware of what she did, she threw the gun across the room and tried to bolt.

But, as always, he was there waiting for her. Instinct tried to tell her he always would be. She struggled against it, and him, even as he inexorably pulled her close. He clasped her wrists between them with one hand and caught her waist with the other.

"Look at me, Tory. Look at me, love."

Some elemental force pulled her eyes up to his. She quivered, longing to believe the emotions pouring over her like a soothing herbal bath. Tenderness. Devotion. Even . . . She bowed her head on his chest and closed her eyes. He didn't love her. He couldn't. A man who loved her could never have treated her so callously. It was but another trick to humiliate her.

Beau felt her resistance, and, frustrated, he resorted to the last means of persuasion she allowed him. Still holding her wrists, he lifted her chin with his other hand and lowered his head. She turned away and his lips grazed the corner of her mouth. Holding her still, he tormented her, flickering tongue teasing one corner of her lips, then the other, making her long for the full caress he wouldn't give.

She knew what he was doing. Infuriated, she kicked him in the shin. His mouth paused while he wrapped one leg around hers to keep her still. Then he leisurely went back to work.

This time his aim was true. The long kiss arrowed through her lips to lodge in her heart like Cupid's arrow. Instinct banished resistance. Of what use was struggling? This was where she belonged. Here, in his arms. Against his heart, answering this pagan call.

Helplessly, she let her head tilt back and parted her lips to take more of him. Eagerly he accepted her invitation, his tongue thrusting, retreating, rotating, preparing her for the greater intimacy to come. Her tongue answered with innovative parries that made him groan against her mouth.

He tore his lips away to gasp, "Oh, love, you feel so good. I feared I'd lost you. Do you see how right we are for each other?" He pulled back to look at her—and could have kicked himself for his stupidity. *You should have led her to the bed without a word, you idiot!* he railed at himself.

The vague look in her eyes had sharpened to anger. She shoved him away. "I see nothing but your habitual ruthlessness. You'll stop at nothing to humiliate me. The only right thing left for us is to part!" She whirled away to the porthole. The moon bounded off the surging waves like some plump, ghostly rider. How she longed to mount behind it and ride away. She heard his teeth grinding and braced herself for his anger. Instead, his voice was resigned, almost mournful.

"Ah, Tory, why must you make things difficult? Very well, hellion. If it's not a loving you want, a fucking you will have. But either way, you spend the rest of this voyage in my arms."

Tory turned to face him, her hands clenched at her sides, her head high. "I knew it would come to this one day. Rapist!" she spat scornfully.

"Coward!" he hurled back, advancing on her. "Let's see how brave and strong you really are. Reject me and I might believe you really don't care." He caught her when she tried to dash around him. He tugged her head back to glare at her.

"If my only way to your heart and mind is through your body, then by God I'll take it. Nothing will keep me from you. Nothing, do you hear?" He unpinned her hair as he spoke, then wrapped a handful of the living fire about his hand.

Immobilized, she silently resisted when his lips took hers. He laughed into her mouth, pulling her head back against his shoulder to slant his lips over hers. Again and again he kissed her, soft kisses, hard kisses, drugging kisses, that drained her of strength. Her head whirled with the need to breathe, to answer the irresistible power of aroused male. He broke away to take a labored breath before his lips raged over hers again.

By the time his hands went to her bodice, she was too far gone to even feel them. When she stood against him in chemise and stockings, he propped her weak body against the bulkhead and knelt before her to run his hands down one leg, up the other, following each path with his lips.

"I've dreamed of these legs wrapped around me," he muttered against her flesh. He caught one garter in his teeth and dragged it down to her ankle, then nibbled the bare flesh from knee to thigh, his hands busily freeing her of the other stocking. Stroking, tickling, his hands teased one leg; his lips, tongue, and teeth tormented the other. Up, down, and around he forayed, but his campaign always stopped short of the mysterious forest that was his goal. He parted her legs and ran his tongue up her inner thigh, stabbing the sensitive crease where her leg met her hip. She stiffened against the bulkhead and thrust her hips forward, unconsciously seeking greater intimacy.

"No, not yet." He laughed huskily. He lifted her chemise to blow on the brush that burned for him, sending the flames shooting higher until they singed her very soul.

Nudging the filmy material up with his head, he ran the tip of his tongue along her abdomen, just above that conflagration. She tried to push his head down, but he caught her wrists and held them at her sides. Ruthlessly he teased her, stabbing his tongue into her navel, nibbling the smooth curve of her stomach until she was panting.

His chest heaving, he rose, shoved her legs apart with his knee, and placed her hand where she wanted it. "Tell me you don't want me and I'll leave you alone," he whispered into her neck, rubbing her with the heel of his palm.

His words meant nothing. Not want him? She was on fire for him. Sinan, Sinan, her lover. She struggled to free her hands. When he released her, she showed him just how much she did want him.

Beau thought he'd explode when her untutored fingers brushed against him as she unbuttoned his pantaloons. His pulsing flesh leaped eagerly into her hand. Sighing with pleasure, she curled her fingers around him and sought his lips. With a Herculean effort, he caught her hand and pulled his mouth away.

"Tell me you don't want me, if you can," he gritted.

"I want you. Take me," she pleaded, her lips red and moist from his kisses, her eyes soft.

It wasn't enough, but it was a start. Swinging her into his arms, he stumbled to the bunk to lay her down. He ripped off his clothes so hastily he tore his shirtsleeve. Naked, he pressed his body down upon hers and tried to lift her chemise. He was shaking so badly he was clumsy, so, with an impatient snarl, he ripped the fragile lawn from neck to hem. For one impassioned moment, he looked at her, bare, gleaming, nipples excited, lying ready.

He'd intended to arouse her more, until she was half mad with desire, but he had no more control than a boy. Urging her legs apart, he dipped the hard tip of his shaft into the moist echoing well of her womanhood. Sweat broke on his brow as he forced himself to pause.

Cupping her flushed face in his hands, he ordered, "Look at me, Tory." Her dilated eyes opened to stare into his.

"Who am I?"

"Sinan," she croaked, trying to turn her head away.

"No, Tory. Beau. Say it."

Her eyes closed in rejection, so he caught her breasts in his hands, pushed them together, and buried his tongue between them. He licked around a flushed aureole, but never took the nipple into his mouth even when she arched her back. He rocked his loins into hers, his velvet lance nudging the throbbing seat of her desire. When she was moaning, he consumed her nipple, sucking, nipping, pausing to demand, "Who am I, Tory?"

She knew even through the desirous haze that she could excuse her actions only by pretending things were as they had been. Sinan. This was Sinan. Her first and only lover. She didn't answer.

His lips left her breast, but his hand took over, massaging, stroking as his open mouth trailed down her belly. He moved to her side, bent his head, and sampled the wine of her passion.

A hoarse cry escaped her. This time when he paused long enough to demand, "Who am I, Tory?" she answered, "Beau, damn you. Beau!"

Heaving a sigh of relief, Beau mounted her and joined them with a powerful lunge. He lifted her legs about his waist and burrowed deeper, feeling as though he'd come home. Only when they were as close as two people can be did he pause.

He watched her eyes flutter open. "See, Tory love? It's me. Beau. Siman. One man who wants you." He raised his hips slowly, slowly, then inched back gradually until he was buried to the hilt. The gentle, thorough strokes left not an inch of her unplumbed; his mouth left not a morsel of her untasted.

When her hips thrust upward impatiently, signaling her need for deeper, harder contact, he laughed and obliged. "See, love, your body knows me. Listen to it, Tory." And then he had no more breath for talk as he lost himself in her. He tumbled down into the well of her womb, relishing the long, slick slide, climbing out again to the cold only to dive deeper the next time. And when the echoes of her pleasure began to resound around him, he immersed himself and mixed his own male essence with her feminine fluid. He threw his head back to cry out in triumph, in joy, as the stream died to a trickle. Spent, happy for the first time in weeks, he slumped against her, praying his seed would take sturdy root.

When her body was calm again, Tory's mind resumed control. She stared down at the wheaten head cradled on her shoulder, wondering why, after everything, it was still so dear to her. It felt so right to have him nestled in her. So damnably right. She clenched her hand on the need to caress his head.

Deliberately, she whipped up anger. He hadn't cared for her in the mountains; he didn't care for her now. She was but a receptacle for his lust.

Very well, they would use each other. He owed her. Since her body enjoyed his, and since she would probably never let a man near her again after she returned to England, why should she not utilize him like the stud he thought himself? Thus, when Beau withdrew and propped himself up on one elbow to look down on her, she looked back steadily. She didn't even flinch when he brushed her tumbled hair away from her brow.

But when his eyes absorbed every pore of her face with a

hunger as basic as his passion, she couldn't bear it. She didn't trust his tenderness, or her own response to it.

She crossed her arms behind her head and said coolly, "Well, I must admit, Beau-Sinan, that was a fucking to remember."

He flinched as if she'd slapped him. His eyes narrowed to glittering slits. His hands bit into her shoulders, but she went on as if he had not reacted at all, "You're right. Why should I deny us release? I eat, I sleep, I drink. You told me to choose. So I choose. You can fuck me any time you want." For a moment she thought she'd gone too far. He reared over her like an avenging god, filling her eyes with his magnificent, panting chest, her nostrils with the scent of musky male. But then he took a steadying breath.

Releasing her, he stood, feet braced, to taunt, "Very well, mistress. Lie to yourself if you must. I care not, as long as I get what I want." He blew out the lantern and climbed back into the bunk beside her, wondering if his words sounded as false to her as they did to him.

Apparently not, for she agreed calmly, "Fine. What better way for us to end our association?"

"Fine. Sport with me again, my lusty lady." And he spent the rest of the night showing her how much pleasure they did indeed have to share. Only when at last he had allowed her to drift into exhausted sleep did he let his guard down. Cradling her in his arms, he planted a loving kiss on her brow. Caressing her warm, soft belly, he whispered, "Use me well, my only love." And he stared over her head into the darkness for a long time before sleep veiled his anguish. Even then, he held her prisoner in his gentle arms.

In the nights that followed, Tory allowed her body the freedom she denied her heart. In his turn, Beau was slow and devastatingly arousing, spending himself in her with a pleasure he took care to pretend was purely physical. Though he found joy in her body, his heart rejoiced not, for he knew she intended to leave him once they reached London.

Tory, too, seemed to find their affair bittersweet. She always responded passionately to his advances, but afterward, he had to force her to stay in his arms. They both grew haggard through emotional tension and lack of sleep.

Since Tory was intimately involved with the man she'd been avoiding, she often walked along the deck and ate her meals with McAllister, Helen, and Jarrod. She was puzzled at the intimacy between Beau and Helen. They spoke and touched like friends—or more—of long standing, yet Tory knew better than anyone that there was nothing sexual between them. His prowess as a man was indubitable, but even he could surely not have energy enough for more than the three times daily he usually took her. Why, then, had Beau risked his life for this woman?

She saw him watching her watch them, so she bit her lip over her questions. Jealous? Ridiculous. She wasn't jealous. Curious, that was all. At least that was the justification she used when she questioned Jarrod one day as they sat alone at luncheon.

"Who is Helen? Of what relation is she to Beau?" she asked idly as she nibbled a hard sea biscuit. The closer they came to England, the worse became the food.

Jarrod kept his eyes on his plate. "I cannot say. The master instructed that you ask him."

Tory almost choked as she tried to swallow the hard mouthful too fast. "I'll not ask him the time of day, the bastard. And well he knows it."

When Jarrod looked uncomfortable, she changed the subject. They were discussing the horses when the object of Tory's . . . curiosity entered.

She was a beautifully serene woman. Fair of face, slender of body, and sweet of smile, she was surely tempting to any man. They'd exchanged few words, and Tory wanted to keep it that way. However, when she rose from her half-finished plate to leave, Helen raised a staying hand.

"Please, wait. I'd like to get to know you better."

Tory sat back and met that deep blue gaze. She cleared her throat. "What do you want to talk about?" Jarrod looked from one to the other, then tactfully slipped away.

"A subject I suspect is dear to us both: Beau."

Tory's face blanked of all expression. "Dear to you, perhaps."

Helen smiled sadly. "Ah, my dear, if you really believe that, you lie to both of us. My cabin is near yours. I hear your sounds in the night." When Tory turned a virulent red, Helen patted her hand. "I don't mean to embarrass you. They are familiar sounds to any woman who's lived in a harem, as I have, and nothing to be ashamed of. But I've watched you, Tory. Beau has told me your story. You're too strong a woman to find such pleasure in the arms of a man you despise."

"By what right do you say such things to me? My relationship to Beau is none of your concern," Tory cried, leaping to her feet. She braced her palms on the table and leaned over it to finish, as if goaded, "Or is it? Has he given you that right? I wouldn't put it beyond the bastard to sport with two women at once. Why did he risk his life for you if you mean nothing to him? Why?"

All of Tory's torment was plain in her unguarded words and expression. For the first time, Helen felt anger at Beau. "Do you mean to tell me he hasn't told you of our relationship?" she asked slowly, frowning.

Tory braced herself. "He has not."

Clicking her tongue impatiently, Helen rose to face Tory. "You've nothing to fear from me. The relationship between us is indeed close and of long standing," Helen said deliberately, staring at Tory. When Tory closed her eyes in pain, she nodded once in satisfaction and concluded blandly, "I'm his sister."

Tory's eyes flinched open. She sagged limply into a chair. But then her eyes narrowed as she realized how Beau had once again lied to her and manipulated her. If this time it wasn't a sin of commission, it was surely a sin of omission, and its effect on her had been as heinous. He'd known she was jealous, and had reveled in her torment.

Helen sighed as Tory cursed. She moved to sit beside her. "Don't be too angry. His motives, if not his methods, are pure." When Tory looked at her askance, Helen concluded simply, "He loves you. He's hurting at this estrangement between you, and he's trying to end it."

Shock glazed over the bitterness in Tory's eyes. Her mouth opened eagerly, then snapped shut. Her eyes went hard again. "No, I don't believe you. If you're his sister, of course you'd champion his cause, though why he won't just leave me alone is a mystery to me. He's had ample revenge. For that matter, why should I trust you? Doubtless you hate me as well for leading your poor misguided husband astray."

Helen stiffened. "I hated you at first, for making Henry so unhappy. But there at the end he seemed to become genuinely fond of me. Given more time, I think we might have been happy together." Her voice trailed off on a sad intonation.

Guiltily, Tory bit her lip. Helen had been through much, partly because of her, yet she seemed to bear no ill will. "Forgive me, Helen. I have no quarrel with you, and I'm deeply sorry that your marriage was unhappy because of me. Truly, I never intended to hurt Henry. We knew each other such a short period of time . . . When I found out how he felt, I was so shocked that I fear I rejected his proposal clumsily.''

Helen nodded understandingly. ''I believe you, Tory. And please believe me when I say this: Life is too short and precious to waste on pride or recrimination. My brother is a wonderful man. Everything he has done to you has been motivated by his sense of honor.''

''Oh, yes, he raped me out of a sense of honor!'' When Helen raised a skeptical eyebrow, Tory flushed. ''Oh, very well, it wasn't rape. But it was a cold, heartless seduction. He used me, Helen, without a care or thought for my feelings.''

''No, Tory, without a care for his own.'' When Tory looked confused, Helen leaned forward. ''He knew the dangers involved in becoming your lover—that you'd hate him and could threaten his mission, indeed, his life. He accepted them because he wanted you so very much. Think about that when we reach England.'' Patting her hand, Helen rose and left Tory alone.

And Tory thought. She thought until her head ached, but she always came to the same distasteful conclusion: Beau had manipulated her from the beginning. He was still using her for his pleasure, then taunting her to jealousy of Helen. How could she put her trust in a man like that? He'd already hurt her almost more than she could bear. She didn't dare allow him near her again. She rose to go on deck, wondering wearily why her sound sense didn't relieve the constant, gnawing pain in her heart.

That pain never went away, except, briefly, when she was in Beau's arms. But afterward, it always returned with greater intensity. Thus it was that, when England's familiar shores came in sight, Tory exulted—outwardly. Inwardly, in the private corners of her heart that she kept locked away, she despaired. She looked at Beau's fine profile and tried to tell herself she was glad that soon she'd never need to see him again. But she had to turn away and close her eyes to keep the tears at bay.

Chapter 15

England! Tory's eyes watered as they entered the mouth of the Thames to follow its broad course to London. Other ships—brigs, barks, schooners, frigates—sailed before them, sails spread like the wings of joyful birds soaring home after winter.

Home at last. To Greaty. And away from Beau. As soon as they cast anchor, she turned to the shore boat, but a tall figure blocked her path.

Arms crossed over his broad chest, Beau said sternly, "London's going nowhere. We shall get you home soon enough."

"*We* . . . ?" Tory repeated with foreboding.

"Yes. As in me . . . I. You're not leaving my sight."

Tory inhaled, steadying nerves and temper. "I thought we'd agreed that once we reached England, we would part. I apprehend your word, as usual, is not to be trusted."

Something flickered in Beau's eyes—something that looked remarkably like hurt, but his tone was nasty. "We find what we seek. And if you'll search your memory, you may recall that I never agreed to part when we arrived. Quite to the contrary. I must pay my respects to your grandmother. I'll change and return shortly. Make your good-byes now, for Jarrod and Helen will soon be departing to America."

Only then did Tory realize they'd had an audience. McAllister, Helen, Jarrod, and even some of the crew watched openly. Tory gritted her teeth, but forced a smile.

She offered her hand to McAllister. "My thanks for everything, Captain. I'm sorry this day didn't come sooner and that you and the men suffered so. When I've obtained a new yacht, I'll be in touch, if you still want to be my captain."

Privately McAllister thought she'd soon be moving to America, but he knew better than to say it. Instead, he shook Tory's hand gently. "Aye, lassie, I'll be yer captain again, gladly." He released her and gave a mock shudder. "As long as ye dinna take it inta yer head t' sail the Mediterranean."

Tory laughed. "I deserved that. No, I've learned my lesson well. I'll take pleasure voyages in safe waters from now on. I'll have a large sum deposited in your name at my bank. Divide it among the men as you see fit in small recompense for their captivity."

McAllister didn't insult either of them by trying to refuse. She needed to make amends; they needed the money. "Thank ye, lassie." When Tory would have turned to Helen, he winked and added, "And my best t' ye an' the braw lad."

Pretending sudden deafness, Tory held her hand out to Helen, who ignored it and embraced her. "I've enjoyed knowing you Tory. I hope to see you again. Soon." Helen turned to stare over the railing.

As she looked down into Jarrod's sad face, Tory teased shakily, "And you, you little rascal. Take care of yourself and come see me if you're ever in England again."

Jarrod looked up at her with serious dark eyes. "I won't have to, mistress. I'll see you in Philadelphia." He stood on tiptoe to kiss her cheek shyly; then he dashed below.

Were they all in collusion? Tory wondered, dabbing her tears on her sleeve. Why were they all so convinced that she and Beau were meant to be together? Why should she trust him again? What had he done to earn her confidence?

When Beau came back on deck, Tory blinked. His hair was dazzling in the sunshine. His white shirt was starched, his mathematical perfectly tied, his dark blue vest and pantaloons beautifully complemented by the sky-blue jacket that fit without a wrinkle over wide shoulders. He was, to all appearances, a Corinthian with the physique to match. Had Tory just met him, she'd have been enchanted by his virility. But this was not their first meeting; it was their last. She clambered into the shore boat, ignoring his outstretched hand.

It dropped to his side, clenched, then released, slowly. Beau turned to McAllister. "I'm grateful for your help on this voyage, McAllister, and that you'll handle the port authorities. They'll be curious indeed, for I doubt they've ever seen such a vessel. I'd appreciate it if you would tell them the truth, that we used this ship to escape Algiers, but leave out my role." Beau handed McAllister a wad of pound notes. "This should cover her moorage for a few weeks. When I'm ready to leave, I'll sail the *Scorpion* home."

McAllister stuck the currency in his coat and thrust out his hand. "I'll do my best, laddie." He bobbed his head toward the rail. "And I wish ye health and happiness wi' yon lassie. I'd best be lookin' for another position, aye?"

"I hope so, sir. If you've a hankering to join the merchant marine, you've but to say the word. We can always use a wily captain like yourself."

"Thank ye, Beau, but I prefer t' work on private vessels. But if ye e'er need my help, ye've but t' contact me at the Red Lion Inn, East India Docks. I've rooms there."

"Thanks, McAllister." Beau clapped him on the shoulder. "Health and happiness to you as well."

Beau turned to Helen. He frowned. "Where is Jarrod?"

"He ran below. He's upset at leaving the two of you. Must he come with me?"

"I can't let you go alone, and I don't know how long I'll be here. I've ordered a man to escort you to a hotel. We have an account there. I'll meet you tomorrow morning and take you shopping. Your attire is not quite up to snuff, m'dear."

Helen grimaced as he tweaked the sleeve of her tunic.

"Wear a cloak and stay in your room until I can obtain a maid for you." He kissed his sister on the cheek. "I'm so glad to have you safe again that I want to be very certain nothing happens to you. Tell Jarrod I'll see him tomorrow."

Straightening, Beau flashed a smile bolder than he felt. "I'd best be off before my beloved tries to leave without me." Waving, he climbed over the rail and down the ladder into the boat, where he seated himself across from a fuming Tory.

Judging by the long-suffering look on the face of the crewman who immediately began to row, he'd been right. Beau folded his arms and leaned back. "So you couldn't charm this fine fellow into leaving without me, hmm? Tsk, tsk. Perhaps you've lost your famous talent for flirting."

Tory gritted her teeth and ignored his needling.

"Still, you're free to try it on me." When she gave a distinctly unladylike snort, he added dryly, "It's plain you need the practice."

Tory snapped, "Would you be quiet? I've had a surfeit of your crude, rude company. God, I can't wait to see the back of you." She snarled at the crewman, "Hurry up!"

Beau paled a little, but his reply was equable. "How odd. It seems to me you've always preferred the *front* of me."

When the crewman went goggle-eyed, Tory turned as red as

her slippers. She longed to rip this sarcastic beast to shreds, both verbally and physically, but she mentally counted to twenty.

Patting a bored yawn, she sighed, "Indeed, you've had your uses. But even the most solid of, er, fronts becomes a bore after a while." Tory was pleased when Beau clenched his knees as if he wished he held her throat instead. He turned to stare at the approaching quay. Tory did likewise, ignoring her churning sense of regret that it must end like this.

By the time the hackney dropped them off at Grosvenor Square, the air between them fairly crackled with tension. Beau lifted Tory down despite her attempts to pull away. She jerked away so fast that she stumbled. Beau paid the driver.

He watched Tory dash up the steps and yank the bell. Their recent intimacy hadn't softened her a whit. She would fight him, and her feelings, to the bitter end. Would the duchess be his ally? She would not be pleased to hear that he'd bedded but not wedded her granddaughter. But perhaps that would work in his favor, too, when she discovered how badly he wanted to do both. Somehow he had to persuade the duchess to let him stay. Only then would he have a chance of regaining Tory's trust. He followed Tory up the steps.

When the door opened, the erect, elderly butler was so shocked he forgot himself. "Miss Victoria!" he cried, holding out his arms.

"Hemings!" Tory ran into them without a second thought. His age-spotted hands trembled as he patted her shoulders. Collecting himself, he put her gently away.

His long, thin face was flushed, his sharp gray eyes bright, when he said fervently, "Forgive me, my lady. I'm just so delighted to see you."

Tory squeezed his arm. "And I you. Where's Greaty?"

"In the yellow salon. I'll fetch her immediately. We've all been so worried about you."

"Don't be silly. I'll go up." She dashed up the curving staircase, so eager to see Greaty she didn't realize Beau was hot on her heels.

She threw the door wide and erupted into a genteel little tableau: Three elderly ladies sat chatting to her grandmother, cups of tea decorously held in manicured hands, gray ringlets primly capped. Tory barely saw them.

Greaty looked up in shocked reproof when the door burst open. Her cup fell from her hand to shatter on the highly polished parquet floor. She swayed in her chair, whispering "Tory" in a voice faint with relief.

Falling to her knees, Tory put her arms around her grandmother's plump waist, their mutual tears staining Greaty's magnificent purple taffeta gown. Neither noticed. Greaty traced the lines of Tory's face with a trembling hand. Hazel eyes locked with misty turquoise in a look of such love that the ladies drew out their handkerchiefs.

"My prayers have been answered at last," Greaty quavered, hugging Tory. Then she set her back to chide, "Child, you've aged me twenty years. If you *ever* do anything so foolish again—"

Tory buried her head in Greaty's small but sturdy shoulder to sob, "I'm so sorry. I never meant to cause such grief. I just couldn't bear to marry Cedric."

"It's all right, Tory. I was wrong to try to force you. You're home safe again, and that's all that matters." But Greaty's eyes were on Beau, who stood near the door, watching their reunion with tender possessiveness.

She pulled Tory away to smile. "So, my dear hothead, you've met Beau at last. Though not under the circumstances I'd hoped for." Greaty looked from Tory to Beau.

Tory stiffened, all her softness hardening. She stood. "Yes, we met at last." Tory, too, looked at Beau, her eyes dry and accusatory.

Forestalling the threatening tempest, Greaty rose and cast a significant look toward the watching women. All three held their lorgnettes to their eyes. They listened, bug-eyed as pugs scenting a treat.

"Ladies, forgive us, but you all know how worried I've been about Victoria. Tory, make your curtsy." Tory did so, standing with her hands laced together afterward. Two of these women were the worst gossips in the *ton*, and she had no interest in being any more of an *on-dit* than she obviously was already.

The ladies twittered, "By my troth, it's good to see you so obviously healthy!" and, "Victoria, you've given us all such a turn. You must tell us about your adventures!"

Greaty cut off the innuendos by walking to the door. "Excuse us. We have much to discuss. After Tory has rested, I'll hold a ball to welcome her home. You'll all be invited, I promise you."

The duchess made no attempt to introduce the tall, handsome man who stood silently watchful, and that did not go unremarked by the visitors. There was an element of familiarity in the way he looked at Tory and in the duchess's acceptance of him. Gushing their relief at seeing Victoria home again, they reluctantly filed out. The trio in the room knew the news of Tory's return—and of her escort—would spread like wildfire.

Closing the door behind her callers, Greaty leaned back against it to eye Tory, then Beau. "It's plain to see your time together has not been peaceful."

"No, you're right about that," Tory agreed bitterly. "It's been one grand lie from beginning to end. I lost my yacht, my jewels, my crew, and—" She choked on the words and turned away.

Greaty's eyes narrowed on Beau's guilty face. "Does she mean what I suspect, sir?"

At Beau's nod, Greaty slumped against the door. Tory eyed Beau with such rancor that she didn't see the guilty look pass across her grandmother's face. Then the duchess, too, looked at Beau, her hazel eyes hard.

"You, I collect, are to blame?"

"Yes, Your Grace. But I want to make amends. I'll marry your granddaughter tomorrow, if she'll have me." Beau took a pleading step toward Tory, but she whirled away from him.

Greaty saw pain in his eyes before he assumed an indifferent expression and threw himself into a chair. "But I'm apparently not good enough for Lady Victoria Alicia Grenville, crude American that I am."

The duchess shook her head slightly at Beau and put her arm about Tory's stiff shoulders. "There will be time enough to discuss this later. You, sir, will stay with us."

"No!" Tory protested. "I don't want him here. Send him away, Greaty." She shrugged off her grandmother's arm, then went curiously still.

Greaty raised a brow at the way Beau ran a silk handkerchief through his hands. It was more like a scarf than a handkerchief; surely it was an odd male accessory. The way he slid it slowly through his fingers was sensual in the extreme. Greaty looked at Tory's pale face and made a mental note to pursue the subject. Later.

"Come, child, your room has been kept ready. I'll have bathwater and a tray sent up immediately. We'll finish this conversation when you've rested." She walked Tory to the door, pausing to pin a commanding look on Beau's sprawled figure. "And you, sir. Wait here. I'm not finished with you yet."

"As you wish, ma'am." His fingers never paused in their stroking as he watched Tory walk up the stairs.

Tory forced herself to walk steadily under that sensual stare. As Greaty helped her undress, she explained about Becky. "If that scoundrel is to be trusted, she should follow shortly."

Greaty didn't comment, but Tory's bitterness troubled her. When the knock came at the door, she let in the maids. She kissed Tory's cheek. "Rest, darling. I'll see you at supper."

Downstairs she stalked.

She found Beau in the same position, legs spread before him, hands still worrying at that blasted kerchief. "Whatever your virtues, it's plain that courtesy isn't one of them," she said tartly, closing the door behind her. "Didn't your mother tell you how to act in the presence of a lady?"

Flushing, Beau put his legs together and rose. "You're quite right, Your Grace. Forgive my rudeness, but your granddaughter is enough to make any man forget his gentlemanly instincts."

"That, sirrah, is abundantly evident. Do you think Tory suspects I sent you after her?"

"I'm not privy to your granddaughter's thoughts, ma'am."

"Nor should you have been 'privy' to anything else, sir," the duchess retorted. "Had I doubted your honor, I'd have thought twice about requesting your aid. Why didn't you keep your hands to yourself?"

Beau began to pace the floor. "I intended to, ma'am. But I didn't count on our reactions to each other." From the corner of his eye, Beau saw the duchess sit down and spread her skirts with a satisfied air.

He turned to glare at her. "There's little censure in your manner, ma'am. To be blunt, you seem little surprised and less put about at the news of your granddaughter's, er, ruination."

"I'm not happy about it, I admit, but neither am I surprised. I knew the two of you would be sparks to tinder four years ago. That's why I wanted so much for you to meet. The blow is considerably softened by the fact that now she'll have to wed you." The duchess looked him straight in the eye. "I sent you after her to save her life, but I'm not devastated at this turn. To be plain, sir, when a filly refuses a fence, you lead her the long way about to pasture. We've but to finish what you've begun."

Such blunt speaking took even Beau aback. His eyes widened as the puzzle pieces fell into place at last. "I could never understand why you and my father asked me to intercept her. You surely knew she'd lose her yacht, her crew would be imprisoned, and she'd do well to keep her virtue."

"Of course I knew. But far better you than a genuine pirate who would never have stood for her temper. She'd have been dead within a month. I assure you, my only thought was to save Tory when I asked Robert to send you the message."

Those acute eyes gave nothing away, but Beau knew the duchess well enough not to take her words at face value. He sat down to pin her with a level stare of his own. "Wouldn't it have been much simpler just to ransom her, as you did most of her crew?"

The duchess's eyes flickered. Beau slammed his hand down on the arm of his Louis XIV chair. "Damn you and my father. Do you realize what danger your matchmaking put us in? Now I understand why he insisted that I visit you four years ago, and why you decreed that we attend that cursed masked ball."

"Of course. It took you long enough to find the right of it," the duchess said without apology. "And naturally my granddaughter *would* appear at her worst and then fix her interest on the wrong man."

The duchess folded her hands complacently. "But I haven't lived over three score years without learning to recognize when a man is strongly attracted to a woman. When you first saw Tory, you stiffened as though you'd been poleaxed. Unfortunately events did not proceed as we'd hoped."

"I wouldn't be surprised if you'd encouraged Tory to flee," Beau snapped, his pride still rankled at the way they'd both been manipulated.

The lively mischief in the duchess's smile reminded Beau irresistibly of Tory. "Now you credit me too much, sir." Her smile faded. "I'd never put Tory in such danger even for the best of reasons. Besides, I didn't know you were in the Mediterranean until I summoned Robert to ask for his help."

"How providential," Beau grated.

The duchess fixed him with a pointed stare. "Indeed. Providence plays a part in any life. Only a fool doesn't take advantage of it."

"Granted. But I can't help wondering in which direction you wanted to tilt the scales of destiny: interception or succession."

Clarissa didn't pretend to misunderstand him. "Both, sirrah. And it seems fate was kind."

Stuffing the kerchief back in his pocket, Beau resumed his pacing. He touched a Wedgwood bowl here, a Limoges vase there. He was no stranger to the luxury of this salon, with its hand-painted silk wallpaper, gilded molding, Italian marble fireplace, and expensive fixtures, for his family home in Philadelphia boasted similar elegance. But his home and the wealth it symbolized had been earned with sweat, toil, and the ultimate sacrifice; this wealth came through generations of exploitation, and it had bred generations of arrogance.

Robert Cochran had lost four sons in the War for Independence in fighting that arrogance. Why in heaven's name did he want his only surviving son to ally himself with a product of it? And why in heaven's name would he himself consider it? His actions had not allayed Tory's disdain for his country. This was the woman he wanted to spend the rest of his life with?

As Beau stared out the window, the setting sun strung the treetops with red-gold cloud streamers. So did Tory's hair look unbound, flowing about the downy softness of her shoulders and breasts. He remembered her laughing face creased with mud; he remembered her eyes half closed as she tossed her head and danced for him; he remembered her pleasured cries as he plumbed the depths of all they had to give each other. And he knew that, whether fate or their matchmaking relatives had united them, whether she scorned him and his country or would come to accept both in time, he wanted her. He wanted her body; he wanted her respect; he wanted her heart; he wanted her child. By any reckoning, the only way he could have them all was in marriage. Despite his own doubts, he would bear her kicking and screaming to the altar if necessary.

Decisively he turned to the duchess. "Sometimes providence needs a push, ma'am. As you well know." When she flushed at his sarcasm, he relented. "I want nothing so much as to wed your granddaughter, though I fear our union will be stormy."

"The happiest usually are. You love Tory, then?"

"For all the good it does me, yes. But she doesn't believe it. She thinks I wanted only to humble her, and initially, I admit, I hoped to do exactly that. But the first time I took her was in love. I swear it. I just don't know how to get her to believe it."

The skeptical gleam in the duchess's eyes faded at the frustration and pain in his voice. "Have you tried telling her?" she asked more softly.

He withdrew the kerchief from his pocket to stare at it. "Not in so many words. It would do no good anyway." He bound the kerchief tightly about one hand, an odd little smile flickering on his lips. "Still, if providence is really smiling on me I may have an advantage over her she can do nothing about."

The duchess leaned forward eagerly. "Yes?"

Beau told her.

Tory had barely opened her eyes after her nap before Beau's voice echoed in her ears, "I'll marry her tomorrow if she'll have me . . ." How she would have liked to pretend she'd never met Beau Cochran, much less heard the words that, even now, made her quiver with a longing to believe in them, and him.

Precisely because she was so afraid, she forced herself to rise. He cared for nothing but himself, like all her other suitors. He'd avenged himself royally on her body; now he thought to take advantage of her wealth and position. Wealthy and powerful though his family was in America, the heiress to the Grenville merchant fleet would be a welcome addition to the Cochrans' balance sheet. Had Beau not come to England four years ago to pursue connections in the English shipping community?

Well, he would not use her again. Finally she understood why he'd been so eager to become her lover again on the voyage. It wasn't her he wanted, but a hold over her. An illicit relationship of recent standing gave him far more leverage than their brief magical idyll. The possibility that he could have an even more tangible hold over her now was something she couldn't face . . .

Tears pooled in Tory's eyes as, inevitably, she dwelt instead on the one time in her life she'd been truly happy. How euphoric she'd been, dreaming like a child building a sand castle. But truth had come, a bully in the night, to smash that dream like the temporal and fragile thing it was. She wanted to wail at its passing, but she would not. Could not, for if Cochran knew her distress, he'd never leave her be. Somehow she had to get rid of him so she could lick her wounds in private. She had to talk to Greaty.

Wiping her eyes, she went to her wardrobe and surveyed her gowns. Selecting an elegant gold silk with a sea-green lace overslip in the latest Empire style, she prepared for battle in the ancient female way: powder and perfume her war paint, silks and laces her armor, a fan her broadsword. She gave up on her hair after a halfhearted attempt, for Becky had always dressed it. She brushed it until it hung like a supple copper mantle over her shoulders, pinned one side of it back, pinched off a yellow rose from the arrangement on the dresser, and stuck it on the side of her head to hide the pins.

For the first time in weeks, she felt a shadow of her former self. There, in that cheval mirror, was the Tory who'd so blithely left England an aeon ago. Tilting her chin at the right angle, she brought the fan up to cover all but her eyes. She lowered it hastily and turned away from her reflection.

She could pretend all she wanted to that she was the same, but her eyes told a different story. They expressed a new sensuality, but even more troubling, a sadness, a knowledge that life was more than a challenge to be met with conviction. Life was also a trial by fire, as she'd learned after immolating herself. Tory snapped her fan shut and hung it on her wrist.

Soon she'd be as heart-whole as she'd been six months ago. But as she descended the stairs, she knew, despite her bravado, that nothing would ever be the same—because she would never be the same. She'd left part of herself back in that sunny mountain glen. Perhaps the best part. The part that dreamed, loved, laughed, and gave of herself unselfishly. The part that Sinan Reis had brought to vivid life; the part that Beaufort Avery Cochran had crushed beyond redemption.

Greaty and Beau awaited her in the salon. Beau stiffened in the act of raising his glass of sherry to his lips. Tory dipped him a mocking curtsy, then went to kiss her grandmother's upraised cheek.

"Child, you look much more your old self. Do you want me to hire you a temporary maid until Becky returns?"

"No, Greaty, I've become accustomed to dressing myself and can manage until she comes."

The duchess nodded approvingly as Tory went to pour herself a glass of sherry. The old Tory wouldn't have suffered the inconvenience. She'd have expected, and demanded, all the rights and privileges she'd never been denied.

When the butler announced dinner, Beau thumped his glass down on the mantel. He offered Tory his arm, his black jacket and gray knee breeches somber but elegant. "Ma'am, may I escort you?"

Tory set her own half-finished glass down on a table and smiled a distant refusal. "Thank you, no. My grandmother is higher in rank. She should have the honor."

The outstretched arm stayed as steady as the green eyes. "I have two arms," he pointed out gently.

Tory couldn't bear the treacherous gaze, or her own treacherous response to it. She snapped, "One to match each of your faces, no doubt.

Still the arm didn't waver, but the stare hardened a bit. "Think me Janus if you like, Tory. Actually I'm pleased you liken me to the god of new beginnings. Did you know he's the porter of heaven?"

Groaning, Tory whirled and flounced into the dining room. Alone. By choice. She tried to comfort herself with that thought through each remove, but the best food she'd had in months tasted like sawdust. She excused herself immediately after the meal.

The duchess was getting into bed when Tory, attired in one of her most elegant negligees, went to her room. Greaty dismissed her dresser and patted the bed beside her. "I was wondering when you were going to talk to me. Don't you think it time you told me what happened?"

Tory sat and twined her long fingers with the duchess's short ones, debating what to say. "You know most of it, Greaty," she said at last. "I'd like to put that time behind me, so let's not discuss it any more. That's not really why I came to see you." Tory released her grandmother's hands to fold her own in her lap. "Greaty, you must send him away. Surely you see how it . . . distresses me to be around him. I'd think you'd be crying for his blood instead of welcoming him."

The duchess was not fooled by Tory's spurious calm. Watching her closely, she answered, "If he were any other man I'd probably do exactly that. But I've known his father since he was in short coats. Beau is much like him. He wants to make amends by wedding you, Tory. And frankly, I think he's a perfect match for you."

Oh, God, nothing had changed, Tory thought in despair. Like a cat chasing its tail, they'd come full circle only to arrive where they began. Something had changed, however, as Tory proved by saying calmly, "I, however, do not. I could never marry a man who tricked me, seduced me, not once but twice, then had the gall to expect me to fall into his arms so he could bilk me of my status and wealth. No, Greaty, I will not wed him." She rose and sailed to the door.

Greaty watched her granddaughter with mixed worry and approval. This was no spoiled termagant having a tantrum; this was a woman asserting her rights. Greaty found she much preferred the new Tory, but she also knew this Tory would be more formidable. She called imperiously, "Wait, Victoria!"

Tory turned politely, her hand on the knob.

"There's something else to consider. Gossip is rampant about what happened to you in Algiers. You must make a match with someone to, er, regain your good name." When Tory made a moue of distaste the duchess sighed. "I know the *ton* has silly rules, darling, but even I can't quiet the talk without your co-operation. I suggest we accept callers and let them see Beau's . . . standing with us."

Why not? Tory thought. He'd used her. She didn't really care what the *ton* thought. All she wanted to do was retire to the country. But Greaty did care. If a few subtle hints of intimacy would help quiet the gossip, then she had no objection. But it could never go so far as an engagement.

"Very well, Greaty. But a few selective hints is all I'll stand for. I'll not marry that arrogant American, no matter what. Understood?"

"Do you think I'm deaf, child?" Greaty snapped back. "Leave and let me get my rest. It's obvious I'll be needing it." After Tory left, Greaty blew out the candles and settled down. No matter how she shifted, however, she could not get comfortable in her vast feather bed. Guilt and worry plagued her in equal measure. She was, as always, acting in Tory's best interest. But she was grimly aware that Tory would be outraged if she knew how much the duchess had had to do with bringinq that "arrogant American" back into her granddaughter's life.

Only when Tory reached her room did she realize that Greaty had never agreed with her refusal. She, too, tossed and turned as she worried about Greaty's odd tension . . .

The next day they had their first guests, the Misses Winslow, wealthy spinster sisters who were as kind as they were empty-headed. The elder sister, a short, plump woman with frizzy hair that gave her a marked resemblance to the poodle she carried under one arm, kissed Tory's cheek.

"It's *so* gratifying to have you back, Victoria. *Such* a tragedy. But you seem recovered. You always had such a strong constitution, you lucky girl . . ." The woman complained of her recent ailments until her short, thin sister interrupted.

"Yes, Alicia, I'm sure Victoria will be most interested to hear your remedy another time. But we mustn't monopolize the conversation so and bore Mr. Cochran. I'd like to hear about your adventures, sir. Did you truly rescue Miss Victoria?''

Both sisters watched avidly as Beau went from his position at the mantel to stand behind Tory's chair. He put a possessive hand on her shoulder. "Perhaps it would be more accurate to say she rescued me, ladies."

When two identical pairs of washed-out blue eyes widened in shock, Beau concluded, "From a lifetime of loneliness." He rubbed Tory's shoulder and bent to kiss the top of her head. Fortunately he was the only one close enough to hear her gnashing teeth.

"How romantic," the sisters sighed, so dazzled by the tender look on Beau's handsome face that they didn't notice the anger on the pale face of his "beloved." They left soon after to spread the exciting news. "*Such* a handsome man. From one of the wealthiest families in America, and *so* taken with Victoria. We'll see an announcement soon, no doubt. *What* a romantic tale—he rescues her from a fate worse than death then weds her as a gentleman should."

The gossip spread pandemically. Town was light of company, so Tory's return was even more of an *on-dit* than it would have been during the full season. Beau played his role masterfully, blending the right amount of mystery and fondness to keep the gossip mill running. He tried to stay as close by as he could.

When Baron Cedric Howard was announced, however, Beau was at the docks, seeing Helen and Jarrod off on their voyage to America. The duchess was resting in her room. Tory was alone.

She hid her dismay well and held out a cordial hand. "Cedric, how good to see you again."

He kissed her cheek, holding her upper arms to eye her critically. He smiled. "Glowing, simply glowing. One would never know you'd been imprisoned these past five months. It would almost seem you . . . thrived. Perhaps I should have carried you away over my saddlebow. Would you have looked more favorably upon my suit then?"

Tory drew gently away. "I deserve that." She sighed, backing several paces to sit down. She waved him into a chair. "I truly regret having left you in the lurch, Cedric, but I didn't know what else to do. I . . . was not ready to wed."

The pleasant smile on Cedric's lips did not warm his icy dark eyes. "Rumor has it you've changed your mind."

A small start betrayed Tory's nervousness at the subject before she folded her hands and responded, "You know how unreliable rumor is. I've made no firm decisions as yet regarding my future."

Cedric rose to put his hands on the arms of her chair and lean close. "Then I may still hope?"

Why did those large dark eyes, gazing at her so soulfully, send a chill up her spine? Tory wondered. There was nothing of menace in his manner, yet she felt threatened. She cleared her throat. "I could not encourage you in that, Cedric. Very soon I'll be retreating to the country. I've neglected my stud long enough."

Leaning so close his breath brushed her face, Cedric murmured, "Until then, Victoria, you owe me another chance."

"She owes you nothing, sir. Unhand my . . . Victoria immediately." The harsh, aggressive tone matched Beau's stance as he strode into the room.

Cedric straightened slowly. "Ah, we meet again." He looked Beau up and down. "As rude as ever, I see."

Beau went to stand protectively over Tory. "But with one very large difference." When Cedric looked bored, Beau smiled. "Now I'm her suitor, too."

Surging to her feet, Tory cried, "Enough! Both of you! I'm no bone to be fought over." She turned to Cedric. "Thank you for coming. Again, I regret any embarrassment I might have caused you. My grandmother is giving a ball soon. I hope you'll attend."

When Cedric approached to kiss her cheek, Beau drew Tory under one arm. She wrenched away and glared at him.

Cedric saw Beau's flash of pain and felt Tory's trembling when he bussed her cheek. Interesting, he thought. "I'll be honored, Victoria."

Favoring Beau with the curtest of nods, Cedric left. His eyes were both hard and thoughtful as he whipped his horses with more force than was warranted. So, the chit was as much a handful as ever. Cochran didn't have her shackled yet. Unsurprising, particularly in light of the tension between them. He knew when a woman was afraid to be touched by a man; he knew when a man longed to touch a woman.

If they hadn't been intimate, he'd eat his best beaver. But perhaps he could use her resentment to his advantage. Both of them needed a lesson in manners. Victoria had left him a bare two days before they were to wed. He'd never been so humiliated in his life. Now that she had returned with another man, he was being laughed at even harder. That she had obviously allowed Cochran far more liberties than she'd ever allowed him merely increased his rage. He'd had to fight for the slightest kiss. But damme, she was desirable. She'd always believed he pursued her for her wealth. Indeed that was part of her attraction. But Cedric had wealth enough of his own. He would never consider shackling himself to a woman he didn't desire.

There was the rub. Despite the ridicule she'd subjected him to, he couldn't completely disdain her as she deserved. One look at her and he felt the old, gnawing need, stronger now because obviously she was no longer an innocent. Yes, one way or the other, she would be his. She owed him. He would still wed her if he could. If not . . .

As for the man who'd taken what should have been his, well, he had much to learn of England and Englishmen. His hands clenched on the reins as he remembered yet again Cochran's impudence at the masked ball four years ago. To have Victoria transfer her allegiance from him to such a one made him doubly angry. There was an accounting to be made. By both of them.

Two days before the duchess's ball, Tory was wound as tight as the strings on the pianoforte in the drawing room. For weeks now, Beau had taunted, teased, and flirted with her until she thought she'd go mad. Only the knowledge that she had to go to the ball kept her from fleeing to the country. That, and pride. This was her home; she was no mouse to let a ruthless hawk chase her out of it.

Tory was too busy controlling her emotions to consider the increasing familiarity between Beau and her grandmother. She did sometimes wonder why they watched her so expectantly, however.

When Becky returned the day before the ball, she discovered why. After the tearful greetings, the assurance that all was well, the duchess drew Becky aside for a private conference. That evening, Becky, limping on a cane, helped Tory prepare for bed.

"Lahtil sends greetings and thanks to you and Beau."

"Then Kahlil was successful in winning her?"

"The dey was so grateful for his honesty in turning Beau's cache over to the treasury that the price of one slave seemed little enough reward. When Kahlil's service expires—in another moon or so, as he would say—the dey will accept his resignation, with regret."

"Was Kahlil able to discover the whereabouts of Ismail's sister?"

"Not yet, but he's making inquiries. He, too, sends his regards. And, er, hopes for your obedience and that you may bear many strong sons."

Tory's hand went with a will of its own to her abdomen, but she forced it away, along with her suspicions, and took the brush from Becky to finish her own hair. "Both his hopes will come to naught, I'm afraid," she said coolly.

When Tory set the brush down, Becky put her hand on top of Tory's and met her eyes in the dresser mirror. "On both counts, Tory? Are you certain?"

Comprehension fell on Tory like a brick wall. She whirled on the seat. "So that's why they watch me. And they've enlisted you as their spy. I thought better of you, Becky." Tory leaped up and went to plump her pillows up with savage blows.

Becky followed her to the edge of the bed. "Hardly their spy, Victoria," she said in a hurt voice. "If you're with child, it will soon be obvious to everyone. They only have your best interests at heart."

"Their own machinations, you mean. Set their minds at rest. I'm not breeding. I had my menses right after we returned and am due again soon," Tory lied without compunction.

When Becky lifted a skeptical eyebrow, Tory got in bed, turned away and muttered, "You'll see. I'll gladly show you the evidence when it happens."

Becky kissed the top of her head. "Very well, Tory. I'm so glad we're both home at last. Sleep well."

Tory was left with her conscience for company, and it gave her no peace. She'd lied to them, but she could no longer lie to herself. She'd missed two months now, and the conclusion was inescapable: She was pregnant. Dear God, wasn't her life enough of a mess without this? She had no one to blame but her own unruly passions. She was no green girl, not to know the risks. She couldn't even really blame Beau, for she'd turned to him as eagerly as he'd taken her. Godlike as he thought himself, even he could not decree conception.

Beau's child. Tory's hand crept to her belly. Despite her resentment, she welcomed this growing life. Her own life would have purpose at last. Still, this child would be a constant reminder of Beau, a fact she no longer despaired of. True, they had no future, but they'd had a past, some of it very happy. For the child's sake, she would remember that.

But Beau must not know. He would never leave her if he learned the truth. Somehow she had to fool him and get rid of him before her condition became obvious.

The intimate supper party preceding Lady Victoria Alicia Grenville's welcome-home ball was the most sought-after event of the little season. Had captivity tamed even Tory the Terror? Those of the Upper Ten Thousand in attendance expected her to be a pale, twisted shadow of herself. They were disappointed.

Tory was in her best looks. Beau was on his best behavior. The foods, wines, and decorations were the best good English gold could buy. Nevertheless, what should have been a triumph for the duchess ended in disaster.

The evening began propitiously. The duchess grinned when Beau went stock-still at sight of Tory in the gown the duchess had ordered made for the occasion. The palest ice blue watered silk fell from Tory's abundant bosom in shimmering folds to her ankles, where silver-strapped sandals peeped. The puffed sleeves and low, heart-shaped neckline were unadorned, but the underskirt was elaborately embroidered with silver thread cleverly worked to resemble hawks. The eyes of the birds were set with opals while the background leaves and trees were interwoven with aquamarines and pearls. A magnificent parure of matching aquamarines and pearls completed the ensemble. Tory's throat, wrists and ears glittered as brightly as her eyes. The tiara sparkled with every turn of her head.

The significance of the hawks did not escape Beau, but he doubted if Tory had made the connection. She knew he was called the Hawk in Algiers; she did not know his family crest depicted a winged hawk bearing an olive branch in its talons. He looked closer. Yes, those stylized tree limbs definitely resembled olive branches. Beau wanted to groan. Subtlety was not the duchess's strong suit. However, since crests were not flaunted in America as they were in England, he doubted if many others would make the connection.

His eyes swept over Tory again. His heart fell to his shoes. She was as beautiful, and as unattainable, as a dream. This was the woman he'd always remembered before seeing her again, the woman he feared to make his wife. This sophisticated beauty was in her métier here. Philadelphia had amenities aplenty and social events to match, but its best would seem a poor substitute for this.

She was no closer to forgiving him than she had been when they left Algiers; if anything she was more remote. He preferred fury to the icy civility she'd treated him to in England. The duchess forbade him to use the only advantage he had over her.

"Even I cannot countenance such behavior under my own roof," she'd warned him. "Besides, if your only hold over her is one of the flesh, you'll never win her. She's too strong to be satisfied with such a shallow relationship. No, Beau. You must win her to your side by other means."

Well, all other means had failed. What in hell was he to do? Beau offered his arm to her now, his face set. "My lady, may I escort you to the salon?"

She appraised his tall frame attired in brown velvet coat, gold silk vest, and knee breeches as if she'd never seen him before. Reluctantly, she took his arm.

He felt her tremor at that tiny contact, and some of his despair abated. She still wanted him. He felt it. That alone gave him reason to hope. And he might yet have another advantage . . .

Had he known why Tory looked at him so searchingly, Beau would have been both shocked and elated. She was wondering what their child would have of him. Would a boy grow up to have his strong shoulders, erect bearing, and dauntless chin? Would a girl have that lush honeyed thatch of hair and those clear green eyes? When Tory almost giggled at her next thought— perhaps the girl would get the shoulders, bearing, and chin—she realized how close she was to hysteria. She dropped his arm as soon as they reached the salon.

The assembled guests rose at her entrance. The duchess had gone all out for this dinner. Twenty removes were planned; the chandeliers and sconces on the walls blazed with the steady light of the best wax candles.

The setting had nothing of a battleground about it, but Tory knew better. This was the scene of the battle for her reputation. For Greaty's sake, she resolved to be on her best behavior. She greeted the guests, trying to ignore their veiled censure. Tory had been through this ritual so many times she could do it in her sleep, but this time was different. This time the men were more familiar, the women less friendly. Tory realized that curiosity, as much as Greaty's influence, had brought them here. What did a woman look and act like who'd been abused by a pirate? Or maybe even by more than one pirate? Tory read their thoughts as if they were emblazoned on their foreheads. For the first time she began to consider what such cruelty could mean to her future. Not for herself; for the innocent life she carried. Her smile became strained but it stayed in place.

Tory arrested her hand when it tried to wander to her abdomen, and clasped Cedric's hand instead. She'd never considered him an ally before, but at least there was no condemnation in his eyes. She greeted him enthusiastically for that.

"Cedric! I'm so glad you came!" He led her to a corner of the room to talk privately while footmen passed out drinks.

"You are in looks, as usual, my dear. A stunning gown, if I may be so bold." He put up his quizzing glass to examine the embroidery, ignoring Beau when he walked up to stand beside Tory.

He let the glass drop. "Most . . . illuminating." His flinty eyes struck sparks off the jade-green glare.

Puzzled, Tory looked from Beau to Cedric. She'd assumed Greaty had chosen the unusual design by coincidence, having no way of knowing Beau's piratical nickname. Yet Cedric seemed suspicious about the embroidery's significance. Her puzzlement growing, she observed the barbed exchange.

"Does she know you've put your stamp on her, Cochran?"

"I had nothing to do with the gown's design. It was Her Grace's idea." Beau's eyes narrowed. "You seem to be the only person who finds it noteworthy. I wonder why."

"Why?" Howard smiled superciliously. "It should be obvious, my dear chap. I've made it my business to discover everything I can about you."

Why was she always snarled over? Tory wondered wearily. "Gentlemen, if you desire to brangle, kindly retire."

The duchess, gowned in gold satin and cream lace, glided up from talking to several guests to agree. "The purpose of this evening is to quiet scandal, not cause it. If you two rapscallions persist, I'll have the footmen show you both out." She smiled at them, but her hazel eyes were rapier-keen. When both men bowed, she nodded regally. "Howard, your arm. Dinner is served."

Tory waded through the rich meal, conversing lightly with her neighbors. But her discomfort grew apace with her indigestion. No longer did the men discreetly eye her low-cut bodice; they ogled it. The nausea that had been troubling her of late returned in full measure. Finally she could take no more. After one bite of dessert, she excused herself and retreated to a small salon near the dining room. She sat down in a high-backed chair before the fireplace.

She was brooding on Cedric's words when the man himself materialized beside her. "My dear, why are you hiding here? Come, face your accusers with your haughtiest glare and they'll not dare to utter a word against you." He took her hand.

"Cedric," Tory said, watching him closely, "you seem deuced interested in my well-being when you've every right to be furious with me. I had not realized you were such a forgiving man." Did she imagine that tightening of his mouth?

"You've suffered enough for your foolishness. I want only to see that nothing hurts you again." He pulled a chair next to hers and sat down. "I think you're not as headstrong as you used to be, my dear. I feel we could deal together extremely, if you'll give us another chance. Besides, a match is the best way to save your good name."

"I got into this mess alone, and that's the way I prefer to get out of it," Tory said baldly, too nauseated for politeness.

"Indeed? Apparently Her Grace doesn't agree."

"Enough riddles, Cedric." Tory wiped her clammy brow with her hand. "If you've something to tell me, out with it."

Lifting his monocle, he eyed the embroidery on her gown. "Exquisite workmanship." His enlarged black eye bored into her. "Don't you know you wear the symbol of Cochran's family crest? You might as well be branded, my dear."

Tory's eyes widened with horror, both at his words and at the realization she'd lost the battle with her stomach. She leaped to her feet, flung up the window, and spent the lobster patties and wine in the shrubbery.

The glass fell from Cedric's bugged eye. He peered at her waist. Slim as ever, but if she was in the early stages . . . fury surged through him in a black wave, for he had little doubt who'd fathered the brat. Removing his handkerchief, he wet it with water from a pitcher and wiped her face and mouth when she leaned, spent, against the wall. He pocketed the kerchief, lifted her chin, and put one arm about her shoulders.

To the man who entered in search of Tory, she and Cedric seemed to be in the first throes of a passionate embrace. Beau's tension found release in fury. He stalked across the room and pried Howard's arm away.

"Leave her alone," he growled, standing over her like a bear guarding his honeycomb.

Howard's hands bunched into fists, but before he could answer, Tory screamed, "No, *you* leave me alone! Get out! You manipulative bastard, you don't care what you have to do, whom you have to hurt—"

The duchess sailed into the room and snapped, "Hush, child, they can hear you in the dining room." She took in the scene at a glance, then said decisively, "This has gone too far, Victoria. You can afford no more scandal. You *must* wed. Let me make the announcement at the ball."

Tory's voice, composed now but hard as nails, pinned Greaty to the spot. "You're right. It has gone far enough. There will be no ball, and certainly no announcement." When Greaty straightened haughtily, Tory continued fiercely, "Why can't you ever trust me to make my own decisions? I thought this time things would be different, but you still want an heir, no matter the cost to me. You'll do anything to . . ."

When the duchess's eyes flickered, Tory trailed off. She swayed under the shock of comprehension. Beau reached out to steady her, but she shook him off. "You sent him after me, didn't you? Somehow you knew he was in the Mediterranean, and you sent him with your blessing, just as you brought him to meet me four years ago. You gave him leave to terrify me, to imprison and beat my crew, for your own twisted designs."

Beau closed his eyes and groaned. Cedric looked from one woman to the other.

Tory's laugh held no humor. "Tell me, ma'am, did you also give him your blessing to bed me?" She turned on Beau. "And you, you came to me on the ship for the same reason. Didn't you . . . ? *Didn't* you?" When Beau bit his lip, she braced her wobbling body by grabbing the chair beside her.

"Victoria," Greaty began in an unwontedly pleading voice, but Tory interrupted.

"Well, your plan worked beautifully, to a point. I'm not breeding, ma'am. And no power on earth would make me wed the instrument of your scheme." Trembling with the force of her emotions, Tory went to the desk in the corner and removed a letter opener. Methodically she ripped into the exquisite embroidery of the gown, slashing until the petticoat showed under the triangular gash. The duchess moved to stop her, but Beau's hand clamped down on her wrist.

She kicked the jewel-studded material away. "See the results of your meddling, ma'am? I hope your deviousness pleases you. It makes me ill." Her mouth working in pain, Tory dashed her tears away and quavered, "You were the one person in this world I thought would always love me, that I could always trust. What a fool I've been. What a stupid fool." She stumbled out of the room. She ignored the trio hastening after her and didn't even notice the guests congregating in the hall. She'd built her whole life on a foundation of sand, and it was sinking about her. If Greaty would betray her so, then no one and nothing was to be trusted.

She locked her door and dressed in her nightgown. Opening a drawer, she removed the jeweled dagger she'd taken from Beau such an age ago. What a sentimental fool she'd been to keep it, but now it would serve her well.

She lifted her nightgown, dipped the knife in a pitcher of water, and sliced a small gash in her upper thigh. She held a wadded rag to the gash, wiped some of the blood on the sheets, then rubbed more on the back of her nightgown. She tossed the rag in the wastebasket and got in bed to stare dry-eyed into the darkness.

For the first time in her life, she knew what real loneliness was.

PART V

"Oh my heart! Why are you set upon
making the waters rise to the mountains?
You are the fool who pursues the sun!
Cease to love a woman who will never say yes
to you."

—Saharan nomad song

Chapter 16

The dowager duchess of Westmont was not in her best looks. Her gray hair was askew, her morning gown was wrinkled, and her haggard face for once showed its age as she paced the breakfast room. Neither she nor Beau had slept last night. Hemings had spent an awkward few hours turning away the ball guests, but the social scandal troubled Clarissa not a whit as much as Tory's state of mind. A state for which she was partly to blame.

Beau, too, feared they'd pushed Tory too far this time. Her set expression as she climbed the stairs last night haunted him, for he'd seen it before—the day she learned his identity. But this time she had even more reason to be upset at what was, to her at least, a betrayal. The duchess had been in her life much longer than he had. . . .

But Tory would never believe Clarissa had acted out of love. And it was him, in the end, she'd blame. A sad little smile curved his lips at the irony of the situation. Usually it was the woman who used pregnancy as a means of entrapment; Tory was as justifiably furious as any wronged suitor.

Beau pulled the handkerchief out of his pocket to stare at it, fearing that what it represented—passion, joy, and tenderness—would never be his again. He'd have only memories now. Any hard-fought ground he'd regained had been lost last night. She would never forgive him. But if she didn't wed him, what would she do?

Tory entered on the thought, pale but composed. When Greaty went to greet her, she nodded. "Ma'am. I trust you slept well?" Tory selected a hearty breakfast from the sideboard and went to the table.

Greaty sat down with a gloomy look at Tory. "No, miss, I did not, as you well know. And yourself?"

Pretending interest in her food, Tory replied steadily, "Yes, as a matter of fact I did. Decision is a great sleeping draft."

"And what have you decided?" Greaty asked warily. Beau

stiffened and placed his fork just so across his plate, not looking at Tory.

Popping a morsel of buttered scone in her mouth, Tory chewed, then wiped her hands and mouth on her napkin. She gave every appearance of enjoyment, but inwardly she prayed she would not throw up in their laps. "I'm going to Fairleigh. I'll move the stud there."

"Hiding will accomplish nothing, Tory."

"Hiding, ma'am? Or seeking peace? It's plain I'll have none here when you put the interests of a rogue over those of your own granddaughter." Tory's voice shook on the last. She quickly took another bite of scone.

Greaty glanced from Beau's set face to Tory's remote one. She knew that look. Tory's mind was made up, and neither God nor man would sway her. Still, she had to try. Greaty covered Tory's hand with her own. "Child, I've always had your interests at heart. You're making a great mistake. Give Beau a chance."

"As he gave me a chance?" Tory burst out. "He knew who I was from the beginning, Greaty. He ruthlessly seduced me, even tried to make me pregnant to further his own ends. Well, I'll be used no longer. Not as a brood mare to breed your heir, not as a stepping stone to his ambition. If you want to cut me off, do so. Now I'm twenty-one I can live quite easily at Fairleigh on my mother's bequest. In fact, I'd prefer it. At least if I ever meet a man I can love, I'll know he loves *me* rather than my assets."

She shoved back her plate. "Now I have an appointment to keep, but first I have one last thing to say." She stood and leaned her palms on the table to pinion the duchess with rapier eyes. "You irrevocably damaged our relationship last night, but I may eventually forgive you if you accede to my wishes now. Send him away. He's a painful reminder of things I want to forget. If you truly have my interests at heart, prove it." She went to the door. Not once had she looked at Beau.

And he could not bear it. Leaping to his feet, he blocked her path. He wanted to shake her until her icy composure shattered, but all he said was "Do you really believe I want to wed you because of ambition?"

"What other reason could there be? You've used me in every other way. Why else could you want a child on me?"

Beau hesitated. Pride reared its ugly head, but the gut instinct he always heeded warned it was time for one last gamble. He'd risk all on this throw; if he lost he'd concede defeat. He caught her shoulders in his hands and backed her into the wall, pressing himself against her. "You're wrong, Tory. I have many reasons, but none are material." He bumped his hips into hers. "See what you do to me? I slept not a wink last night, but I've only to see you to want you."

The growing hardness was undeniable. A thrill of gladness shivered up her spine, but she quelled it. She'd not be hurt again. She tilted her head against the wall. "So? I thought we'd agreed it was a bodily function. I enjoy your body as well, no matter how I despise you."

Beau gritted his teeth, then said passionately, "You're not capable of such coldness. Don't condemn us both to unhappiness, love. I wronged you, but I want nothing more than to spend the rest of my life atoning for my offense." He eased his hand between them to rest it on her soft belly. She flinched, but he caressed her. "For the sake of the life that might be growing here."

She turned her head away. "For the brat you planted in lust," she said nastily in an attempt to deny her own feelings.

A gentle hand turned her face around. "For the child planted in love, Victoria Alicia Grenville." Her eyes leaped to his face. She'd known such tenderness from him only once before, during that stolen idyll so very long ago.

"I sought it not, but you've bewitched me, my love. If you send me away now, you condemn me to loneliness. I want to wed you, I want to see your belly grow big, and be there when you bring my child forth. Not because I want your wealth, but because it will be a part of you and me, our spirits mingled to dwell on long after we depart this earth. I want to grow old with you."

Lies, lies! the hurt, angry part of Tory screeched, but the gentle, loving side Sinan had nurtured begged her to heed Beau. She searched his face as if her life depended on it, as it well might. She'd thought nothing he could say would sway her, but she'd never dreamed to hear such an avowal from him. Did she dare believe it?

While she wavered, the door flew open. Becky rushed into the room. She didn't see Beau and Tory pressed against the wall beside the door. "Oh, Your Grace, what will we do? Tory is not increasing. I found . . ." Her voice trailed off as she followed the duchess's gaze.

A quiver of pain crossed Beau's face, but he took a deep breath and said, "Well, love, what's it to be? Will you allow me another chance, with honor this time?"

Her self-inflicted cut throbbed, but it was nothing to the wound in her heart. She would only heal by amputating herself of this infection. Tory shoved Beau away. "You don't know the meaning of the word. I don't want your touch, your child, or any reminders of you. Even if I believed you spoke from the heart, I'd not change my mind. Go. Savor your victory over me, for you'll get no other." One hand pressed to her mouth to stifle her sobs, she ran from the room. Becky hurried after.

The duchess slumped in her chair and closed her eyes. He'd come close, so close. If only Becky hadn't interrupted . . . When she glanced at Beau, the look on his face brought tears to her eyes. Samson shorn, Atlas shrugging, or Prometheus chained surely could have known no greater despair. It seemed obscene to see such utter defeat on the face of a man as strong as Beau. The duchess averted her eyes.

"Well, ma'am," he said at last, his voice devoid of emotion, "further conflict would serve no purpose. I've done enough damage to your relationship with your granddaughter. It's best I leave before I do more." He rose heavily, but the duchess jumped to her feet and caught his arm.

"Beau, don't go. She'll calm down. I know her. She's fighting you so hard because she cares so much—"

A harsh bark of laughter cut her off. "If she cared any deeper, ma'am, she'd plant a sword in my gullet. No, I'm making her unhappy to no purpose. I took her under false pretenses, but I leave her with only truth between us. Since she doesn't want my love, I've no choice but to give her hope of happiness with someone else." His voice grew gravelly at the end, as if the words were stones sticking in his mouth.

If the duchess had doubted his feelings, she did no longer. She watched him walk steadily up the stairs, wondering if Tory would learn too late what she had lost.

When Tory came down to order her carriage, she stiffened at the sight of the small valise in the hall. She gripped the newel post of the stairway to steady herself. She knew what that innocuous case meant: He was leaving.

I'm glad, I'm glad, she repeated to herself, but the sweet victory tasted more of charred defeat. If he gave up so easily, she was truly well rid of him. Later she would realize how chaotic her thoughts were, for Beau had cajoled, flirted, seduced, and even blackmailed to win her, but at the moment she knew only that he was leaving.

Booted and caped, he exited from the salon, Greaty following, dabbing at her eyes. He paused. For an eternity of heartbeats, he and Tory stared at each other. Tory felt her life pass before her eyes in that moment. She remembered the first time she'd seen him, then the fear, rapture, and agony that had led to this cold finality. She closed her eyes, her heart pounding so hard she felt sick.

Beau looked Tory carefully up and down. One strong hand stuffed itself in a cloak pocket. Then his face went blank. Politely he walked to the foot of the stairs, where Tory still hovered. His voice was husky but even. "I bid you farewell, my Amazon. I wish you happiness now and in all your years ahead. Perhaps someday you'll think of me a little more kindly, as I will always think of you. What I did, I did for love of you. Believe it or not now, but I swear it's true."

He took her stiff, cold hand and bent to kiss it. He held it to his lips for a long moment; then, still bent, he cupped it to his cheek. His eyes closed tightly.

Tory looked down at that sun-tipped head bent over her hand and wondered why she still stood, for surely her heart had burst. She felt nothing but a great numbness and the creeping warmth where he touched her. Then even that was gone as he released her and stood erect.

Vaguely she sensed that he was offering her something. She took it automatically. She looked down at it, and the agony lancing through her proved her wrong; she was still alive, for there was more yet to bear.

Rustily, she croaked, "Why do you give this to me?" She ran the kerchief through her hands as he so often had.

"It is the tradition when a relationship ends. I have no need of it, for the look of you when you first gave it to me will always dwell in my heart. Keep it as a memento of what not to feel, if you like."

When she looked up at him, he gritted his teeth and mastered his bitter tone. "If you ever have need of me, send it and I'll come forthwith." He backed up a step, swept one last look over her, and bowed. "Good-bye, Tory. God be with you always."

He picked up his valise, nodded at Becky and the duchess,

and went to the door. When the butler opened it for him, he exited without looking back.

Tory wiped her eyes, then held the kerchief to her nose and inhaled. Taking a deep, shaky breath, she put it in her cloak pocket and descended the last step. A small, rigid figure blocked her path.

"You're a fool, girl. You're a Grenville through and through, and you'll only love once. Your pride will be a cold comfort to you in the years to come." When Tory didn't answer, the duchess shook her arm. "You've won! Why aren't you crowing?"

"Yes, I've won," Tory agreed. In the same dull tone, she requested her carriage. She stumbled to the door, flinching at Greaty's curt reply.

"No, Tory, you've lost. Someday, when it's too late, you'll see that."

As Tory rode to the physician's, she reflected that someday had already arrived. Even when they stood in the hall she'd known she was making a mistake in sending him away. She'd tried to root him from her heart, but he was planted deep as a stubborn weed. She'd shrivel and die before cutting him out. She knew that now. But it didn't make her choices easier.

It wasn't too late to call him back, part of her said. But when she exited the doctor's an hour later, she knew it was too late. They had hurt each other too much to trust easily again. How could she ever know now why he would have truly wed her? For the child, for influence, or for the only reason she'd accept. If she felt such agony now, did she dare risk far more in future?

She was too upset to notice when a burly, ill-kempt man went into the doctor's lodgings as soon as she'd left, then exited a few minutes later rubbing the bruise on his fist.

Tory was puzzled by Cedric's thinly veiled contempt when he called on her the next day. At first.

Usually he at least pretended respect, but now the aggression, which she'd always suspected, was overt. He contrived to brush against her, no matter how she inched away and glared. And his suppressed air of triumph bothered her even more.

She interrupted him rudely. "Really, Cedric, I can sit without your support. Come to the point."

His smile was mocking. "Direct as usual. Very well, m'dear . . . I've dared to hope since you sent that cursed American away." He pulled her into his arms despite her struggles and emoted,

"Oh, my dear, give me the privilege of repairing your good name. I care not if you've been . . . soiled. I still want you for my wife."

He couldn't have couched a proposal in terms more calculated to offend Tory. "You insufferable prig. Unhand me!" She wriggled free and retreated to the fireplace to glare at him. "I'm surprised you can bear to touch my 'soiled' flesh. I didn't want to marry you six months ago, and I don't want to now. Please leave before you further embarrass us both."

"Embarrass *you*! You arrogant little—" Cedric seemed to choke on his own wrath as he towered to his feet. "Do you have any idea of my humiliation when you fled so close to our wedding? You owe me, and by God, you'll pay!"

Tory hid her fright under a haughty toss of her head. "I owe you nothing. Now leave, else I'll summon the servants."

After one more menacing step, Cedric got a grip on himself and blew a brittle laugh. "The haughty lady to the last. Well, we'll see how haughty you are, m'dear, when all London hears of the bastard you carry."

Tory stared at him with dislike. "You had me followed?" Somehow she was not surprised he knew.

"Of course. I've suspected your condition since you threw up in the shrubbery, and I knew you'd soon want to confirm it." He appraised his manicured nails. "It was most convenient for you to send Cochran away before he knew. Now, after we wed, no one will suspect who the real father is. Of course, we'll know. But that needn't hamper our domestic bliss, and I'll get plenty of true heirs on you myself."

Shaking, Tory went to the door and flung it open. "Get out! You'll not be admitted here again. Do your dirtiest, for I care not what you and your ilk say of me."

Cedric sauntered to the door. "You will, sweet Victoria. You will." He went, humming a jaunty air.

Dear God, what was she to do now? Tory's knees barely supported her to a chair. She hadn't a doubt that if she didn't wed him, he'd trumpet her condition to the world. She'd planned to retire to Fairleigh and concoct a quick wedding, with widowhood shortly following. She knew her servants would never betray her. Now . . . She shivered, remembering the lust mixed with rage in Cedric's black eyes. How right she'd been to run from him.

If she left London, the gossips would rejoice, but they'd have no proof. Surely even the sticklers wouldn't heed Cedric when he bore such a grudge. Even if many did, what matter? She'd make a life for herself and the baby at Fairleigh. Tory ignored the niggling voice that begged, *Tell Beau. He has a right to know.* He would insist on wedding her. She'd not be a duty to him any more than she'd be used. *But he said he loved you*, the voice reproached.

Because Tory longed to believe that so much, she didn't dare. After the babe came, she could leave it with Greaty and go to America to see him. If he asked her again to wed him, declaring himself without knowing of the babe, she'd have no more doubts. Now she needed solitude, mental and emotional peace, to prepare herself for the physical trial to come. She would know naught of peace if she wed Beau now. Tory went upstairs to order her bags packed.

The duchess secretly hoped Beau wouldn't sail in two days as he planned, so she tried to dissuade Tory. As usual, she might have saved her breath.

The next morning, Tory was ready early. At least she was *up* early, after a fashion. Doggedly, she crept down the stairs, holding on to the railing.

Greaty came out of the breakfast room still wearing her dressing gown. That alone told Tory how upset her grandmother was, for she never came belowstairs so attired. She frowned at the sweat on Tory's brow and came forward to feel her forehead.

"No fever. Why are you so pale, child? Come have some breakfast and you'll feel better." The duchess ignored Tory's protests and pulled her into the small, charming chamber on the front of the house.

Tory took one look at the attractive array of dishes on the sideboard and bent double. She had but a sip of water to lose, but the dry heaves racked her for several minutes.

After a frozen moment of shock, the duchess helped her granddaughter to a chair, ordering a footman to clean up the small spot on the polished floor. A big smile banished her weariness as she sat next to Tory.

"When, child?"

Tory leaned her head back and opened her mouth to deny it, but one look at the duchess's face made her swallow the lie. "In about seven months you'll have your heir, ma'am. Will you be as proud when he's branded a bastard?"

The duchess's euphoria receded. She bent a stern look on her granddaughter. "Only your own stubbornness makes it so. Let me send for Beau. Why did you lie to us? How could you hope to keep such a secret?"

"I intended to tell you as soon as he was gone."

Greaty sighed at the revealing statement. "Do you hate him so, then?"

"Hate him?" Tory repeated wearily after a long silence. "I told myself I did for a long time, but the pain I felt on telling him good-bye made me a liar."

The duchess rose so fast her chair overturned. "Praise God! Beau wouldn't tell me what ship he was taking, but McAllister knows. I'll send for him immediately . . ." Her babbling trailed off when Tory gripped her arm.

"No, ma'am. Let him go. I can't wed him now."

"What?" the duchess squawked. "Have you gone mad, gal? You carry his child and you love each other. Of course you must wed."

"I love him, but how will I ever know if he loves me with the child between us?"

"Don't be daft. He told you so himself."

"He's lied to me before."

Feebly, the duchess righted her chair and sat down. "What do you intend to do?" she asked dispiritedly.

"Go to Fairleigh. After the child is old enough for me to leave with you, I'll go to America to see him." When the duchess opened her mouth to protest again, Tory cut her off with a curt "I'm determined on this, Greaty. Please let me live my life as I see fit." The warning was veiled but clear.

Greaty's protests sat ill in her stomach, but she swallowed them. If she interfered again, Tory truly might not forgive her. She spread her hands in surrender. "You're being foolish, but I yield. I'll have my bags packed. We take Becky, of course."

"No, Greaty, she can follow when her leg is completely healed. There are servants aplenty to help me there. Besides, you need to stay here." Quickly Tory told her about Cedric's threats. "You must use your influence to discredit him."

The duchess paled, then reddened. "The upstart! I'll see him ruined for this." She cleared her throat. "Er, Tory, please forgive me for trying to make you wed him." The words were gruff, unaccustomed, but obviously sincere.

A sweet smile curved Tory's lips as she looked at her grandmother's bent head. "Of course, ma'am. He's a wily devil. Few seem to know his true nature, and he was always on his best behavior around you. I listened to my instincts."

The duchess still seemed shaken at Tory's close escape. When she walked Tory to her carriage a couple of hours later, she gave her an unwontedly fierce hug. "Take care of yourself, child. I'll come to Fairleigh as soon as Cedric is bridled. I'll not have him spreading poison about my granddaughter." Her eyes dropped to Tory's waist and took on that pleased gleam again. "Or my heir."

Relieved they'd at last made peace with each other, Tory kissed her grandmother's cheek. "Good-bye, Greaty. Don't worry about me, and I'll see you soon." Tory kissed Becky's cheek as well. Still yawning, she had just come down the stairs. "Take care of yourself, Becky."

They waved as the family's finest traveling coach, attended by two outriders, swayed off down the street. When, a scant hour later, Cedric Howard arrived, the duchess was prepared for battle.

She harangued him for fifteen minutes before allowing him to speak.

He looked abashed. "Forgive me, ma'am. I spoke out of anger." He stared sadly over her head. "The child should have been mine. I was jealous. But I know I'll never have Victoria for my wife now. Perhaps soon I'll learn to accept that." He looked back at her. "May I see her?"

"She's not accepting visitors. If I hear a word of scandal, Cedric, I'll know whose door to lay it at." She punctuated the warning with a hard look.

"Not a word will pass my lips. Should Victoria feel more the thing, send word to my club. I'd like to apologize." Bowing, he took his leave. Only when the door had closed behind him did he smile cattily.

The duchess fidgeted with the lace at her sleeve in unaccustomed nervousness. She should have felt victorious, but Cedric had been entirely too repentant for the scoundrel she now knew him to be. What did he know that she didn't?

By the time she found out, it was too late. . . .

Luckily Tory wasn't hurt in the carriage accident. On the narrow country road, the coachman couldn't avoid the dray in time and landed them in the ditch. A rear wheel splintered, but Tory was cushioned by the padded panels and seats. The coachman tugged open the free door, his frantic expression easing when he saw her struggling to sit up.

After helping her out and venting his rage on the disgruntled farmer, he returned to Tory. "We'll go no farther with this carriage, my lady. Shall I send to the White Swan for another? It's a short piece up the road."

Tory sat down on the embankment and nodded. "Yes, we've gone too far to return to London now." One outrider departed as ordered. A nondescript but comfortable coach arrived an hour later. The outrider would stay to see to the coach and himself take it back to London.

They set off again, only the coachman and one outrider attending. Shortly after, the coachman realized they were being followed. He whipped up the horses to verify his suspicions. Sure enough, the two pursuing riders urged their mounts to a gallop.

He lashed the nags, but they were tiring, and the riders soon pulled even. One brandished a pistol. "Pull 'em up, if'n yer values yer life."

The coachman ducked one shot, but the next caught him in the arm. He cried out and dropped the reins. The weary horses slowed to a stop. The outrider pulled his own weapon and fired, but the bouncing motion of his horse as he pulled him up threw off his aim. The other rider knocked him out before he could reload. He slumped to the ground.

Tory was reaching for the door when it opened and the trussed coachman was thrown in beside her.

"If ye unties 'im, I'll kill 'im," the burly rascal warned, slamming the door. There was a lurch as something was stowed behind the luggage flap. Then the coach moved on.

Tory was too furious to be afraid. She wetted her handkerchief with the water flask and dabbed at the coachman's wound. He groaned. His eyes fluttered open.

His face crumpled as he remembered what had happened. "Your ladyship, forgive me. I tried to outrun them—"

She shushed him. "You've nothing to apologize for, Thomas. If anyone is to blame, it's I." She had a very good idea who'd paid these men to kidnap her, and she'd played right into his hands by leaving. No wonder Cedric had been so sure of himself. And with reason, for, unless one of them escaped, it would seem the earth had opened and swallowed them after they hired the coach. There would be nothing to tie Cedric to her disappearance.

Of his plans for her, she did not let herself think. When she'd made Thomas as comfortable as she could by loosening his bonds, she clasped her arms about her waist and prayed.

The two hirelings were too busy sharing an ale jug to hear the telltale whisper from the rear of the coach. Tory didn't catch it, either.

There was no more evidence of Hubert's escape than a grunt as he hit the ground and rolled away from the coach slowing around a bend. He moved the knife from his belt back to his boot, where the men had not thought to search. He shook his head to clear it, noted the coach's direction and the area around him, then turned and began a ground-eating trot.

The duchess was at the breakfast table when a commotion at the door roused her from her gloomy contemplation of her plate. Frowning, she watched as the door burst open and Hemings, with none of his usual equanimity, led a limping, bruised Hubert in.

"Your Grace, forgive this rude intrusion, but Hubert has news of the most shocking import," Hemings said, almost stuttering in his haste.

Hubert removed his hat and squinted at the duchess out of one blackened eye. "Yer ladyship, it's sorry I am ta be the one ta tell ye this, but yer granddaughter 'as been kidnapped."

The napkin fell from Greaty's lap. One hand went to her throat as she croaked, "By whom? Do you have any idea where she's being taken?"

"No, but I can tell yer exackly where I were when I jumped off the coach. I 'adn't enough coin ta hire a horse, so I been the night getting 'ere."

Whoever had orchestrated this scheme had planned carefully. One name came immediately to mind. The duchess turned to Hemings.

"Send word to Baron Cedric Howard immediately to call on me. Fetch McAllister as well. Hurry, man!" she snapped when Hemings moved too slowly to suit her.

She turned to Hubert. "You've done well, my man. Your wages will be increased. Now go, clean yourself, and eat; then return here. I'll need you to guide us to where you jumped off the coach." Bobbing his head, he went.

When Cedric was admitted, the duchess was torn between relief and dismay at the sight of him.

His expression puzzled, he kissed her hand. "Why did you send for me, ma'am? Is something amiss?"

"It seems Victoria is missing," the duchess said coolly, watching him.

His shock looked genuine when he gasped, "My God, when? How did you find out?"

"Yesterday. One of my servants escaped the blackguards."

Limply Cedric slumped into a chair. Then he surged to his feet. "By God, they'll not get away with this. What can I do to help? Shall I fetch the watch?"

"Not yet. If I need you, I'll send for you. Please go, for I've much to do," the duchess said wearily. Cedric was a superb actor, but every instinct she possessed warned her that he lied. Still, if he'd kidnapped Tory, why was he waiting to go to her? They had but one hope to find her quickly . . .

Still seeming shaken, Cedric bowed and exited. He drove his curricle away at a decorous pace, unaware of the groom on the prime blood following him. The man thought it most curious that, as soon as he was out of sight of the house, Cedric used his whip mercilessly.

Two hours later, McAllister hurried to the docks, praying he'd be in time. If Beau's head ached from their two-day carousal as much as his did, maybe he'd decided to delay his voyage. McAllister pulled his horse up to the *Scorpion*'s berth—in time to see the xebec turn up the river.

He yelled, "No, Beau, wait!" The wind and dock noises drowned out even his stentorian voice. McAllister swept his hat off and threw it on the ground. Then, cursing, he picked it up and turned to go back to the duchess.

Tory shuddered when another rat ran across the room. She pulled her feet up on the straw mattress and huddled under the thin blanket. The early November morning was chilly, but she'd not been offered even a cup of tea since her supper last night of hard bread and harder cheese.

Her captors had allowed her one candle to light this hovel. The windows were boarded, so she needed it even now, in full daylight. She jumped when the harsh laughter sounded again, but the footsteps she feared didn't approach.

Tory rubbed her chilled hands together, battling her usual nausea and, more intimidating, fear. It was the waiting that reduced her to a mass of quivering nerves. Why had Cedric taken her, if it was indeed he? But he had no need of her money, and his consequence as an Englishman would never allow him to do anything that would ruin him in the eyes of his peers.

That could only mean that whatever he planned to do with her would leave no trail. The chills running up and down Tory's spine increased until her teeth chattered . . . Dear God, she had to get out of here.

Tory's knees knocked together when she stood. She searched diligently, but there was nothing heavy enough to batter open the shutters, which were nailed shut from the outside. The door was bolted, and she'd have to evade her jailers even if she could open it somehow. She slumped down on the bed, the closest she'd ever been in her life to total despair. Even her captivity in Barbary had not been so unnerving. For there, she'd had Beau.

Like a light flickering in a cavern, she let his bright memory guide her now. How she loved him. When her very life was forfeit, she knew how precious that life was and how foolish she'd been to let pride rule it.

Yes, he had tricked her, but he'd had cause. And he seemed genuinely sorry. Wasn't she forgiving enough to put the past behind her in her yearning for a future with him? Had it not been for the babe, she'd go to him as soon as she escaped. As she would escape, she told herself staunchly. She knew she could trust him with her life; her heart had not the same assurance. But trust or not, he was the only man she yearned for. Both comforted and troubled by the thought, she dozed off.

The sound of the door opening woke her that evening. She started erect, then swayed under the wave of nausea incited by her empty stomach. The candle had burned down, and she squinted against the sudden lantern light. Her heart dropped to her toes.

"Have you had a pleasant stay?" Cedric asked.

Running her tongue around the inside of her mouth to wipe the sourness away, Tory replied coolly, "Lovely, and precisely what I expected from such as you."

"Actually, you deserve less, but I'm ever generous to my mistresses. Until I tire of them, of course. Still, you'll learn to make do, no doubt. Slaves are not accorded many luxuries." Cedric came a step closer, set the lantern down beside the bed, and unbuttoned his coat.

Tory took several deep, calming breaths. So that's what he planned: to get his fill of her, then sell her into slavery. "I escaped from bondage once. I can do so again. You'll never get away with this."

"But I already have. The fools I hired were careless, but your servant has no idea where you are. So effective to double back, you see. No one will think to look for you this close to London. Besides, your estimable grandmother saw me this very morning herself, to her disappointment, I might add. She has no reason to tie me to your disappearance. I'll appear in London regularly. When I can draw myself away from your bliss." He drew off his shirt and bent to remove his boots.

"Come, undress yourself and show me what you learned in the harem." When she stayed frozen, he cocked a cruel smile on her. "No? Just as well. I've always wanted to humble that haughty pride of yours. Doing so will lend a certain piquancy that may even help me forget you've been so well used."

Fury came to Tory's aid. There would be no Beau to save her this time, for she knew he'd sailed on the tide. Only God and her own strength could help her now. Tory leaned back on her palms and put her feet casually on the floor. When Cedric leaned over to grab her, she kicked him as hard as she could in the disgusting bulge in his breeches.

He howled and fell to his knees, grabbing himself. Tory ran for the door and was relieved to find it unlocked. The two burly men Cedric had hired looked up in shock when she burst into the room. She dodged one, but the other blocked the outer door. Her glance flicked from side to side, but there was no other exit. She backed away as the men stalked her from either side.

She closed her eyes in despair when a harsh voice hissed from the bedroom door, "Strip her. When I've had her, you can each take a turn. More than a turn, if you like. You'll learn the *hard* way you're but a woman, my dear." The endearment was both terrifying and obscene. Worse, he accompanied the descriptive with a crude gesture.

Tory took little comfort at his obvious pain as he limped toward her. She gamely tried to evade the brutal hands reaching for her, but she was cornered. Despairingly, she screamed. The name that dwelt in her heart burst from her lips like a dying woman's prayer.

Incredibly, it was answered. The outer door slammed back on its hinges, and McAllister and Beau stormed into the room, a pistol in each hand. One of Cedric's men made the mistake of grabbing for the knife at his belt; it was his last. With a grunt of satisfaction, McAllister watched him fall. The other man threw his pistol on the floor and put his hands above his head. Cedric, however, tensed on the balls of his feet.

After a comprehensive glance at Tory, Beau fixed a predatory, ruthless gaze on Cedric that said much about how he earned his nickname. "Do it, please," he pleaded, his hand tightening about his pistol butt.

McAllister collected the pistol from the floor and tossed it out the door. Slowly, Cedric raised his hands.

"Very wise," Beau sighed in disappointment. "Tory, come here." For once Tory obeyed without question. When she reached him, her strength gave out. He caught her as she sagged, holding one pistol steady with his other arm.

If the protective arm quivered a bit, Tory was too upset to notice, nor did she see his lips move in a silent prayer of thanks. McAllister hustled Cedric's man to the door.

Cedric asked idly, "How did you find me?"

"You're not as clever as you think yourself. One of Her Grace's grooms followed you here, then galloped posthaste back to tell her where you went. Luckily, I had just arrived at the duchess's house."

"Luckily," Cedric repeated dryly. "May I at least dress myself before I meet the magistrate?"

"Certainly. But you'll not meet the magistrate. You'll meet your Maker."

Sniffing, Tory wiped her eyes and moved back, looking up at the granite chin above her. "No, Beau. He's not worth it. Let him pay for what he's done with the king's justice."

"Justice is uncertain, at best, for peers of the realm. But Howard can't cheat my sword."

"But if it's learned you killed him, the reason will be wondered at. I'd rather this not become known. Not for his sake or mine but for Greaty's."

"We'll say we dueled." Beau shrugged. "It will be true enough."

"And what if I kill you, Cochran?" Cedric gibed, walking into the bed chamber to retrieve his shirt. Warily, Beau followed, watching as he shrugged into it.

"Then the king will get his chance to prove he can still mete out justice. But you won't win, Howard. I'll not leave Tory a widow before she's a wife."

Two pairs of eyes flashed to his face, one startled and hopeful, the other vengeful. Cedric sneered, "How honorable that you'll marry this bitch just to give your brat a name."

Tory closed her eyes in humiliation, so she didn't see the shocked delight on Beau's face. "Tory?" he asked huskily, taking a step toward her. He glanced at her middle, giving Cedric his opening.

Cedric threw the lantern at Beau's head. Beau ducked, but the lantern shattered against the wall. A sliver of glass imbedded itself in the skin under his eye like a hard, unforgiving tear. He squinted, and his aim was thrown off as he fired. Tory screamed. By the time McAllister rushed back in from tying up the surviving kidnapper, Cedric and Beau were struggling for the remaining pistol, and a hungry tongue of flame was licking up the wall. McAllister aimed, but, in the vicious struggle, he was afraid of hitting Beau.

They were both tall, muscular men, and their strength was evenly matched, but finally Beau wrestled Cedric's hand down, raised his own knee and slammed his foe's wrist against it. With a grunt, Cedric dropped the pistol. Beau cricked Cedric's arm behind his back, turned him around, and marched him out of the hut. McAllister helped Tory, who was bent almost double from her coughing.

They left none too soon, for the abandoned hut's dry timbers went up like a bonfire, spreading from the chamber to the living area. Beau watched the flames, then he accepted a pistol from McAllister and released Cedric with a disgusted shove.

Out of the corner of his mouth, Beau said, "Get the swords, Mac. This fire will attract an audience I'd prefer to do without, so we must hurry."

McAllister helped Tory to a large boulder on the edge of the clearing before obeying. Beau kept his pistol stuck in Cedric's back as he spared her a concerned glance. "Are you all right, sweet?"

Tory nodded gamely, but physical and emotional deprivation were catching up to her. She settled herself to watch without arguing further. She knew that look on Beau's face of old. His mind was made up. He would duel to the death. Surely God wouldn't take him from her now when she'd just found him again, she prayed.

Beau handed McAllister the pistol and accepted the wrapped swords. He unfolded the blanket, offering Cedric his choice.

"What if I prefer pistols?"

"There's a vast difference between us, Howard. You're a knave aping a gentleman; I pretend to nothing but what I am: your executioner. I care not if I plug you or gut you; I just want to get the business done. To use pistols we'd have to wait for daylight. Besides, you struck the first blow when you attacked me. I'm perhaps overly generous in allowing you first selection, but the weapon matters less than the man who wields it." The matter-of-fact tone was as insulting as the words.

Inhaling furiously, Cedric grabbed each sword, tested it, and selected one. "This suits me fine. I want to watch you suffer before you die."

"Bloodthirsty cur, aren't you?" Beau chided mildly as he drew off his coat and tested the other sword. He glanced at his opponent. "Perhaps you never heard, but Tory wasn't just rescued by me. She was captured by me." Beau executed a mocking bow. "You see before you Sinan Reis, late corsair captain of Algiers. A title I won by my sword."

"Beau, you shouldn't have told him that," Tory groaned.

"So little faith in me, my dear? He'll not live to tell the tale, I assure you."

Cedric seemed paler in the fire glow, but his arm was steady when he assumed the on guard position. "That explains much. It inspires me anew to dispatch you forthwith. It will be amusing to see the anger of the Upper Ten Thousand when they realize they've had a pirate foisted off on them as a gentleman." He saluted mockingly.

Tory's nails bit into her palms as the two blades clashed, then disengaged with a menacing hiss. McAllister uncurled one of her hands to catch it in a comforting clasp.

"Do not fash yourself, lassie. Beau will win wi'out a scratch." McAllister watched the duel with a deal more serenity. But then he'd tested Beau in battle; Tory hadn't. But then his happiness didn't depend on the fragile heartbeat coursing through Beau; Tory's did.

Flames popped and crackled behind the two fencers, limning them in shimmering rivulets of blood. Cedric thought he saw an opening and lunged, as Beau had intended. He entangled the blade, almost tearing it from Cedric's hand.

Cedric pulled away just in time. He attacked with more wariness now, thrusting right, left, then right again. Though Beau gave ground, Cedric couldn't shake the feeling that Cochran was toying with him. Feeling became certainty when Beau slammed his blade almost to the ground and stood waiting for him to recover instead of slicing into the opening.

Fury overrode caution. Despite his many faults, Cedric was no coward. "You miserable excuse for a man, you'll not take me without cost," he panted. He slammed Beau's blade aside so hard it flew too wide for him to block Cedric's vicious follow-up lunge.

But Beau knew it was coming. He backed up a tiny step that saved his life. The tip of the sword pierced his breastbone, but he didn't even wince. He twisted away and brought his sword up beneath Cedric's, knocking it skyward.

Tory gasped at the bright red dot on the end of that blade. It trickled down the steel and gleamed wetly in the glow of the flames. A matching patch spread over Beau's shirt. McAllister leaned forward almost as tensely as Tory when the two men engaged again.

The close escape cleared Beau's head of the reckless rage. His own cruelty had almost cost him dearly. Anger was no friend to the duelist.

It was time to end it.

Beau's face set into hard, remote lines. He didn't hear the flames roar louder as the roof of the burning building caved in; he didn't see Tory break into tears of distress. He knew only the movements of Cedric's body, the telltale tensing and flexing that he read like a book. The next time Cedric engaged him, Beau batted his sword away, preparing the coup de grace in his mind. He built up to it with a deceptively simple series of feints, but even Cedric's weary senses knew the end was near.

And, as Cedric panted and barely fended off Beau's thrust, for the first time in many a year he remembered one of the biblical truths his devout mother had striven to impress on him: "They have sown the wind and they shall reap the whirlwind." Understanding came too late. The whirlwind was borne to him on Beau's sword. It swooshed past his feeble guard and funneled into his chest, swift and sure as Beau intended. In the blink of an eye, it returned Cedric to the dust from which he was made.

Not nausea, not pride, not exhaustion kept Tory from running to Beau. He threw his bloodied sword aside and tried to catch her so she wouldn't stain her dress on his own blood, but she burrowed into him as if he were hearth, home, and happiness. As he was.

"Beau, Beau, Beau," she whispered, running her hands over him to assure herself he truly stood whole before her.

He silenced her babbling in the only way he knew. The passionless kiss they shared healed as it asked forgiveness for the past and promised hope for the future. Gladly they both gave and took in equal measure. When Beau put her gently away from him, his eyes were bright.

"Well, that's answer enough to my most important question, I hope. When will you marry me?"

A little of Tory's glow faded. "For the babe?" she asked softly.

Beau's heart sank at the entreaty in her tone. Pain stabbed him as he realized Tory's love for the unborn child was already greater than whatever feelings she bore for him. For the child's sake, she would wed him. But if that was the only reason she'd accept, it would have to do. Someday, please God, there would be more.

"Aye, for the child's sake," he muttered, running her tumbled hair through his fingers.

Tory buried her face in Beau's chest, biting her lip over more tears. The worst had happened, but she hadn't strength enough to deny herself any longer. Surely he would grow to love the mother of the babe he wanted so? "Whenever you like," she whispered into his chest.

McAllister interrupted. "We'd best go, laddie. If I mistake not, we'll soon ha' company." Beau patted Tory's shoulder, then helped load the body into the rear of their carriage. They stopped long enough on the hasty trip to turn the live and the dead kidnappers in to the local squire with the explanation they'd tried to rob them. When they returned to London they took Cedric's body to his lodgings explaining to his horrified man that he'd lost in a duel, then turned to Grosvenor Square.

"Why didn't you sail this morning, Beau?" Tory asked.

"I hired a crew and sent the *Scorpion* on with a message for my father." He pulled her into his lap while McAllister drove. "As for why I didn't go . . ." He nuzzled her neck, whispering, "A vixen called me back. Even drunk, you haunted me. I knew then I couldn't leave. I was determined to tree you if I had to bay at the moon to do it. I returned in time to set out after you with McAllister. To your grandmother's relief, I might add."

Tory rested her head against his broad shoulder, wishing with all her heart that Greaty had waited to tell him about the child. But one thing she'd learned the hard way in the past months: Wishing for something didn't make it so. Sometimes all one could do was live one day at a time. Besides, she had reason to hope. Had he not come back for her even after she'd rejected him cruelly? *Before* he knew of the child?

This knowledge comforted her when Beau was questioned about the duel and held briefly by the authorities before the duchess intervened. It became imperative for Beau to leave before a scandal could devolve. The knowledge comforted her during the hasty wedding when McAllister escorted her up the aisle of the tiny chapel. It sustained her when they made their good-byes to Greaty, Becky, and McAllister, promising to return soon after the babe was born.

But the comfort lost its effect when they boarded their ship, for Tory was to face a lonely voyage. Beau had been generous. He'd booked her the best cabin.

He'd booked himself one, too.

Chapter 17

Tory found no comfort in the fact that the very elements seemed in sympathy with her. After yet another lonely night, she stared at the sea surging to engage the looming horizon like an angry primordial beast. What had she done to make Beau so distant? Had he only wed her for wealth and status? For it certainly seemed he'd lost interest in her since taking her safely to wife.

On their wedding night three weeks ago, when he'd casually rejected the one thing she knew he enjoyed of her, she'd stared at him in shock. "What did you say?"

His back was to her, so perhaps that was why his voice seemed muffled. "I . . . er, want you to be as comfortable as possible. These bunks do not accommodate two. You need not fear for your safety. I'll be right next door, and this is a tightly run ship."

Even then, Tory reflected bitterly with the advantage of hindsight, she'd been obtuse. She had not been able to believe he no longer wanted her. So she had walked up to him and put a hand on his shoulder. Her heart had pounded at her own daring, but faint heart never won fair gentleman, she'd paraphrased whimsically to herself. "Surely if we slept close enough together, we'd be comfortable."

His muscles stiffened under her hand. Slowly, a searching gaze was turned on her. She blushed and looked away.

He removed her hand and patted it in a manner that seemed patronizing to her. He propped his shoulders and one foot behind him on the door and drawled, "I would term little of our relationship 'comfortable,' least of all our sleeping habits. But this is for the best, m'dear. Trust me."

Tory hid her hurt under a haughty facade. "So I have done in the past. At my peril."

"In the past I had no right to ask more."

"So that's it! You think because of this"—Tory held up her left hand and twisted the band of emeralds and diamonds until it sparkled in the candlelight—"I must subjugate everything to you, even my mind? Haven't I every reason to doubt you? Do you think to use your conjugal rights as a carrot before a witless donkey? Well, sir, I am not so easily led by my appetites. Any of them." She looked at him defiantly.

"Woman, you have a positive gift for misunderstanding me! Sometimes I opine you do it deliberately." Beau held up his hand and began to refute her points one at a time. "One: Now that I am *privileged* at last to call you my own, subjugation has no place between us. Only sharing." He shook his head when she would have interrupted. "Two: I've never once lied to you since you discovered who I was." He raked her up and down with a look every woman knew. "Three: I want nothing more than to assert my conjugal rights. Now. Often. In every way imaginable, for you are the most apt pupil I've ever had." He grinned as her skin darkened to match her wine taffeta gown. "But we have all the years of our lives ahead of us. It's time we establish an affinity for other things as well. Do you not agree?"

Then Tory had been appeased—as he'd intended, she knew now. She'd been helpless against that rough velvet voice. "You're probably right. But if not now, when?" She hadn't meant to sound so eager . . .

He threw back his head and laughed, his male triumph too joyful to raise her hackles. He walked up to her, still chuckling, and hugged her, then held her away to look into her eyes. "When you trust me and mean the vows we spoke today."

Tory's eyes narrowed. "Which ones?"

"Why, love, honor, and, er, what was that other one? Ah, yes—obey. Most definitely obey," he drawled provokingly.

She ducked from under his hands, breast puffed like a pouter pigeon's. But she smiled sweetly. "Of course, master. What is thy first commandment? Shall I hang up your coat?" She pulled it from his broad shoulders with such force that the form-fitting garment tore at the shoulder.

"Oh, dear, how unfortunate. Leave it with me and I'll mend it." She tossed it in the corner. Next she lifted his satchel and, huffing, lugged it to his cabin. "Let me unpack for you." She opened the sea chest and tossed his starched cravats and ruffled shirts on the bottom, throwing his extra boots on top. He winced.

That chore done, she stood, shook out her skirts, and looked about. She swooped down on his hat. "Here, let me hang this up." She pretended not to hear his muffled protest. The hat fell the first time she hung it, so she rammed it down hard on the peg the next time. There was a distinct tearing sound as the crown of the beaver top hat, unlike Beau, wisely took the path of least resistance.

When Tory looked around, Beau held up a weary hand. "You win, ma'am. I'll concede whilst I still have a wardrobe to protect. Your point is crystal clear."

"I'm glad you take it, sir. My notions of obedience may not match yours. Your notions of trust may not match mine. Perhaps some women can give one without the other, but I cannot."

"But if the twain shall meet, Tory? What then?"

"Why, then . . . then we may have a marriage in truth," she whispered. And she'd slammed out of his cabin before the disappointed tears fell. She had so hoped this voyage would be a tender new beginning for them. She'd been ready to meet him more than halfway, ignoring even her outraged pride. Yes, he'd married her for the babe, but she could make him rejoice in their union for other reasons—the marriage bed, for example. At least, so she'd planned.

He'd sabotaged those plans nicely. He brought her tea and biscuits in the morning to help settle her stomach, lunched with her, and made civil conversation. He dined with her by candlelight, looking supremely romantic—and acting dull as ditchwater. He had not so much as touched her hand. He never argued or sent her one of those wicked glances and sensual innuendos that made her toes curl. In short, he wasn't the Sinan she'd come to love or the Beau she'd hesitantly wed. He was as courteous—and as boring—as any of the suitors she'd avoided like the plague.

And this was the man she was to believe cherished her? The man who wanted her "now and often, in every way imaginable"?

"Poppycock!" Tory grumbled to herself as she stood at the railing. "He has more the air of a man who's gotten what he wants. I believe he'd wish me good riddance were it not for the babe." Tory was too preoccupied to note the approach of the subject of her thoughts.

For long moments Beau watched her, wondering if she wanted him a fraction as much as he wanted her. He longed to carry her off and consummate his rights. But he'd taken her twice out of his own selfish needs; he would not do so again. Until she cared for him as much as she wanted him, it was best for both of them that she sleep alone. He had wed her in haste, but he would woo her in leisure, as he should have done in the beginning: chivalrously. It was time to consider emotional needs over physical ones. Connubial bliss was no substitute for love. Besides, since Tory considered his words suspect, surely she'd see how he loved her when he sacrificed his desire to woo her as she deserved?

Oh, but how she tested his resolve. The wind whipped her hood back, freeing a fiery curl that warmed her cheek. She absently tucked it behind her ear. Her breasts, slightly fuller with pregnancy, lifted with the motion, thrusting against her gray kerseymere gown.

Closing his eyes, he tried to cap the longing springing up from the deepest stratum of his soul. Think of the future, not the present, you rutting goat, he snarled inwardly. You've treated her like a possession long enough. Only patience will win you the love you want so much. He opened his eyes to see the wind molding her Empire-style gown to the tiny swell of her abdomen. She was beginning to show. She was due in late May, so she wasn't quite four months along.

How he longed to touch her. Yes, as any lusty male desired his wife. But more, in the tenderness of devotion—the confident clasp of a hand, eyes meeting in unspoken but shared thought, the affectionate brush of a soft cheek to a whiskered one. And he wanted most of all to strip her and cherish her as the mother of his child, to trail his hands and mouth over her, learning the wondrous changes they'd wrought together.

He dared not. She'd slipped away from him this past three weeks, despite his wooing. The most logical explanation was the one he wanted most to deny. The closer they came to Philadelphia, the glummer she seemed. Did she dread life in America so very much? Would she despise the quicker pace, more open society, and freer manners? He considered demanding the truth, but he'd faced death with less fear. It was too soon to risk all. He turned and walked away.

Thus, when they sailed up the Delaware on December 18 to dock at Philadelphia, there was little of the newlywed about them. Beau was grim as he helped Tory to the wharf; Tory was pale and tense. It was not a good beginning.

His parents met them, for Beau had sent word of their marriage and arrival. Beau frowned. They were both dressed head to toe in black, their expressions matching. Where was the joy he'd expected? Robert was haggard, and Miranda had tear stains on her cheeks. She twisted a damp, frilly kerchief in her gloved hands. What the devil was wrong?

Aware of the irony of this moment, he drew Tory forward when she hung back. He, who'd always disdained idle English ladies, was bringing one home as his wife. And her name was Tory to boot . . . "Mother, Father, I present my wife, Victoria Grenville Cochran."

A twinkle banished the melancholy in Robert's eyes. "Now, that's the best news I've had in years. Young lady, I can't tell you how glad I am to welcome you to this family." He ignored her outstretched hand and drew her into a strong embrace. He was as tall and dark as his son and his strong face had much the look of Beau's.

Miranda, a tall, fair woman with longish but attractive features, burst into happy tears this time. "Oh, Beau, we were so worried about you!" She released him from her fierce hug to take Tory's hands and look at her searchingly.

"Why, she's every bit as lovely as Her Grace always claimed. Bless you, my dear, for taking this rascal on. He's in need of a firm hand."

Tory relaxed at their genuine warmth. They, at least, were happy she was among them, even if their son was not. "Thank you, ma'am."

"Father, what's amiss?" Beau asked, frowning at the mournful, muffled peal of the Christ Church bells.

Miranda's eyes watered again. Robert patted her shoulder. "Washington is dead," he said grimly to his son.

Beau hissed in a shocked breath. Tory saw him swallow several times. "When? how?"

"On the fourteenth. His cold worsened into lung fever. Bleeding could not save him." The three Americans clasped hands and bowed their heads in prayerful homage to the man who'd been first in American hearts.

Tory was also sad at the loss of the great leader. Washington had been admired, behind hands and doorways, even by many Englishmen. Had it not been for him, she knew, there probably would be no America now. Her eyes watered. Would that every soul who passed this earthly vale left so many to mourn his passing.

Tactfully, she looked around to give the Americans time to compose themselves. The log wharves were cemented with earth and stone. Even the dockworkers seemed subdued as they toiled with cargoes of rice and cotton. Over the foul smells Tory caught the scents of coffee, tobacco, and tea. Crates of scotch whisky and Spanish sherry were unloaded reverently. From another vessel, men carried off furniture. She might have been standing on London's docks, such was the diversity. Robert looked up when she stood on tiptoe in an effort to peer beyond the docks. He released his wife and son to stride over to her.

Smiling, he took her arm. "What a poor greeting we've given you. Forgive us. But we revered him so."

"I understand, sir. I, too, admired him."

Beau twisted his head around at her comment.

Robert assisted her into the black coachee with red trim awaiting them. The red leather cushions were plush and comfortable, the doors paned with real glass. It was as elegant as her grandmother's best. Robert kept up a commentary as they drove west into the city, away from the Delaware.

"As you are probably aware, William Penn himself helped select the site of Philadelphia for his 'greene country towne.' He remembered the plague of 1665 and the fire of 1666 in London, and he wanted a site that would not burn easily and would be wholesome for the inhabitants." Robert slanted a sly look at Tory's attentive features. "Of course, even more, as a Quaker he wanted a place of refuge free from religious persecution by your sundry kings and queens.''

''Assuredly,'' Tory agreed blandly. ''But had it not been for the daring of an Englishman, Sir Walter Raleigh, who can say when this land would have been available for Penn to settle?''

Robert made a fist and brushed her chin. ''What a facer! Of course, we both know how ended Raleigh's spirit of enterprise.'' He made a lopping motion with his hand and quirked an eyebrow.

''Round to you, sir,'' Tory conceded. ''However, there's a line past which initiative becomes arrogance—as you Americans so graphically proved when our Parliament displayed its own enterprising spirit. It was a little matter of taxation without representation, I believe?''

Grinning hugely, Robert bobbed his head. ''Rousted royally! I take your point. Whether it's enterprise or usury depends upon which side of the ledger one occupies, hmm? One item I hope we will agree upon, my dear: You are a definite asset to this family.'' The pair, having made each other's measure, smiled in reciprocal admiration, but then Tory glanced at Beau's tense features.

The elder Cochrans looked intrigued when she said dryly, ''A question your son and I have debated before, but have yet to settle.'' Beau turned to the window when his parents eyed him curiously.

Miranda glanced at Tory. No namby-pamby English miss was this. If she'd handpicked her son's bride herself, she could scarcely have done better. She looked back at Beau. Obviously he loved the girl, yet he watched her as if she were volatile. He seemed to view his wife's and father's bantering as a daggers-drawn confrontation. Helen had told her what she knew of Tory and Beau's relationship when they'd received word of the marriage a few days ago, so she had not expected a harmonious couple. But there was something in Beau's face that went beyond worry, or even anger. It could best be termed fear. Of what? She worried over the matter as her husband resumed his lecture.

''Many streets running east-west are named after our indigenous trees. You'll see lombards planted along the streets, for instance. Their shade is most welcome in the summer, which can be quite warm. North-south thoroughfares are numbered. Virtually all of our streets are straight, unlike those in so many of your English cities.''

As he spoke, Tory watched the passing scenery. The city was larger than she'd expected, but it was, and would be until next year, the capital of America. Then, Beau had informed her, the government was moving to the dismal swampland named after Washington. He shared other Philadelphians' contempt for the new capital, but building was proceeding.

Tory liked the city's open, organized aspect. Its public squares and regular streets were so unlike the crooked, crowded lanes of many European cities she'd seen—including London, in many respects. The streets paved with roundish stones were higher in the middle so as to allow good drainage. The sidewalks were elevated brick affairs, which she could imagine were attractive in spring when the trees and flowers were in bloom. On corners and in front of buildings she saw lampposts supporting four-sided lamps that would be easier to clean than the traditional globes. The houses were attractive, red brick with white trim and shingled roofs, all of similar design.

"I think you'll be pleasantly surprised at how much there is to do here. We've theaters, a fine library, museums, hotels, and dancing assemblies. Virtually every type of good is imported through our port, and some of the finest farmland in America surrounds us, so our foods are of the freshest."

Soon they drew up before a three-story Georgian mansion on Chestnut Street. Robert exited first, holding up a hand to help Miranda down. Beau went next. Tory hesitated, then put her hand in his. As she bent to exit, their eyes were on a level. She wondered at his pleading look before he gently lifted her down. She sighed. Would she ever understand him? What did he want of her when he looked at her so?

Robert led the way up the steps. "Beau, your mother has redecorated your room. Why don't you show Tory up? Then come see me in the library."

Tory blinked at sight of the imposing black servant who let them in the house. She'd seldom seen blacks, and never one as proud as this. From the top of his curly head to the tips of his gleaming shoes, he was every inch a butler in control of his dominion. Beau greeted him warmly.

"Elias, it's good to see you. And how is your missus?"

In almost perfect diction he replied, "Expecting our third any day now, Mr. Beau. It's glad we all are to have you back." He took the men's hats and the ladies' capes as he talked, and hung them in a recess under the curving cherrywood stairway. He nodded politely when Beau introduced her. "Welcome to this house and land, Mrs. Cochran."

Bemused, Tory nodded. Beau smiled as she looked after Elias's retreating back. "Slavery was outlawed some years ago in Pennsylvania. Elias earns an honest day's wage for an honest day's work." His tone grew harsh. "You will soon discover, I hope, that we're not quite the backwater bumpkins you think us."

Tory opened her mouth to deny the unfair assumption, but he'd already turned away. "Come, so you can wash and rest. Dinner is served at seven."

Shrugging, Tory took one last appreciative look at the commodious paneled foyer with its fine red and gold japanned secretary, Chippendale chairs, Oriental carpet, and crystal chandelier, then followed Beau up the stairs.

He turned left down the pine-floored hallway. The new silver Argand lamp sconces, fueled by whale oil and a hollow wick so they wouldn't smoke or burn down, were arrayed along the plaster walls. He opened the third door. Their room was a soothing study of contrasts between masculine and feminine, old and new. Tory was touched that her mother-in-law had tried to make her feel at home in the limited time allowed her.

The massive four-poster had new hangings of peach cotton embroidered with navy flowers. They were an obvious attempt to lighten the navy velvet drapes at the windows, which had probably matched the old hangings. The towering highboy with its imposing, carved pediment had been pushed aside to make room for one of similar but more feminine style. Tory opened a drawer and found it empty, awaiting her use. Beau's small shaving table had likewise ceded supremacy to her veneered mahogany commode dressing table with folding mirror.

The old, valuable Persian carpet of gloomy hue before the fireplace had been counterbalanced by a peach and blue hooked rug next to the bed. The nautical souvenirs, statues from exotic lands and scrimshaws, legacies of Beau's voyages, had been lightened with Dresden figurines and Wedgwood bowls and vases. Tory fingered a pretty shepherdess that stood on the table next to the navy sofa before the fire.

"I'm sorry to have discommoded you so. I hope you won't feel crowded. Er, in any way." She glanced at the huge bed, then hastily away. Her heart thrummed in hope. She hadn't realized they'd be sharing a room, but surely he'd find it hard to keep his distance now, in such intimate, attractive quarters?

Apparently not. He, too, refused to look at her as he stretched his long length out on the sofa. His feet hung off the end and his shoulders almost overflowed the narrow seat, but he said evenly enough, "You shall find the bed quite as comfortable as I will find this couch." He waited, holding his breath, for her to naysay, but no protest came. When he peered over the back of the couch, she was staring out the window at the gardens and hothouse at the rear of the property.

They jumped at a loud knock. At Beau's call, a manservant entered with Tory's first trunk. "Er, I'm sure my mother has hired you a maid. I'll, um, send her up." He fled.

Tory busied herself unpacking, but the activity did not lighten her heavy heart.

Downstairs, Beau smoothed his own perturbed expression away, asked Elias to send Tory's maid up, then went to the library. Robert was puffing at one of his favorite Virginia cigars when Beau entered. He blew the fragrant smoke through his nostrils and smiled a welcome from behind his massive writing desk. A large globe stood in one corner of the book-lined room. Glass fronts protected the tomes. Comfortable leather chairs were grouped before the desk.

"I'm damn glad you're home, Beau, and that you were able to find Helen. She's visiting friends, but will return for supper. It's like old times to have you both here again. With a new addition I highly approve, by the way."

"Well you should, since it was at your instigation that I fetched her."

"And I was petitioned by Clarissa. Truly I felt the danger to Victoria outweighed the danger to you. I have great faith in your abilities."

"I don't want to disillusion you, but it's only by the grace of God we all made it out whole. Physically, at least. As for the emotional reckoning still to come . . . If you wanted me to make a match with the girl, why didn't you just say so?"

"Because you would have avoided her like the plague. Besides, we merely took advantage of the situation, we didn't plan it."

"Just like you didn't plan for me to meet her four years ago when you sent me to England to investigate new contracts?" When Robert shrugged sheepishly, Beau slammed a fist into his palm. "You and the duchess should sport wings and cherubic features to give a fellow warning." His tone was accusatory, not teasing.

Robert tilted his head to one side and watched his son take great, restless strides about the room. "By the look of you, I'd say you think us more horned, tailed, and cloven-hoofed," he countered dryly.

"And so it may prove, for there's naught more hellish than a marriage of one-sided love," Beau burst out.

"On whose side? Yours or hers?"

"Mine, of course. Mother saw it immediately."

"What makes you so sure Tory doesn't return your affections? Helen seems to think she does."

"Because I told her several times of my devotion and she rejected me. It's a miracle she finally agreed to wed me."

"Well, then, why are you so glum? A lady of her wealth and standing doesn't wed for no reason. Clarissa told me of her recalcitrance."

"Oh, she had a reason, all right," Beau said quietly. "She carries my child. It's due late in May."

Robert sucked in a puff so hard it went down the wrong pipe. He coughed and wheezed until his eyes watered; then he stubbed out his cigar in the silver ashtray and shoved his rotating chair with the marble rollers away from the desk.

When he'd gotten his breath back, he clapped Beau on the shoulder, beaming. "It's high time you set up your nursery. Clarissa must be ecstatic."

"Oh, yes, she's glad, you're glad, maybe even Tory's glad . . ." Beau trailed off.

"You're not?"

"Yes. But I want Tory's devotion first as my wife rather than as the mother of my children."

Robert frowned at Beau's bent head. "The source of the trouble between you goes back to your capture of her, I take it. Tell me what happened." The men took chairs opposite each other. The sun was lowering in the sky when Beau finished.

Digesting Beau's tale along with one of the sugared plums he was so fond of, Robert mused, "I didn't realize you'd taken her in such dislike because of Henry. You were . . . not exactly honorable in . . . knowing her under such circumstances."

Since Beau had chastised himself far more harshly, he didn't squirm under his father's stern gaze. "I loved her by then, and

I'd come to the conclusion that I'd misjudged her as well. But I can't convince Tory of that.''

"You're not so different from any other newlywed couple. Devotion, loyalty, and love grow only with time and vigilance. Treat her tenderly and she'll respond. I don't think she would have wed you just because of the child, from what I've seen and heard of her.''

Robert rose to open the liquor chest against the wall and pour two glasses of Madeira. "Now we must discuss how to appease those who are angry with us for 'interfering' in foreign affairs.''

Beau accepted his glass. "Yes, Terence explained Congress had been apprised of my mission.'' Beau's eyes glittered when he asked, "Who do you think told them?''

"I was told by a fellow Republican that Lewis Fuller informed Congress of our, er, as he put it, 'egregrious, unauthorized interference in foreign affairs by private citizens,' '' Robert replied, naming a prominent alderman, one of Philadelphia's most fervent Federalists, and a longtime political and business enemy of the Cochrans.

"How could he have found out about it?''

"I think he became suspicious at the way I received your dispatches. I took precautions that now, with hindsight, seem foolish. I didn't think it wise to have the courier come to the warehouse, so I arranged to meet him at the Indian King. Casually, I thought, but someone, either Fuller or one of his cronies, must have found it odd that I met with this stranger on such a regular basis, although he was not an employee or business associate. A few queries would have told them that he shipped out shortly after our meetings.''

Beau groaned. "It's a damn sorry state of affairs when a man can't conduct business in a quiet tavern without looking to his back.''

"Nevertheless, I should have been more cautious. The last dispatch was stolen.'' Beau cursed. Robert continued grimly, "The courier's purse was taken, but I suspect the motive was political. While I have no proof that Fuller hired the ruffian, how else could he have known?''

"Have charges been brought against us?''

"Not yet, but they're being considered, if the authorities can decide what laws we've broken. Until the Federalists tried to smother dissent with their cursed Alien and Sedition Acts, we would have had little to worry about. But our barrister has informed me that one statute, the Logan Act, forbids private citizens from entering into negotiation with an enemy in the time of war.''

''But we're not at war with Algiers, and my actions could hardly be construed as negotiations.''

''Not from our view, perhaps. But what if we're soon at war with Tripoli, as Terence fears? His father has told him to come back as well, but the damage may already be done. What's really at issue here is not foreign affairs but domestic ones, just as the Alien and Sedition Acts are but disguised attempts to crush Republican opposition.'' Robert held his glass to the firelight to eye the wine'e clarity, but his mind was obviously focused inward.

''Much has happened while you've been away, Beau. The political climate has been poisoned by the Acts, and Pickering and his ilk are using them ruthlessly. Bache died in the fever of '98, and William Duane became editor of the *Aurora*.'' Robert brought his glass down to smile admiringly. ''His calumnies have been more harsh against the Acts even than Bache's, and he's doing a marvelous job of carrying the Republican banner for Philadelphia. Indeed, for the country.''

Robert's smile faded. ''But his effectiveness has of course incited Federalist fervor to silence him. They've twice trumped up charges of sedition against him this year alone. He was acquitted on charges of inciting riot by posting petitions for signatures against the Acts, but he's since been charged with seditious libel on two different counts. I'm of the opinion he'll be acquitted again, but the trial has been delayed until June.'' Robert sipped contemplatively.

''Now you can see why I ordered you home. I fear our opponents will use us as scapegoats to show the extremes to which Republican notions of liberty will take the country. After all, we took it upon ourselves to spy upon another country—one with which we're supposedly at peace. That hardly shows great faith in the Adams administration, or belief in the virtues of a strong central government.''

Slamming his glass down on the table next to his chair, Beau leaped to his feet to pace. ''Dammit, I risked my neck for my country, and I return to find myself condemned for pursuing the very causes so many fought and died for. We might as well be in England, subjects of the Crown, if we violate our own Constitution so readily by denying our editors freedom to speak according to their consciences.''

"I don't quarrel with that, but I'm not the one you must convince. I don't need to remind you that most of our fellow merchants consider us radicals for espousing Republican views when we own one of America's largest merchant fleets.''

Beau whirled to glare at his father. "The old elitist view that only the wealthy and powerful are fit to rule is the canker that's rotted many a country from the inside out. Are we to parrot slogans we don't believe in merely to reassure our associates?''

Robert said mildly, "I can hear you, Beau, as can the entire household.'' When Beau gave a frustrated groan and collapsed back into his chair, Robert continued. "Your idea of selling the *Scorpion* was brilliant. We refurbished her. She didn't bring as much as I'd hoped, but the sum should bolster our contention that we desperately need a navy if we're to promote the cause of liberty.''

"More like we'll be accused of bribery,'' Beau said, tapping his fingers together as if he couldn't sit still.

"Not unless they so accuse many other worthy Philadelphians who subscribed the funds to build a small frigate. Besides, it will be easier to justify our actions, since your mission was so successful. You saved Tory, you found Helen, you mapped the Algerine defenses . . .'' Robert's voice trailed off at Beau's sudden stillness.

"Beau?'' he growled. "You *did* complete the map, did you not? Terence sent word you'd shown him one.''

"I made two. I lost one in a fight with an old foe before I even left the harbor.'' Beau gripped the arms of his chair. "I gave Terence the complete copy before I left Algiers. Didn't you get it?'' Glumly, Robert shook his head.

Beau groaned and rubbed his aching temples. "It was to go out in the next dispatch. Was that the dispatch that was stolen?''

This time Robert nodded. Their eyes met grimly. "I'll reconstruct what I can from memory,'' Beau sighed, "but it won't be near as accurate, of course. We must find that map. I risked too much to draw it.''

They silently contemplated this latest disaster. "I doubt more action will be taken until January, what with Washington's death and Christmas,'' Robert said at last. "We'll keep our noses to the wind and scent whence it blows. Since the fervor died down over the XYZ Affair, opinion seems to be going our way.

McKean was elected governor this year," Robert smiled when Beau whooped his approval, "and, with Duane's help, we may be able to build a strong enough coalition to put Jefferson in office next year. I may be wrong, but it's beginning to seem that Federalist use of the Alien and Sedition Acts to stifle us has had the salubrious effect of uniting our sometimes fractious voices into one outraged cry."

"I'll not hide like a coward, if that's what you're suggesting."

"Not at all. You need to show Tory about. When the assemblies begin next month, in fact, you may find her an asset, providing, of course, her condition doesn't keep her from dancing."

Robert frowned when Beau laughed bitterly and said, "Oh, yes, her ladyship should do a wonderful job of soothing Federalist sensibilities, what with their fawning over anything English." Beau rose and put his empty glass down with a snap. "If you'll excuse me, Father, I'll change for dinner."

He stalked out, leaving Robert confused and concerned.

As he walked upstairs, Beau reflected again on the irony of his position. How could he have been bedazzled by a woman who represented all he despised? A woman who'd made her low opinion of the country he loved quite plain. This aristocrat, who wore her rank of titled lady like a crown, was to suddenly change to an obedient Republican wife? He snorted. Not likely. Far from championing him, she would instead please his detractors by voicing her own English-biased sentiments. If his own wife criticized him, why shouldn't his political enemies do the same? On this at least he would insist on obedience. She might stay a Tory to her grave, in politics as well as name, but by God she'd give him outward loyalty.

Beau cruised into their chamber to engage her. He foundered midstream, the wind taken out of his sails and his lungs. Tory's maid was helping a newly washed, perfumed Tory out of her wrapper, leaving her clad in chemise and stockings. An artful mass of fiery curls fell from the crown of her head to coil about her pearly shoulders and neck. The firelight outlined her body in disturbing detail. Beau's eyes consumed her. It had been so long since he'd seen her thus, longer still since he'd touched her as he wanted to. Everything but that need flew from his head.

Tory turned from appraising her hair to smile at her new maid, Celie, who was Elias's eldest daughter. "Celie, you're as talented as any London hairdresser. I'm pleased—" She gasped at sight of Beau standing just inside the open door. She knew that look. She swayed under the violent relief. Celie reached out to grab her, but Beau was quicker. In one leap, he had her by the shoulders and was lowering her to the edge of the bed.

"Leave us," he said to Celie. She obeyed, and when the door had closed behind her, he sat down beside Tory to rub her hands. "Were you about to faint?"

Yes, Tory yearned to reply, with longing for you. Instead, she shook her head. "No, I'm just hungry."

"Ready yourself, then, and we'll go down. Helen should have returned by now, and I know she's anxious to see you."

"I can't. You dismissed my maid." Tory peeped at him, hoping he'd take her meaning.

He did, but not in the way she intended. His lip curled. "I see. Your ladyship can't dress herself. Well, it won't be the first time I've played lady's maid. Which dress do you wish to wear?"

Tory pointed to the red velvet dress lying over the back of the sofa. While he fetched it, she shrugged into her petticoat, the mass of soft material hiding her impish smile. Perhaps they would be late to dinner . . .

He drew the dress over her head, being careful of her hair. He seemed to be an inordinate time fastening the tiny pearl buttons up the back. Did he tremble when she brushed against him?

"There," he gasped, backing up a safe step.

Slowly, Tory turned. He stiffened, his eyes gluing themselves precisely where she wanted them: to the extremely low-cut bodice. The gown was not overly daring, for the creamy fullness of her breasts was veiled by a red tissue-silk panel ending at her throat, where a high jet-bead collar glittered with her every movement. More curlicue beadwork trimmed the bodice where silk met velvet in a style so cunning that Tory's breasts thrust temptingly forward, like apples held out for his delectation.

His reaction—breath quickened, nostrils flared—pleased Tory. She was glad she'd decided to use her attributes before she grew heavy with child. She took an eager step forward, her mouth open to suggest they stop this foolish avoidance of each other, when he turned away with a smothered oath.

"You go on down. I'll follow as soon as I've changed."

Tory ignored the warning and followed him to his chest.

He slammed through drawers, removing a clean shirt and cravat. Next, he went to the armoire to take out a severe black coat and knee breeches. He ripped off his coat and threw it over a chair, then sat down on the edge of the bed to take off his boots.

Only then did he realize she was still there. He froze in the act of lifting his knee.

"Well," he barked. "What do you want?"

"Ah," Tory stammered. "I, ah, thought I might help you." Suiting action to words, she dropped to her knees before him and grasped his boot.

He gritted his teeth when her breasts swayed, glittering enticement, as she tugged the boot off. His nostrils quivered at her scent, and when that full, soft warmth fell against his stockinged leg after she took off the other boot, it was all he could do to keep from pulling her astride him. His mouth worked, but the words to send her away would not come. He sat, a helpless prisoner of her and what she made him feel, when she knelt between his spread legs to unbutton his shirt. He was too occupied in trying to calm his rioting passions to realize that her hands shook or that her eyes dilated more with every loosened button.

When the shirt fell open, she shoved it off his shoulders and held it on his arms to imprison him. She buried her face in his soft chest hair glistening in the firelight, rubbing her nose back and forth, inhaling his clean male scent. A rumbling grew in his chest like a volcano about to erupt, but Tory took no heed. She released his arms to touch the muscles quivering with tension. He caught her hands.

"Madam, unless you want to find yourself ridden the night through, I suggest you desist," he warned hoarsely.

Tory's eyes, soft and fetching as dew-washed gentians, smiled up at him. "Maybe that is indeed what I want."

"Victoria, don't play these games with me now. Our future is at stake, and we must both be very careful what wagers we make with it." He moved her aside, rising to rip off his shirt and put on the clean one.

"Games?" Tory repeated. "What games?"

"Bait and retreat. What else would you call your behavior since our marriage?"

Angry now, Tory rose and brushed off her gown. "I have no idea what you're talking about," she snapped.

"No? Then why else did you treat my tenderness with such disdain on the voyage here? The more gallant I became, the more distant you acted. What else could motivate you but the intent to torment me as punishment for what I did to you?" Savagely Beau pulled his cravat so tight he coughed.

"Oh!" Tory squealed. "You stupid mule!" She marched to the door, where she turned to glare at him. "Not everyone is as devious as you, Beau Cochran. Some of us enter into obligations with the sincerity they deserve." She slammed the door with such force the little Dresden shepherdess quivered.

Beau's fingers paused. What the hell had she meant by that? She'd as much as admitted that she married him because he'd fathered her child. Was she implying more or seeking to wound him? Beau finished tying his cravat, unaware it was askew. He shrugged into his vest and absentmindedly buttoned it up crooked. He pulled clean stockings over his muscled legs, not noticing that the laundress had washed them with something red so that they glowed a pale but decided pink. Lastly, he shrugged into his jacket, forgetting to turn the cuffs up neatly. He stomped downstairs, determined to make Tory tell him what she'd meant by that last tantalizing remark.

Since he was late, everyone awaited him in the dining room. The oval cherry parquetry table and matching sideboards reflected back the brilliant Austrian crystal chandelier suspended above. The upper portions of the plastered walls were papered in a soothing blue Chinese design to correspond with the everyday blue and white Canton ware. Elaborate plasterwork decorated the ceiling and moldings.

Helen saw him first. She ran to him, calling his name. He caught her waist and whirled her around. "Now this is the sister I remember." He approved the modish blue silk gown that matched her sparkling eyes.

After kissing his cheek, she backed up a step to look at him. She blinked. Her mouth quivered, but she said only "I'm so glad to see you, Beau. I saw Jarrod at the warehouse today and told him you'd visit soon. He wouldn't live with us here despite our invitation."

"And how has the little rascal adjusted to Philadelphia?" he asked, pulling her chair out for her. He was careful not to look at Tory, so he was unaware of how she stared at him, mouth agape. His parents, too, looked him up and down. Robert took his seat at the head of the table and rolled his eyes heavenward.

Miranda giggled, but her eyes were soft when she glanced from Beau to Tory. It was high time a woman shook that arrogant confidence. She settled back in her chair to watch the fun. When Beau would have taken his old seat facing the mirror above the sideboard, she waved him into the chair next to Tory, facing the door.

When the first course of clam chowder had been served, Helen answered Beau's question. "Father thinks Jarrod has an affinity for figures. He speaks English beautifully, and he's learning to write and read it fast. But he's not happy, Beau. He doesn't like the cold, and he's having a hard time making friends."

"I'll stop and see him first thing tomorrow. Is he living above the warehouse?"

"Yes."

"And how is Bobby?"

Helen's mouth lost its worried twist. "A perfect little angel." When everyone laughed, she added sheepishly, "A *loud* little angel, perhaps. I've obtained a new nursemaid for him, and he seems to be behaving better."

"It's having his mother back that's made the difference, dear, as you well know," Miranda insisted.

Helen flushed with pleasure. She turned to Tory, whom she had greeted before Beau came downstairs. "Mother told me your news, Tory. I'm so pleased for you both. There's no feeling on earth like hearing the cry of one's firstborn." After Tory thanked her, Helen winked at Beau and gave him a broad grin of approval.

You'd think she'd done the deed herself, so pleased was she, he thought irritably. It was a wonder McAllister hadn't tried to take the credit as well. Why did no one credit him with wit enough to handle the vixen?

He allowed himself to look at her. Her hair shone like Saint Elmo's fire. But was she sailor's delight or warning? He no longer knew, for this ache in groin and heart was not conducive to rationality. Perversely, he resented her beauty, forgetting that he himself had put her beyond reach. The need to resolve their conflict was so strong he forgot their witnesses.

He chunked his spoon into his empty bowl, unmindful of his mother's frown, and turned to the source of his torment. "Well, madam wife, isn't it time you elaborated on that last comment to me?"

Decorously Tory put her own spoon on her soup plate. "You may take it at face value, sir. Unlike some people, I say what I mean."

"Which tells me precisely nothing except that you still haven't forgiven me."

Tory bridled. She wasn't a redhead for nothing. "I commit myself to making our marriage work and you accuse me of harboring resentment? What would you have me do?"

"Live up to your vows."

"Ooh!" Tory cried, throwing her napkin down to leap to her feet. "You dolt, what do you think I was trying to do earlier? Things will never change between us. Always, always, you'll think the worst of me."

Hope surged in Beau's heart at her words, but her next comment dashed it.

"Well, sir, perhaps I should make an effort to justify your fears." On that ominous note, she turned on her heel and stalked out, skirts rustling.

Silence prevailed at the table. Miranda opened her mouth, but Robert shook his head. He said mildly, "Your sojourn in Algiers must have taxed you more than I realized. I thought we raised you better, Beau."

When Beau looked at him vaguely, Robert realized he was so far gone he'd forgotten they were there. Robert grinned ruefully when Beau's eyes focused on him. "Aye, lad, women are a sore trial, but what a reward they can be to a man with patience enough to win them."

"Really, Robert, do you have to be so patronizing?" Miranda protested. She was infuriated when, for once, both men ignored her.

"Did Mother ever try you so?"

Robert nodded. "She was a rare handful when we first wed"—he glanced at his wife and twinkled—"until I trained her to her proper place."

"Robert!" Miranda protested louder, truly shocked. His wink appeased her not a bit.

"I don't know what's troubling you and Tory," Robert said, "but I see your temper is on a short leash. She has enough to adjust to, and this is an emotional time for her. Stifle your natural exasperation and be patient."

Beau propped his elbows on the table and his chin on his knuckles. "If I'd ever believed a woman could have me at such sixes and sevens—"

The man-to-man talk was interrupted when Miranda rose to her full, regal height. "Come, Helen. This rarefied air is stifling. Let's go see Tory." Helen sent a darkling look to her male relatives and joined her mother at the door.

Miranda paused to say coolly, "Before you two scheme too hard, I suggest you look in the mirror, Beau."

Frowning, Beau obeyed. He gasped and turned beet red. He slammed his palm down on the sideboard. "Damn her!"

Miranda glared at him. "It's to yourself you should be looking, my fine man. It seems to me you've mistaken who needs patience." Arm in arm, the two women swept out of the room.

The serving maids looked confused when they brought in the rest of the dinner, for there were only two glum males to serve it to.

Upstairs, Tory turned from putting on her dressing gown to the knock on the door. A flushed Helen and Miranda stood there. They drew her to the sofa and sat down with her before the crackling fire.

Miranda took her hands. "Tory, we're delighted you're here. You're a perfect mate for my son."

"I'm flattered, ma'am, but I fear Beau does not feel the same." Tory stared into the fire, her face somber.

Miranda released her hands and swiveled on the couch until she could see Tory's face. "Will you not confide in us? What was that exchange at dinner about?"

Tory hesitated, looking from one concerned, pretty face to the other. Why not? she thought. Who could know Beau better than these two women? Succinctly she explained everything that had happened since Helen left England. When she finished, Miranda nodded.

"It's as I thought. Beau barreled over your quite natural objections and now can't understand why you balk. Bravo, my dear! I've never seen my son so confused. It's good for him to want something he can't have, for once."

"But he *can* have me. I . . . even offered myself to him."

Miranda's smile faded at Tory's anguish. Beau's love for her was plain as a pikestaff to anyone who knew him as his mother did, but loyalty to her son forbade her to tell Tory. Besides, it would do him good to suffer a little. Things had come too easily to him. When he won Tory, he'd value her all the more.

"Have you done so before?" she queried gently.

"Not since I learned his identity. I fear our child was conceived at a time of great conflict between us. Now he doesn't even seem to want me."

"Oh, he wants you all right. So much he barely knows if he's coming or going. Didn't you notice the way he was dressed at dinner? I assure you, he doesn't normally play the court jester. Usually he's quite elegant.'' Miranda's eyes twinkled wickedly.

Tory recalled how Beau had looked, stock askew, wearing pink stockings, and she had to laugh. "Did I really discomfit him so that he didn't even know what he was wearing?"

"Indeed you did. I had to tell him to look in the mirror. And then, of course, like the rest of his species, he blamed you." Miranda sniffed.

"Oh, he did, did he?" Tory tapped an impatient drumbeat on the sofa arm, no longer amused. Decisively, she turned to her in-laws. "What do you advise me to do?"

Helen knew that gleam in her mother's eye. "Mother, surely Beau has enough to worry about with the political situation . . ."

"Nonsense. He's just like your father. Neither man values what he wins too easily."

"I would hardly call Beau's courtship easy."

"Courtship?" Tory echoed. "Decree from up above, more like. He's given me no choice in our relationship from the beginning. First he was my master, then he was my seducer, and now he thinks to play autocratic husband. I'll have none of it."

Miranda smiled approvingly. "Exactly, my dear. I had the same problem with Robert. Even now he delights in goading me. But despite our years together, he's still not quite sure how far he can push me. Our arguments are sometimes quite fierce, but neither of us would have it any other way. And such a marriage is the only kind that will make Beau happy."

"What are you suggesting I do?" Tory asked.

"Lead Beau a merry dance. He's downstairs right now planning how to bring you to heel." When Tory's brows snapped together, Miranda went on, "And he'll be mightily disappointed if he succeeds too easily."

Tory played with her robe's sleeve, staring into the fire. Perhaps they'd been so at odds since their marriage because they'd stepped out of the roles that had first attracted them. She would not win the love and devotion she craved by becoming the clinging woman who had obviously bored him in the past. Beau didn't know how to deal with her when she was compliant; she didn't know what to make of him when he played the mealymouthed gentleman. Miranda was right. Beau was a man who needed challenges, and she was a woman who rose to them. What could be more fitting?

She turned to kiss Miranda's cheek. "Thank you, Miranda. I

see now what's been wrong between us. I changed the rules of our relationship and didn't even know it. No wonder Beau is so confused.'' Her smile was pure mischief. ''Not that he'll find me any easier to understand now.''

Helen stifled her own reservations and hugged Tory. ''I hope you're doing the right thing, Tory. There is one thing you're both leaving out of your calculations.'' Miranda and Tory looked at her quizzically.

''Beau's feelings. He doesn't feel confident of his power over you. Right now he needs a loving and supportive wife rather than a combative one.''

After her in-laws left, Tory got into bed to stare at the ceiling. Was Helen right? What if Beau saw her actions as evidence that she'd never be happy with him? Yet what else was she to do? She'd all but torn his clothes off tonight, only to have him accuse her of playing games. Tory felt the small swell of her abdomen. She only had another month or so before she became ungainly. She'd best make use of it. She drifted off to sleep on the thought, troubled by dreams of Beau sailing away from the wife he scorned.

Chapter 18

Tory appraised herself in the glass. This first Tuesday in January would mark her debut into society, and she wanted to make a good impression. Not least of all on her handsome, irritating, wonderful, impossible husband. Beau had avoided her like the plague, rising early to go to the docks, and retiring after she'd gone to bed. On the rare occasions when she saw him, he no longer reacted to her goading as he had in days gone by. Instead of rebutting her sallies with a bold remark or bolder caress, he snapped his teeth together over a growl and turned away.

Tears gathered in Tory's eyes. What if she'd already lost him? Beau was more a mystery to her now than Sinan had ever been. If he loved her, surely he'd respond to her sallies; if he didn't, surely he'd be less touchy, even indifferent. But a fastidious man who dressed as he had for that first dinner, who snapped at her and flinched from her touch, was not indifferent. That, at least, she knew. She could only persevere in using her advantages—the beauty that had once attracted him and the proximity of marriage.

Tonight she would use both. When they danced together, he'd have to touch her. She'd get some reaction from him this night if she had to cause a scene to do it. Her eyes dry now, Tory curtsied to her image. Her velvet gown was the same shade as her eyes. The long sleeves were banded with silver braid at intervals, forming rows of puffs down each arm. The same braid trimmed the low, square neckline and circled the bodice just beneath her extravagant bosom. The full cut of the Empire gown gave her a medieval look that was accented by the coronet of braids through which she'd woven a string of pearls. A pearl and diamond choker, Beau's Christmas gift, encircled her neck.

Miranda, dressed in pale blue silk, and Helen, in fine white cashmere, entered as she turned away from the glass. They stopped and stared at her with delight mixed with a little envy.

"My dear, you are the first stare of fashion and will put us all to the blush tonight," Helen said.

"You've no need to feel embarrassed. I've seldom seen better in a London ballroom. Is this your first appearance in society, Helen, since returning?"

Helen's face lost its animation. "Yes. I'd rather not go, but Mother insists."

"You've brooded long enough, Helen. The best way to quiet gossip is to face it. Doesn't she glow, Tory?"

"Indeed so, ma'am. We'll band together, Helen, for we are a unique breed, are we not? How many Christian women can claim to have escaped a Barbary harem?"

Helen's face regained its color. "Truly I hadn't looked at it so." She locked her arm with Tory's and smiled teasingly. "Tory the Terror, tonight may you reign."

Tory wrinkled her nose. "I've always hated that sobriquet, but tonight I'm mightily tempted to live up to it."

Miranda agreed, "Perhaps you should. My son is being even more pigheaded than usual." She joined the banter with a mock curtsy, then draped Tory's spencer of matching velvet lined with silver fox about her shoulders. "Your robes, Majesty." She handed Tory her blue and silver lace fan. "Your scepter." Helen giggled when Tory, with a wink, set her head at a haughty angle and stalked to the door. Her demi-train and tall bearing were indeed majestic.

So thought the man who watched her glide down the stairs, his hands thrust into his pockets as he blanked all expression. His worst fears had come true. They had not been here two days before she became the capricious coquette of old. She must indeed have been taunting him that first night when she so sweetly offered herself to him, for since then she'd been anything but accommodating. His hopes that marriage and pregnancy would mature her into the helpmate he needed had been vain. She would never be happy here. She resented him for having taken her away from England. That he desired her more than ever only complicated matters. Under the circumstances, how could he confide in her about his political difficulties?

For days now he'd struggled against his fears, but, seeing her thus, they almost overcame him. Victoria Alicia Grenville would never become plain Tory Cochran, no matter how he wished it so. Though he longed for the earthy, practical Tory he'd known so briefly in Algiers, he loved this London lady also. But what havoc she could wreak upon him! Particularly this night, when he came face to face with his enemies . . .

His parents and sister, after observing the eye battle waged by the newlyweds, tactfully went out to the carriage.

Thus Tory was left to face the brooding stranger who both thrilled and chilled her. She faltered on the last step. His black velvet jacket and gray knee breeches fit him without a wrinkle. He had eschewed his usual cravat for a white ruffled shirt that threw the tough male features into sharp relief. He was magnificent, this man who was her husband only in name. She longed for him to consummate their vows, but her very need made her angry when he so obviously didn't feel the same. She, too, donned a haughty mask.

"Sir, I'm flattered you grant me your presence. In truth, I thought you'd forgotten you have a wife."

"Indeed, madam? Perhaps because you little act one."

Tory's eyes widened. Was he as unhappy with their stalemate as she was? She descended the last step and walked toward him. "Beau—"

He interrupted harshly, "But I expected little else from Tory the Terror. Perhaps we should not have wed, after all." He turned away to shrug into his cloak.

The words stopped her in her tracks. She swayed under their

devastation. Then, recovering, she snapped open her fan. When he turned to offer his arm, he saw only blue eyes glittering at him over lace. "La, sir, if it's Tory the Terror you want, you shall have her. She pines no more to act the wife than you yearn to be a husband." She snapped her fan closed and swept out the door, ignoring his outstretched arm.

Beau frowned at her odd tone. When he climbed into the carriage to sit next to her, she looked through him with queen-like dignity. However, when he took her hand to apologize, she snatched it away and gazed out the window.

They made the short trip in silence. Robert was hopeful that they could gain some advantage tonight over their enemies. Helen was pale at the thought of the avid curiosity she would encounter, and Miranda was worried about Beau and Tory.

It was not a festive group that entered the Oeller Hotel assembly room.

An attendant took their cloaks. Beau hissed a shocked breath when Tory turned toward him. When she saw where he looked, she spread her fan before her breasts.

"Sir, by your own decision, you have no right to look at me so. Pray take yourself off," she whispered fiercely. She turned her back on him and went to Helen's side.

Robert didn't hear her comment, but he couldn't miss Beau's reaction to it. "Beau, remember, patience is the thing." He touched Beau's arm. "We must keep a cool head tonight."

"Patience, hell," Beau snarled. "She's run wild long enough. It's time she was broken to bridle." He strode toward his wife, but she and Helen were mobbed by Philadelphians.

"Helen, it's so good to see you again," gushed Beth, a petite brunette, an old rival for Henry's attentions. "I must say, your tribulations have left no mark. How . . . proud Henry would be of your, er, stamina."

Avidly the bystanders watched to see how Helen would react to the innuendo. When Beau made a move to elbow his way through the crowd to his sister's side, Miranda grabbed his arm and shook her head.

Helen paled. She shrank away, but then Tory gave her hand an encouraging squeeze. Bobby's chubby, laughing face popped into Helen's head. If she let these people shame her now, what kind of example would she set for him?

Helen met Beth's malicious blue eyes, a steady little flame burning in her own. "Yes, I do think Henry would be proud of me. A woman of lesser mettle''—she looked the brunette up and down—''could easily become petty and selfish, blaming her own unfortunate state upon those she envies.''

All eyes turned to Beth. She bridled, for her father's fortune was not large enough to coax anyone of proper ''connection'' to wed her. ''Why you—'' She got a grip on herself and cooed, ''I'd rather be unwed and respectable than—''

''Yes, you obviously enjoy your fortunate condition.''

Beth was routed by the laughter, the one chastisement she could not bear. She exited, her face flushed. Men and women alike looked at Helen with new eyes. This was not the reserved young girl who'd left them three years ago. They respected someone with grit enough to emerge a stronger person from such an ordeal. The gentlemen greeted Helen warmly. If their ladies still watched doubtfully, at least they no longer scorned her. The woman was, after all, a Cochran. They could hardly shun her without insulting the entire family.

Pink with triumph, Helen moved to introduce Tory, but Beau forestalled her. His smile became fixed when she stiffened at the possessive arm he dropped around her shoulders, but he seemed the proud husband when he said, ''Please welcome my wife, Victoria Grenville Cochran, to Philadelphia.'' He fended off long conversations—and questions—by introducing Tory around.

However, both caught the comments swarming about them like bees: ''Heiress to the Grenville fortune, you know,'' and ''I never thought Beau would marry a London belle,'' or, ''They say he rescued her from a harem,'' rebutted by, ''No, my dear, I heard he kept her there while he played the pirate. Damned impudent even for a Republican.''

One graying merchant, his paunch as puffed up as his consequence, barely bobbed his head when Tory was introduced. ''Knew your grandfather, I did. He'd be disappointed in you, miss.'' Beau tried to draw Tory away from the old Federalist, but Tory was not one to ignore such a challenge.

''Why whatever do you mean, sir?''

''You, an Englishwoman, should be truer to your name.'' He sent Beau a disdainful glance.

Again Beau tried to move her on; again she balked. He could only watch, his heart sinking to his shiny, silver-buckled shoes, and wait for his wife to show her true colors. He was so certain she was going to humiliate him that he tensed. The shock of her unexpected reply rippled through him.

"What could be truer to English values than respect for champions of liberty? Don't forget it was Englishmen who forced King John to sign the Magna Charta, which I understand influenced your own American Constitution."

While Beau was staring at her classical profile, wondering if he'd heard her aright, a new voice intruded. "And it is radicals such as your husband who would circumvent those values now with their own usurpation of authority."

The people remaining in the anteroom turned to the newcomer. Hostility emanated from Beau in a palpable wave, giving Tory pause to her retort. Some instinct warned her to take the newcomer's measure. He was a tall, handsome man, a bit older than Beau, with thick chestnut hair and long, rakish sideburns. His pale gray eyes had a worldly air abetted by the cynical twist to his thin mouth.

Beau recovered his composure quickly. With a mocking bow, he said, "What powers you credit me with, Fuller. To hear you tell it, I'm organizing a revolution."

"Such scorn for the government's authority can hardly be interpreted otherwise."

"Perhaps not to someone with your twisted way of thinking." The insolent remark drew gasps from the audience.

Fuller took an angry step forward, snarling, "Damn your impudence—" But he was interrupted by a dignified voice at the door.

"Gentlemen, you know the rules." One of the assembly managers, a white ribbon across his chest to identify him, pointed at the framed list on the wall. "I'll have no disputes, political or otherwise. Refuse to comply, and you'll be asked to leave."

Both men bowed an apology under his stern look.

"Now, your tickets, please, for the dancing is about to commence and these ladies have still not drawn for places."

A moment later, Tory found herself in the assembly room, Beau still vibrating with rage at her side. "What was that all about?" she whispered.

"Later," he answered. After signing the subscription list, Tory accepted from another manager a folded billet with a number. When she turned to question Beau again, she found that he'd deserted her to hover on the sidelines. Tory saw him heartily greet a late arrival, a tall man with brown eyes and hair. Then

Robert introduced both men to a stranger of smaller stature. Tory sighed. Her plan to make this all a romantic evening for the two of them was certainly coming to naught. She took the opportunity to look about.

The square room was papered in the French style, gods and goddesses grouped in compartments around the walls, set off by pillars and festoons. The polished floor reflected scores of candles, and a handsome music gallery was tucked in one end so the musicians didn't intrude into the dancers. They were tuning up for the first dance.

Helen approached to explain the rules. "This is somewhat different from the balls you've attended in London, Tory. You'll dance with one partner all evening unless you obtain permission from a manager to accept another invitation. On no account leave your set."

"But whom will I dance with?"

The answer came with a flourish of woodwind and strings. A manager strutted to the center of the room and began calling out names and numbers. Helen stepped into the first set, flushing a little at the honor of being in the lead, for she would be allowed to call some of the dances. Tory saw the tall man Beau had greeted take his place beside her.

While she was puzzling over his identity, her name was called. She went forward to meet her partner—and groaned. What a fine to-do. She'd looked forward to dancing with Beau and instead found herself partnered with his enemy. Still, her smile was pleasant.

He put a hand inside his blue satin jacket and bowed low. "Lewis Fuller at your service, ma'am."

Tory curtsied. "Victoria Cochran."

"And how do you find Philadelphia, Mrs. Cochran?"

"A charming city, almost as lovely as London."

A fervent sigh greeted this comment. "Ah, London. No city on earth can compare with it, even our own city of brotherly love."

"Why, thank you, sir," Tory said, genuinely touched at such an accolade from an American.

"And you, ma'am, represent the best of both."

Tory raised an eyebrow at the smooth compliment. She would not balk if he wanted to get in her good graces, for she sensed he could be a formidable enemy. She'd learned in London salons that civility drew more confidences than anger. It never occurred to her that Beau would view her efforts differently.

"I am exceedingly flattered, Mr. Fuller. Are all Philadelphia gentlemen as gallant as yourself and my husband?"

His pleasant smile went cock-eyed. "As to your husband I cannot say, but you surely would instill gallantry in the coldest heart." He took her hand to kiss it.

From the sidelines, Beau looked about for his wife. He had not expected to dance this evening, but he was curious as to who would be her partner . . . He stiffened with rage and took a step forward. Tory pulled her hand away from Fuller's lips with a laughing remark, but seemed not to mind his touch a whit when the first country dance began.

Robert caught Beau's arm, shaking his head. "It's a nasty turn, Beau, but I'm certain Tory will be circumspect."

Beau remained grim, for he was certain of no such thing. In truth, the sight of Tory enjoying Fuller's company made his stomach churn with more than worry. "I wouldn't put it past the bastard to have bribed the managers. Else chance has blessed him indeed."

The smaller man at their side said coolly, "For the moment, perhaps. But the Federalist star is setting, if I've anything to say to it."

"Which is a very great deal, William. Such a furor you stir up! What invective is hurled upon you!" Robert nudged Beau, who still frowned at the dancers. "The cause of Republicanism was favored when William Duane came back to us to lead the *Aurora*'s battle cry."

Duane, a handsome man with curly hair, wide-spaced, piercing eyes, a broad high forehead, and a hawklike nose, shrugged. "I but allow my pen to voice my conscience. As others use their sword." Duane nodded his head toward Beau.

Beau turned his head at Duane's wistful note and replied, "Which I may yet live to regret, if Fuller has anything to say to it."

Duane laughed. "We may end up standing at the bar side by side before the Senate, Mr. Cochran, if the Federalist majority wins the day."

"Beau, please. Now Terence has returned, they surely have little ground for prosecution."

"Under these blasted Acts, that's not stopped them before. You can say many things of the Federalists, but you can't fault their determination. Still, if you do as your father suggests, you may win public opinion your way. And I can certainly attest to the power of it.''

"Come, Beau, let's be off to the game room and put our plan into effect," Robert suggested.

But Beau hesitated. Tory was in her element, glittering there beneath the candles. She and Fuller seemed cordial in the extreme. Every instinct Beau possessed bade him separate them. The knowledge that he and Tory had not consummated their vows ate at him as he watched her sway under Fuller's hands. Terence glanced at him over Helen's head. Beau plucked his earlobe and nodded toward his wife and Fuller. Terence, who was next to them, nodded before smiling down at Helen again.

Feeling slightly less tense, Beau followed Robert and Duane to the game room. The atmosphere there was quiet as serious games of commerce progressed. The muted rumble of voices dimmed when they entered.

Beau went directly to Frederick Cummins, who was an assistant in the newly formed naval department and an Adams appointee. "Pardon the intrusion, sir, but I have an issue of some moment to discuss with you." Cummins, a small, spare man, looked up at Beau coolly.

"I cannot imagine what we have to discuss, sir. I do not even know you personally, and as for what I know of you. . .'' The way his words trailed off would have been a set-down to a less determined man.

Beau didn't bat an eyelash. "What I wish to discuss is not of a personal capacity but of an official one."

"By God, sir, it's a little late for you to be thinking of acting through proper channels," Cummins snapped, shoving back his chair and rising. The clink of coins stilled as every eye in the room turned toward them.

"And what 'proper channels' was I to act through, sir? There was no navy to enter when I left three years ago."

"That does not excuse taking the laws of our land and circumventing them for your own use—"

"My own *use*? Of a surety, I had much to gain and nothing to lose by allowing myself to be captured. Only my life!" All Beau's frustration rang in the rebuttal. Even the Federalists in the room shifted uncomfortably at the truth of the statement.

Cummins waved away Beau's objection. "You'll have opportunity aplenty to defend yourself after the forthcoming resolution in the Senate.'' Cummins snapped his mouth shut, looking chagrined at having let his anger overcome him.

Into the brooding silence blasted Duane's angry voice. ''Ah, brilliantly blind to the end, as is the rest of the Adams administration. May I remind you, Cummins, that your own Federalist slogan has been 'Millions for defense, not one cent for tribute'? Why do you now condemn a man for doing more than orating his sympathy for such values?''

''You stay out of this, Duane! Your seditious libel will be called to account soon enough.'' Nevertheless, Cummins's voice was more reasonable when he turned back to Beau. ''It's not your goal I find repugnant, but your means.''

''Very well, if you'll excuse me a moment, I'll see if my 'means' meet more with your approval.'' Beau hurried out.

Robert took up the battle. ''You know very well that when Beau left not a single ship had been launched. Congress was still debating even the need for navy and being parsimonious with the funds already voted. We had no official means of enforcing respect for our merchant vessels. Why is it so wrong for the owners of those vessels to devise a private way to assist in ensuring their safety?''

''Hear, hear,'' boomed Grant Chippenham, Terence's father. He rose from his table to join Robert and Duane.

''And what, pray, has your interference accomplished?'' asked a new voice from the door. Fuller, two glasses of punch in his hands, entered the room. ''I'm told the dey of Algiers is complaining bitterly to our consul about the planting of a spy in his midst. He used to assist us with Tripoli and Tunis; now he's threatening to encourage them to break their treaties.'' Fuller set the glasses down and turned to glare at Robert.

Chippenham, a tall, thin man with a head of thick brown hair, spoke up. ''My son can attest to the fact that Tripoli's Bashaw needs no encouragement. Nothing less than a frigate or brig-of-war will satisfy him. That's the problem with bribery, gentlemen—where does it end? We did not send our sons into danger lightly. Surely with their intimate knowledge of how these corsairs do battle and the detailed maps they've brought back—'' He stopped with a wince when Robert's foot squashed his toes.

''We've recently proved our fighting mettle in this quasi-war with France,'' Robert said forcefully. ''We not only had need of a navy, gentlemen, we had need of men to lead it, as events have proven. I should think we'd be commended for our fore-sight instead of calumniated as bungling fools.''

There were murmurs both of scorn and agreement from the other men in the room, who'd long since thrown in their games to listen. When Beau reentered with a small satchel, he paused at the hubbub, his eyes lighting on Fuller. Deliberately he walked to the table before him.

''I, too, heartily endorse the new navy, and I would have been glad indeed if I'd had it to enforce the rights for which I lost four brothers.'' Beau looked at the Federalists in the room one by one, his eyes boring into Fuller last. He deliberately kept his voice soft. ''I ask you, sir, are we to mouth our independence and continue to be laughed at from Whitehall to Algiers, or shall we enforce respect by force of arms if necessary? Is it not odd that the dey of Algiers sought a treaty only *after* hearing that we'd at last funded a navy?''

While Fuller was fumbling for a reply, Beau thunked the satchel down on the table. ''Gentlemen, I say respect is given to those who demand it. I would remind you I was beaten, chained, and spat upon during the last three years while aiding my country. However, I sincerely regret any offense or confusion I might have caused and hope this civil responsibility will meet with your approval.'' He upended the satchel.

Shiny gold eagles rolled and tinkled merrily across the table, landing in a large, glittering heap. ''From our own mint. Every dollar is a donation from the family Cochran to the navy fund. If the worthy citizens of Philadelphia have already subscribed enough for the frigate even now being built in their name, let this go to another vessel. For I predict, gentlemen, that our country will need many such vessels in the years to come to defend the values we died for.''

Most of the listeners were businessmen who knew almost to the penny the size of the donation. Beau had them all in the palm of his hand. Fuller knew it, too; his rising color attested to his growing choler.

Beau added with a grin, ''And the source of these coins is most appropriate—you see before you the worth of the xebec *Scorpion*, late cruiser of Bobba Mustapha, dey of Algiers.''

The room burst into spontaneous applause, joined even by the staunchest Federalists. Beau winked impudently at the laughing crowd. ''I fear His Excellency would be most disconcerted if he knew the fate of his worthy vessel. But it seems an appropriate turnabout. We funded a vessel to be used by the Algerians against us; now the dey has unknowingly done the same. Poetic justice, is it not, gentlemen?''

Even Cummins nodded in agreement. ''This is most generous of you, sir, and I'll see the Senate is informed—'' But his quasi-apology was interrupted by an icy voice.

''Justice, hell! More like bribery!'' Fuller slammed his fist down on the table, and the gold jumped. Several pieces rolled to the floor. Cummins picked them up and put them back in the satchel, sending his ally a darkling look as he did so, for this contribution was by far the largest they'd seen and deserved praise instead of condemnation.

Beau straightened to his full height and propped his hands on his hips. No one noticed when Tory peeked in the door, then eased into the room.

''And bribery is a sin you are intimately familiar with, is it not so?'' Beau said quietly. Too quietly. Several men called for silence when they missed the comment, for Fuller reacted oddly to it. He started, then went very still.

''Much can be accomplished with a few dollars in low places,'' Beau went on. ''Lives can be ruined. Three years of work wiped out.''

Tory was as confused as the rest of the group, with the exception of Robert and Chippenham. They eyed Fuller narrowly. But after the start, he didn't react.

''I haven't the slightest notion what you're talking about,'' Fuller said calmly.

''Haven't you? Shall I be plainer, then?'' Beau took a step until he and Fuller were standing almost nose to nose. ''These gentlemen would be most interested to hear the fate of one of our couriers—''

Fuller cut him off with a furious ''By God, sir, I know not what you accuse me of, but I mislike your tone!'' He stepped back to raise his arm, but before it could land, a figure in flowing blue velvet hurried up to pull Beau away.

''Fie on you, sir,'' Tory said lightly, pinching Beau on the arm. ''Stirring up trouble in your usual inimitable way, I see. You've deprived me of my dancing partner long enough.'' She patted the spot where she'd pinched him and took a step toward Fuller, but found herself caught around the waist.

''You, madam, will stay out of what does not concern you,'' Beau ground out. ''Leave us.''

Stunned, Tory paused in the circle of his arms. Had the dolt not sense enough to see she was concerned for his safety? Tory pulled away and turned to meet those green eyes she could no longer read. Surely this time he had no reason to look at her with such distrust. She was no unknown London belle; she was his wife. Or was she? Perhaps he did not regard her so. Perhaps he never would.

She had to know, one way or the other. "And who could be more intimately concerned, pray? Should I stand by and let you be wounded or killed without lifting a finger to stop it?"

Beau was jolted at her lack of faith in his abilities and wit. This was her idea of loyalty? To make him look like a fool in need of protection? And to do so by flirting with his adversary? His reply was harsher than he intended. "I don't need your help. Go back to your gaiety, madam."

Tory's white teeth bit hard into her lower lip, but then her face took on her Tory the Terror look. "That's plain speaking indeed. Well, husband mine, I'm not one to stay where I'm not wanted." She walked up to Fuller, took his arm, and smiled prettily. "Mr. Fuller, sir, persist in this quarrel if you must, but I have need of you healthy if we're to take our places again. Our steps match so well that it would distress me to have to seek another partner, even should I find one this late. Would you have me be a wall-flower?"

Triumph flamed in Fuller's eyes when Beau stiffened. Cockily, he extended his arm. "Tory"—he used the familiar name deliberately—"how can I refuse such a charming request?" The pair sauntered out.

It took Duane on one side and Robert on the other to hold Beau back.

"Get a grip on yourself, Beau," Robert hissed in his son's ear. "The pair of you have caused comment enough. I only hope you haven't undone all the progress we made this night."

Indeed, many of the men were shaking their heads. True, Tory had interfered in men's business, but she was, after all, a new bride and unsure of herself. Many of the men Beau had almost won over looked at him doubtfully again. Had living with savages changed the boy?

Beau's face was grim when he bowed. "Forgive the squabble, gentlemen. I hope to discuss this more anon, but for now, I must see my wife." He disappeared through the door. Robert, Chippenham, and Duane followed, leaving a roaring room in their wake.

A cotillion had been called. Beau waited, propped against a pillar, for it to end. He saw Tory glance at him once, then turn back to her partner with even more animation. His anger flared hotter. How dare she slight him among his peers and then flatter his worst enemy! Somewhere in the back of his mind he knew that he'd incited her deliberately because he was no longer able to bear this armed truce. If it required out-and-out warfare to teach her whom she belonged to, so be it.

The cotillion ended, and he waited tensely for the couple to come to the sidelines, but with barely a pause, the orchestra struck up another dance. Robert saw Beau's intent in his eyes and grabbed his arm, but Beau shook him off and strode purposefully onto the floor, drawing gasps from dancers and spectators.

Beau didn't know that Terence had pulled Tory aside before the cotillion to explain some of the political maneuvering that was going on and Fuller's part in it; he didn't know Tory had been drawing Fuller out during the dancing; he knew only she was enjoying herself in another man's arms after spurning his.

What happened then was inevitable.

A rough hand on Fuller's shoulder spun him away, throwing him off balance. Beau grabbed Tory's wrist to tow her off the floor. Her cry of outrage drowned out the manager's protests. Before Beau and Tory could reach the door, Fuller regained his balance and charged after them, upsetting the pattern of the dance. The music whined to a stop as the musicians, curious at the commotion, peered from the gallery to see what was amiss.

Fuller's insult came clearly: "You bastard, I'll—"

Beau's fist stuffed the words back into his mouth as, still holding Tory's hand, Beau knocked Fuller sprawling. "That's just a sample of what you'll get if you don't keep your paws off my wife," he muttered, and he pulled her behind him to the door through the shocked crowd. Tory kept her head high under the curious stares.

When two of the managers blocked his way, Beau confronted them. "Yes, yes, I'm banned from the assemblies for the rest of the season!" He drew the subscriptions for himself and Tory from his pocket. "Take them and gladly!" He crumpled them into a ball and tossed them in a corner. And then they were gone.

Robert, Miranda, and Helen hastily collected their wraps to follow, but the carriage pulled away with a clatter before they reached it. "Damn the boy, what's gotten into him?" Robert snapped, jamming his hat on.

Miranda smiled serenely and patted his arm. "He'll not hurt Tory, my love. Don't worry. Shall we go inside and enjoy ourselves? Doubtless he'll send the carriage back for us." Reluctantly Robert obeyed.

Helen blushed when she entered to find a relieved Terence grinning at her.

"How glad I am you aren't going to let that hothead spoil the best evening I've had in years," he said. "Dance, my dear?"

Some distance away, in front of the Cochran residence, Tory disdained her husband's hand and stepped down from the carriage. In silence, as they had driven, they mounted the stairs, fortifying themselves for the fight to end all fights. Beau slammed their bedchamber door behind them and locked it, turning on his pride, his torment, his hope of happiness with a far from appreciative gleam.

"By God, what was the meaning of your behavior this night?" he roared.

Tory yanked open her spencer and threw it as far as she could send it. "Why, I'm but living up to your opinion of me as a faithless, brainless chit." She whirled away to tug at her necklace clasp.

"I never said you were brainless," Beau growled.

Tory's fingers paused. "Do I deduce from that generous statement that you consider me faithless?"

"What reason have you given me to trust you? Since that first night, you've scorned my bed—"

The unfairness of the accusation made her leap forward to confront him, her face as white as her pearls. "*I've* scorned *you*? Sir, you've daily made your contempt of me obvious. Why should I offer myself to your ridicule when you can scarce keep a civil tongue in your head when you're around me?"

"You don't invite civility. You invite what any husband should give a recalcitrant wife, and by God, madam, if you don't watch your step, you'll have it."

"Are you threatening me with violence?"

The quietness of her voice warned him, but he was too upset to heed it. He waved a contemptuous hand. "You prove yet again what you think of me. Have I ever given you reason to think me a woman-beater? Of my own pregnant wife?'' When she didn't answer, he went on. ''There are many ways to curb you that don't require violence. I should have brought you to heel long ago. You're not the sole proprietess of your fate now, my dear. You belong to me and it's time you admitted it.''

When her long lashes veiled her expression, he watched her suspiciously. Her eyes were guileless when she looked at him again, but she inched closer to the table before the couch as she spoke. ''May I remind you I'm your wife in name only, sir, by your own decision? When you deserve my loyalty, I will give it. Until then, I must ask you to leave.''

He blinked. ''Are you ordering me from my own room?''

''We're fooling no one by this farce. Surely you'll be more comfortable in a bed instead of on this sofa.''

''I'll be the judge of that,'' he said, planting his feet.

''Now, that, sir, you do royally, but I'll have no more of it. Out!'' He had to leave before she burst into tears, she thought.

If I leave now, she'll never let me in again, he thought. ''No.'' His eyes went over her, and her haughty beauty made him yearn to rumple it. His body stirred as he longed to make imagination reality.

The sensual storm that had been building apace with their anger hovered over their heads, awaiting a last lightning retort before venting its fury.

Unwisely, Tory flashed, ''You've no rights here when you hold me at arm's length like a child—'' She broke off when he moved fast as a devil-wind. She just had time to pick up the Dresden shepherdess before he engulfed her.

He caught her hand when she tried to throw the figurine at him, pinning her to him with his other arm. ''Very well, my dear, if my gentle treatment bothers you so, I'll amend my ways.'' He snatched the shepherdess and threw it against the wall. He smiled, a hungry predator's smile, when she flinched.

''You're at arm's length no longer. As for thinking you a child—'' He snapped the flimsy laces of her dress. The bodice gaped, revealing her low-cut chemise and petticoat. Pinning both her struggling arms with one hand, he plunged the other into her underclothes.

They groaned in concert. Tory's struggles ceased. Beau's rough possession became a gentle seeking. As quickly as that did the fury between them change to that other, but no less tumultuous, urge.

Her softness filling his palm drained every hard feeling out of him. Here was Tory, the same Tory who'd won his heart, yet a new Tory, too; Tory, the mother of his child. Since words always failed them, he resorted to a more basic communication.

How she'd pined for this kiss. Women dreamed of such tenderness, for a lover who asked rather than demanded, who gave rather than took. Tory forgot all but the need to answer him with the reply burgeoning from her heart.

And so they stood for minutes on end, arms and legs entangled, mouths sealed in a kiss that did much to heal their mutual pain. They would never remember who took those few steps to the bed. Nor did it matter, for there was only one ending to a bonding such as this. Too long had pride denied it to them.

Beau fell on his back, pulling Tory atop him. He caressed the supple spine bared by the low-cut undergarments, looking down at the twin globes pressed against his chest. He pulled her higher to bury his nose in the silken valley and inhale her sweet scent. Her breasts fell forward, almost escaping their scanty covering, as if begging for his lips. Groaning, he obliged, kissing, muttering endearments.

"Oh, lady hellion, I've missed you so, longed for you. I. . ." He lifted his head and clasped hers to bring it down, sighing into her mouth the words he could not stifle. Did something deeply feminine hear them and trigger her response? He wanted to believe it so, but whatever the reason, she went wild in his arms.

She twined her fingers in his hair, pulling it in her eagerness to meld her lips to his. It was she who nibbled at his lips, teasing them until they opened. Her tongue flickered hotly inside to ignite him in turn. Their tongues dipped and swayed together like married flames, sending heat throughout their bodies. For the first time in months they were warm, and they writhed against each other in frantic need to get closer to the hearth.

After loosening her hair and tossing the pearls on the floor, Beau flipped up her skirts, trying to find smooth skin, but he was frustrated by the layers of clothes. He tugged ineffectually, his hands shaking. "Help me," he pleaded into her mouth.

She raised herself up and peeled the rumpled velvet gown off over her head. The straps of her chemise and petticoat slipped over her shoulders, then farther still as he slid his hands down her arms. She didn't notice when he freed her breasts, for she was intent on opening his ruffled shirt. The tiny pearl buttons

slipped beneath her sweaty fingers. She had the shirt halfway
open when she grew impatient and ripped it the rest of the way.
Buttons went flying.

A rumbling laugh shook the broad bare chest. "Am I to be
raped, then?" He clasped her breasts possessively.

"If necessary. Talking to you is useless. You respect initiative,
so why should I not improvise?"

"Ah, but what we're doing is not new, my dear. Men and
women have been doing it for millennia," he teased, trying to
pull her down to his mouth.

She resisted. "Have they? In just such a way?" When he
chuckled harder at her pretended offense, Tory smiled, her eyes
as agelessly wise as an Egyptian idol's, and lowered her breasts.
The laughter choked in his throat when she rubbed her erect
nipples against his own.

He clamped his arms about her and nudged the scented hollow
of her neck with lips and nose, muttering, "You win, witch.
Never was there a woman like you. Ah, what a spell you cast
upon me." Never let me wake up, he thought.

There was no more time for banter then. Beau pulled her
under-clothes up to her waist, growling, but she lifted away before he could push them up over her head.

Easing back until she straddled his thighs, she opened his
breeches, then his undergarment. His passion reared free like a
miniature tower soaring for the heavens. Frantically he shuffled
through the layers of fabric about her waist, sighing his pleasure
when he found her. He fingered the moist folds, throwing back
his head, eyes closed, when she caressed him likewise.

Thus he didn't see her hesitate, then bend. An ageless instinct
she didn't seek to deny, or even understand, guided her. She
lowered her lips to that yearning crest.

Ripples of fiery hair washing warmly over his groin were his
only warning. His eyes flew open; his fingers paused. "Tory,
what are you—" His teeth bit his lower lip to stifle a cry. The
feel of her warm mouth on the flesh that throbbed for her was
almost more than he could bear. Then she opened her lips to
take him inside her mouth, and he knew he could not bear it,
that he'd dissolve into a boneless mass. Nothing ever had, or
ever would, pleasure him so again.

But she proved him wrong there, too, as she had so many
times before . . .

Her face as flushed as his, she wriggled over him with a lithe movement of her hips. He soared into her, an inch, another, then a fathom and a mile, until his tower of flesh pierced the heavens to find the sun.

He was the source of Tory's existence, too, and never had she known that more surely than now. She flung back her head with an exalted cry and rocked about him, welcoming his fierce attempts to find her white-hot core. One final thrust and she burst around him, bathing him in elemental heat. The golden shower drew him upward until he, too, spent his all in a spectacular death. Then, formless bits of stardust, they floated back to earth to coalesce again as humans enriched by the experience. Shyly, Tory tried to lift away, but he stopped her with gentle hands on her waist.

"Thank you, love. But let me see you, too." When he tried to tug her clothes over her head, she stopped him.

"Please, blow out the candles first."

He cupped her breast. "Why, darling?"

But she moved away without answering, fluffing up her pillow. Confused, he did as bidden. He threw off his clothes, then removed hers. He couldn't see, but he could feel. Lord, could he feel! He savored her curves and valleys. Had she always been so soft, so very womanly? He thought not, for he'd relived the feel of her again and again in his mind. Surely her breasts had never been so full, her hips so voluptuous. His hands went to the rounding abdomen, pausing when she sucked in her breath. He couldn't resist a quick kiss there despite her efforts to turn over.

He would have questioned her reticence, but she drew his lips down over hers until he forgot everything else. He was starved, and here was bounty. What else could he do but savor it with every fiber of his being?

The night was long, but not long enough for their stored passion. Time and again they coupled, then disengaged, certain they were too fulfilled and weary to do aught but sleep. But then he would wake, or she would wake, and they shared yet again the treasure trove of lovers.

When dawn sent seeking fingers through the curtains, Beau was awake. He watched Tory sleep, her skin glowing in the pink light, her shoulders peeping above the blankets. He hesitated, but he could bear it no longer. He had to see her. He eased the covers down to her feet.

Propping himself on one elbow, he ran his fingers over her to help his eyes learn what his hands already knew. Her loveliness stunned him, but he was eager for the slight mound of her belly to swell. How hungry he was to see her big and beautiful with his child.

Tory woke to the feel of warm lips traveling over her belly. She stretched, enjoying them—until she remembered. She blushed as pink as the dawn from head to toe, pushed him away, and pulled up the covers. "Don't," she begged, afraid to look at him. She'd still not come to terms with her bodily changes, and it embarrassed her for him to see them.

Puzzled, he crossed his arms on his pillow and leaned over to look into her face. "Whyever not? I thought we settled all that last night."

"Settled what?"

"My husbandly rights. You're truly mine now."

The glow left by the night grew dim in the cold light of day. So satisfied he sounded, so smug. Had the heaven they'd shared meant so little to him? "That you planted the seed in me does not give you the right to gloat over my ugliness," she said coldly.

"What in heaven's name are you babbling about?"

"Why else have you left me alone so long? I'd almost decided you'd lost interest in me, until last night. And why did you choose then to assert your 'rights'? Are you a dog protecting your bone?"

Beau was hurt and then angry. He'd all but worshipped her last night, yet she harbored such ugly suspicions this morning? Why did she always think the worst of him? "You've too much meat on you to be a bone," he snapped, rising.

Tory's dim glow was snuffed. She sat up against her pillows, wrapping the sheets about her breasts. She waited for a better answer, but all he did was slam about the room, throwing on his clothes.

"Beau, why have you slept apart from me so long?"

If he hadn't been hurt and tired from lack of sleep, he might have admitted he wanted everything this time. He loved her too much to possess her body a third time, but never her heart. But such words were tantamount to a confession he wasn't ready to make and she obviously wasn't ready to hear, so he snarled, "Because I didn't feel I had a wife, but a shrew who gave me no loyalty. You may have been born an Englishwoman, my *lady*," he gave her a mocking bow, "but you're wed to an American now. Make the best of it."

"You talk as if our two countries are still at war and I am the enemy."

"Your behavior last night had a remarkable similarity to . . . consorting. Fuller is more English than American. His family opposed the war from the beginning to end, and even now he'll do anything to further English causes. Is it any wonder I'm troubled you find him so amicable?"

Tory thought anger would choke her, but her voice was steady when she asked, "What, pray, would you have me do to prove my, er, loyalty?"

He crossed his arms over his chest and stated, "Take an interest in my affairs. Support my views before my peers instead of making me look the fool. Don't give aid and comfort to my enemies."

So nothing had changed, despite last night, Tory thought bitterly. Even when she labored in his behalf she was accused of betrayal. Yet was not she the one who'd been betrayed? Every time he gave her that temporal ecstasy, he did so with ulterior motives: the first time, revenge; the second, to make her pregnant; and now to set his stamp on her. In her own way, in her own time, she'd give him what loyalty he deserved. She'd help cause this mess he was in, so she must help him out of it, but she owed him nothing more. Since there was no love lost between them, there would be naught else, either. She eyed him narrowly.

So sturdy and inflexible he stood, like an oak marked for toppling. He made Tory itch to find an ax. She'd cut him down to size before they were much older . . . She rose to wrap the sheet about her, feeling at a disadvantage now that he was fully dressed. She threw one corner of the sheet over her shoulder and tucked the other underneath to free her arms. "As you command, lord and master," she droned, salaaming. "The next time a man yearns to kill you, I'll not say him nay."

"Dammit, woman, you deliberately misunderstand me!"

"Do I, Beau? You ask for blind obedience without giving me reason to obey." The words rushed out then. "Your friend Terence tells me more of your affairs than you do. But even without his explanation, I knew Fuller wished you ill. Of what use is it to antagonize him? A charmed snake is less dangerous, and easier to manipulate, than a threatened one."

Tory turned away in disgust and went to her dressing table to brush her hair. "Believe of me what you will. In truth, I'm almost to the point where I no longer care. Perhaps you were right. We never should have wed. Too much in the past stood between us and too much stands between us now. You should have taken an American to wife, since you hate my country so. Were it not for the babe. . ."

Beau's hopeful gleam died. "Yes, were it not for the babe, you would not be here." The harsh words dropped like stones in a pond, sending ripples outward that inundated the fragile understanding they might have formed.

Pride took his steps to the door despite his yearning to go to her and plead for her love. Pride made her turn away and pretend she didn't care when the door closed behind him. And pride kept them icily polite to one another in the weeks that followed. They saw little of each other, for Beau was occupied with business and compiling a defense for his actions if he should be called before the Senate. As she grew with child, she grew in resentment toward the man she still foolishly loved. Her wandering about Philadelphia, sometimes with Helen, sometimes with Jarrod, kept her body occupied, but not her mind. However, not even her anger mitigated her concern for Beau.

Terence visited often, and he answered her questions readily. "There's been less outcry against me," he explained, "because the whole affair was Beau's idea and because the Bashaw never discovered my mission. I also brought back a detailed map of Tripoli harbor and a listing of her manpower and vessels. Beau would be on stronger ground if we could recover his own map." He explained Fuller's suspected role. "Beau broke into his warehouse last night, but found nothing. If Fuller didn't burn the map, he's got it hidden at his store or home." Helen brought Bobby in to play with him, distracting him from Tory's thoughtful frown.

Beau's donation had quieted only some of his critics. Duane's championship of him in the *Aurora* had fired Federalist ire. As their political fortunes waned, they grew angrier against one who should have been their ally. Led by Fuller, they grew bolder as winter trudged into spring. Beau's surly behavior to all did not aid his cause. The resolution calling for a fine and imprisonment against him that had been defeated in the Senate after his donation was presented again.

This time, it was given a fair chance of passage . . .

Chapter 19

Market day! A watery spring sun peeked down on Jarrod and Tory as they strolled side by side. How different this market was from Covent Garden. There was little clamor here on Market between Third and Second, and no filth. Entrances had been chained off so the commerce would not be disturbed by traffic. The brick footpaths were swept after every market day. No spoiled goods were allowed.

Even now market clerks, who were paid by the city to regulate the proceedings, bustled about their business. One sampled butter. He frowned at the vendor and ordered the man to dispose of the rancid product. Another listened to a dispute between a mob-capped woman selling sausages and a portly young man who claimed her scale was unfairly weighted. The clerk examined the scale closely and proclaimed it sound. Fuming, the young man slammed some coins down on the stall, accepted his package, and stomped away.

Tory bought fresh, crunchy apples for herself and Jarrod, then ambled on, ostensibly casual. After purchasing potatoes, butter, and rice, she swung her basket and turned casually down White Horse Alley. In the middle of the street, above a door, hung a sign: Fuller Imports.

Jarrod stopped in midstep when he saw where she was headed. "Miss Tory, why do you go there? You know the captain doesn't want you associating with that man."

Tory turned to look down at her little friend. "Jarrod, I've long since given up trying to understand what the captain wants. Only from Robert and Terence, never from my husband," she emphasized bitterly, "do I know anything of him." She drew Jarrod into a doorway when they attracted curious looks.

"It's my fault Beau lost that map, Jarrod. I know you've been helping him by keeping an ear out at the docks, but you can help him even more, now. Fuller would be suspicious if Terence or Beau set foot in his shop. But he is not likely to suspect a pregnant woman and a young boy of spying on him."

Jarrod digested this. "But if anything should happen to you the captain would never forgive me."

"So he's set you to guard me, has he? I wondered why I could scarce set a foot out the door without you following me. For my protection or because he doesn't trust me?"

"Because he's concerned for you, Miss Tory." He gave her a pleading look.

"I wish I could believe that," Tory muttered. She recalled Beau's increasingly grim silences and grimmer stares. She'd seen Fuller casually about town on a number of occasions; once she'd invited him for tea. Beau had come home unexpectedly that day to see her serving tiny cakes to his enemy in the parlor. He'd gone still, then erupted out of the house. That evening he moved his clothes to an unoccupied bedchamber.

Since then they'd not exchanged ten sentences. Tory was hurt that he trusted her so little, but she was more determined than ever to prove him wrong. When she produced the map, Beau would have to eat his words and his suspicions. She hoped he would choke on them.

She shook off the melancholy and turned a bright smile on Jarrod. "Well, little friend, are you willing to help me save the captain's neck?"

When Jarrod nodded, Tory bent down and lowered her voice. "This is what we'll do . . ."

It was ridiculously easy for Tory to distract the sole clerk with a request to see the newest Canton ware. Meanwhile, Jarrod wandered casually from the display of Oriental jars and bowls to a case of Wedgwood dishes, inching nearer the rear office all the while. However, when he tried the door, he found it locked. Tory met his eyes across the shop, nodded casually at a window, then carried a platter to the front of the shop to appraise it in the light. The clerk followed her, his back to Jarrod.

Quickly Jarrod unlatched a window on the side of the shop, then strolled back to Tory. They left a few minutes later, Jarrod carrying the platter and bowl Tory had purchased.

Safely down the street, Tory said, "I'm coming with you to-night."

Jarrod stumbled and would have gone flying if Tory hadn't braced him. "No, *sitt*!" he shouted, so upset he used his old form of address. "You cannot endanger yourself so. Besides, how, er . . . You're too . . ." He went bright red and gulped.

Tory glared at her mounded belly. "You're right. Climbing in the window in this condition would not be easy." She nibbled her lip, then brightened. "But I can wait in the carriage so I'll be close by if something goes wrong." When Jarrod opened his mouth, she shook her head. "No more arguments, Jarrod."

So it was that, after dinner that night, Tory rose before dessert. When the family looked at her in surprise, for she loved sweets, she smiled wryly and patted her stomach. "I've little inclination to look more like an elephant than I do."

Robert smiled at her. "If you're an elephant, you're a lovely one. Isn't that so, Beau?" He nudged his son.

Beau nodded, but didn't look up from his plate. Liar, Tory thought bitterly. You can't even bear to touch me. Her smile was brittle. "I'll say good night now. I've a need to retire early."

Beau's head came up at that. "Are you well?"

"Just tired," Tory answered. He looked back at his plum tart, and she decided she'd imagined the concern in his eyes. She hurried to her room, collected her cloak, locked her chamber door, and slipped down the stairs, feeling thankful that the doorway to the dining table gave no view of the hall. She heard Miranda arguing with her son as she crept by.

"Beau, what's gotten into you? Why do you avoid Tory so?"

Tory would have given much to listen to his reply, but she had to hurry out the door. After hailing a hired carriage, she fetched Jarrod, then directed the driver to take them to the middle of Elbow Lane, where she'd have a clear view of the shop and the street intersection. She handed Jarrod candle and flint.

"Hurry, and be quiet and careful. I'll be waiting."

She hung out the window of the carriage. By the light of the street lamps, she could make out Jarrod's wriggling legs as he boosted himself over the sill. The tiny flicker of light as he lit the candle looked like a blaze to her.

Minutes dragged like hours. Tory's nerves grew more taut with every tick of her bodice watch. When a street light illuminated a tall figure walking their way, she cursed. He advanced another dozen steps . . . Without pausing to think, she clasped her cloak about her and hurried down the carriage steps.

"Mr. Fuller," she called, rushing toward him. "I'm so glad to see you. Perhaps you can help me."

He took her arm to steady her. "Certainly, ma'am. But what do you do out alone at this time of night?"

"You may have heard about Jarrod, the little boy my husband brought back from Algiers?" He nodded. "He's been having problems with some of the local lads, and I fear he's gone to confront them. Two of them work at the Indian King.''

Fuller frowned. ''I came from there. I meet colleagues there every Tuesday after market. I saw nothing.''

''Still, sir, would you mind escorting me? I would not like to enter the tavern alone.''

''You shouldn't enter it at all, but I understand your concern. Come with me.'' When they'd walked the short distance to the tavern, he suggested, ''Wait just inside the door.''

Tory obeyed, avoiding the curious stares as Fuller searched the premises. When he reported that Jarrod was nowhere to be seen, she sighed. ''Perhaps he changed his mind and went back to his rooms. Thank you so much.'' She leaned on his arm as they strolled back to her carriage.

His nostrils twitched at the scent of her delicate perfume. He looked down at the bulge in the front of her cloak and clenched his hands. She was too good for Cochran. She deserved a husband who knew her worth instead of one who made her the talk of the town with his neglect. Big with child or not, she was one of the most beautiful women he'd ever seen.

The words came out almost of their own accord. ''Will you be attending the theater this Saturday, ma'am?''

''Alas, no. My family let their box lapse, since they seldom used it.''

''But I have one. I'd be honored if you'd be my guest.'' When she frowned a little, he added hastily, ''You and whoever else of your family would care to attend.''

Tory opened her mouth to refuse, but then they came in sight of the carriage. Jarrod was leaning against it, hands in his pockets. When she glanced at him, he scuffed his foot on the cobblestones and shook his head. Helen had pointed Fuller's house out to her once; it stood near the Chestnut Street Theater. Tory turned to smile up at Fuller's attentive face.

''I should be delighted, sir. May I bring my sister-in-law?''

''Of course, of course. Is that your little friend?''

Tory started in apparent surprise. ''So it is.'' She rushed forward. ''Jarrod, you gave me a fright.'' When he opened his mouth, she covered it with her hand and gave him a warning look. ''Not a word out of you. Get in the carriage. We'll discuss this in a moment.'' After thanking Fuller and arranging a time for his carriage to fetch her and Helen, she let him help her up. She waved as they jolted off.

"Nothing?" she asked Jarrod, watching him play with the pick he'd used to open the office lock. He shook his head. She leaned back thoughtfully. That left only one place to look . . . She dropped Jarrod off at his rooms without mentioning her plan.

Tory was relieved to see the hall empty when she used her key to get into the darkened house. She was unlocking the door to her room when a hand clamped down on her shoulder. She cried out when it spun her about. She met the glittering gaze of the man she least wanted to see.

"Where the hell have you been?"

Tory saw the pain that his anger didn't quite hide, and almost she told him the truth. Then his hand dropped as if it had been burned. He actually backed up a step. Her mouth closed; her chin went up. "That is none of your concern."

He grabbed her before she could open the door, then backed her up against it to press his lean length into hers. "You're my wife. I have every right over you. This is mine." He shoved her cloak open and flattened one large palm over her belly. When a vigorous thump answered his touch, he gasped and drew his hand away.

Her lips twisted. "One biological moment of lust doesn't give you license to order me about, any more than it gives me reason to obey you. What else have we to link us except this child? Precious little, it seems to me."

His voice was harsh. "Lust? 'Twas not my lust, madam, but your own. 'A fucking to remember' was your crude appraisal, as I recall."

Tory could stand no more. Trembling, she shoved him away so hard he staggered back. "Yes, and why not? But I've paid tenfold for every moment of pleasure you ever gave me. No more, sir. I've too much respect for myself to let you use me again." Her voice went soft. "And too little for you." The door snicked shut behind her. There was the distinct sound of a bolt being shot home.

It was that sound that sent Beau over the edge. For weeks now he'd tried to contain his pain and rage, tried to trust her when she gave him no reason to. Even tonight, when any husband would surely have been justified in questioning an errant wife, she twisted his words and turned them back upon him. He'd been so moved to feel his child kicking lustily within her, but she couldn't even share that with him. He lifted his foot with the thought and slammed against the door, again, again.

A nightcapped Robert and robed Miranda hurried from their room down the hall. "What in tarnation are you doing?" his father cried.

"Stay out of this," Beau snarled, raising his foot one last time. The sturdy oak door split at last. He charged into the room, picked up a struggling, furious Tory, and carried her down the hall to his new room, where he laid her on the bed and locked the door behind them.

Miranda grabbed Robert's arm when he would have followed. "No. It's time they had a good loud fight. That's surely preferable to their silent rift. They need truth to bridge it. Come back to bed, Robert." With a last worried glance down the hall, he obeyed.

Tory folded her arms over her swollen breasts and glared at her adversary, for even Sinan Reis had not been such an enemy. "So your true colors show at last. You were entirely too much at ease as a pirate. Well, go back to your seafaring with my leave, but I'm no longer your booty!"

Somewhat calmed now that he had her in his bed where she belonged, he propped one arm on a bedpost and growled, "No, but you're even more my property. Now not only the laws of the sea bind us; the laws of God do also."

"Spout platitudes all you like—" She broke off with a gasp when he swooped down next to her.

"Platitudes, hell," he snarled, lying by her side to pin her arms over her head. "It's truth and you know it. I'll make you admit it yet if I have to . . . have to—"

"You'll not coerce me, you bastard, physically or otherwise."

"No, my dear. I wouldn't harm a hair on your head. But you're my wife, and by God, I'll sleep apart from you no longer. There will be no more late outings. I know not what you were doing, but I can't believe you met a lover. Probably you're looking for some other way to bedevil me. You really hate me for bringing you here, don't you?"

Tory squeezed her eyes shut. She would not cry, she would not. He obviously believed she no longer had the power to attract men, but he was still taking no chances. When she'd gotten control of herself, she opened her eyes.

He'd tossed off his clothes while her eyes were shut. Hands on hips, he glared at her. She swallowed as her eyes coursed down that magnificent form. His fine body hair glittered in the candlelight until he looked like a magnificent, gilded David, as perfect as if Michelangelo had just set down his chisel. Weakened with a rush of love and longing, she shrank bonelessly against the pillows.

It took her a moment to realize he was undressing her. She put her hands over his, but he gently pushed them away. "No. I've given you more than enough time to adjust, and all you do is drift farther away. Besides, you're too far along with child. I'd not risk harming you or the babe."

Those warm green eyes drew her in out of the cold. She hadn't the will to deny him any longer.

"Let me look at you, hold you. That's all I ask." Her chemise slithered over her head. The silence was filled only with the sound of labored breathing. Tory buried her cheek in his shoulder when his hands drifted over her from neck to heels, passing with a butterfly flutter over her distended stomach. Again the child kicked in response to its father's touch. This time Beau's hands stayed put, warm and tender.

It was that tenderness that conquered Tory. She turned her head to look at him. His face was shadowed by the bed hangings. She blinked. Before she could be certain that she saw moisture in his eyes, he blew out the candles. He got into bed, pulled the covers over them, then cradled her back against his chest.

"Sleep, little mother," he whispered into the nape of her neck.

Tory snuggled against him, then gasped. That hardness pulsed against her, strong and eager as of old. She rubbed her buttocks against it to be sure she wasn't dreaming.

He stiffened. "Be still," he growled.

She relaxed, truly relaxed, for the first time in weeks. So he didn't find her repulsive after all. Many things a man could pretend to, but not that. He wanted her, fat and ungainly as she was. Tonight he'd broken down a door to get to her; he'd forced her to lie with him. If he was still attracted to her, why had he behaved so oddly these past months? She was too tired to puzzle over it now. But, one way or the other, she'd find out . . .

Over the next days, she watched him carefully. He was polite and gentle, but talked not at all unless she spoke first. If she hadn't known better, she would have thought him unsure of himself. She scoffed at the notion. The man who'd defied his country and suffered torture for his beliefs could surely not be intimi-

dated by one woman—and she his own wife. Yet when night
came, he slept with her in his arms as if he couldn't bear to be
apart from her. Often she felt his hunger rearing against her. She
knew there were other ways to satisfy him beyond the usual one,
but she was too shy to suggest them. What did she know of this
distant protector?

When Saturday came, she was still at a loss. However, at least
now she had hope. Words indeed had always served them ill, so
she had not questioned him. Actions, however, said a great deal
. . . and her actions this evening would be concrete proof of her
loyalty and devotion. As she dressed, she dreamed of how proud
he would be when she handed him the map.

After Celie had fastened her upswept hair with turquoise-inlaid
combs, Tory appraised herself. Fat she might be, but her skin
had never been so glowing or her eyes so clear. The gathered
front of the cream taffeta gown was paneled with turquoise lace,
and the elbow-length sleeves and low neckline were trimmed in
the same lace. Tory eyed the low bodice uneasily. She tried to
pull it up, but her breasts refused to cooperate and peeked out
impudently, as if awaiting only the proper moment to show
themselves.

Sighing, Tory accepted her fan and light dress cloak. She met
Helen, dainty despite her height, in blue velvet the color of her
eyes. Robert and Miranda had gone to visit friends and knew
nothing of their plans. Beau was working late at the docks.

Tory flipped her cloak back so Helen could see her dress. "Do
you think this too daring?"

Helen raised a brow. "It's certainly revealing. If we can indeed get into Fuller's house, he'll not be watching *me* closely.
But if Beau sees you with Fuller, dressed like that . . ."

Tory refastened her cloak. With luck, Beau would return just
in time to get the map waved under his nose. "Well, he won't.
Are you sure you want to help me, Helen? I hate to involve you,
but I can't believe Fuller is really dangerous."

"Don't be silly. If Beau hadn't had to rescue me so hurriedly,
he might have gotten away without alerting anyone to his mission. Besides, I'm tired of being coddled. I didn't survive three
years in a harem for nothing." She sniffed.

Tory knew Helen argued with Terence about his over-
protectiveness. She suspected he'd asked her to wed him, but
Helen's pride was bruised. The gossip about her was dying as
she resumed her old routine, but Terence still shielded her as-

siduously. Both women had something to prove to the men in their lives.

As they alit at the Chestnut Street Theater, Fuller met them, offering Helen one arm and Tory the other. Tory appraised the building admiringly. It was of Palladian style, marble-trimmed, its entrance flanked by imposing columns.

"Why, how lovely it is. But it looks familiar . . ."

Fuller grinned. "And well it should. It was modeled on the theater in Bath."

"Of course!" Tory snapped her fingers.

They joined the glittering throng of people crowding up the marble steps. Tory sat between Helen and Fuller. She allowed Fuller to help her off with her cloak. An in-drawn breath rasped through the audience hum, but she was too enchanted with the theater to heed it.

England had few better. The front boxes were arranged like the tiers of an amphitheater; pit and gallery seats were staggered. Over the wide stage was an emblem bearing the motto, "For useful mirth, and salutary woe." The box fronts were gilded and draped, as was the soaring ceiling.

Tory turned back to Fuller. Her smile faded at his stare. She snapped her fan open. "Which play are we to see tonight, sir?"

"*She Stoops to Conquer,*" Fuller answered.

Helen broke into a coughing fit. Tory fluttered her fan in front of her face to hide a grin. Goldsmith must have been laughing in his grave, she thought. But she would stoop as low as necessary to save Beau . . .

She lowered her fan to smile at Fuller guilelessly. "I believe we have an interest in common, sir, other than our love for the theater—old jewelry."

"Indeed, it is a passion of mine. My mother began collecting it, but I've added a great deal over the years. I have a necklace that's rumored to have belonged to Cleopatra herself. To my regret, I've no wife as yet to help me display it." His eyes dropped to Tory's bosom.

She forced herself to sit under his admiration. "I'd love to see your collection. I lost most of my best pieces when I was captured in Algiers."

He shook his head. "How unfortunate. You must see mine soon."

Sooner than you think, Tory hoped. "I would be honored." She winked at Helen, who pinched her and gave her a warning look in return. But Tory was satisfied that he suspected nothing. They settled back in their seats as the play began.

Fuller was in the midst of a hearty guffaw when Tory stiffened beside him. He turned to look down at her, frowning when her teeth clenched her lower lip.

He bent to whisper, "Is something amiss?"

"No, just a twinge. I'm certain it's nothing." A moment after he looked back to the stage, she gasped and clutched her abdomen.

He put his arm about her. "But you're not well. Let me see if I can find a doctor—"

"No, no, if you will just escort me outside. This stuffy air is making me ill."

Fuller helped her up and put her cloak about her shoulders. "Of course."

His solicitude made her feel guilty, but what choice had she? She had to get into his house. If he hadn't taken the map, she would offer her true friendship, Beau's reaction be damned; if he had taken it, any trick she played on him to get it back was justified. Helen followed, looking as tense as Tory felt.

Outside, Tory wavered under his guiding arm as he walked her up and down. She took deep breaths of the cool spring air, but clapped her hand over her mouth and looked at him sorrowfully.

"I think I'm going to be sick." She waited until he blanched, then added, "If only I could lie down. Perhaps a cup of tea would help."

He fell neatly into the trap. "That's easy enough. My house is a short distance . . ." He looked at her diffidently.

"Helen will join us, and right now I want to lie down too much to worry about gossip."

"Good. Should I call for the carriage?"

"Perhaps walking would help me."

Fuller's house was down Chestnut, just past Christ Church's soaring steeple. His entryway was paneled with cherry and lined with oils. Fuller led her to a drawing room and gently seated her on a blue velvet fainting couch that complemented the cream and royal blue interiors.

After he'd ordered tea, Tory fumbled in her cloak pockets. She looked up at him helplessly. "I seem to have misplaced my kerchief. May I borrow one? Some water, too, perhaps, to dip it in."

"Of course. I'll get you one of mine."

He'd scarcely cleared the doorway before the two women erupted into action. Tory lunged to the alcove; Helen tore open the drawers to a dainty writing desk against the wall. They peered behind furniture and even tried twisting the lions' heads on the marble mantelpiece. Nothing. They were sitting down again when Fuller entered carrying a small ewer and clean handkerchief.

"Here you are." Tory took the kerchief absently after he'd dribbled some water on it. She folded it over her eyes and lay back, thinking furiously. If he hadn't burned the map, he most likely kept it with his valuables.

When tea was brought, Tory drank hers quickly and set the bone china cup and saucer down on the carved table next to the couch. "I feel much recovered, Mr. Fuller. Thank you for your consideration." She absently stuck the kerchief in her pocket and rose, her loose cloak falling off her shoulders.

Fuller picked it up. "We've missed too much of the play to go back now, but can you not stay a little longer?"

"I am fatigued." When his face fell, she added as if in afterthought, "However, I *would* like to see your jewelry collection."

"Excellent. This way. It's locked in my study."

The book-lined room was redolent of leather and old paper. Both women sat down, watching him expectantly. Fuller paused in crossing the room and turned instead. Tory was elated at his wary look. She knew as surely as if he'd told her that he'd just remembered who they were.

"Ah, forgive me, ladies, but perhaps you could wait outside a moment."

"Of course." Tory bent to the keyhole when he closed the door. She had a clear view of the desk and the left side of the room, but could not see him. She and Helen listened, closing their eyes to concentrate. There came the sounds of a key turning, the tinkle of glass, then . . . Their eyes flew open.

That last sound was one like no other. To their ears, it was music, mundane as it was—the sound of crackling parchment.

The rest was ridiculously easy. When Fuller readmitted them to the study and laid an impressive array of ancient hammered-golden jewelry on the desk, Tory asked to try on a Celtic necklace. She rushed back to the drawing room to look in the mirror, Fuller following with a smile. Alone in the study, Helen hurried to the large Oriental jar displayed in a glass case beside the fireplace; it was the only glass container on the right side of the room.

When Fuller and Tory returned, she gave Tory a sweet smile and made their excuses. Fuller walked them to the door, then lingered low over Tory's hand. Tory suffered the touch, unaware of the spectators across the street who had just exited a nearby taproom.

On arriving home, Tory and Helen bent their heads over the map. They recognized Beau's hand in the writing of the legend. Helen rolled the chart back up and handed it to Tory. Jubilantly they patted each other on the back.

"When do you give this to Beau, Tory? Don't expect a great deal of gratitude from my stiff-necked brother. He'll be angry he didn't find it himself."

Tory stuck the map under one arm beneath her cloak. "When he comes to our room, I imagine." She patted a yawn. "All this excitement has worn me out. Thanks again, Helen." She was but three steps up the stairs when the front door crashed open. She started and turned. Helen froze at the foot of the steps.

Two sets of inimical eyes glared at them. One brown, one green, both condemning. "What the hell were you doing at Fuller's?" Beau snarled to Tory.

"You lied to me, Helen," Terence said angrily. "The way you're dressed tells me you've been to the theater, yet you refused my invitation."

Tory opened her mouth to defend herself, but Beau rushed on, "Answer me, woman! You're comfortable with dandies like Fuller, aren't you? Admit you wish you'd wed someone you could manipulate."

Her mouth snapped shut; her chin went up; her temper soared. "I admit nothing except that you're blind, deaf, and as stupid as a camel. Would to God you were dumb as well." She marched up the steps.

When Terence took Helen's arm, she shook him away. "I'll not listen to your nonsense, either. What I do with my life is no concern of yours."

"It will be soon enough. Damme, woman, you need a keeper. Don't you understand that Fuller is trying to ruin us? Why do you socialize with him?"

"I understand too well. You and Beau are both alike. Well, I hope you'll have joy of each other, for you'll get little from either of us.'' She stalked up the stairs after her sister-in-law.

Terence ran a hand through his thick brown hair. ''It's probably not what it looks to be,'' he muttered. ''They're doing this just to spite us.''

''Tory knows how I feel about Fuller. She knew I'd be angry if I found out where she'd been tonight. Why else didn't she tell someone she was attending the theater with him? That's bad enough, but for her actually to enter his house and allow him to . . . to maul her—''

''Beau, he merely kissed her hand. And I'm certain they had a good reason for going there.''

''Oh, yes? Well, there's only one way to find out.'' Beau prowled upstairs like a great cat in pursuit of dinner.

As soon as Tory reached her old bedchamber, she secreted the map in the bottom drawer of the highboy under her chemises. Then she straightened and, two spots of red flagging her cheekbones, marched to Beau's room and removed all evidence of her recent occupation. A stack of clothing in her arms, she went to the door—but not out.

The look in Beau's eyes would have frightened her once upon a time. Now she was too angry, too disillusioned, to care about the peculiar animadversions in what passed for his brain. Not one word had he allowed her in defense of herself. Very well. Let him think what he liked. She had half a mind to burn the map herself. But even in her anger, she knew she wouldn't. She loved him too much, fool that she was. That knowledge only made her angrier.

''Stand out of my way,'' she spat, much as she would have spoken to an insolent lackey.

He braced his hands on either side of the door. ''No. Not until you tell me what the hell you were doing with Fuller.''

''Oh, are you ready to listen, now?'' She smiled sweetly. ''But I'm no longer of mind to explain.''

''Tory!'' he roared, his voice echoing from rafter to floor. His beloved didn't turn a hair. His tone rose another notch. ''By God, woman, if you don't tell me what you were doing, I'll . . . I'll . . .''

''Yessss?'' she encouraged. When his mouth worked helplessly, her smile widened. It was not a nice smile. ''Why, Fuller and I had a romp in bed. Isn't that what you're waiting to hear?''

She heaped the clothes over one arm and patted her belly with the other. "This got in the way a bit, but we managed."

Beau snorted, some of his anger fading at her outrageous lie. "And what did Helen do?" He nodded down the hall to his shamelessly eavesdropping sister.

"She watched," Tory said. She raised her voice. "Didn't you, Helen?"

"Er, well . . . that is—"

"And what does his chamber look like?" Beau asked dryly.

Tory faltered but a moment. "Ah, it's a handsome room, of purple and crimson, with silk sheets on the bed and cherubs holding back the drapes."

She'd just described to a tee one of the most elite whorehouses he'd ever been in. Beau choked back a laugh and said gravely, "And it had a painted ceiling, I suppose."

Tory nodded. "Yes, with satyrs and nymphs chasing one another."

"*Chasing* one another?" he repeated with a droll look.

She had the grace to blush. "Ah, they were . . . were . . ."

When Beau opened his mouth, she covered it with her hand and glared at him. "You know very well what they were doing, and I'll not have you say that awful word again." She jerked her hand away when he bit it gently.

"But this is *so* enlightening," Beau murmured. "And Fuller wore the obligatory dressing gown, I suppose?"

"Er, yes. It had dragons embroidered on it."

Beau's mouth quivered at the vision she conjured up, but he stilled his laughter. He moved back a pace to cross his arms over his chest. "And what happened then?"

Tory cleared her throat. "Ah, we, you know . . ."

"No, I don't know. Enlighten me."

"You surely don't want to hear all the details."

"Yes, I do. I'm curious as to how my wife, who's to deliver in less than a month, cuckolded me. What position did you use?"

Miranda, Robert, and Helen, had congregated down the hall and were listening with varying degrees of appalled amusement. Even Terence, who'd come upstairs in pursuit of Helen, stood among the spectators. Neither Beau nor Tory noticed them.

Tory wished she'd never started this. She searched her mind frantically. None of the positions Beau had taught her would work in her current condition. "Ah, the frontal?"

Beau shook his head. "Impractical."

"Sideways?"

"Unlikely."

"Standing on my head, then," Tory snapped, goaded. Snickers drifted down the hall. Tory glanced at their audience and blushed, but Beau wouldn't let her evade his questions.

"That, my dear, sounds intriguing. You'll have to show me. I'll be the woman, and you can be the man, since you're not happy with the way things are." His amusement faded abruptly. "Enough. Now tell me the truth. What were you doing at Fuller's? You didn't discuss my current difficulties with him, did you? Do you miss England so much?"

Tory was puzzled at the question—until she realized he thought she had sought Fuller's company because he was a fervent Anglophile. She was Beau's wife now, and her first loyalty was to him, yet he gave her no chance to show it. In full view of his family, each of whom she'd come to love and respect, he accused her of abetting Fuller's case against him. What would he suspect her of next? She gritted her teeth, so furious that even her pain at his distrust seemed a bagatelle under the urge to stomp his arrogance into the ground. Her eyes fell to the garments in her hands. He wanted to play the woman? Very well.

"Here," she trilled. "Let me satisfy your curiosity." She sorted through the garments, keeping several and throwing the rest on the floor. She draped a filmy wrapper over his shoulders and tied the pink bow in the front. She rose on tiptoe and stuck a frilly mob cap over his brown head. Then she stood back to appraise him, one finger to her cheek.

She seemed not to notice the fire crackling in his eyes. She snapped her fingers. "I know what's missing." She bent, picked up a pair of embroidered house slippers and stuck one over each of his ears. "There. Your horns." She turned his stiff body around so the audience down the hall could see him.

She was pleased at the disgusted groan that shook him as he caught sight of them. They looked at him with quivering mouths. Miranda had to turn away.

Robert asked, "Have you both run mad?"

A rumble began in Beau's chest, growing louder as he ripped off the slippers and flung them against the wall. The cap and wrapper followed. He kicked them away and turned on his wife, his jaw flexing. Very gently he took her shoulders.

This time he didn't yell. This time Tory *was* frightened. "Very well, my dear, I hope you've enjoyed your little jokes. But the last laugh will be mine.'' He nuzzled her cheek, pulling back with a nasty smile when she shivered.

"You are to go to our cabin on the Schuylkill tomorrow. You will stay there until I join you. You will pass the time in womanly pursuits, sewing for the child and such like. When I come, we'll talk further.'' He put her away from him, his eyes sharp enough to draw blood.

Indeed, Tory felt as if she were bleeding inside, but her head stayed high. "I'll go if and when I please. I wouldn't let you browbeat me when I was your slave, and I'll certainly not allow it now when you accuse me of the most base crimes. Until I receive the respect due me as your wife, I'll give you none as my husband.''

There was a long silence. Green eyes tried to cow brilliant turquoise ones, but neither flickered. No quarter asked, none given. Then Beau sighed so deeply his chin met his chest. His face went blank. His mouth quivered once, then stilled.

"Very well, Victoria Alicia Grenville. It's plain a Cochran you'll never be. I'll trouble you no longer.'' He turned on his heel and walked down the hall to where Terence stood listening with the others. "Have you a spare bed?'' he queried. "I think it best for all concerned that I make myself scarce for a while.''

A volley of protests sounded—from everyone but Tory. She stood frozen in place, her face as icy white as an alabaster death mask. Even when two heavy sets of footsteps trod down the stairs, she didn't move.

Helen put her arm about her. "Tory, he didn't mean it. He'll be back.'' Miranda and Robert agreed, making excuses for Beau, but Tory barely heard them.

She retreated to her big, lonely chamber and lay dry-eyed, staring into the dark. So easily he cast her from him because she wouldn't bend her neck under his boot. She had never bowed to him. Why would he expect her to do so now? And if he didn't care about her, why had he been so gently protective? Their child kicked and rolled, as if sensing its mother's agitation. Tory put one hand over it. "He doesn't want us, little one.'' The words echoed in her mind discordantly, lacking the ring of truth. No, something else was amiss, and as she remembered his words tonight, she finally understood what it was.

Incredibly, he really doubted her loyalty; he really thought that she, as an Englishwoman, would be sympathetic to the Federalist cause even if it meant betraying him. It hurt that he thought so little of her, but she had, after all, antagonized him. Somehow she had to find a way to prove to him that her loyalties lay with him, and only with him. She was no longer certain that simply giving him the map would suffice.

Those next few days were the longest of her life. She debated driving to Terence's, but then Robert passed on to her some interesting news: Beau was to take his written defense of his actions and the new map he'd drawn from memory to the Indian King Tavern, where Fuller and his cronies met every Tuesday. Robert, Terence, Grant Chippenham, and William Duane would accompany him to assist in one last public confrontation. Their barrister would take another copy of each document to the Senate to be read on Beau's behalf before the vote the next day.

Tory left the study, her face animated for the first time in days. When Tuesday dawned, she was torn between nervousness and resolve. As she dressed carefully that night, she felt much as Caesar must have when he crossed the Rubicon.

The Indian King Tavern taproom was full that muggy night in early May. The patrons were a mixed group. Rich and poor puffed on cigars and pipes, swigging from foaming tankards of ale. Coarse stories made the rounds from table to table and were laughed at by dockworker and merchant alike.

Despite the convivial atmosphere, however, the political split between merchant-Federalist and common man–Republican was evident even in the seating arrangement. On one side of the room United Irishmen, wearing their badges of plumed feathers and black cockades, mingled with laborers and farmers. On the other, richly garbed men sat in muted conversation. The two sides eyed one another warily, Republicans distrusting Federalist use of power, Federalists leery of Republican ability to govern.

Into this atmosphere came Beau and his supporters. The United Irishmen saw them first. Their leader, a stalwart fellow with pepper-red hair, hurried toward Duane, who was a captain in their Republican Greens regiment. "Captain," he whispered, " 'Tis dangerous for ye t' come here. Ye know the Senate wants t' clap ye in irons."

"Thank you for your concern, Patrick, but I'll be fine. Go back to your table, please," Duane replied. The man obeyed reluctantly.

Beau looked sharply at Duane. He'd been so involved in his own problems he'd not read the *Aurora* lately. "What does he mean, man?'' he asked, pulling Duane out of the taproom into the shadow of the stairs and beckoning his father to join them.

Brows lowered over his piercing eyes, Duane growled, ''The Federalist scum will do anything to quiet the *Aurora*, for they see their end coming in the next election. The majority has run roughshod over Republican opposition and set up a special committee to investigate my 'criminal writing.' I appeared before them once, but they've already judged and condemned me without benefit of counsel, so I'll not appear before them again. They've charged me with contempt and issued a warrant for my arrest.''

Beau cursed. Duane leaned forward to tap Beau's chest. ''So you see, my friend, they think to make an example of us both. I have my own reasons for being here tonight. I'll not let them cow me, nor do I recognize their brand of 'justice.' So far I've managed to avoid them and continue writing. No one knew I was coming tonight, so they'll not have men on hand to take me. I've endured worse—beatings, even the Black Hole of Calcutta, when the British found my pen's ink too acidic. I believe in the ideals this country was founded on, and I'll not see the same injustice done here. Too many printers have already been terrified into silence or servility. But men are still found who dare to speak truth.''

''I'd not have you in further trouble on my account.''

''Our causes are similar, Beau. We are both persecuted for being men of conscience. I tell you: 'For modes of faith let graceless zealots fight; his can't be wrong, whose life is right.' ''

Stirred by William's ringing words, Beau realized yet again what a powerful ally this man was. If Duane couldn't help propel Jefferson into the presidency, no one could.

Robert added, ''I invited the Greens tonight. And many Philadelphians have signed a petition urging the Senate to reconsider its resolution against William. The Federalists have become oppressive because they see the writing on the wall, Beau. Their greedy usurpation of power is going to wrest it from their hands.''

Duane nodded his agreement. ''They call me the leader of the 'Jeffersonian Mobocracy' and spreader of 'the contagion.' Well, I tell you, sir, that if contagion I be then may they succumb quickly.'' Duane's slight Irish accent was stronger than usual.

"Come, let us commence." Fire glowed in his eyes, and Beau could see how he relished the fight.

Silently the group went back into the taproom. Beau walked straight to the two groups of merchants. Fuller saw him first. His slumped spine straightened. Beau wondered at the flash of foreboding he saw on the man's face. But to his credit, Fuller rose to face Beau squarely.

Behind him came several cries, "It's Duane! Fetch the constable!"

The group of Irishmen, however, had already risen to block the door. " 'Tis a private talk they want, and even sich snooty 'gentlemen' as yerselves can show them common courtesy, I'm thinkin'," drawled Patrick from his position by the door.

The grumbling subsided as the Federalists, almost a dozen in number, realized they would either have to listen or force their way out. They reseated themselves and glared at the Republicans.

Beau made a quick survey of the group. Good. Two senators, Cummins, and several of the wealthiest, most influential merchants of Philadelphia. And, of course, Fuller, who sat down but remained watchful.

"Gentlemen," Beau began politely, "I am here this night to suggest one last time that we be reasonable men. Can we not put aside our political differences and remember first we are all Americans?"

One senator, a well-fed, priggish man, snorted. "But we are not, sir. Duane is from Ireland and is a dangerous radical. With him as your champion, how can we believe you are not in sympathy with his sedition? Indeed, you proved your contempt for Adams and us by taking the law into your own hands. And now you ask *us* to be reasonable?"

Duane stepped forward. "I am sick unto death of being considered a dangerous alien. I was born in this country, sir, and all my years abroad do not change that. Your taunts, threats, and subversion will not silence me or chase me away. I'm as much an American as you." Duane sent a contemptuous look up and down the fuming senator. "More so, to me way o' thinkin'." The deliberate brogue was a taunt.

Beau clasped Duane's shoulder. The editor clamped his jaw together and stepped back to Robert's side. He waved a hand. "Go on, Beau. Forgive me for interrupting."

Moving to the table, Beau slapped down a roll of parchment

and sheaf of paper. "My mission was not a total loss, gentle-men, and I ask that you take that into consideration tomorrow." He tapped the paper. "In here you'll find a detailed history of my years in Algiers. I recount the treatment of prisoners, the chain of command, the discipline aboard Algerine cruisers, cor-sair raiding tactics, and the best way to repel them. I include a section on the dey, his political strengths and weaknesses, his latest inclination on what nation to grant favored status to, and an estimate of the current state of his treasury. This information has been submitted to the full Senate by my barrister to be read tomorrow before the vote."

"All of which information we can obtain from our consul," said the other senator, an effete blond.

"Come, now, sir, our consul knows little of the way the dey thinks, how his officers operate, and nothing of their discipline at sea."

"Very well, I grant that information could be helpful if we go to war with them. But only your blasted interference has created that possibility—"

Terence interrupted the blond. "The dey will remain peace-able only so long as his greed is fed. And I predict, gentlemen, that Tripoli will become even more demanding over these next months. Are we to supply the Bashaw and the pasha the same incredible terms? For that's the only way we'll appease these pirates. I ask you, sirs, can we afford *not* to go to war with them?"

Beau leaned his palms flat on the table and looked each sen-ator in the eye. "We sent over a million dollars to Algiers alone—almost a sixth of our entire government expenditure last year. Is this the price you're willing to pay for this spurious 'peace'?"

Rumbles of anger sounded all over the room, even from some of the Federalists. For the first time Cummins spoke. "I agree, Cochran, these pirates are become insatiable, and if they take more American ships, it's my opinion the navy will be ordered to punish them. If only you had gone through proper channels—"

"What proper channels? We had just concluded a treaty with Algiers. Had we asked permission of the War Department, it would not have been granted."

"All the more reason to punish you now, for you knew you went against the wishes of the government," the plump senator rebuked.

Beau straightened. "You forget one thing, gentlemen. I had a very good personal reason for going to Algiers. My sister was being held captive there. Do you also deny my right as a citizen to rescue her?" He looked the Federalists in the face one by one. Fuller looked away. Beau was puzzled at his silence. He'd expected Fuller to be most vociferous, yet he'd said not a word.

Cummins shifted uncomfortably. "No one denies you that right. But you didn't have to spy as well."

"But I did. I lost my best friend, Henry Stoville, to those pirates. Paying tribute to them through the ages has done naught but make them more arrogant. I believed then, and I believe now, that it's time to 'repel force with force,' as Jefferson advised years ago. I'll make no excuse for my actions, nor will I pretend that I would not do the same again. And if war does become necessary, I'll be first to offer my services. All I ask is that when you vote tomorrow, you take into account not only my reasons but also what I have accomplished."

"Why did you not bring back a map, as Terence did?" asked Cummins.

Beau looked at Fuller's bent head. How he would have loved to accuse Fuller of his act, but he had no proof. He could only answer, "I made two copies, and both were unfortunately lost." Fuller looked up, his gray eyes startled.

Puzzled, Beau continued to watch Fuller as he spread out the parchment. "I drew this map from memory, and while it's not complete, it gives us some idea of the way the Algerine defenses are laid out. Doubtless the dey has ordered the guns to be moved by now—"

"Your excuses for your incompetence are no more convincing than your justification for your actions!"

Beau let the parchment roll back up. He straightened slowly. "At last you speak, Fuller, if such braying can be termed so. I didn't expect you to agree with my reasons, but surely even you will grant me the right of self-defense."

All eyes went to Fuller. He leaped to his feet, scraping his chair back. "So it's been granted. Now get out and wait for the Senate's decision. And if you go into hiding like this coward" —he shot a disdainful look at Duane—"I'll lead the search for you."

Duane muttered a curse, but Robert took his arm and held him back. "Look at their faces, man. Let him rage. He's losing the support of his own associates," he whispered in Duane's ear.

Indeed, both senators and Cummins were looking at Fuller oddly. His face was red with his frustration, while Beau stood with a casual hand on his hip.

"You're in a mighty hurry to be rid of me. I wonder why?" Beau asked the room at large.

The answer came from an unexpected quarter. "Because he fears that his own cowardly act will be exposed." The feminine tones reverberated in the tense silence. All eyes turned to the door, where the Greens parted to let Tory enter the male sanctum.

Those who had not seen Tory sat a little straighter; those who had seen her looked from Tory to her husband. Beau stood as if turned to stone, still facing away from the door.

Tory had listened for some time and had acted at the most dramatic moment. She refused to be embarrassed by the whispers and masculine stares. Her eyes glowed like votive candles, lit with purpose and devotion. They remained fixed on Fuller's whitening face as she walked to Beau's side.

She glanced at Beau, but looked quickly back at Fuller. She tossed back her light summer cloak, revealing her pink muslin dress embroidered at neck and hem with red roses. Her coppery hair was caught up with fresh red roses that should have clashed, but somehow didn't. Instead they complemented her rosy cheeks, the femininity accented by her rounded belly.

Every eye remained on her as slowly she drew her other arm out of her cloak. She turned away from Fuller to hold out the roll of parchment to her husband. "This, I believe, belongs to you."

Numbly he took it and unrolled it to hold it to the candlelight. He rolled it back up and handed it to Cummins. "This is the original map I drew—the one that was stolen. Where did you find it, Tory?"

Fuller seemed to have recovered his composure. He pushed his chair out and sprawled rudely before her. "Yes, *Tory*, tell him where you found it."

Tory met his challenging stare without flinching. "I am Mrs. Cochran to you." She felt Beau start, but her attention remained on Fuller. "As to where it was found—why, in your own study, where you hid it after hiring a thief to rob Beau's courier."

Gasps sounded, and the whispering grew to a buzz that was

silenced by Fuller's oily retort. "Indeed, love? So now you resort to lying so as to wreak your petty vengeance. I regret your anger at my change of heart about our, er . . ."

Beau growled and took a step toward Fuller, but Tory caught his arm. "Let him squeal like the cornered rat he is. No one will believe his filth."

Tory reached into her cloak. "The night we attended the theater, I was seen by your own servants—as they will doubtless testify—entering your home with my sister-in-law and departing with her shortly after."

Pulling a handkerchief out of her pocket, she tossed it on the table before Cummins and the two senators. "He gave me this that night when I pretended to feel unwell. You'll see not only his initials, but the crest on which he so prides himself."

She smiled mockingly into Fuller's rigid face. "You thought your charms so persuasive, did you not? Poor man."

Tory's goading worked. Fuller leaped to his feet, white with rage, and shouted, "You slut! You pretend to refinement and nobility, but you're as low-born as your husband!"

Before Beau's raised fist could fall, Tory caught it. "No, Beau, he's not worth it." She ignored Fuller and turned to the dismayed Federalists. "If you need further proof, sirs, I can show you where the map was found."

Cummins shook his head, his mouth curled with distaste. He moved his chair away from Fuller. "No, ma'am, his reaction makes it obvious that you tell the truth. Agreed?" The two senators nodded glumly.

"I'm not precisely sure what laws have been broken, Cochran, but I can investigate the matter if you wish," one of the senators inserted stiffly.

"That won't be necessary, Senator. Fuller will be punished enough where it will really hurt him." Beau took Tory's arm and led her from the room.

After they had left the tavern, Fuller began an agitated defense of his actions, but he got no sympathy from his former associates. The use of such tactics, and then lying about them by trying to besmirch the reputation of a lady who'd been defending her husband, could not be tolerated. Especially in a man one must trust to do business with.

Robert, Terence, and his father also exited, but Duane paused to look back at the senators, his Greens a bulwark on either side of him. "I'll be busy this night, gentlemen. I suggest you read the *Aurora* tomorrow before you vote." He bowed and exited.

The two senators stepped around the still stuttering Fuller and went to the door, well aware of their position. If Fuller's action was publicized, they, as his business associates, would seem manipulated at best and conspiratorial at worst if they voted against Beau . . .

By the time they reached home, Tory's nerves were shrieking with tension, for Beau had said not a word during the carriage drive. He seemed remote instead of relieved. If this didn't bridge the breach between them, she didn't know what else to do.

Retreating to her chamber, Tory left Robert and Beau to explain the evening's events to Miranda and Helen. She dressed in one of her prettiest negligees and sat down to brush her hair. At last she heard footsteps ascend the stairs. She tensed when they paused outside her door, but they passed. A door closed; then all was silent. Tory glared at herself in the mirror. Her mouth firmed. Rising, she tied the ribbons on her cream lace robe and stalked to the door.

When she slammed Beau's door open, she found him staring out the window into the darkness. "So, husband, do I get not a word of gratitude or praise?" She crossed her arms over the mound of her belly and waited.

He turned to face her, his features grim in the light of the candles. "You would get both, if I knew your reasons for acting as you have. Why the dramatic revelation? Why did you let me squirm like a worm on a hook, worrying about your relationship with Fuller? Why didn't you tell me what you were doing?" Tell me you love me, he pleaded silently. Tell me you weren't just acting to protect the father of your babe.

Tory stabbed her finger into his chest. "I might ask the same. I've learned more of your affairs from your family than I have from you." Tory stepped away. Her angry tone softened. "You wanted proof of my loyalty as your wife. Surely I've supplied it. I'll always be English, but that doesn't mean I can't be a Cochran, too."

He shrugged. "I appreciate that, as far as it goes. But how many of your actions were done out of an angry need to get back at me, to make me feel guilty?" When she flushed, he turned away again. "I thought so. Well, madam, you've succeeded. I apologize for mistrusting you. No man could ask for a greater champion. You played the avenging angel beautifully this night."

''What else would you have of me?'' she cried.

Everything, he longed to reply. I can't bear to see you heavy with my child, wearing my ring, supporting my cause, yet so little my own. All of this is not enough, my love. I thought it would be. I was wrong. His throat ached too much for speech, so he shook his head, still looking out the window at the gloomy garden.

So he didn't care after all, Tory thought. Pain pierced her like a stake through the heart, but her head went a notch higher. She said huskily, ''So, we're at quits. You regret having wed me. I can't offer the blind obedience you want. I never pretended I could. If my loyalty and respect are not enough, then there's no hope for us.'' She stumbled to the door, hoping, praying he'd stop her. He didn't. She returned to her room, wondering vaguely what she was to do now that her marriage was over before it had really begun.

Beau stood listening to her retreating footsteps. Then he put his palms flat against the windowpane and leaned his forehead against them. She was right; loyalty wasn't enough. She was so much woman. She called to everything male within him. Right or wrong, he wanted all of her, not just body and mind, but heart and soul as well.

Tonight had proved to him beyond all doubt that he could no longer bear to live with her, yet without her in the only way that mattered. She'd been so lovely, so proud and perfect. It had been so painful to watch her standing staunchly at his side. He'd looked at the envy on the other men's faces and wanted to laugh. If they only knew what torment it was to be wed to such a woman. Having only half of her was worse than having none at all. She became more desirable to him daily, yet ever further out of reach. If she didn't love him now, she probably never would.

He had to face that truth at last. He'd coerced so much from her, but he could not coerce the one thing he wanted most. There was only one thing left to do . . .

PART VI

"The lips of the one I love are my perpetual
pleasure:
The Lord be praised, for my heart's desire is
attained."

—Hafiz, from *A Book of Love Poetry*

Chapter 20

The banks of the Schuylkill burst with greenery. Fine country homes graced its slopes: Here a two-storied white house slumbered within a lacy tree embrace, there a brick abode dwelt high on a rolling hill. Spring-fed, the Schuylkill rushed over shallows alive with leaping shad. The faint roaring Tory had heard since leaving Philadelphia grew louder every moment until the falls came in sight. Tory ordered the coachman to stop.

This was the limit of the river's navigable course from Philadelphia, and Tory could see why. Water gushed over cliffs to agitate the river into white foam, veiling, then revealing jagged black rocks. The rock-and gravel-lined banks glistened with mica specks in the morning sun.

They proceeded on to the cottage, turning up the Wissahickon Creek, which wound a gentler though serpentine course through lush hills and projecting rocks. Everywhere new life abounded. Trees lifted leafy arms in worship to the sun; lambs gamboled in pastures; tender green seedlings sent tentative shoots up neatly plowed rows. New trees, new animals, new plants. It was even a new century, but for the first time in her life, Tory felt old. Without Beau's love, what did she have to look forward to? The child kicked her as if in reproach. Tory folded her hands over it protectively. They passed a barnyard where a newborn colt suckled its mother. Tory felt her breasts tighten at the sight.

Soon she, too, would know what it meant to be a mother, but the joy she'd expected was missing. Beau had all but sent her away. Despite the life lowering within her to prepare its path to the world, Tory felt alone as never before.

Her in-laws had protested this morning when they'd come down the stairs to see her trunks being loaded by the coachman. Tory had shaken her head at their entreaties to stay until Beau returned from his early visit to the docks.

"I think it best to go now. We . . . spoke last night. Besides, I've but three weeks left, and I'd like time to settle in the cottage before the baby comes. I want to get to know Mattie better as well.'' Miranda's and Helen's trusted midwife had retired to her country cottage. She was old but capable, and Tory liked her. It had been agreed long ago that when May came, Tory would go to the family seat in the country. She'd not only be more comfortable in the clean river breezes but she'd be safer, too, for soon yellow fever might visit its summer wrath upon the city as it often did.

Robert took her arm and murmured, ''But don't you want to hear the outcome of the vote?''

''Do you really doubt the outcome now, since Duane will make all known today?''

''No, Tory,'' Robert admitted. ''But you have as much to do with that as Duane. I didn't get the chance to thank you last night. Let me do it now.'' He drew her into his arms and hugged her. ''Tory you may be, but a man could not ask for a more loyal wife.''

When her eyes misted, his smile faded. ''My dear, what's amiss? Won't you let us help?''

Tory pulled away before she succumbed to the impulse to sob in his strong arms. ''It's nothing. I'm just emotional.'' She turned to go to the door, then looked back at Robert. ''Can you send word to the cottage after the vote?''

''Of course. Are you sure you want to do this?''

''Yes. Good-bye, all. I'll expect you at the cottage after the babe is born.'' With a last brave smile, she waved and exited. Robert, Miranda, and Helen went to the front windows to watch the carriage drive away.

''Robert, she shouldn't be alone right now. We must do something.'' Miranda gave a little sob. Robert caught her hand.

''Don't worry, love. I don't know what happened between them''—Robert released her and took his hat off the hook behind the door—''but I'm going to find out. I've a certain two-legged mule to see.'' Setting his hat at a decisive angle, Robert stomped out.

Tory rocked on the front porch, watching the sun's alchemy turn the river to molten brass. Wind rustled the shrubs and trees beside the house, accenting the busy insect clatter. Diana rose opposite Apollo, smiling as if looking forward to her nightly dominion over him. The evening star winked beside her golden cheek like a single diamond earring.

Mattie, Elias's mother and the midwife, came out of her small cottage behind the larger house to give Tory a cup of herbal tea. "Here, child, drink this. It will help you sleep."

It was obvious from whom Elias got his looks, Tory thought, smiling up at the tall, regal black woman. "Are you going to spoil me so shamefully for the entire three weeks?"

"Humph! Every woman needs spoiling at this time in her life. Some folks need reminding of that." Mattie tapped her cheek. "Drink." She watched sternly until the cup was empty. She took it, ordering, "Time for bed."

"Not yet. I want to enjoy the view."

"Very well, but not long. You need your rest. Don't forget to summon me if you need me." She'd rigged up a cord beside Tory's bed that went to a bell on the side of the house. "Good night, child."

"Good night, Mattie. Thank you for your care for me." The midwife's white teeth flashed in the gloom; then she went down the porch steps, her stride still energetic despite her full head of white hair.

Tory rocked, and slowly the peaceful night and hypnotic sway relaxed her. Agonizing over what had happened and what would come served no purpose. She had an ordeal to live through before she could plan for the future. She would think of Beau no longer. She wouldn't. But when she nodded off, his name was on her lips.

It seemed minutes later that strong arms lifted her and carried her into the house. Tory burrowed her face into the shoulder she recognized even half asleep. "Beau, darling," she whispered against him, too softly for him to hear. He set her down on the wide quilt-covered bed and removed her dress. When he would have pulled her petticoat off as well, she awakened fully and stopped him.

"No. I'll manage. Why are you here?"

He straightened. "What kind of monster do you think me to desert you at such a time? I always intended to be with you. You shouldn't have left without telling me. Of course I want to be here when my heir is born."

The warmth in her eyes cooled. "I see. Well, far be it from me to deny you. But you've three empty chambers to choose from." She couldn't bear for him to hold her any longer when he wanted only the child she carried.

His face was shadowed in the dancing candlelight, and his

voice seemed muffled when he said, "As you wish, milady."
He stalked to the door.

"Wait," she said anxiously. He paused, hand on the knob,
but didn't turn. "How concluded the vote?"

"In my favor, by a two-vote margin. So you see, milady, you
saved my hide. What a pity you have no interest in it." He
slammed out.

Tory hugged a pillow, tears falling hot and fast. Always they
were at cross-purposes, from that first meeting in a London ballroom to now, when she was about to deliver his child. Why was
it that even her attempts to put things right drove them farther
apart? She didn't understand him, not one bit. And, no closer
than he allowed her now, she probably never would.

That despairing certainty grew over the next days. Beau was
as gentle and kind to her as any pregnant wife could wish, bringing her breakfast in bed, helping her in and out of chairs, fastening the buttons she couldn't reach. But when she didn't need
him, he disappeared to fish in the river, hunt in the woods, or
visit friends downstream. He might have been a doctor hired to
tend her, so remote was his care.

And it drove Tory crazy. Damn him, and damn his duty. If
she hadn't been so burdened, she'd have gotten out of his life
for good. She began rising before he brought her tray, sitting
next to the sofa arm so she could lever herself up, and wearing
dresses she could pull over her head. If anything, he drew further
away from her then. Occasionally, however, she caught him
watching her oddly. Almost hungrily, as if storing up memories
like a bear stuffing himself before hibernation.

Tory grew so tense she couldn't sleep. But no matter what
time she finally drifted off, she still saw a light flickering under
his door. She couldn't help thinking she was missing something.
Somehow, his behavior made sense, if she could only find the
critical link.

When the baby came a week early, the feeling grew stronger;
Beau's behavior was most peculiar for a man who cared only for
the child. . . .

Tory's eyes flew open in the middle of a sound sleep as pain
racked her body. She waited for several more intervals, but when
water gushed between her legs, she knew this was it. She pulled
the cord. The bell outside pealed but once before her door
slammed back against the wall.

Dressed only in a red robe, Beau rushed in. "Tory, what is it?" he cried.

Tory forced a smile. "Your child is impatient. Get Mattie."

But Mattie trotted in a second later, as neat as if she'd been expecting this. As she had. She threw the covers away from Tory and felt her abdomen, then she parted Tory's legs and lifted her nightdress.

"Ah, shouldn't you send Beau out?" Tory whispered to Mattie, flushing at the indignity of her position, but planting her feet as requested.

"Out, Mr. Beau," Mattie ordered over her shoulder.

Beau didn't budge. He stood, holding a candle high in one hand, like a lighthouse beaming into the darkness. Tory saw wax drip down on his arm and flinched, but he merely wiped it away impatiently. That was her first clue to his state of mind. She peered at him, but then another pain took her.

She breathed as Mattie instructed. When the pain receded, Mattie helped her rise. The midwife glanced at Beau impatiently. "If you must stay, make yourself useful. Change the sheets."

White-faced, he set the candle down and did so. Efficiently Mattie helped Tory put on a clean gown. As Tory climbed back into bed, she looked up at the man who stared down at her as if she might explode any moment.

"I'll be fine. You can go if you like."

Huskily he answered, "No. I'll stay to help."

"But there's nothing you can do—" She gasped and grabbed his hand.

He held her tightly, stroking her forehead with his other hand. "Yell if you want to, love. I'm here. I'll not leave you."

And he didn't, not through that long night, not even when dawn came. All through the pain that tied her intestines into knots, then pulled, pulled, Tory noticed how haggard he grew. When her pains came so close and sharp she had to scream, he started as if punched. But never, not once, even when his face contorted as he watched her agony, did he release her hand. When the head came, they cried out together.

A few moments later, Tory held a bloody, ugly, squirming, squalling bundle. Joy such as she'd never known coursed through her weary body, washing away the dregs of pain and resentment. She peeled the blanket away to examine the tiny boy. Ten toes, ten fingers. All there, thank goodness. She dropped her head back on the pillow and smiled up at Beau.

She blinked. There were tears in his eyes—but he wasn't looking at the baby. "Beau?" she asked uncertainly. "What's wrong?"

Mumbling an excuse, he staggered out. Tory looked at the baby's red-gold head. "He didn't even hold you, little one."

Mattie heard her. "He's fair wore out, Miss Tory. I've never seen a man more afraid of losing his wife in all the babies I've delivered."

That gave Tory even more to think about. She felt like an explorer who'd traveled thousands of miles and had sighted his goal. She was afraid to name the hope burgeoning in her breast, bringing vigor back to the heart that had felt numb for weeks. Womanlike, she resolved to test it.

Mother and son were fresh and sweet-smelling the next time Beau entered. Dressed in clean breeches and white shirt, he reminded Tory of the pirate who'd won her heart. But the way he hesitated by the door was behavior Sinan Reis would not have countenanced. Boldly he would have walked in to kiss them and claim his due. Only something radical, something powerful, could have wrought such a change. Her heart pounding, she sent him a flirtatious smile.

"Come, husband, see your handiwork." When he crept to the side of the bed, she held the sleeping baby up to him.

He stuck his hands behind his back and shook his head. "No. I know nothing of babies. I might drop him."

"Then you must learn, for I'll not have other people raise my children, nor will I allow you to be an aloof father." Tory kicked the covers back and stood. She swayed, wincing as her sore muscles protested.

Beau blanched and caught them both in his arms, scolding, "You little idiot, it's too soon for you to . . ." But she looked at him so searchingly that his voice trailed off. When he was certain she could stand, he stepped back.

His eyes ran over her. Even with her stomach still swollen and her eyes shadowed by her ordeal, she looked lovelier to him than he had ever seen her, standing there holding his child. Oh, God, how could he bear to lose them? He looked from Tory's delicate features to the child who had inherited her coloring but his chin, eyebrows, and mouth. A despairing thrill ran through him. Here, in this room, he had all a man could ask for, yet he had no right to claim it. He had taken so much from her. Even the child she cooed over had been forced upon her.

Her soft voice was a welcome distraction. "What shall we name him?"

"What do you have in mind?"

"I'd . . . like to name him Beaufort Grenville Cochran. For Greaty. Oh, little one, I can't wait until she sees you. She'll be so proud." Tory kissed the babe's brow.

Pain quivered across Beau's face. He agreed dully, "Yes, it's a proud name for a proud heritage. When do you go?"

Tory frowned. "Go? Where?"

"Why, back to England."

"During the worst of the heat, I suppose. I'm eager to see the foals my mares have dropped. The countryside is so beautiful in summer . . ." Tory reminisced, looking forward to sharing England with her family, until a howl from Beaufort distracted her.

She nibbled her lower lip, glancing shyly up at Beau. Then she sat down in the rocker near the bed and opened her wrapper. Mattie had told her to let the babe suckle as often as he liked so her milk would come in. Tory drew the wrapper off one shoulder and lifted Beaufort to her breast. She jumped when he clamped down on her nipple, but stroked the velvety head with one hand. She peeped up at her husband. Her mouth parted in a soft gasp. His eyes glistened as he looked down at them longingly, as a dying man might look at his last sunrise. Then he turned on his heel and left.

The following day, the rest of the Cochrans came to see the new member of the family. Miranda and Helen pampered Tory and the baby shamelessly; Robert gave Beau a cigar as if he were the proud papa. Through the chatter, Beau's silence glared. He seldom looked at his wife and child.

Robert tried to relax the increasingly strained atmosphere by recounting the latest news about Fuller. "He's moving his offices to New York. Duane's editorial before the vote was devastating to him. Before the day was out, he'd lost half of his contracts."

"Good. He deserves no less." Tory glanced at Beau, but he was staring out the sitting room window. "There's something that's always puzzled me. Why do you suppose he kept the map? He must have known how it would implicate him if it was ever found."

Robert shrugged. "Perhaps he hoped to sell it, or trade it for a Mediterranean contact. Who knows? But it's lucky for us he kept it.'' Robert's voice grew hard. ''Isn't that right, Beau?''

Still Beau didn't answer. Robert slammed his hands on his knees and rose. He took his son by the arm and dragged him from the room. Tory stared after them. They went down the front lawn and paused by the creek's edge. She saw Robert berating Beau, Beau shaking his head stubbornly.

Helen took the baby back to Tory and stood in front of her, shifting from foot to foot. Tory forced her gaze from the window to her sister-in-law. She looked from Helen's rosy face to a smiling Miranda. ''Well, it seems I'm not the only one to be congratulated. It's Terence, isn't it?''

''Yes, we're to wed in August.''

Tory rose to press her cheek against Helen's. ''I'm so happy for you.'' They talked about the wedding plans until Beau and Robert returned.

Impatiently Robert interrupted, ''There will be time for this later. Tory needs her rest. Come, Miranda, Helen.'' Robert didn't even look at his son, though he kissed Tory and Beaufort, then escorted his wife and daughter to the door.

As their carriage drew away, he slumped back against the squabs. ''The boy's stone deaf or crazy. He insists on captaining our first voyage to China, and he won't tell Tory he loves her. Persists in thinking that she must make her own choices, that he's forced her too many times. If she's still here when he returns, he'll tell her then of his feelings.'' Robert took Miranda's hand.

''Mandy''—she knew how upset he was when he used his intimate pet name for her—''what if she goes back to England as he fears?''

Miranda kissed his lined but firm cheek. ''Didn't you notice the way she looked at him, dearest? She admitted to me he's yet to hold the baby, but she didn't seem upset. In the past, his apparent indifference was devastating to her, but now she seems intrigued by it. She's beginning to understand, Robert. I predict that before the month is out, they'll be billing and cooing like a certain other couple we know.'' She glanced at her daughter, who smiled back, unabashed.

''I hope you're right, my love. I hope you're right,'' Robert replied, patting her hand.

● ● ●

A month later Tory turned before her mirror in the lantern light, wondering if she was close enough to her old form to seduce her husband. Her breasts were heavier, her stomach the tiniest bit fuller with a few white lines on her lower abdomen, but other than that, she looked the same. In a way, she thought, she looked better. For now there was nothing of the girl left; she was all woman. She reveled in the knowledge and prayed Beau would find her body pleasing.

Tory drew the peach lace nightdress over her head. Sleeveless, it plunged to a deep vee and was banded under the bosom with gold and peach braid. The lace robe tied high at the throat with the same braid. Tory brushed her hair until it crackled, her thoughts on her husband.

They were still at the cabin, but the healthier Tory grew, the less she saw of Beau. She knew he was only waiting for her to recover in full before returning to Philadelphia. But he would not be returning any time soon. She hugged herself in delight at her new knowledge.

She'd tested her insane theory so often that she was almost certain of its veracity. If she brushed up against him, he flinched away, but looked at her with longing in his eyes. If she tried to hand the baby to him, he stuck his hands in his pockets and made a lame excuse. But she saw how he watched them. She remembered his fear during her labor; she remembered his jealousy. She'd never understood his behavior before because she'd never found the key.

Now she had. He avoided her, spoke to her in monosyllables, and flinched at her smallest touch, not because he cared too little, but because he cared too much.

That explained everything.

Tonight, Tory thought, smiling at herself dreamily, the truth would out. In the midst of passion, when even the awesome barrier of his pride was lowered, she would ask him how he felt about her. He would not be able to lie to her then. And when he had admitted his feelings, she'd be free to admit hers.

Perhaps she was being cruel, keeping him in suspense, but she wanted to be at her best for him so they could celebrate their reconciliation in the warmest of ways. Besides, she thought, eyes twinkling impishly, he deserved to suffer a little for what he'd put her through.

When the knock came, she was ready. But instead of getting in bed, where he always kissed her cheek and wished her good night, she stood before the window, one elbow propped on the high sill, looking out. Her pose looked casual, but she'd worked on it for an hour. She stood quiet as he entered, knowing the summer breeze blew her negligee back from her figure, which stood in profile to him. Her hair rippled in the candle flame like living fire.

Slowly, she turned to face him. He got two steps before going rigid. Green eyes coursed her length, pausing on the gentle rise and fall of her breasts. With a strangled "Good night, Tory," Beau backed up a pace.

Tory lifted languid hands to the ribbon at her throat and pulled. With a supple shrug of her shoulders, the robe slid down her body and pooled at her feet. "Close the door, husband. Beaufort should sleep for several hours." When he didn't respond, she smiled and walked forward, her gown flowing about her legs and hips, to reach around him and shut the door.

She leaned into him; he shrank against the door. "Woman, it's too soon . . ."

"I would say it's far too late. We've surely set a record, sir, for marital abstinence. One night we've had together in all the months of our marriage! But that's easily enough rectified. All we need to do is put aside the pride that's kept us apart."

He met her eyes, growling, "But what have we to replace it? Aye, we've passion aplenty between us, but I find that's no longer enough. For me, at least." He put his hands on her waist to move her aside. Tory placed them on her hips instead. He drew in a shocked breath. His eyes darkened.

"So, passion is not enough?" she murmured. "Have you more to offer?"

He clenched his teeth and tried again to move her aside. Again she resisted, pressing her body into his.

When he gave a frustrated groan, she smiled up at him wickedly. "I must admit to a certain fondness for this turnabout," she teased, grasping his shoulders to pull him down. "But how much better I like my present role." Tory pressed her lips to the pulse beating in the hollow of his neck, whispering, "Resistance is useless, as you warned me so many moons ago. You'll end in my bed anyway."

She trailed her mouth up his neck, licking around his Adam's apple, taking a nip out of his stubborn chin, then standing on tiptoe to kiss him. He tried to turn his head aside, but she buried her fingers in his hair and forced his head down. Soft, eager lips opened under his, her tongue darting out to tease the corner of his mouth. She felt the tension draining away from him; it was replaced by a tautness of a different kind. His mouth opened. He hauled her close, kissing her with all the dammed-up passion of months of loneliness.

Sighing her bliss into his mouth, Tory rubbed herself against the hardness thrusting against her abdomen. Unsteadily she unbuttoned his shirt, kissing the honey-dotted skin as she went. She bared him to the waist and went for his belt, but he grunted and started away, lifting her into his arms. Tory's head fell back against his shoulder. He explored the velvety column of her neck with eager lips, trembling as if with ague as she purred her pleasure and arched her throat back.

They fell across the bed. When his hands went to the ribbons on her gown, she helped him. However, when she tried to unfasten his belt, he took her hands to his chest. Enchanted with her rediscovery of the harmonious curvature of his torso, and delirious at his hand play, she didn't realize how quickly he fanned her passions to an unbearable heat without allowing her to stoke his own.

His stubbly face chafed already quivering nerve endings as he kissed her from her curling pink toes to her sighing, passion-swollen mouth. "Beau," she moaned, struggling for coherency. But then she forgot her purpose. When she tasted the milk he'd brought to fruition when he planted his seed in her ten months ago, everything else faded away. There was only Beau, and this moment. Feelings mattered now. Words could come soon enough.

Beau battled his feelings. He shuddered in pain-pleasure, rapture-remorse, as the sweet taste of the milk and the sweeter taste of Tory filled his mouth. Oh, God, he wanted her! He'd give ten years of his life for the joy of loving her one last time. But he could not. It was too soon after the baby, nor could he risk making her pregnant when this might be the last time he saw her. If this was all she wanted of him, then he would give it, keeping tight rein on his own needs. Maybe someday she'd see the significance of his sacrifice.

So he built her passion to fever-pitch, stroking her hips, inner thighs, and their joining with hands, then with lips. She gasped when he cupped her buttocks and knelt on the bed between her legs to give her that most intimate of caresses. His tongue savored the sweetness his touch had wrought. He lapped and teased the little nubbin until it grew as hard as his own desire. When she was moaning, her hands clenched in his hair, he suckled. Tory cried out and stiffened. She convulsed, her nails digging into his scalp. She felt as if she shattered into bits. Slowly, then, as her breathing returned to normal, she drifted back to earth, coalescing piece by piece until her sum was greater than the parts of her former whole. For now, she was different, more complete than ever before.

Now she was a woman loved.

Only a man who adored could give so unselfishly. She stroked the brown head resting on her belly. She felt him, hot and heavy against her leg, thrusting through the coarse material of his work breeches. She yawned, tired with the release that had come after so much tension, but she wanted him to find it, too. However, when she tried to pull him up, he shook his head, rubbing his lips against her belly.

"Sleep, love. I can feel how tired you are."

A wide yawn spoiled her denial. "But what about you?"

"Don't worry about me. I've gotten everything I deserve."

That was a peculiar way of putting it, Tory thought. She tugged on his hair until he levered his long length beside her. But even then he turned her about and snuggled against her back so she couldn't see his face.

He stroked her arm soothingly. "It's happiness enough to hold you like this. Go to sleep."

Tory's eyes closed. There was something in his gentle tone, in the poignant way he cradled her, that troubled her, but she was too tired to worry. Cotton fluffed in her brain, cushioning everything but the need to sleep. Morning would be soon enough. Maybe even the middle of the night . . . Smiling at the thought, she drifted into her deepest slumber in months.

When dawn came, Tory stirred as the comforting warmth at her back faded away. Footsteps quietly retreated. They went to Beaufort's room, paused for endless, aching moments, then dragged outside. The front door closed.

Tory would never know what woke her. Perhaps some bond stronger than that of body or even heart; a bond that linked their deepest thoughts in a mystical way. But her eyes flew wide, and she knew as surely as if he'd told her that he was leaving. That was what had bothered her about his touch last night. He'd bidden her the sweetest good-bye a man could give.

She heard the sound of the carriage drawing away. She leaped out of bed and ran to the window to see the coachman tooling the light coach down the river road toward Philadelphia.

Hands on hips, naked as the day she was born, Tory scowled after it. "Well! If it's a coward you are, Mr. Cochran, then it's a reckoning I must force you to face." Wearing her Tory the Terror look, she went to her trunk and rummaged through it. She'd packed all her belongings when she left Philadelphia, not knowing if she would ever return.

When she found the items she sought, she smiled. Dressing quickly in pants, shirt, and boots, she picked up one token, her eyes misting at the memories it evoked. She stuffed it into her pocket, strapping the other item to her thigh, then hurried to Beaufort's room.

He was sleeping in the magnificent mahogany crib that had been his father's. He gnawed at one plump little fist, and she knew he'd be awake soon and screaming for his breakfast. She blew him a kiss. "Bless you, sweetheart, for sleeping through the night. You knew your parents had things to settle, didn't you? Well, they'll be settled soon enough, and you'll enjoy your papa's arms for the first time."

Tory hurried out to fetch Mattie and saddle Orion. The road wound a desultory course beside the creek. She'd be able to cut Beau off by traveling across country. She knew exactly where to await him.

Beau rested his head against the seat of the carriage but he knew he wouldn't sleep, despite the fact that he'd slept not a wink last night. He'd spent those long hours leaning over Tory, wishing he could hold back the dawn. He'd ached with desire; the heartache was much worse. Perhaps this parting had been destined, as had the passion, the anger, the pain they'd shared. They'd deceived and tormented each other too much to ever find conjugal peace. How much better for them both if he'd never blocked her voyage that fine June day over a year ago.

Beau shook his head wearily. No, that was a lie. Despite this agony, he didn't regret having known her. Her spirit, her heart, her mind, and her body would always dwell in that special place each man kept within him for memories too precious to forget, or even to share. If things had been a little different—if he'd told her sooner who he was, if he hadn't forced her to wed him—perhaps he would now be where he belonged. Beside her, watching her succor the child they had created.

But it was too late for regrets. Tory didn't love him. A woman who loved didn't refuse to sleep next to him; a woman who loved didn't leave him so that she could bear their child alone; a woman who loved surely would have spoken of her feelings last night after he had pleasured her. But then, why should she love him? He'd given her scant reason to, he thought bitterly. He had forced many things upon her, but he couldn't force that. And he loved her too much to make her stay. It was time to let her go back to the England she loved, triumphantly bearing the Grenville heir. If she didn't return, he'd go to see her. After his rawest wounds had healed.

Too much had happened in one short year. His feelings for her would never change, but perhaps absence would make her value him more. If she seemed to miss him, he'd suggest they try again, and this time he would treat her differently. If she didn't want to return with him, then so be it. He'd see his son whenever he could, for he could not give up the child completely.

Of the other possibility—that she might still be here when he returned from China—he did not dare let himself hope.

The shot, when it came, startled him out of his depression. He bolted upright, growling, "What the hell?" The coach came to a bone-jarring halt. Beau was reaching for the door handle when the coach turned about and jounced off in the direction from which it had come. Beau banged on the ceiling and yelled for the coachman to stop, but there was no response. He pulled the heavy curtains aside to see a bright, sparkling morning, but naught else.

When they pulled up at the cottage, he was fuming. He jerked open the door and leaped down without using the steps. He stomped around to the driver's seat, mouth open to rebuke the coachman. His mouth opened wider. He blinked.

Orion, pawing and snorting, white coat gleaming, rounded the coach to block his path. Atop him sat a figure he'd have known in his dreams. Tory was dressed in breeches, shirt, and riding boots. She had a red kerchief tied around her head and knotted under one ear. A gold earring dangled from the exposed ear. She had a pistol in the belt cinching her narrow waist, and *his* jeweled dagger was strapped to one slim thigh. The smile on her lovely face could only be termed wicked. She lacked only a saber and a ship to complete the picture of a female pirate captain raiding the Spanish Main.

Dismounting, she tied Orion to the cottage rail and dismissed the family coachman. As he barreled off, muttering to himself, Tory swaggered up to her captive and bowed deeply, sweeping one hand before her.

"Victoria Alicia Cochran, wife of a most cowardly husband, regretfully informs you, sir, you are my prisoner." But when Beau still stared at her, mouth agape, she nodded in the direction of the cottage. "Inside. We've a ransom to discuss."

Dazed, he stumbled ahead of her into the cottage, his brain whirling with confusion. What game did she play now?

When he reached the tiny salon, he turned to face her, but she shook her head. "The bedroom." She smiled sweetly at his startled look. Mattie, who'd been sitting with Beaufort, looked from one to the other and melted away.

Beau's temper began to burn at Tory's self-satisfied air. He was still trying to adjust to losing her. Why was she making his good-bye so difficult? He crossed his arms over his chest. "No. If you want to talk to me, do it here."

"No?" Tory raised a brow. She pulled the dagger and fingered the tip, eyeing him evilly.

Despite his anger, his sense of humor was tickled at her mimicry. Lips quivering, he mocked, "What a fearsome pirate you make. But if you want to complete the menacing picture, next time I suggest you fasten your shirt, so a man will be thinking about being cut to ribbons instead of certain other things." His eyes caressed the cleavage exposed by her partially unbuttoned shirt.

A slow, sensual smile stretched Tory's lips. "You noticed, did you? I thought you might."

His eyes flashed to her face. "Tory, dammit, what the hell are you doing?"

She gestured with the dagger toward her chamber. "Inside, and you'll find out soon enough."

Snorting resentfully, he obeyed. Tory followed him, tossed the dagger on the lowboy, and stood, thumbs in her belt, looking up at him. He looked back, trying to pretend indifference, but his eyes betrayed him.

The growing tension between them was shattered by an angry wail. Tory looked dismayed; then she shrugged. She stuck her hand in her pocket, pulled out a square of material and advanced on him. He stood his ground, but drew in his breath sharply when she stuck a finger in his belt, tugged his trousers open and dropped the square inside.

Patting it, she gave him an enigmatic smile. "A memento to remind you whom you belong to until I honor you with my attention again." She sauntered to the door, looking back over her shoulder at him. "I suggest you remember your words to me when you gave it to me and think on them while I'm gone." She exited. To his amazement, she locked him in.

He backed up two steps on weakened legs and collapsed on the bed. He pulled the square from his breeches and spread it out. There, wrinkled and stained, was the kerchief that had traveled so many miles with them, passing from her to him, him to her. He did indeed recall giving it to her—and the words he had spoken.

She'd been standing on the stairs in her grandmother's vast town house, her face icy pale as she listened to his good-bye. He'd kissed her hand and given her the kerchief that represented so much for them. He'd said, "If you ever have need of me, send it and I'll come at once."

If you ever have need of me, if you ever have need of me. . . . The words echoed in his tired brain. He surged to his feet, the kerchief crushed in his hand, and ran to the door. Remembering it was locked, he scrambled out the window and rushed back into the house, to Beaufort's room.

There, in a rocker, sat his pirate lady, luscious breasts bare as she suckled their son. He didn't even note the incongruity of her attire to her present activity. When she looked up at him, he knelt beside her, dropped the kerchief in her lap, and cupped her knees.

"Do you mean what I think you mean?" he croaked.

She switched Beaufort to her other breast before answering. "What do you think I mean?" she countered.

"Tory, don't play with me. I cannot bear it." He was as white as the kerchief.

She sighed. Wanting him to speak first was a little thing, perhaps, but a woman liked to cherish such a moment. If she had to bribe a confession out of him, it would tarnish the memory. She finished feeding Beaufort, burped him, and stood. Holding their son on her shoulder, she looked at Beau's pleading face. He towered to his feet.

"How can you be so strong and intelligent, but so obtuse?" she asked, exasperated. "Luckily I'm a little more intuitive, else I might have let you ride out of my life without lifting a finger to stop you."

Tory walked up to him and handed him the baby. He hesitated until she ordered coldly, "Hold your son, or you're less than the man I think you."

His hands trembling, he reached out and cradled the warm, squirming little body. The expression on his face brought tears to Tory's eyes, but she cleared them away.

"And you were going to let pride take all of this away from you. How could you, Beau?" She took Beaufort, changed him, placed him in his cradle, and led Beau back to her chamber. She unlocked the door, then closed it behind them. She didn't realize she'd forgotten to button her shirt.

Bright green eyes tried to hold her challenging stare, but he coughed and turned away. Her anger abated. Her heart in her eyes, she went to him and gently turned him to face her.

She cocked her head to one side and coaxed huskily, "Come, my captive, your ransom is a simple thing. Free us both. Three little words. Are they so difficult?"

His eyes glazed over as he stared down at the love she no longer tried to hide. Afraid to believe it, but desperate enough to test it, he snatched her into his arms. "Tory, Tory, I love you, I adore you, I . . ."

Sighing her satisfaction, she pulled his head down to meet his lips. Silence prevailed, but Tory felt as if the birds, the trees, the very earth sang in concert with her joyous heart. Passionately they pledged their troth anew, as if they had just exchanged their wedding vows. In truth, only now did they really know their meaning.

Breathless, they drew apart and stared at each other. Beau ran a tender finger down her cheek to her gold earring. "What a pirate you make. You have captured me, woman, body and soul.

Forgive my stupidity, but I truly don't understand. How long have you loved me?''

"I gave myself to you in the desert because I knew I loved you." Tory rubbed her cheek against his hand, too happy to reproach him. "That's why I was so hurt at your deception."

Beau winced and sat down on the bed, pulling her into his lap. "God forgive my selfishness. I wanted you so much. I tried to pretend you weren't worthy, but I couldn't fool myself for long." He kissed her brow. "I can't begin to tell you how low but exalted, all at once, I felt when I took your virginity. I couldn't delude myself any longer then."

"You mean you wed me because you loved me?" Tory asked in dawning wonder.

"Of course. And I labored to make you pregnant for the same reason—to tie you to me."

Tory pretended to be insulted. She tweaked his nose. "Labored, mmm? You make it sound like one of the labors of Hercules."

He laughed, some of his tension receding. "Indeed it can be." He nibbled her ear. "You're an insatiable wench. But I'm so hungry for you that I'm more than equal to the task." He whispered more endearments, but she put her hand over his mouth.

"Not yet. I want to know why you were so remote after I helped you with Fuller."

His happy smile faded. "Because I thought by then I'd lost all hope of winning you, and I couldn't bear your sweet support if it was given only out of a sense of duty." He scooted back to lean against the brass headboard and cradled her closer in his arms.

Contrition and love warred in his eyes when he burst out, "I'd forced so much from you—your desire, your virginity, your trust, your hand, our son. How could I continue to treat you so if we were ever to be happy? I had to leave you to make your own decision."

Tory kissed his scowl away. "Oh, my darling, I was unfair to you as well. Thank God I finally realized why you acted so strangely."

He shuddered at how close they'd come to a long separation. "Forgive me for not telling you sooner how I felt, but I viewed that, too, as wheedling for your love. I wanted you wholly,

Tory. If that's selfish, I'm sorry, but that's the way you make me feel."

Tory dropped her eyes to hide her satisfied gleam at seeing that look again on his face. Her Hawk was back, never to leave her again, she hoped.

"I'll learn to live with it." She sighed.

His arms tightened about her. "Damn right," he muttered, bending to plant possessive lips on the upper curve of one breast. "Now that I know you love me, you'll never have reason to doubt my feelings again."

Tory squirmed her hips over the swelling in his breeches, then she bolted from his arms before he could stop her. "Well, now that's settled, we've packing to do. Shouldn't we return to Philadelphia?" Leaning against the lowboy, she crossed her ankles and fluttered her lashes at him.

Grinning that slow Sinan smile, he rose and hooked his thumbs in his belt. "Now I've paid me ransom, I've a mind to collect me own. You're obviously hale and hearty, me pirate beauty." He stalked toward her, licking his lips.

"But, sir, I won you by superior force of arms. I owe you naught." She stood erect and glared at him.

"Aye, your weapons are awesome," his eyes caressed the flushing skin of her bosom, "but it's been many a moon since you tested mine." He gave an explicit little bump with his hips.

She needed no reminder of the bulge there. She thought she would fly apart with happiness as his moss-green eyes clashed with his fierce scowl. Ah, what a man he was. What fun it would be being wed to him. What fights they would have. What passionate apologizing they would do.

"Ah, so it's swords you want to cross, is it?" she asked archly. She looked about as if to find one. She shook her head. "There seem to be no swords available. I guess we'll have to wait for another day." She turned as if to exit.

Large hands pulled her away from the door. Picking her up by the waist, they tossed her down on the bed. A very long, very dear, very aroused body followed her down.

Beau pressed her hand against his bulging breeches. "See, my vixen, we've a sword, after all. At your request, I'll gladly share it with you," he whispered throatily.

Secure at last in the love beaming at her, Tory murmured,

"Yes, my hawk. Lend me your blade. We'll test it together." And they did.

The Hawk had his lady; the lady had her Hawk. As to who had done the taming, neither could say, nor did they care. Taming or roaming wild and free, they were together. And that was all that mattered.

CAPTIVATING HISTORICAL ROMANCES!

Colleen Shannon ————————————————

"A sparking new talent!"—*Affaire de Coeur*

☐ *THE HAWK'S LADY* (ON SALE FEBRUARY '89)
   1-55773-158-6/$4.50

☐ *THE TENDER DEVIL* 0-441-80221-4/$3.95

Elaine Barbieri ————————————————

"Barbieri has pleased readers over and over."
                                    —*Lovenotes*

☐ *TARNISHED ANGEL* 0-515-09748-9/$4.50

Karen Harper ————————————————

"Her talent... grips the reader with vivid images that
remain alive and vibrant."—*Affaire de Coeur*

☐ *TAME THE WIND* 1-55773-132-2/$3.95

☐ *ONE FERVENT FIRE* 0-441-58679-1/$3.95

Please send the titles I've checked above. Mail orders to:

BERKLEY PUBLISHING GROUP
390 Murray Hill Pkwy., Dept. B
East Rutherford, NJ 07073

NAME _____

ADDRESS _____

CITY _____

STATE _____ ZIP _____

Please allow 6 weeks for delivery.
Prices are subject to change without notice.

POSTAGE & HANDLING:
$1.00 for one book, $.25 for each
additional. Do not exceed $3.50.

BOOK TOTAL	$_____
SHIPPING & HANDLING	$_____
APPLICABLE SALES TAX (CA, NJ, NY, PA)	$_____
TOTAL AMOUNT DUE	$_____
PAYABLE IN US FUNDS. (No cash orders accepted.)	**144**

If you enjoyed this book, take advantage of this special offer. Subscribe now and . . .

GET A *FREE* HISTORICAL ROMANCE
—— NO OBLIGATION(a $3.95 value) ——

Each month the editors of True Value will select the four best historical romance novels from America's leading publishers. Preview them in your home Free for 10 days. And we'll send you a FREE book as our introductory gift. No obligation. If for any reason you decide not to keep them, just return them and owe nothing. But if you like them you'll pay *just* $3.50 each and save at least $.45 each off the cover price. (Your savings are a minimum of $1.80 a month.) There is no shipping and handling or other hidden charges. There are no minimum number of books to buy and you may cancel at any time.

send in the coupon below

Mail to:
True Value Home Subscription Services, Inc.
P.O. Box 5235
120 Brighton Road
Clifton, New Jersey 07015-5235

YES! I want to start previewing the very best historical romances being published today. Send me my FREE book along with the first month's selections. I understand that I may look them over FREE for 10 days. If I'm not absolutely delighted I may return them and owe nothing. Otherwise I will pay the low price of just $3.50 each; a total of $14.00 (at least a $15.80 value) and save at least $1.80. Then each month I will receive four brand new novels to preview as soon as they are published for the same low price. I can always return a shipment and I may cancel this subscription at any time with no obligation to buy even a single book. In any event the FREE book is mine to keep regardless.

Name _____

Address _____ Apt. _____

City _____ State _____ Zip _____

Signature _____
             (if under 18 parent or guardian must sign)
Terms and prices subject to change.